THE DARK LEGION

MICHAEL HOLLADAY

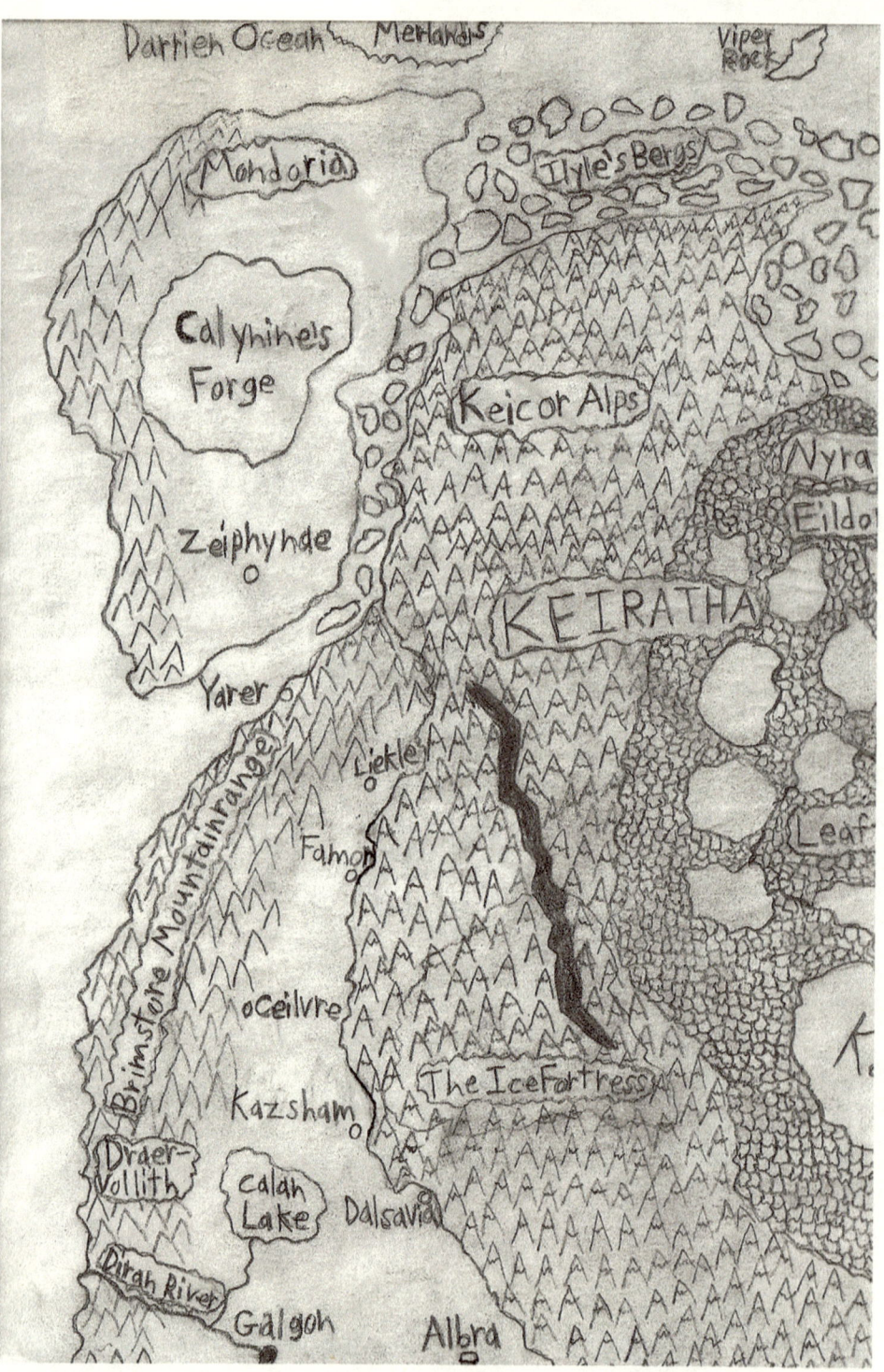

VALVASSA
Jergh
Vlazrahm
Halecear Bay
Kirtchaz
Iszalli
Nyrah Forest
Eildon Lakes
The Fire Realm
Border Line
Modrezra
Ancient Archimage's Grove
Malmeir
Azreilliav
Lamahl's Cesspool
Leaftorn
Zahkrahm
Border Line
Kalba Lake
Malldem
Zeilkru
Veilzanor
Oukrahm
M.H.

The Dark Legion
by Michael Holladay

Signalman Publishing 2011
www.signalmanpublishing.com
email: info@signalmanpublishing.com
Kissimmee, Florida

Cover design by: Kate Danailov

ISBN: 978-1-935991-22-9 (paperback)
        978-1-935991-23-6 (ebook)

Library of Congress Control Number: 2011940179

Signalman
Publishing

To my remarkable parents, Doc and Polly.
Without them, I would be nothing.

Acknowledgments

I firstly must thank all those who cheered from the sidelines in anticipation. I am astonished that they'd stay with me through all these years as I strove to make dreams reality. Thank you all for bearing with me.

The Frankland and Hubbard families, for proofreading and giving any feedback they felt was necessary.

John McClure and his team at Signalman Publishing, for their ceaseless dedication in readying and then releasing *The Dark Legion*.

John Kudrick, my editor, for going through the bogginess of my story and abridging all longish sentences, removing superfluous commas, and altogether honing the quality of the characters and circumstances.

And above all, my gratitude goes out to my entire family, who asked almost every time the status of my book. They gave words of encouragement to aid me through the process, never minding my estrangement when writing called. I hereby dedicate this book to them. Without my family—and friends—I never could have finished this.

May Light Be Your Path,
Thareous, the Son of Haverin

Pronunciation Guide

Aildeimor—ail-DAY-more

Anazeil—anna-zail

Artheil—AR-thee-ill

Galthoria—gal-THOR-ee-UH

Haverin—HAV-er-in

Ianvorr—eye-uhn-VORR

Ingrezl—in-greh-ZUHL

Jaldor—JAHL-dorr

Jallaca—jahl-la-KUH

Jurtithan—jurr-ti-THAN

Keiratha—kair-ath-UH

Keirn—kee-AIRN

Kielkanur—kail-KAY-nur

Kielthavra—kail-THAV-ruh

Kyjre—KHI-jur

Lefanarí—lef-an-AHR-EE

Malluesaer—mall-us-SAY-ER

Mareinia—MAH-ray-nee-UH

Nahilmara—nah-hill-MAHR-UH

Quaron—QUAH-run

Varkin—VAR-kin

Vellar—vel-lar

Thareous—thair-ee-us

Theldaneru—thel-DAY-neh-roo

Yelva—yell-VAH

Zakumahk—ZAH-koo-MAHK

FINDING

Ragged breathing sounded down the hall. Clawed feet pounded on the icy floor as the blue creature ran on all fours. Her winged serpentine body curved when rounding a bend. A group of her kind, walking toward her, parted so that she could get by. She gave no thanks. There was not time for it.

At last she came to the threshold of the Great Hall. Here the head brother of her species took residence. He was actually no relative to her; "brother" was just a term of respect for males. Such was it also with the "sisters," or females.

She stopped at the entry and forced herself to remember why she came. It returned to her a second later. And there she stood, reflecting a matter of immense importance while standing before the place she had to be. Chiding herself on the inside, she went under the doorway in a brisk walk.

Four columns of ice held up the chamber she entered. They formed a path to the being on a frosty throne: a beast with huge wings, spikes going down his back, horns jutting from his head, and a massive body. Argent scales encased him from snout to tail. White, pupil-less eyes of light regarded the unannounced arrival.

For a moment they both stared. Then the blue being bowed and spoke. "Silver One ... he has been uncovered. Our brother has been found! After these thirty long years the elves have discovered him!" Her voice broke with emotion. "We can realign him to the rest. He may at last be freed!"

The breath seeped from the larger creature in a hiss. "Be not so quick to rejoice. Our relations with the Royal Family are not at all well. One ill move would cause something we could never reverse. This is war. Do you not remember our motives for going into hiding?" A sigh escaped him. "I wish to evade any chance of this. The land would soon tear apart, should we battle each other."

"I know this," the blue one said. "I knew you would react thus. So I came to request a rescue mission. Brother Ianvorr has suffered captivity long enough! I implore you to allow me just this!"

"That is the sort of move—of action—I meant," the Silver One said. "This is what I know: Ianvorr is held in Galgon. The king and queen rule from there, in case you have forgotten. Attempting any release for our fallen brother would be a grave error. The rulers might deem it an attack upon the Capital of Keiratha."

"How knew you he was in Galgon?" the female demanded. "And how long?"

"Since the day he was taken there," her superior said. "These past three decades you searched for naught. He always was within saving. You often approached me for an inkling of hope. I lied every time to you. Now the truth is obvious. I cannot pray you forgive me; I do not even own remorse to my deeds. For I did what was best for our kind and the other classes. I disallowed you from being the originator of a war."

The blue beast's eyes narrowed, but she held within the onslaught of ire that assaulted her heart. "What, then, should I do, Silver One?" she questioned. She beat her tail on the ice floor, giving liberty to some of the pent-up energy she felt coursing through her veins. "What would you have me do? You know I love him. Or is that it? Have you kept this from me because you—"

"No such thing," the argent being said. "Heed what I must speak. Had the elves not have found this out and related it to you, I would not utter a word to you. But now you possess this knowledge, so I must order you not to act on impulse. The knowledge itself is incentive enough to do this. Hostility is to be the only result."

She did not know what to make of this. "What are you trying at?"

"You should wait until the proper time," he said, bringing his head down some. "That is less than a month, during the Convergence Ceremony. At that time, as you know, Galgon's citizens gather to celebrate their unity. Go then and confront King Jaldor as the activities begin. Do whatever is necessary to have him free Ianvorr."

Rapture flew through her like a sudden burst of wind, dissolving any remaining tendrils of anger within her being. "I shall do as you command." She bowed and turned to leave without his permission. She had to plan how this was to be done at the Ceremony. Her lover was to be returned to her in a matter of days! After that day he would never again leave her side.

The female dragon once more sped through the halls, this time propelled by joy. To where she went was not important. She only knew that she had to be with Ianvorr. Thirty years of lovelornness and ghostly memories left her thirsting for him. Soon he would be the water to revive her soul.

In the Court of the King

Time. Days, weeks, months, years. All flowing without repose, all coming together and separating into extensive lengths. Memories of past occurrences haunting the halls of the heart. Like ghosts they wandered and wore down the victim. They wore down Ianvorr the Powerful with longing and growing bitterness. This beast that once won the hearts of the people was now torn from his pedestal. Yet he did not retaliate.

No, memories told him he should not. For from what he remembered, he had been a part of a great order. These years of isolation had made him doubt bygone experiences. His order, the Omnipotent Ones, was only a dream to him these days. Ever since his capture it seemed a gap between the sleeping and waking.

Ianvorr stared out the partitions of his cage. His wardens spoke amid themselves. He heard—and understood—every word. They gestured at him, taunting him in their quiet tones. They always conversed in whispers, as if afraid of him. They knew anything said could kindle the wrath within Ianvorr.

He turned his head away, extending a wing some. His confinement had little room for him to move about in. The ceiling was also a little low. At least it provided enough space to stretch out his limbs. Still, he felt cramped all the time.

A plume of frosty breath shot from his nostrils. It formed a cloud and curled away on some ephemeral breeze. Ianvorr glanced down at his paw and saw the white scales covering it. The lung-choking haze he exhaled—with which he could shape things—was ice. With it he could free himself if he wished. Only he could not.

Escape might bring suspicion upon the Omnipotent Ones. King Jaldor would throw his soldiers out on a tremendous search for them. Finding even one would give him the chance to deliver his message: war was waged. In his old age the monarch was rumored to be rash. The slightest notion caused him to follow capricious decisions.

This complicated Ianvorr's plan to get out and rejoin his brethren. It did not stop him, though. For he retained a reason for requiring to. The previous night he dreamed to be amongst a congregation. In it the tyrant of another land addressed his minions. The schemes Ianvorr overheard put him in a state of shock. They also provoked him to burst out of his cage and fly away. The others had to be told.

So he came up with a workable method: the Convergence Ceremony. He would break out then. His order had to be informed or the land Keiratha, would be obliterated. Such had transpired in the kingdom the tyrant ruled.

Jaldor would never believe his story. For this reason he had to confide in someone else. Ianvorr already knew who this to be. Thareous, son of the Master Magician Haverin, a boy eighteen years young. He would stop by soon. The youth had visited him for almost a month now, every day. A girl sometimes accompanied him—Princess Nalla, about the same age as the lad. It was difficult to tell their status of friendship.

Of course, Thareous would likely find some measure of delight in learning of Ianvorr's ability to articulate in the human tongue. For thirty years he had uttered no word. The smallest formation of sound might spawn an interrogation concerning the Omnipotents' whereabouts. As it was, mankind appeared to have forgotten that dragons could speak.

That is, it seemed, all but one. When visiting alone, Thareous himself oftentimes tried to get a word out of Ianvorr. The caged beast held his impassive facade while smiling underneath. In spite of the stares from the sentries, the lad would not quit. Ianvorr did not mind; he liked a balm from these tedious days.

A cry drew the Ice Dragon's attention elsewhere. He saw Thareous sprinting through the southern threshold, Nalla in tow. The guards drew their swords and ran at the pair. Yelping, Thareous let the princess go and took a step back. "No! It is not as it seems. I—I—we …"

Nalla stepped around him, stopping before the guards. Her face pinched up about her cobalt eyes. With a hand she tossed back her golden hair, tousled by the run. "You are dismissed. He has done nothing to me. We wish to speak alone."

"But Milady—"

This soldier was cut off by an authoritative glare from Nalla. "If you do not trust us together, then remain. If I can be believed, leave us be. I do not tolerate men pretending to be something they are not because of my rank."

"Yes, Your Grace," they muttered, leaving one by one.

"Now," Nalla said to Thareous, "*what* is this about?"

"I think the dragon can speak like you or I," he said.

Ianvorr's eyes widened some at this. He busied himself by observing his keepers vanish down a hall. Trying not to grin at Thareous's perseverance proved difficult. Then he became intrigued by the princess's reply.

"This is why you drug me from my room?" Nalla asked. "People saw us. They might have suspected we were eloping. And all you care about is this giant ... creature?" Her face flushed as she caught him staring at her. "Why do you think this, Thareous? Why is it you are so convicted to this?"

The Ice Dragon switched his eyes to the boy. Could he have let his guard down once? Had his intelligence been marked?

"For the longest time I have maintained suspicions it could vocalize," Thareous said. "I have wondered days on end what tamed him. From what I know, he was once a mad beast. Look at him now! He is as gentle as the wind that stirs your hair."

Ianvorr watched Nalla bite her lip. "What have you deduced from this?"

"That he has the judgment of a human," Thareous said. "He may even be smarter than our kind. No one can tell for sure, save the Omnipotent Ones, an order he used to be in. My father tells me they are a rebel group."

You little guttersnipe, Ianvorr thought to himself. The lad had attempted to lure him into defending his organization. Perhaps he should oblige the scoundrel. A few words to put him back in his place would serve him well. He ignored this urge and lay down in a way that he could view them both.

Thareous himself turned from Nalla and walked up to the cage. "I know not your name or your past. Either is kept secret to ensure the Omnipotent Ones' safety. I am not one wishing to see you or them harmed. So please let me know I have not been chasing the wind all this time. Help me to show you that I am a friend."

Fear took the Ice Dragon's heart and petrified it. An ironic resemblance to what his breath could do. A second later he realized the fear to be hesitancy. Why did he hesitate if he already trusted Thareous? Because he knew the boy was a friend, but was unsure where his allegiance lay.

Now Nalla approached. "I swear, everything within my power will be done to protect you. No weapon is to touch your scales. Your reticence is understood by us. We also understand if you do not confer with us."

Ianvorr shut his eyes and listened. He had to be sure the guards were out of earshot. From what he could detect, they were. So his lips parted to expose lines of sharp teeth and he moved his tongue. In a rumbling tenor he released his secret. "The Omnipotent Ones are not traitors. They are protectors." Next his inscrutability crumbled into an expression of cognizance. "My name is Ianvorr the Powerful."

When neither human could overcome their awe, the Ice Dragon continued. "For three decades I have been kept in this cage. It is because of a detestable deed I committed—under the power of a wicked sorcerer—that the king ordered me confined. For that I have endured my sentence with patience. Now I must escape and return to my kind. An evil is upon us."

Thareous looked away, blinking, not quite comprehending. He seemingly had been given too much to process at once. "What is it you speak of? What evil is upon us? What did you commit—why are you here?"

"All this shall be answered in time," Ianvorr said. "At the moment just know that I am the reason the Omnipotent Ones hide. War would be waged had I broken out sooner. In a few days I will leave. I wish the two of you to come with me. King Jaldor would do anything to find where the Omnipotents are. This is why you must accompany me. I shall not have youths such as yourselves interrogated."

"Can you not at least tell us what this evil is?" Nalla questioned.

The Ice Dragon faced her, blue eyes of light centered on hers. "Valvassa, our neighboring enemy land, is invading. Its ruler, the Dark King Zakumahk, comes here with an army of fiends. He is determined to take over Galgon for his own ill purposes. I have seen this by a sight no others in my class attain."

"Thus war comes anyhow," Thareous said.

"This is so, Young One," Ianvorr said. "Only it is graver, far more lethal. Should the king be told, he would not believe a word of it. Therefore I plan to leave on the day of the Convergence Ceremony, at noon. Join me if you will. I entreat you, though, should you choose to remain, say no word of our conversation."

With that he moved back into his apathetic state. Thareous and Nalla did not speak until they were well away from the courtyard. Ianvorr knew that the fact of an impending war shook them. It would be difficult to relate this to anyone.

******

Over the next few days they persisted in visiting Ianvorr. Nalla always sent the guards out while they spoke with the Ice Dragon. As he updated his plans, he considered leaving the princess behind. She could tell her father of the invasion after he and Thareous escaped. "The rest of this world is too dangerous for you," Ianvorr told her. "So you shall stay."

Unbeknownst to them the guards grew suspicious of Nalla and the company she kept. They assumed the worst to be happening, although Thareous was not known to seduce women. Captain Ahlk, the sentry who countered Nalla, evaluated this as he paced under the watch of his men. "This cannot continue. We know not what goes on in there."

"Perhaps we should spy on them," a soldier said.

"Nay," another said, "they need their privacy."

"Well, something must be done," a third said.

"Something will," Ahlk said, smashing a fist against a flat palm. "Our action is another thing." His face twisted as he tried to think of the best recourse. Only a frustrated grimace came. "Why can I not ...? Of course ... of course."

"What is it?" asked the second man who spoke up.

"He is the only man who can help us," Ahlk said, almost to himself. "He is the one who can barricade those two from absconding to the court." His shoulders leveled out as he braced the others for the news. "Men ... the king ... He must be told."

******

Jaldor huffed on his throne, his hoary beard trembling when he breathed. His knuckles were whitened from clenching the arms of the royal seat. His forehead wrinkled as his eyebrows met. "Captain, what lies do you bring into my hall? My daughter would never fall for such a lout. She is too proud. Do you defy these statements?"

Ahlk lowered his head and shook it. "I have to, Your Majesty. It is my duty to make sure the White Dragon is guarded. We have been ejected from his courtyard whilst Princess Nalla and Thareous are alone."

Next to the king, sitting straight in her opulent throne, Ingrezl asked to speak. A nod from her husband gave her leave, so she proceeded. "I fear that you both are correct. Nalla has never felt strong emotions for anyone. Now it seems she is in love with an unexpected lad. What, therefore, is wrong if she has acquainted herself with a fellow?"

"It would depend on how she acquainted herself," Jaldor said. "That is no comfort for me." His eyes flashed with sudden realization. "Where are they now?"

"As far as my knowledge goes, in the courtyard still," the captain said.

"This is all I will hear," the king said. "She should be with her sisters, Keirn and Mareinia. Retrieve her this instant! Whether her yokel beau trails her is not my concern." After Ahlk bowed and left, the king turned to his entourage. "Scribe, now is when your nib should flow most fluidly. Let it be told to the generations hereafter that blasted court will never again be accessible. Only the guards are to enter and defend it to the death."

Without warning the queen whirled on him. "This is unfair. I was a commoner too. You chose me as your wife and supporter. Both have I been. I scorn them now. Your decree is unpremeditated."

Hot wax lay on the envelope bearing the new statute. A servant conveyed it to Jaldor, who pressed his signet ring down into it. Then it was carried back to the retinue, where a eunuch took it. All the while the king studied the parchment. He ignored his wife, who scowled and looked away.

Minutes passed before footsteps broke the silence, echoing down the halls outside the throne room. Nalla entered a second later with Ahlk holding the door for her. She offered no thanks—only a glower and an insult. Thareous was not far behind. He passed both of them and went before the king and queen, then bowed. Jaldor pursed his lips and waited for the commoner to speak.

******

"Your Highnesses," Thareous said, "it is not as it seems. Your daughter and I are merely friends. We needed time to speak—to get over past feelings. You know how love is. It can take days, and hours of each, to transmute into friendship. So we went to a place where we would not be beleaguered by crowds."

The lie coming from his own mouth astonished Thareous. He did enjoy Nalla a lot, had even dreamt of marriage and a family with her. In spite of this he knew he had to protect Ianvorr. To Thareous it seemed that they formed a stronger pact than brothers, than mentor and pupil. Nothing would rupture their bond.

Much more to his surprise, Jaldor appeared contented by his answer. It seemed the old man could not find the right words, so he gave in. "Very well. Without this account I would have ordered you separated. Still, I must command you stay away from Nalla. I, knowing it full well, deem love *will* catch back up with you."

Thareous had done his best and bowed, fearful of angering the king. "As you wish. I shall see your mandate fulfilled."

"That is not all," Jaldor said. "The White Dragon's court is forever closed. The guards may attack anyone who resists. I have asked you both here to give you a fair warning. It is law, Nalla. You can no longer dismiss the sentries. I have granted them total power over that area. Now everyone leave. I must speak with my daughter."

Outside of the throne room Thareous's mind was a haze. *I cannot see Ianvorr anymore? How am I to know when he is gone, if ever? Will I get to speak with him again?* The last question made his heart sink into a pit from which it was unable to scale.

The Way of Magic

Memories of the new decree assailed Thareous as he awoke the next morning. He was eager to visit Ianvorr that day and even more to be around Nalla, whom he had admired since the age of thirteen.

All morning he was out of sorts and unwilling to help his mother, Anazeil. At age thirty-four she was quite beautiful and admired by many. Her sea-green eyes sparkled even in the toughest times. Still, he growled whenever compelled to help.

Haverin held several terse discussions with his son, though nothing terminated his petulance. At last he grabbed Thareous by the collar, shoving him into a wooden chair. "What is with you?" he demanded. But Thareous only gave him an expressionless look and said nothing. "Is this about Nalla?" his father finally said.

Silence was his reply.

"Blast it, boy, answer me!" Haverin roared.

At this Thareous winced, but could not bring himself to admit his troubles.

As Thareous's stubborn silence continued to swell, Haverin's impatience did as well. He knocked an earthen vase off its stand. It exploded to tiny shards. "This is going to be you if you do not answer straightaway," he said.

Sighing, Thareous realized he had no choice. "It is not only Nalla. The dragon is also involved. King Jaldor set up a new decree that nobody could visit it anymore or they would be attacked and arrested." He exhaled and let a smile play across his face. "I say it is worth dying to see that marvelous beast again!"

The Master Magician frowned, looking uncertain as how to proceed. So he changed the matter. "Thareous … I deem it is time I taught you the arts of magic."

An awkward moment ensued. Thareous could hardly speak. "Why did you not teach me before?" Thareous had begged him to do this in the past.

Each time he was refused. To travel in his father's footsteps was a dream, which diverted present worries.

"Because you were neither old enough nor strong enough. Magic is concentrated through the Power of the Will," Haverin said. "It is proper I teach you its strengths and weaknesses, freedoms and restraints."

"Do I need to learn a new language to acquire this power?" Thareous asked.

"No, magic comes from here," Haverin said, pointing at his head. "The Power of the Will, or the mind. With it you can do many great things."

"Am I going to have to communicate with dark spirits?" He would lose all interest if that were the case.

Haverin glowered. "Occultism is punishable by the same terms as heresy—burning on a stake to death. To avoid this, think of what you want to develop and focus on that. Now watch my example as I meld back my cause of destruction."

His eyes shut like curtains. A whitish orb extended from his mind and picked up the shards of the vase. It forged back into its original form. Thareous watched in amazement as its reformation occurred. Every detail was more improved than the former. The orb sparkled in his vulnerable eyes.

With the retransformation complete, Haverin sank into a chair. After a moment he turned to Thareous. "We will begin our lessons tomorrow. Most Magicians your age tire fast. They use that as an excuse not to study these arts. I expect the opposite from you to be held as an example to your lineage. Rest today and train with all your heart on the morrow."

"Yes, Father," Thareous said. "My anger will be gone by then. To answer your earlier questions, my heart burns to court Nalla. Even more so than seeing the dragon."

Haverin half-smiled at his son. "Princess Nalla shall await you. As for the dragon, hope is lost. That statute can never be repealed."

"I know. Still ..."

The Master Magician rose to embrace Thareous. "My reasoning cannot help you," he said. "All you can do is respect the authority. Forget about this dragon, also. There is not any other recourse."

"I am worried King Jaldor might do something to him."

"He would not dare. The people would have to say something about it. They abhor inhumanity. This talk must end, for I am late for the training hour at the fields. Finish helping your mother and go do as you like in town. Farewell."

******

Unsure of what pleasures he might find, Thareous just walked. Following a packed crowd down Bakers Street, he took a left to the Square. It was less busy since the streets had different trades. Down an alley his eyes caught a shocking scene.

Four adolescents surrounded Nalla, faces contorted into sneers. Thareous placed them as a band of infamous scamps he knew of. Their father was the commander of the Galgonian Army. Thareous had heard that the father forever told his sons that they had to be tough to survive. *Would they have the audacity to harass a daughter of the king?* Thareous wondered. He paced forward to find out, ears cocked.

"Your family has done aught but vilified Galgon's honor!" raged Yal, the apparent leader of the group. "Laws disallow pleasure. We take a cluster of grapes and get warned. We start a fight in the bar and get beaten. This is unjust."

"We can still have fun right now," the second oldest, Blugn, said. He smiled through rotting teeth and reached out to caress Nalla's cheek, moving his head forward. She froze.

Yal struck his brother's arm. "Are you mad? This causerie is just to get her to deliver a message." He whirled on the princess. "Tell your father to drop the laws or drop dead." He spat in her face. "Curse him and your progeny!" he snarled, then extended a hand to rub the spit in.

A hand grabbed Yal's wrist, twisting it back. The other three brothers turned to Thareous, the attacker. They halted. Thareous landed a punch across Yal's jaw and pulled Nalla away. They ran out of the Square. When they entered onto Bakers Street, Thareous kept her to his side, not making any contact. "What happened?" he asked.

"They do not like my father making new laws. They called him rash."

"So I heard, but how did they come to stopping you?"

"I was recognized. They surrounded me. They insulted me."

Thareous growled and began to walk. "Why are you even out of the palace?"

"I sneaked out for a walk," Nalla said. "My father is having a meeting, my mother is visiting the noblemen's wives, and my sisters are playing with their daughters. It is certain I am to be noticed missing. I shall not mention you or—"

"They have to be punished," Thareous said.

"I know, but you would be included."

The people in front of them clustered, muttering.

"What is this?" Thareous questioned.

Nalla peered over a bystander's shoulder and gasped. Thareous followed suit and took in the scene. A corpse lay on the streets, a pool of blood around him.

"That was one of the guards of the dragon's court!" Nalla said. "He is ..."

"Dead, Your 'Ighness," an old, skinny man finished for her. "Wargur was 'is name. 'E used to be my son's best c'um."

"Can you dictate what got him?" Thareous asked.

"See fer yerself." He gestured toward three wide gashes about the size of a dragon claw. These were lined on his torso, all parallel. Dried scabs had formed within the wound and kept any more blood from flowing out.

"What could have done this?" Thareous questioned.

"The dragon in the heart of the city. Or one of the beastie's friends. This might be 'is first victim. More lives are in danger so long as we let 'im live, I tell yuh! Just look at Wargur. 'Is body lyin' lonely like an' all ..."

"Do any of you plan on taking a course of action?" Nalla asked.

"Nothin' illegal, Milady. We are debatin' about a spyin' network in one of the four thresholds. We can keep an eye on the guards, an' 'em on us."

Thareous's mind raced. *Ianvorr could not have done this!* "King Jaldor will hear of this. You know how furious he is if the citizens take the law into their own hands."

"Why do you bring up the king?" a voice from the crowd asked.

"The guards will see you," Thareous said. "He will be told, then off with your necks."

"What are yuh drivin' at?" the skinny man queried.

"Gentlemen, ladies, you can do aught without first seeing the king," Thareous said. "Your notion is, in fact, unlawful."

"Thareous Haverinsson, the boy 'oo used to visit this beast," the skinny man said. "Of course! Yuh wish to protect 'im 'cause of this."

"And you are?"

"Malko Ronjersson. Been a father fer twenty-five years. Served in the Guard fer twenty of 'em an' 'ave been retired for the last five."

"Master Malko, you all have a choice to make," Nalla said. "Knowing the way my father handles things, there shall be three years in the quarry. Is this what you want—to have your families cope for themselves since their providers made a foolish action?"

"No, Your Grace," came the broken responses of the crowd.

"Let us all come to an accord: we will not tell on you if you do not tell on us," Nalla said. "This means we will not report your plan if you do not tell the king we were together. Our meeting was quite by accident."

"I believe I speak fer us all when I say we accept," Malko said. "We will take the body to the soldiers an' tell 'em what 'appened—wit' slight exaggerations."

At that the crowd lifted the corpse and left.

When they were out of earshot, Thareous said, "Get back to the palace."

Nalla backed away in alarm. "I wish to spend the rest of the day with you."

"Out of the question. Do as I say. We were never seen together."

"Oh, very well. Good day."

Thareous glowered as he watched her depart. Each of her movements filled with grace and elicited his passion for her. *One day I shall have a family. Whether noble or substandard I care not. I do want her as my wife.*

******

The next day Haverin and Thareous entered the Magicians' training field—a huge coliseum. With several other Magicians there to train, orbs flashed overhead, intent on destroying clay targets directed by telekinetic conjurers. They hovered about like a swarm of angered hornets.

Haverin led him to the center of the field. "Before we begin our lesson, I will clarify why the Magicians were instituted. During the rupture of a rebel group, the Omnipotent Ones, King Jaldor required another force than the soldiers. He turned his attention to the Way of Magic and had us learn it.

"My father, Frendur, was the best. He led the Magicians into battle against the imprisoned dragon. They held him back for hours. He managed to penetrate their lines and escaped. How, we know not. At least our fears are now over."

"You never told me how Grandfather died," Thareous said.

"Old wounds," Haverin said. "He never recovered."

"Because he was the best, he received the title the 'Master Magician'?"

"Aye. The king awarded him with the designation since he researched the Way of Magic keenly," Haverin said. "It was passed down to me. I want you to carry it on."

"I shall," Thareous said.

"We are about to reveal if you have potential," Haverin said. "Close your eyes, clear your mind, think of what you want to happen, and create an orb. Use your mind to guide it into the targets. This is the most basic exercise." He backed away to allow his son some space.

Thareous did as directed and excused anything that might distract him. He thought of an orb—what color he cared not. He painted it into a rainbow. He could make out the faint light through his eyelids. Some sort of energy hummed in front of him.

He moved it an inch ere letting it go off into the open air. An intuition opened his mind to the area. Wherever he guided the orb, he could feel the presence of anything breathing or moving. Bits of clay scattered down on his shirt like rain.

Feeling his focus diminish, he opened his eyes. The Magicians stopped practicing and stared at him. He glanced at his father, seeing that he, too, was mute. An uneasy moment set in. He feared he had done something wrong. *Did the orb strike someone?*

Then a tremendous cheer erupted. Magicians rushed forward to congratulate him. Thareous looked around, trying to summon to mind his accomplishment. It soon struck him: the targets. None were left. He had shattered them all in his first attempt.

Haverin lifted his hands, signaling silence. The rock-shaking ovation settled. "Hear now, men of Keiratha, a hero has risen to smite our enemies, to encumber their forces. Such a hero should be rewarded. Ergo, I hereby dub my son Thareous a Magician. He understands the Way of Magic."

"Hear, hear!" the enormous assembly bellowed in approval and acclamation.

Awareness

Ianvorr lay down in his cage. The skin-stinging haze drifted beyond the partitions. The guards repositioned themselves to avoid it. Heavy in thought, the Ice Dragon did not notice this.

His attention lay on a young sentry polishing his blade. The Head Guard Ahlk addressed him to the others as "Vellar." Many of the guards gasped; they had recognized the name. A warrior-king from long ago bore that same calling. The father of Jaldor, Vellar had been idolized by many for a steadfast keeping of justice and peace. Apparently the young guard before them was named after the great hero.

He was a lean lad with a clean-shaven face and tan hair almost at his shoulders. A gauntleted hand ran a rag over the steel of a double-edged blade. Wargur's replacement was indeed a wonder to behold.

From what Ianvorr had picked up from the guards' whispering, Vellar was known well around town as the only child of the First Division Officer Rhallanas. This notable soldier had earned his spot as second-up in the Galgonian Army after years of service. Ianvorr held special interest for his boy.

The squealing of hinges snagged the Ice Dragon's head to the side. Six guards rushed into the cage. They brandished cudgels and spears. Their eyes shone with intolerance. The rest remained outside the cage.

"Shove yer spearhead up 'is jaw!" one snarled. "This shall teach 'im to blow that frigid breath at us!"

"If we had some giant thread, then we could sew it shut," another said. The others laughed with him.

Vellar arose after seeing what had happened. "Are none of you going to do anything about this?" He flung this question at the indifferent bystanders. A truncheon smashed against the hinges of Ianvorr's jaw, delaying an answer. The dragon made no action. The low ceiling permitted him to rise six yards.

Dropping his unpolished sword, Vellar took up a bow and strung an arrow. "Stop this at once, you mob!" he ordered.

The six revolters peered his way. One stood firm. "Why cares you of our actions, boy? You are not the captain."

"I care because I am following the orders of the king," Vellar said. "He does not approve inhumanity or a brood of weaklings."

"Who do you call weak?" the staunch guard sneered.

"All of you, since you cannot brook some cold."

A bell tolled in the distance. The six guards filed out. Captain Ahlk appeared at the eastern threshold. "Time for lunch, men. Ten minutes as usual. Come with me." All the soldiers fell in and marched out of the courtyard.

Ianvorr watched as Vellar hung behind, no doubt in case any of the maltreaters should return. Only a rumbling voice met the young sentry. "Thank you for saving me from further torment."

Vellar's head arose and he turned around, eyes wide.

Ianvorr sat as high as he could, seeming to smile back. "Yes, I can speak. I have watched you since you came. I wonder, can you keep this discreet?"

"Wha-what discreet?"

"The knowledge that I can articulate."

Vellar nodded. "I can."

Ianvorr chuckled at his timidity. "Come, young one. I will not kill you if you tell. It is just better the king not knows."

Still he remained diffident.

"Would it make you feel better if you shot me in the heart?" Ianvorr asked. "Go on. You retain your bow and shaft."

"That I cannot do," Vellar said.

"You do not trust me. Why is this any different?"

"Because it is inhuman!"

"Then you trust me after all?"

Vellar settled with an "Aye," and laid his weapons down.

Upon hearing this, the Ice Dragon straightened. "By the elves' copse, the dwarves' warren, and the giants' summit, I am Ianvorr the Powerful. Ten tyrants have fallen under the smite of my claws. Countless invaders were slain by my wrath. Of my brethren I am the last of the first and considered the greatest warrior amongst us.

"I have a message that I wish for you to herald to Thareous Haverinsson, son of the Master Magician. Where he lives, I know not. Any guard can tell you. His father is famous. When you get there, repeat this to him: in three days, as the Convergence Ceremony commences, I am to escape at noon. The guards shall be too busy feasting. I will sail straight through the ceiling.

"I wish to bring you and Thareous with me. The king will question you after he learns of my flight. I have yet to decide our destination. Know it will be safe from the Galgonian Army. Say not a word now, for the others return."

＊＊＊＊＊＊

The dragon's caution came too late. Quaron, the guard who had contested Vellar, listened to everything since the introduction. He had heard something and stopped at the outer corridor. After Ianvorr spoke, he felt a change of heart—and saw a means of escape.

Because Quaron led the revolters into the cage, he would be held responsible. Jaldor would punish their cruelty by death. They had been charged to protect the dragon from harm, after all. He suspected that Vellar would report it to Ahlk and that in turn the captain would relay the news to the king. What if Quaron showed the dragon could give voice?

A plan edged up in his mind. He would have to confront Jaldor, tell him of his suspicions, and carry out the concluding action, should it be granted. Vellar would be an obstacle. But he could best him.

He was stirred back to reality. The footfalls of his companions drew nigh, echoing throughout the lengthy corridor. He weighed the possibility of any of them telling the king. They had seen and experienced how irate he could be. After working with someone for fourteen years, you come to know them well.

＊＊＊＊＊＊

At the end of the day Thareous collapsed into a chair, exhausted from the exercises in the training field. His eyes turned heavy, his sight bleary, his body disinclined to stir, and he dozed off. As soon as he did, a sharp tapping rattled the front door.

He arose and walked across the stone floor. Since Haverin was still at the fields and Anazeil in the marketplace, he had to greet the visitor. He wrapped his palm about the handle, opening the door. A soldier stood outside on the steps.

"Are you Thareous Haverinsson?" the man asked.

"Aye." A note of annoyance thrived in Thareous's voice. "Why are you here? I have not wronged the king."

The soldier nodded his understanding. "I know that. It is something else. A message from a friend of yours."

Thareous fingered his jaw. "Nalla?"

"Princess Nalla? Of course not. It is about the dragon."

"He no longer matters to me," Thareous said, closing the door.

The soldier's gauntleted hand impeded it. "Permit me entry ere you draw a crowd. This cannot be repeated in the midst of others."

The look upon the soldier's face made Thareous step back, for it showed truth. The soldier hurried in and shut the door. "Before we begin, I find it best you know my name. I am Vellar Rhallanasson, lone child of the First Division Officer."

"You are named after the late king—Jaldor's father?"

"Yes," Vellar said. "Anyhow, Ianvorr—aye, he even told me his calling—is escaping on the Convergence Ceremony. He wishes for us to go along with him, for fear the king will interrogate us. He has yet to decide where we should go."

Thareous became thoughtful as they went to the lounge and took a seat. "How did you find out Ianvorr could talk?"

Vellar recounted the event. At length Thareous sat back in his chair, brooding. "Why do you think he has not tried to escape before?"

"I am not sure," Vellar said. "Maybe some of his ilk are coming to get him. But that would attract too much attention."

"Perhaps," Thareous said. "Ask him tomorrow and come and visit me once you are off duty. I want to know why he fears King Jaldor."

"Or why he has reason to," Vellar said. "I shall attend to it when alone."

Echoes of War

Quaron strode down a long corridor lined with guards and suits of armor. Torches slanted in iron rings, their radiance reaching out to where other light failed. Weaponry hung at the walls by hooks. Sunlight filtered in through bay windows, but clear, white drapes obstructed it.

The hallway of a king. If I had a life such as this, I would spend it in pleasure. What do the affairs of others matter to me? I am no meddler. Therefore they could seek help from another prying ruler.

At last he came to the entrance of the throne room. Two hefty guards clanged their poleaxes together. "You are not to pass," the younger said. "The king wishes to be alone with Her Majesty."

"I serve him for the same reasons as you," Quaron said. "I mean to address a certain matter with him."

"I said you shall not pass," the guard said. His left hand went to the hilt of his sword. "Back down this instant, knave."

"What is the problem, Guard?" Jaldor's voice inquired.

"Your Majesty, some ill-eared soldier tries to get through to see you."

"Let him by so I can hear his reasoning," the king said. "Were this not important, he would not endanger his life so."

The sentries returned their poleaxes to a vertical position. Quaron entered via a double-entry door. The throne room was empty except for him, Jaldor, and Queen Ingrezl. No servant stood outside. He must have interrupted precious time. Still, if Vellar became a threat, this was the only way out of execution.

He stopped a few feet from the throne and bowed. "Live forever, Your Highnesses." After the king had beckoned him, Quaron arose. "Sire, I bring news of the White Dragon."

The king scowled. "You came here, imperiling your life to see me, merely to address that brute? You waste my time."

"I have suspicions he can talk," Quaron said, getting to his message before he would be thrown out. The declaration made Jaldor silent. He assumed he could go on. "I guard him. I see the way he looks at us. He appears to note our every move, how many breaths we take."

"Why do you tell us of this?" Ingrezl asked. "What could we do?"

"If this dragon can talk," Jaldor said, "it must be interrogated. I shall send a questioner there in the morn. Now, leave me, eh …?"

"Quaron Xyllanorsson, Sire."

Jaldor's jaw gaped. "Xyllanorsson?"

"Aye, Sire. It is unfortunate; my father turning himself over to our enemy," Quaron said. "But my intentions are far from traitorous."

"Intentions?" Ingrezl asked. "I misremember you mentioning any intentions. What are they?"

"In contrast to His Eminence's plans"—he gestured toward Jaldor—"I wished to question the dragon myself."

"You have no experience," the king said. "How could you bring back any credible results? I think an official interrogator shall do. Hence, your request is denied. Leave now."

Quaron groaned, feigning alarm. "Sire, as soon as the interrogator walks into the courtyard, we will be forced to attack him."

"He speaks sapient council, Husband," Ingrezl said. Her lined face became almost smooth as she frowned. "Your law cannot be circumvented or overruled. Mayhap we should sanction him to use any force necessary."

"Very well," Jaldor said. "Do as you must. Just do not kill it. If that brute can speak, indeed I wish to hear it. You may go."

The wily guard bobbed his head and walked out. Elated thoughts cackled like evil spirits. *Yes! The plan is to be carried out tomorrow. I have taken the advantage of that stupid law and bent it to my own will. I shall have my revenge, torment this "Ianvorr," and get away with it.*

******

The morning of the next day waned. Quaron was late. Ahlk reared nascent suspicions he might have forsaken them. He debated this with the others. They said it was doubtful.

Then Quaron strode in, his baldric woven with a design of a hand lashing out a whip: the symbol of interrogation. Two swords hung from his belt. A spear was in his left hand and a knout in his right. Being fully armored hindered his pace, but only somewhat. Stern eyes flashed beneath a visor.

Ianvorr gazed at him, sensing his objective.

"Hold up where you stand, Quaron," Ahlk said. "Why are you fashioned so?"

"Interrogation, Captain," the guard said. "King Jaldor wishes for me to query the beast—to see if it can talk—since a valid questioner cannot come here."

Vellar stepped forward. "Captain Ahlk, he must be lying."

The head guard rubbed his brow. "If the king did issue this directive, we dare not interfere. We cannot send one to ask him either. None can desert their posts or he will receive fifty lashes. Therefore we can only deem it truthful. Continue, Quaron."

"You cannot allow this!" Vellar exclaimed. He unsheathed his sword and went to challenge Quaron. Two guards held him back at Ahlk's indication. Someone deprived him of his weapons, including his bow. "Let me go! He is going to kill it!"

"Keep that fool at ease," Ahlk ordered.

By now Quaron had reached the door for humans. The hinges protested, but he needed not worry this instance. He unbarred it and went in. Ianvorr hung back. Quaron set down his spear and slid his swords from their sheaths, keeping hold of both a sword and the knout in his right hand.

"One last thing," Ahlk said. "What are you interrogating the dragon about? We know as well as you it cannot utter a word."

"Have you never heard the stories of old?" Quaron asked. "The dragons are protectors, the head of the Omnipotent Ones. The evilest, most vile foes fell under their might. It is said they can speak in the tongue of man. I think this one can as well."

The captain gesticulated him to go on.

"Hear me, White Dragon! You will talk in the midst of my comrades. Your time of secrecy has elapsed. This day, in pain or death, your revelation is to be open to all. You will tell us everything we wish to know. Your tongue will not be held still."

Ianvorr shut his eyes. *You overheard me speaking to Vellar yesterday. You do this to pardon yourself from the noose. Dragons are creatures not to be used.*

Quaron stepped back, shocked to hear a voice in his mind. "Speak in my tongue!" The whip in his right hand cracked upon the dragon's ivory scales. As it flicked back, it entangled about the sword in the same hand and severed in two.

Growling, the guard began to see his plan toppling. *What will it take to get you to speak if not by brute force? I do not want to die!*

Ianvorr opened his eyes to look at Quaron. *You have a poor choice of weaponry. If that was brute force, heed my words when I say neither leather nor steel can sway me. What can, you ask? Your death. For you know of my escape. I cannot have it jeopardized. War is upon us!*

War? Quaron asked.

The neighboring kingdom of an ongoing feud—Valvassa. The Dark King, Zakumahk, musters an army of fiends and marches past the Border Line. I must get away and aid my brethren in this war.

The other guards observed in curiosity.

My father, Xyllanor, is with that army, Quaron said.

Your father is known to me. He is spoken to be traitor. You know your story as a boy: long and woeful. Xyllanor was a respected man until he was relieved of his job for a mistake he did not commit. He aroused a drinking habit and lost control. Each night he returned, poisoned by the spirits of the liquor. He beat you and your mother, Reila. She moved away to a friend's home, leaving him a broken man. He stole away to Valvassa on a ship from the ports of Yarer and found welcome in Modrezra. Ianvorr paused, still staring at the belligerent guard. *You, meanwhile, stayed here, in Galgon for the rest of your life. You bore a secret during that time, a longing desire to flee to your father once more. Going there will count you as an enemy. Do not leave! By Annathias the Crafters shall curse you.*

"I will stay here and fight!" Quaron cried. "This war is not to go by unnoticed in my eyes. My people are to gain another man in arms. The enemy is to fall under the strokes of my sword!"

Ianvorr then decided to disclose his ability to articulate to the other guards, save Vellar. "So it shall be," he said. "The Resistance welcomes you, Quaron, Son of Xyllanor. Tell the others of our conclave. They must report this to the king as soon as possible. Inform him also that the Omnipotent Ones are not your enemy, Captain Ahlk. Zakumahk is."

With that the Ice Dragon fell silent, returning to his pensive air—and leaving the guards murmuring among themselves about his ability to speak in the human tongue. Quaron enlightened them on everything. Every word galvanized their energies. He sheathed his swords, eager to draw the blood of the foe—but not the enemy he had just spoken of to Ianvorr in hearing of his fellow guards. No … as he swore to slaughter the enemy, he referred to his countrymen—the Keirathans.

******

At dusk, after the nighttime sentries came to relieve them of their posts, Vellar went to Thareous's house. The divulgence to all the guards was disturbing. If Jaldor heard of it, a new interrogation would be launched. This would surely lead to his and Thareous's captivity.

When the first knock hit the door, it opened. Thareous bore with him anxious eyes. He had heard something of Quaron's questioning. "What news brings you?"

"All the guards know of Ianvorr's ability to speak," Vellar muttered.

"Come in," Thareous said. "Both of my parents are at the anniversary feast of King Jaldor's coronation. They will be back late. We have time aplenty to discuss this."

"I am sorry. I must leave within the hour," Vellar said, entering. "My father, Rhallanas, will be home by then. He expects me there."

"Let us make this quick. First, how do you think Quaron ever got the notion?"

"I am not sure."

"He no doubt heard you and Ianvorr talking to each other yesterday," Thareous said. "He knew of Ianvorr's plot and therefore attempted to undermine it."

Vellar stared at him. They walked into the lounge, taking the same chairs they had sat in before. "I do not follow you."

"Quaron knows what the king will do. He will send the questioner to the courtyard as the Convergence Ceremony advents. The guards shall be away, gorging with the rest of us. Ianvorr cannot hold out forever. Even if he does, Quaron still knows of us."

"You mean he could be a potential threat?" Vellar asked.

"No, he *is* a potential threat. If the wound opens more, then the plan is in danger of losing all its blood, its significance. We will have to stay here, await penalties, and be sent to the dungeon since we abetted a dangerous beast."

"This conversation is unsettling," Vellar said.

"We shall discuss the thing I wished for you to find out yesterday."

"Why he has not escaped before?"

"Aye."

"Indeed, though it is fortunate that I had time to converse our pearly friend before Quaron's foolish display," Vellar said. "In any case Ianvorr said he feared King Jaldor would make war with the Omnipotent Ones. Now he has special reason to escape. Valvassa marches out to battle at this very city. If we told the king, he would not listen."

"Yes, Ianvorr revealed as much to me about the looming war. But how do you suppose the dragon knows this if he is caged?" Thareous asked.

"This he did not tell me, although he alluded to some special sight he keeps."

"I wondered the same thing," Vellar said. "I asked him, and, aye, he said he has a certain ability to see any places he wishes. During the time in that cage he has been keeping an eye on Valvassa."

"He fears he could endanger the Omnipotent Ones yet has no alternative," Thareous said. "Perhaps because he also told me that he alone had this ability and that no others in his brotherhood retain this faculty."

"Yes, he said as much to me; that he is the only one who bears it," Vellar said. "It is supposed to be a part of some sort of curse."

"I know of the curse," Thareous repeated. "Though he did not elaborate on it."

"He likely did not have time to tell you a lot of things, such as why he is even imprisoned."

Thareous sat rigid in his chair. "Why is he?"

"This he did not tell me," Vellar said. "I have heard talk of a decade-long period where an invincible beast ravaged Keiratha. The Keirathan Army could not stop it. The Omnipotent Ones could not stop it. I believe, to some extent, Ianvorr was that beast."

Thareous said nothing for several seconds, then his eyes grew wide. "Yes, of course; yes, you are right. It was Ianvorr," Thareous said. "He refered to it the day I got him to speak. A sorcerer claimed his mind. It may have been a plot to remove the Omnipotent Ones' reliability."

Vellar nodded and peered at a window in the far end of the room. "We must weigh this another time. My home is a half-hour walk. Father will be expecting me."

They exchanged farewells and Vellar started toward home. Meanwhile Thareous remained stuck to his chair, his mind revolving about what Ianvorr might have been. Thirty years in a cage could have tamed any maniac beast.

******

Quaron walked into his house, unlocking the door with not a key, but his hand. He peered back, making sure he had not being followed, then dashed in as a shadow. Letters written by his father were strewn over his floor. They bore the plea to come and visit him. The way to him would be there in two days, at noon.

I shall be there. I will come and join the Dark Legion. A shadow, blacker than all the night hours, shall come across this land. He will be reawakened. The enemy shall fear him once again. The Omnipotent Ones are to fall.

Removing his armor, Quaron took up his fashion in civilian clothes and went to his bedchamber. Hundreds of letters lay at his feet there as well. They all bore the importunate calligraphy of Xyllanor. Together they would bear up arms and smite the enemy.

Quaron went to a nearby chest and opened it. A cloak, a sheathed steel sword, and panoply lay inside. Taking them out, he slid them into a bulky canvas sack. *It is the time to prepare. The road will be long ere I can meet the Dark King.*

Council with the King

Jubilant throngs amassed in the streets, awaiting the initiation of the Convergence Ceremony. It began when Jaldor presented himself before the multitudes, imparting the day's events. Jousting, horseraces, footraces, archery, sword-fighting, and roaster-catching were enlisted by him.

Thareous and Vellar joined each other in the amphitheater, sitting in a row of bleachers. The Ceremony began with two knights coming out on painted horses, shielded by armor and each bearing a lance and buckler. They charged, lance tips pointed toward the contender. Splinters showered over them when they collided.

In a separate section, hemmed off by a wooden gate, three men chased pigs to be roasted over a fire. There was so much stumbling and rolling that the crowds burst out laughing. The victor claimed his roaster and then walked off the field.

Back in the arena the jousters shook hands after one asserted the "deathblow." Next the races started. It was the ninth hour of the day and Thareous was getting edgy. The horses took up their starting positions first and waited for the signal. The objective was to ride around six barrels placed in different areas.

Jaldor stood, holding up hands for silence, and said, "My fellow Galgonians! It is at this time every year we converge to enjoy a day of festivity! It has come to my ears the food is ready early. We should go and commend the fine cooks by savoring their delicacies. To the banquet hall!"

Arising, the multitudes walked out the entrance, driven by hunger. Vellar and Thareous were at the front of the line and able to make it there in little time. The crowds carried them most of the way. Aromas from countless savories wafted onto the streets and quickened their pace.

Tables piled with food and drink stood before them. Wide platters served as plates so they could amass them with the victuals. Winery of every kind imaginable covered a mahogany. Thareous took a seat at the end of a table. Vellar did the same in front of him. They ate with silence as well as anticipation. Something that might change the plan would happen. They felt it in their bones and told it in their gazes.

Once they had finished eating, they left. It was the tenth hour, two hours until their escape. Servants came to take away the unfilled platters. Uneaten food would be given to the poor.

Back at the coliseum Thareous and Vellar waited for everyone to be seated. The king leaned in his throne at the northern side of the stadium encompassed by his officials. When hearing everyone to be ready, he arose and commenced the races.

As the horses lined up again, a monstrous shadow passed over them. Viewers became curious and looked up. Terrified gasps filled the arena. Thareous and Vellar stared in disbelief. Their intuition was correct; the episode that would alter the course of their plan was about to fall into place. The creature above was sapphire-blue and serpentine. It had the wings of a dragon and horns that twisted behind its eyes. It sailed upon the cloudless azure, almost blending in with the hue of the sky. In one elegant swoop it dove toward the king's platform.

"Get archers!" Jaldor cried.

Below, the riders struggled to control their horses. Three were thrown and injured. One got run over and gripped his arm. The others chased their steeds, which scampered and nickered in the fields.

Bowmen arrived. Spouts of water from the beast washed them away. Jaldor and his officials got up to flee. The creature then landed on the platform. "Keep your feet where they stand, Your Majesty!" a female voice hissed.

The king stopped. His officials got in the beast's way. They quivered like a bowstring. "Why do not you kill us?" Jaldor asked.

"I am not your enemy, Sire," she said, giving a curtsy. She arose, eyes of light stern. "I am Nahilmara, the Sapient Serpent, a kraken of the sea, lover of Ianvorr the Powerful. I share in his curse. I have come to release my long-lost brother."

"Brother?" the king let out in a breath.

"Aye, the one that rampaged the land two scores ago," she said. "An enemy, the Dark King Zakumahk, overtook his mind. We have searched for him since the day his rampage ceased. I have uncovered his location. He is to rejoin us. Send me off with an escort, one who knows where he lies."

Light torrents of water seeped from her maw agape, sliding off the platform. She watched as Jaldor spoke with the other noblemen, acknowledging her potential to destroy the city. Her demands would have to be met, though they were vacillating.

Jaldor ordered his men to step aside. "We all agreed to let him go. I must warn you: if anyone goes into his courtyard, they shall be attacked. Is this worth it?"

"A lifetime without him is worse than death," Nahilmara said. "Fetch the guide. Send none to stop me. This is what I must do."

Vellar turned to Thareous. "We have to get up there."

"We can follow," Thareous said. "Come on. It looks as if we will have to go early. Elsewise not at all."

They arose and bounded up the stairway. From the ten floors they were in the third, hurrying down the stairs to reach the base. They came to it. All at once they began their charge again. They broke out of the coliseum through an archway heading down the main street. A shadow surpassed them.

Nahilmara soared above.

"We will make it in time!" Thareous said between breaths. "They will wait for us. They must!" He looked up and saw who Nahilmara carried upon her back. Golden hair flowed in the wind. The sight nearly brought him to a full stop, for the person he saw was very familiar. Nalla rode the kraken. *Why would Jaldor assign her as the escort?*

Their legs pumping, Thareous and Vellar arrived at the marketplace. The shops were closed, but guarded by designated sentries who watched the two should they assume something not their own. They ran on, coming to the Town Square, where they would go through the prosperous segment. They swung into a lane and slowed to a canter. The buildings on either side kept Nahilmara from their eyes. The Royal Quarters towered ahead. In the heart lay Ianvorr's cage. Speeding up a last time, they sprinted harder than before.

Nahilmara came back to their vision. She landed outside the halls to the court. Nalla dismounted and pointed down one of the corridors—the other hall went through the palace. She led the Water Dragon on. Thareous and Vellar fell into a brisk walk.

They passed several suits of decorative knight's armor. This was the armor of past heroes—one had been used by the great warrior-king Vellar. Iron rings held torches up. Voices echoed down the hallway:

"Nahilmara, you were not supposed to come," Ianvorr was saying.

"You cannot decide what I do," she said.

"That is not what I meant," the Ice Dragon said. "I and two others were to escape this day—when the Four Suns merge. They are trustworthy so I have found. Since you came, they should be on—ah! Here approaches them now."

The Sapient Serpent looked them over as they passed the southern threshold. "It is to my understanding these two know of our plight," she said.

"I have told them much as need be," Ianvorr said.

Nalla looked at Thareous in alarm. "Are you saying he is going with you?"

"Yes, we are," Thareous said. "We are going where you cannot. With us danger trails. War is coming. You must stay here and tell your father to prepare."

A blizzard swept past them. The cacophony of metal shattering broke what would be an uncomfortable moment. All eyes fell to Ianvorr, who walked out of the twisted cage, unrestricted and unconfined. "Here you are eyewitnesses of my escape. For you have seen with your eyes and witnessed with your hearts. The enemy shall freeze in their steps; look upon me with fear, see my fury redone, and be felled by my claws. Their legs will grow heavy, their skin numb, their eyes unmoving since I am renewed."

The air grew cold. A chill went over them as each word was spoken. This sensation did not last long, for two figures strode in. Nalla stepped back in horror. The other four just stared on, calculating why they might be there.

"Mareinia, Keirn!" Nalla cried. "Why are you here? This courtyard is restricted."

"We know, Sister," Mareinia said. Her dark hair shimmered in the sunlight. Her brown eyes probed each of them. "We were sent to stop them. Why do you think you were chosen as the guide?"

"We will not fight the princesses of Keiratha," Ianvorr said. "You have no authority here. This is my court."

"We have power beyond any of you!" Mareinia bellowed. The quadrangle darkened as if it was near twilight.

Keirn, Nalla's sandy-haired, fifteen year-old sister, took her place at her side. "O Spirits, the Lost, come to me! Aggregate your numbers and aid me!"

Dark halos formed about her hands. She clenched them into fists and hurled the shadowy energy at Nahilmara, clipping the side of her head. It turned and plowed into Ianvorr's jaw. Thareous summoned a ball of light, hurling it at the sorceress. Keirn flew back several feet, losing her concentration and consciousness.

Mareinia scowled. "None of you will escape us." Her mouth opened. The softest tune flowed forth. It called to Thareous, to Vellar, caressing their minds, beckoning them forth. Entranced, they obeyed the call. Ianvorr and Nahilmara roared; it hurt their ears. Nalla was the only person unaffected.

"Stop this, Mareinia!" Nalla said. "As the eldest I command you to stop or by my right to the throne I shall banish you from this realm!" The melody did not falter. In desperation she leapt onto her sister and landed a fist into Mareinia's larynx. "The next time I give an order, you should listen."

Everyone shook away the trance. Thareous hugged her. "I am proud of you."

She returned the embrace. "Thank you. Father shall not be happy. I wish I could come with you."

"You cannot," Ianvorr said.

They parted and looked at him.

"Why do you say this?" Thareous asked.

"King Jaldor will suspect we kidnapped her."

"We can get Mareinia to tell the truth!"

Nalla sighed. "She would not even if we forced her—unless one of us stayed."

"Partly why you cannot go with us," Nahilmara said.

Vellar looked at Mareinia, who held her throat as if choking. "If we do not take her, she will get into more trouble than she would have if she did not help us. Mareinia will tell how she helped us escape."

Thareous gazed up at Ianvorr, looking hopeful.

The Ice Dragon grumbled in his throat. "Fine. Get behind Thareous. I, being mightier than Nahilmara, can carry more." They scrabbled up onto his back, using his ivory scales as handholds. Ianvorr spread out his great wings and beat them. After Vellar ascended to her back, Nahilmara emulated Ianvorr and rose from the earth. Mareinia watched in despair as they flew heavenward, straight through the ceiling. Rubble rained down overhead. She scrambled out of the way in time.

On the dragons sailed toward the Keicor Alps, their wings acting as masts. Thareous looked down and saw the assemblages in Galgon far below. Would it be the last time? He stared at Ianvorr's shoulder, stupefied as his home shrank away.

******

Behind them a creature, black as the night is dark, skimmed over the clouds. It bore a rider, hidden in cloak and armor. Cold, dead eyes scrutinized the dragons.

Sssoon they shall fall.

Dalsavia and the Keicor Alps

Nightfall crept in as the dragons landed. Eastward, ceaseless blizzards raged, issuing walls of snowflakes. Water melted from the excess snow on the mountains, the Keicor Alps. They settled near Dalsavia, a village ten miles from the frozen peaks.

Ianvorr went hunting, returning an hour later with five male reindeer and set them down so Thareous and Vellar could skin them and assort the meats. One of the pelts would be allotted for gloves and wraps, while the others could be fashioned into coats. The hides first would have to sit out a bit near the fire to dry and cure. Since neither of the dragons bore the ability to blow fire, they had to kindle one. Vellar had a lot of difficulty getting a tiny flame going thanks to the chilly air. Later, Nalla worked on raising a buckskin tent, an odd job for a lady. She had trouble finding the wood to hold it up, so used bones from the deer instead. She showed no revulsion. The dragons ended up lying in front of the tent entrances to help ward off the cold.

When morning came, Ianvorr directed Thareous and Vellar to go into town. Nalla protested, of course. The Ice Dragon said someone might recognize her and report it. So he sent the men away. He and Nahilmara stayed to guard the camp and the princess. Vellar had brought along some money for supplies, much to their relief.

Corruption thrived on the streets of Dalsavia. Men chased females with their skirts held high as if it were a game. Down an alleyway Thareous spotted a boy and girl, each about ten years old, wrapped in each other's arms. Two drunken brawlers sprawled on the muddy road in front of him. He had to break them up and sent them away.

"This thorp is a sink," Vellar said. "Where are the soldiers?"

"Probably where our tipsy friends were," Thareous said.

At last they came to a depot that appeared halfway decent. Chipping shelves and rotten produce filled its inside. Cobwebs and dust coated everyday supplies. They got the best food they could find, paid, and hurried away.

Once outside the town they stopped for breath. Vellar shook his head and pointed at the bag with their provisions. "What a waste of well-earned shillings. Hardly worth guarding our pearly friend."

"You were only on it for two days," Thareous said. He exhaled and straightened up. "Besides, had you not been there, Ianvorr might as well be dead. It was a sign the Fates exist that you were and had a care."

"That is sacrilege if I ever heard it," Vellar said. "Our allegiance lies not to them, but to Galthoria. He is, if you know, the master of mercy and guide of goodness. He is the reason it subsists in the first place!" He paused after seeing Thareous's reaction. "Why do you frown at these words?"

"Because that road is a dead end," Thareous said. "It is an empty path. I have trod it before. It led to insignificance. I felt as if I were chasing the wind. Now I see that self is the greatest guarantee of infallibility."

The flaxen-haired guard was aghast. "This would be asserting everyone to be perfect! Only fools think that. Imprudence is an empty path. Where this stops is not a dead end. It is at a hellish life in Annathias. Is this your want?"

"Do not try to save me!" Thareous snapped. "I am not a bad person. Galthoria will accept me because he should know this. My actions shall ensure—"

"Your actions will not allow you in Kallenalza!" Vellar cried. He panted for a moment to calm down. "Look, you follow your own opinions—secular opinions. These do not certify your safety; they increase your deficiency. All you have to do—"

Thareous yelled as a gauntleted hand batted Vellar's temple from seemingly out of nowhere. His friend fell to the ground, a cloaked being standing over him. This abomination surely had no name to describe it. The head of a snake glowered at him under the lip of a cowl. Sheer strength emanated from a full set of armor. A steel sword hung from his belt in a sheathe.

"You proceed down the right path," he said to Thareous in a sibilant voice. "Sssin is the only reason the Fatesss put us here. Whether our kind is called fools or not, we must follow our heartsss. You may listen to me. I am not your enemy."

"Who are you, then?" Thareous asked.

"That I shall disssclose to you if you come with me," the man said. "As for now, let usss go! I can offer you shelter from this needlesss war."

"I want to fight," Thareous said. "I want to defend Keiratha."

"Defend Keiratha?" the man seethed. "Defend a country that has ridden itssself of dignity? Did you not notice the perversion in Dalsssavia? How can you say this when the war is to arrange change for our homeland?"

Before Thareous could answer, Ianvorr swept from above. "Get away from here, Young Mage!" He landed between Thareous and the man, then lashed his tail out. It struck only air as the enemy became a shadow and vanished.

"Who was that?" Thareous inquired, climbing onto his friend's back.

"A hypocrite," the Ice Dragon said as he picked up Vellar. "We worried when you did not return. I decided to go look for you. My ears detected the words of that charlatan. They were intended to mislead you."

"He requested to take me away from the battle," Thareous said. "Why was that? Why did he not attack me as he did Vellar?"

"You must learn this for yourself," Ianvorr said, taking off. "The answers you seek will be found in the Nyran Forest. It shall come as a great shock to you. You may even reconsider your decision to fight."

"Please clarify this for me," Thareous said. "I am confused. My questions are not quenched by my own replies. Can you provide them for me, then?"

"Not at this time," Ianvorr said. "Later. Later ..."

They flew on in silence. Upon returning to the disassembled camp, the females joined them in the sky. Vellar awoke in Ianvorr's paw and climbed up his arm and shoulder scales. He pulled himself between the spinal spikes ahead of Thareous. Neither traded any words.

A minute later thick black blizzards swallowed them. Flurries of snow beset the humans. The buckskin coats helped very little. Cold intruded every inch of their bodies. The dragons pressed on as hard as they could.

I am sorry for the conditions, Ianvorr said in the mind of Thareous, who showed only a little surprise at the mental rapport suddenly opened by the dragon. *They were formed long ago by an irreversible deviltry. For over ninety thousand years they have surged without end. I should believe they will do so to the end of time.*

Thareous groaned and tried to look down. He could only make out consistent white lines of snowfall and the faded contours of the alps. Beyond that the world was a pasty blur. Any hope of escaping this wearisome prison seemed dead.

As each flake passed, he thought he saw a flicker of motion. *Something is out there*, he told Ianvorr through their mental link. The Ice Dragon responded with a chuckle and barricaded his mind. It did not look as if he was skeptical; it did not even seem to bother him.

To make the matter worse, Thareous noticed the same activity, now closer. *Why does he not care? We could be in danger!* He sensed Nalla and Vellar felt the same way. Nahilmara had her thoughts guarded too. Had the dragons led them into a trap?

Then, before he knew it, the approaching danger set in. Or had it been any danger at all? From what he could make of it, Thareous saw ten facsimiles of Ianvorr. *Ice Dragons!* Thareous thought. *Our pearlescent friend is not the only one of his kind.*

Yes, they are my brothers, Ianvorr said. *They have been sent by Jurtithan to lead us out of the Keicors. So fear no more! We are almost rid of these dreaded storms.*

"Hail, Powerful One!" an Ice Dragon addressed. "Our eminent leader has requested that we—" His voice drowned out with the storm. Thareous wondered who this leader could be. Nothing else was heard past this.

Finally Ianvorr spoke. "The Ice Fortress is now behind us. We should be coming across the margin of the alps anytime. The Nyran Forest is just beyond them. Hold tight! We are about there!"

Almost immediately the fliers broke past the wall of snow. The humans gasped at the emerald canopies and patches of lucent meres. It seemed to fit within a painting, wrought from an artist's conception.

"It is majestic, is it not?" Ianvorr asked, checking their reactions.

A hiss above them caught their attention. "Majessstic?" The mysterious man from Dalsavia sat atop an ebony beast that the dragons seemed to recognize. "Majessstic shall be your downfall!"

And black flame enveloped them.

THE OMNIPOTENT ONES

A mysterious being crept down a hillside, an arrow nocked on his bowstring, eyes fixed upon a deer. His footfalls were silent, his feet dexterous, his legs strong yet flexible. Right now the target faced the other way, grazing. The hunter took cover behind a bush, waiting for the deer to amble his way.

He lifted his head over the crown of leaves and saw its antlers move to the side. Now was his chance. A swift and accurate shot would provide him with meat. Readying his bow, the hunter rose, drawing it in front of him. As he did, monstrous bellows echoed throughout the woods.

The deer raised its head, spotted him, and ran off. The hunter did not care. Danger lurked outside the Nyran. His swore to protect the forest. Following the reverberations, he dashed ahead as light brightened the land. Bushes, trees, and lakes passed by him on either side.

Hilly terrain was his footpath, haste his ally. Great shadows amassed beside him. The leviathans, the Air Dragons, guardians of the forest, gathered. His kind, the elves, joined him at his side. The weald belonged to them.

They formed a single host. Whatever the enemy, they would stop it as one. They advanced, looking almost as if they flew. While they ran, they pulled out their weapons: bows, daggers, swords, and blowguns. The Keicor Alps loomed ahead, terrible storm clouds in a rage.

A cloaked rider pillaged the bags of downed humans. A black beast stood guard and spotted the leviathans. It had bloodred eyes, diamond-shaped and lidless. It unfurled its bat wings and uncoiled its serpentine tail. Spikes like mountains shifted along its spine with each slight movement of its back. Black skin creased as an elephant's hide; its jaws were rotted yellow. With the torso of a dragon, the sable monstrosity lifted itself.

"My rider, enemies approach," the creature, a zarjkakon, hissed.

"They will not impede us," the cloaked rider said. He turned toward the company of elves, unsheathing his steel blade sword. "Let us passs unharmed or so die trying! You might stop me. Yet my pet can ssslay you all."

The elf-archer watched his commander step forward and speak. "One man and his beast cannot break past an army of our kind. You shall not pass."

"Face our fury, then!" the enemy retorted. He charged, his armor grinding. The zarjkakon followed, ebony flames shooting from its nostrils. As they neared, a transparent barricade shot up before them, separating them like a wall. The beast and man stopped before it, careening their sharp instruments at it.

"We stand as one united under the gaze of Galthoria," the Elf Commander said. "You shall not pass. The forest is ours to protect. You shall not pass."

The man hesitated. "Let usss through!"

A giant hand formed itself from the invisible barrier and grabbed him. "You will have much explaining to do before the Tribunal," the elf-archer said. "Intruders are not welcomed to the Copse of the Elves. They are lambasted. So you shall be." As he spoke, the elf willed the hand to let go the man. He fell unconscious. The zarjkakon began to head-butt the barrier. Two hands sprouted and seized the beast's horns.

"See if the others are alive!" the Elf Commander commanded. "If the Silver One has spoken right, these may be the ones we await."

Elves passed through the force field, going out to fulfill their order. As they approached, a young human sat up, rubbing his head. The elf-archer pulled him to his feet and assured him he was a friend. The zarjkakon whirled on them then, its horns snapping off. "If I cannot enter the woods, there is to be carnage!"

It stampeded toward the youth. The elves could not stop it. The leviathans were too far up to do anything in time. The zarjkakon unsheathed its claws. Drool poured down its jaw. Then something happened. It stopped dead in front of its target and was then hurled back. It curled up into a ball and disintegrated into something like a shadow.

The Elf Commander signaled for the barrier to be let down. He walked up to the youth, rubbing his chin. "By Galthoria, you have much unused power. If you be a friend, state your name. I am Karthaiz."

"I am Thareous, Son of Haverin, the Master Magician in Galgon," he said. "We bring back Ianvorr the Powerful. He feared that if he escaped, King Jaldor would claim war upon your kind. But another war is impending."

"Is this confirmed?" Karthaiz the Commander asked. "Do you see Ianvorr?"

The elves searched more thoroughly until coming across his form. "We do, Commander," the elf-archer said. "He is unconscious but whole.

With him we find Nahilmara and identify ten Ice Dragons. Jurtithan sent them to lead their group through the snowstorm."

"There are also two humans, aside from me," Thareous said.

That elf glared at him. "We have searched. Aside from you there is one only."

"Are you sure, Aildeimor?" Karthaiz asked. "This other human, male or female, could be trapped under one of the dragons."

Thareous gasped. "What gender is the one you found?"

"Male," Aildeimor, the elf-archer, said.

"We have a princess with us," Thareous said. "She begged to come along. Ianvorr revoked her pleas. Before we could leave—"

"We know what happened," Karthaiz said. "Nahilmara found out Ianvorr's location by one of our seers. He watched the courtyard until you left. We saw the struggle in lakewater by descrying. The incident was unfortunate."

"Then you knew she was with us," Thareous said.

"Nay," Karthaiz said, "I knew she left with you. You could have abandoned her in a village, Dalsavia perhaps. There the soldiers would find her and take her back to the Capital for questioning."

A grunt made them desert their talk. Ianvorr's light blue eyes cast nearby shadows the opposite way. He forced himself to rise. Snow slid off his side.

"Hail the Powerful One!" Karthaiz shouted.

"Hail him!" the elves and leviathans echoed. "Hail the one redeemed!"

Aildeimor joined in the chant with the others. Vellar was there, but not Nalla. Thareous feared she might not have made it. Then the chanting stopped. A snowy being arose and changed into a human in white garments like those worn by the Royal Family.

"Nalla!" Thareous exclaimed. "How did you do that? I was worried sick about you!" He helped her stand and brushed snow from her gown. It appeared to be untouched by the frozen particles.

"There is something I must admit," she said. "As Mareinia is a siren and Keirn a sorceress, I am a naiad. I can take the form of any watery being at my will. Your father taught this to me so I could protect myself. I am sorry; it was supposed to be secret."

"Never mind now," Ianvorr said. "We must get to Leaftorn. With my second sight I have seen the enemy. They march here. Their numbers surpass ours."

"To Leaftorn it is," Karthaiz said. "Prepare to move out! The Tribunal should hear this as soon as feasible."

To the other Ice Dragons, Ianvorr said, "Return to the Ice Fortress. Tell Jurtithan that we made it and mean to battle Zakumahk here. May the Crafters be with you."

"No, may the Crafters be with you," one of them said. "You need blessing more than curse. You need it to vanquish the enemy."

With that the ten Ice Dragons took to the skies. Ianvorr watched them until they vanished above the Keicor Alps. The light of his eyes flickered, understanding their meaning. "Let us go! For peace wars are fought. For this it is a matter of control."

The elves turned and ran away; the leviathans took off. Ianvorr and Nahilmara waited for the humans to remount on their backs. Before they left, the Ice Dragon looked to his side and spotted something gleaming in the sunlight. "What is this?"

He pawed the figure, gazing over the snaky features. "So, it is the man from Dalsavia. He has followed us through the storms." The memory of the beast sending out the flames over him entered his mind. "And riding a zarjkakon ..."

Then, when he began to lift him, the hood fell. The snake face became human. A gasp shook Ianvorr's sides. "Quaron! He said that he would remain and sway the king into readying for the war. What could have turned him away from this?"

Nahilmara nuzzled his jaw with her nose. "It matters not. He swore an oath—instead of promising to defend his country, he meant to destroy it. But come! The others will be waiting for us. We may discuss this with them."

The dragons launched into the sky, gaining altitude with each beat of their wings. Playful wind sifted through the canopies of the trees, waving at the passing beasts. To their left a group of lakes shimmered in the radiance of the Four Suns. Birds fled the dragons, fearing them to be predators.

In the distance the green contours of the leviathans carried across the open atmosphere. The air there was cleaner, so Thareous noticed. It made him feel as free as a finch, since it was the third time he had ventured atop Ianvorr.

Nowhere below, between the clefts of the trees or the occasional open meadows, could he see a single elf. He asked Ianvorr about it. "Elves are not at all like humans," the dragon said. "They unearthed how to run faster than anything else."

"How can they do this without running into anything?" Thareous asked. "At such great speeds they would collide."

"In truth they have found out how to go through material obstacles," Ianvorr said. "Set up a wall, a force field, or any other blockage, and they cannot be halted."

"Do you suppose they are already at Leaftorn?" Thareous asked.

"I would not doubt it," the Ice Dragon said.

From then on they flew in silence.

******

The arms of night reached out to embrace the land when they finally alighted. An elf ran to meet them. "Lord Ianvorr, the Tribunal is to see you at the morning's first light. For now they bid you rest."

"We will have it," he said. "It would do well to not leave refuse unguarded again, lest it escape." He dropped the comatose Quaron in front of him. "Be sure he is watched well. No one is to visit him save when he is fed. And strip him of his sword."

"I shall do as you ask," the elf said. He lifted up Quaron and ran off.

"You handled that rather well," Nahilmara said.

Ianvorr half-frowned. "I could not have it any other way."

"No?"

"I am not volatile, Nahilmara."

She waited for Vellar to dismount and then extended her snout up to the other dragon. "I never said you were and I never said you were not."

"We will leave it at that."

Ianvorr walked off with Nalla and Thareous still atop him. He carried them off to an unpopulated place in the forest. A band of elves conversed in secret at the other side of a hill. The Ice Dragon sighed. "They know not what advances," he said as his riders slid off an outstretched wing. "Until the Tribunal's verdict they cannot prepare. Preparations are necessitated to no extent!"

"Why do not we tell them that?" Nalla asked.

"Because they would not listen," Thareous said. "I gather elves are incredulous unless proof is given."

"Elves are profoundly precautious," Ianvorr said.

"Indeed we are." Aildeimor stepped from the shade of a beech. "We are wise and guarded. Seldom do we act without premeditation, bar last resorts. The Tribunal is not rash. They are severe and make their decision after everything is heard."

"Are they tyrannical?" Thareous inquired.

"Nay, each of the Three Councilmen are just and impartial," Aildeimor said. "If a serious offense has been committed, only then are harsh penalties doled out."

"They are sure to bear grudge toward me since I ravaged the woodland four decades ago," Ianvorr said.

"Presumably," Aildeimor said. "At late they have been acting somewhat strange. Albeit, in the midst of a meeting, they are composed."

"So others do not grow suspicious of their oddity?" the Ice Dragon queried.

"Aye, and so they do not get replaced." Aildeimor rolled his eyes and fingered a hunting horn at his side. "It is the time we gather our forces from afar. The Omnipotent Ones are not disbanded. Not while Keiratha is in danger."

"Who are the Omnipotent Ones?" Thareous asked. "What is their origin?"

"Guardians of old," Ianvorr said. "We were founded by a young dragon over ninety millennia before. His name is Jurtithan. You shall see why he is called the Silver One. Long have we defended Keiratha from the enemy, Valvassa being the main."

"Why is it they would have to war with the Keirathan Army?" Thareous asked. "Why were you caged? Somehow these two questions are linked."

The Ice Dragon sighed. Icy haze fell over the humans and elf, causing to them shudder. "Zakumahk the Tyrant of Valvassa overpowered my mind a nigh generation ago. He used me to pass great devastation over this land. Villages burned, innocents fell, and Galgon came close to ruin. Jaldor fears my escape might mark my reprisal."

Thareous sat down. "I had no idea of your plight. It distresses me. Inside I feel the burning incentive to avenge you. Why is he invading?"

"From what I gleaned, Zakumahk wishes to drive us from this realm," Ianvorr said. "Valvassa is a death-land. Its terrain is bare and devoid of vegetation. Toxic gases seep from crevices. The land is overrun by fiends, people who were once dead, but now are reawakened. Only they can abide in its conditions."

"How did it ever come to be like that?" Nalla inquired.

"A tyrant from long ago, near the beginning of time, ravaged that land through his Dark Arts," Ianvorr said. "From him I received my curse. He did it in vengeance since Jurtithan slayed a large brigade intent on overwhelming us."

"Who was he?" Nalla questioned.

"Varkin, the most powerful Magician ever to live," Aildeimor said. "How he gained access to such abilities, we know not."

"He is responsible for creating many sins and offenses," Ianvorr said. "He used to have men abducted from their homes to be slaves, his chief wrongdoing. Adultery came second. He would impregnate married women, often widows, and on the streets have sexual intercourse with them. Then he would desert them."

"Galthoria's grace," Thareous muttered. "Such actions should be against the law."

"To have many love affairs is not the matter," Ianvorr said. "How you *choose* to use them is. People can still love another and not break any law. So gallantry is the apposite expression."

They fell into silence, reluctant to talk anymore. At length Ianvorr said, "The hour grows late. We should rest. In the morrow, when the day is young, the meeting is to commence. Sleep well, my friends. May the night bid you restrained dreams." He lumbered off to a clearing not far from there.

Thareous turned to Aildeimor. "Where do we sleep?"

The elf-archer laughed. "We do not live in houses, but with the habitat. As our beds to rest our backs on, we utilize piles of leaves. For coverings to repel the night cold, we use deer pelts. I am sorry there are no roofs to keep out raindrops. We let the treetops do that as much as they can."

"It should be fine," Nalla said. "Though I am used to the comfort of my bed, the warmth of a bedside fire, this will do. Good night."

"Sleep well, Milady," Aildeimor said with a low bow before looking at Thareous. "Good night, Annihilator. This the elves decide to call you for defeating that beast earlier."

Thareous nodded his thanks and lay down. Aildeimor led Nalla off to a thicket closer to Ianvorr than to Thareous. He did not care. For his mind was filled with turbulent musings of his future. *So this is where it begins. I am to ward away a dark army of fiends and redeem peace. How is this possible if I have not faith?*

Council of Fate

"You lie!" cried Yeilth, the lead councilman of the Elven Tribunal. "Valvassa shelters cowards. They would not dare march out against us—not with our numbers!"

Ianvorr lowered his gaze. "My foresight does not lie."

"Foresight?" Yeilth's younger sister, Talleir asked. "No dragons are birthed with this gift. How did you come to claim it?"

"I attained it with my curse," Ianvorr said. "Alongside it comes the ability to turn into a living specter, host material illusions, and converse with spirits of darkness. This I do not use. For they wail into my ears, making them ache to the point that I wish I was dead. Nahilmara shares some of my powers, just not the second sight."

"Tell us what you saw through this second sight," said the third and final tribune, Darjein. "Do not make it long."

"As you wish," the Ice Dragon said. "While I was caged at Galgon, I closed my eyes and saw a gathering. It took place in the court of a castle where fiends met by the thousands. Upon a platform in the center of the room the Dark King stood.

"'Here is the day when Keiratha will fall!' he bellowed. The fiends roared and hooted. 'Down comes the Dynasty, the Omnipotent Ones with it! Arisen is our Overlord, our Majesty, our King ... Malluesaer shall deliver him to us! He is coming! Make way for the Mighty King of Keiratha!'"

Ianvorr paused. "Jaldor is to be deposed. This 'Overlord' will take his place. Zakumahk is set to awaken him. Why they are marching here, I know not. The reason I can guess is to prepare for his coronation."

"From what kind of sleep do you presume he needs arising?" Yeilth asked.

"Death," the Ice Dragon said. "The followers of Malluesaer practice cabalistic rituals, seeking out those dead. If they had the willpower, they could find the burial place of their sought one and revive him by occult means."

The Tribunal spoke with each other for a few minutes until Yeilth rose. "As I said before, they are cowards. Naught ill is transpiring. Thus I hereby annul your plea—"

A mahogany dragon landed in front of the Tribunal's platform, cutting off the leader's decree. "The wyverns need your help."

Ianvorr groaned as his eyes fell on the wyvern messenger. "Oh no!"

Eyes of shadowy light looked back at him and opened into a grin. "Hey, the Powerful One is back!" The wyvern faced Nahilmara. "Your mate is back, Sister. I found him."

"Kyjre!" Ianvorr roared. The elves would have cackled had he not yelled so. "Everyone here knows I am found. Tell us what troubles your kind."

The Fire Dragon dropped his gaze. "The Dark Legion assailed Zahkrahm earlier today and overthrew us," Kyjre said. "We fled. I came here seeking help. The Legion advances still, undaunted, unchallenged."

At this the Three Councilmen huddled to discuss the matter. Yeilth faced the assembly of elves. "I withdraw from my former command. The elves and leviathans will defend the forest. Ever since the day of the Great Wildfire we have been fervent to protect it. So we continue to." Then they strode the platform and vanished into the crowd.

A leviathan appeared from where they departed and ambled toward Ianvorr. "We are eager to follow you in Jurtithan's stead—since he is not here. What are your orders?"

"First tell the elves to gather their weapons and supply these males with swords. Send Princess Nalla with the women and children. She cannot fight, though she, too, is willing to do so. And escort the prisoner Quaron to a hidden coppice."

"Is this all you need?" the Air Dragon, Airalus, questioned.

"We must know how far the Dark Legion is from here," Ianvorr said.

"I shall send out a scout." Airalus went away to fulfill his assigned tasks.

******

A fine sword was presented to Thareous. Its guard curved like bull horns. Its hilt was leatherbound and its round pommel hugged a jade. The iron blade pointed straight up. He swung it out in the open. It clanged into the skean of Aildeimor, who said, "Your weapon is wielded without care. You require practice."

Thareous restrained his blade. "Will you teach me?"

"I can teach you many things," Aildeimor said. "You have only to ask." He sheathed his sword and looked at him.

"Will you teach me to wield a blade?" Thareous asked.

"I shall if you listen to my instruction, advice, and criticism."

"I shall."

The elf smiled. "You and I are going to get along fine."

"After yesterday I surely hope so," Thareous said.

They started down a dingle, passing brush and tree. At last a clearing ringed by evergreens came before them. Aildeimor and Thareous locked blades. "First, let me assess your speed," the elf said. And they clashed.

Their blades met, sending a clang through the metal. Thareous backtracked as Aildeimor stepped forward and jumped to the side. Thareous's sword veered down, clipping the elf's shoulder. Clear barriers shielded both their bodies, so he was unharmed.

They continued to step and parry, working their way down a footpath disguised by grass. Years of disuse had left it to become lush. Tree roots arched out of the ground, threatening to trip them. Thareous, unfamiliar to such training, tired quickly.

Aildeimor, whom seemed to sense his student's fatigue, swung his blows more vigorously. Thareous bore no warrior's strength. How could he survive in the battle if he did not have this? Amateurs lost in the tide of war, as they were apt to just give up. Even some of his best friends had fallen.

Then Thareous heaved his sword aside. "I cannot do this. I exhaust too easily!"

"Let us sit and talk," Aildeimor said. They sat across from each other and crossed their legs. "You grasp your greatest weakness. In battle, fatigue can cost your life. Hesitation results the same. Stamina returns the blows of the enemy twice."

"I have borne tenacity like a grudge, but never stamina," Thareous said. "In truth I have not even learned how to wield that."

Aildeimor remained silent, unmoving.

"Can you not help me?" Thareous asked.

The elf did not shift.

Thareous sensed something to be wrong. "Is an evil behind me?" He was puzzled to receive no indication. Slowly he turned. A yell startled him from where the elf-archer sat. He returned his gaze in front of him. Aildeimor no longer sat there.

All of a sudden a hand grabbed his mouth. "Ignorance is the resolution to resisting impediments when fighting." The hand let him go. "In addition to sparring you shall be learning magic." Aildeimor walked back to his seat.

Emitting a pent-up breath, Thareous settled. "I already know every category."

"Are you certain?"

"As far as I am informed, yes."

"What is thaumaturgy?"

Thareous's eyebrows lowered. "I am not sure."

"The working of anything miraculous: magic itself," Aildeimor said. "If you have never heard what this is, how can you know exorcism?"

"I was taught that," Thareous said. "Exorcism is when evil spirits are driven out of the possessed. Good spirits take their places, ensuring they never return. That also makes the possessed one's mind easier to control."

"You know some magics. Others are untold to you," Aildeimor said. "I have much to do until tomorrow."

"Tomorrow?" Thareous queried.

"When the Dark Legion should be here, if not sooner," the elf said. "Let us not cut into the future. We must focus upon the present. Your training is incomplete, inferior."

"Inferior than most, I suppose," Thareous said.

"Indeed, Annihilator." Aildeimor got to his feet. "Come. It is nigh noontide. Take your blade in hand and come with me. This time, ignore fatigue; resist its calling to cease reflexes. We break for lunch at midday."

They kept with their training. Thareous grew more alert and anticipative. While honing his will to train, he founded an entwined aspect of optimism and approbation. Along with this was the budding fact that he and Aildeimor became fast friends. They would not let this interfere.

When noon arrived, Aildeimor led him back to the populated area of Leaftorn. The scout sent out by Airalus had returned. Ianvorr convened with him about what he had seen. Once all was said, they returned to the others. A marvelous feast of venison, various fishes, and wild-bird eggs was set before their eyes.

Ianvorr stood and addressed the awaiting banqueters. "Elves of the Nyran! It is told to me that the Dark Legion is forty miles from passing into the woods. The Tribunal is not to be found. I recall they led the elves to battle. It seems they have forsaken you."

The elves were speechless.

"Howbeit," Ianvorr said, "I shall take their place while they are away. Should they return, I will re-grant them their positions. They must have a good reason why they ran off."

Karthaiz raised a hand to silence him. "Frostweaver, my troops are your troops. I am your servant in this war. Do you not find it best we come up with some pitfalls?"

"Traps are an excellent idea," the Ice Dragon said. "It may be better if we send out your best archers to waylay them at the border."

Aildeimor walked in front of him. "I am their greatest archer. I am also in the middle of instructing Thareous."

"We can omit you," Karthaiz said. "There are plenty. It shall not go ill."

Ianvorr nodded. "Very well. Gather the bowmen. Have them go to the eastern margin. In my recall about the cartography of the Nyran Forest, the Legion should sneak between the lakes. Post them there. As the enemy advances, pull them back. There is to be no direct assault."

"Consider it done."

At this they began filling large leaves with the food. Cups of stone brimmed with vivid water were passed about. A brief prayer to Galthoria, thanking him for all there, resounded in the calm. Following the "Amen," they ate and settled in to talk.

Their conversation wove too many things. Always the yarn led to the upcoming attack, it seemed. Nerves were high. The next day they would be put to the test. The morrow's night would see a skirmish worse than any the Nyran Forest had ever held.

Thareous noted everything said and done. Then he set down his leaf-plate, having finished, and got up. Aildeimor seemed caught up in talk. Thareous wished to be alone, to ponder over his fate. Getting a taste of a warrior's life made him regurgitate his patriotism.

Aildeimor stepped from behind a tree. "Walk with me. We have much to resolve."

Groaning to himself, Thareous joined in step with him. "What is this about?"

"I sense fear in you. Fear is not supposed to be in us, a part of us, or for us. The solution to its removal is courage. If courage is with you, fear is not. Also, I read from your expression you do not wish to fight. It is your destiny to heed the call of a defender, of an Omnipotent."

Thareous halted. "I am not to be forced."

Aildeimor faced him, shaking his head. "You are not being forced to do anything, Thareous Haverinsson. You were predestined by our late Philosopher Yelva, she who watched the stars each night. Constellations came to her, enabling her to foretell remnants of the future. Yours was the last to come to her."

"What am I predestined to do?" Thareous asked.

"Rescue Keiratha from the greatest danger ever to reawaken," Aildeimor said, brow drawing together. "We are not sure what this danger yet is. Something awful is to emerge from it. It could involve the Supernal Realms."

"The Supernal Realms?"

"Annathias, Kallenalza, and the Middle World," the elf said.

"What is the Middle World?" Thareous inquired.

"The dominion where the Fates rule," Aildeimor said. "It is so called because it is twixt Annathias, which faces west, and Kallenalza, facing east. Galthoria, in Kallenalza, rules over life, the Fates over time and karma, and Malluesaer of Annathias, over death."

"How do you know I am to save the land from certain devastation?" He wished to consume all the facts permitted to him like an insatiable flame.

"Often the Fates move stars to hint to us of the future," Aildeimor said. He ran a hand in the air over him, signifying the sky. "Yelva looked up at the right time and saw a name written in the fields of lamps. It was yours. That night she divulged a secret plot to happen sometime in the future and linked it to you."

Thareous frowned. "I assume preceding fathers named their sons after me in hope they might take up this Torch of Destiny."

"Of great and impoverished," the elf-archer said. "Others who named them did so to deceive people."

"How are you to know I am the right one?" Thareous quizzed.

"Elves can sense the power in the souls of anyone. There is an enormous power in you that waits to be unearthed. It is unnatural, unusual, uncanny. It is true power. Do not let it linger within you. Learn to harness it."

"Show me and I shall," Thareous said.

"Follow me, so we might train more," his instructor said. "Open heart and mind so that focus might spawn. For Keiratha's safety you train to fight and defend."

They practiced until dusk, until the Four Suns rose into the heavens to lighten the Supernal Realms. Then they withdrew back to the presence of friends. Ianvorr inquired of Thareous's progress. Aildeimor said he showed promise. The birth of a warrior began with the visible attempt Thareous made.

******

That night Thareous threw himself upon his leaf-bed. He aspired to drowse his achiness from the long day off. He had never trained so hard in all his life. Without warning a light-blue radiance flooded the area and diminished his sleepiness.

"Get up," Ianvorr said. "We must speak."

He groaned and turned over, levering his back upward, supporting his weight with his arms. "About what? Aildeimor explained everything earlier."

"You are unwilling to take up this fate," Ianvorr said. "I shall deliver a sterner discussion. The enemy impinges over our land. You are not disposed to fight. The blood of a warrior flows in you whether you like it or not."

"Can we not save this for tomorrow?"

"We cannot," Ianvorr said. "Yes, you may be exhausted. You would not be if Nalla was at your side, Young Mage."

Thareous scowled; the Ice Dragon clamped his maw shut. "I am sorry. That was ill-pointed. I meant you should not be distracted. Love can do this to anyone, even those with the bravest hearts."

"Carry on with your rebuke," Thareous said. "The sooner you finish, the sooner the morrow is to come." He bit on his tongue for a second. "And you are forgiven."

"As you say," Ianvorr said. "Aildeimor told me of your fatigue. Inexcusable. Despite your exhaustion you are still amid a fight—a war to begin a series of attacks. You are going to battle alongside us. You shall become an Omnipotent One. It is to be your greatest kismet."

"Will this be the first of our troubles, friend?" Thareous asked.

"The first of our troubles started with taking Nalla with us," Ianvorr said. "Next comes your reluctance—your refusal. This is not the time for petty cowards. If you disincline, I shall be forced to act. If you incline, I will not bother you."

The Ice Dragon turned away, his icy haze weaving a path he already treaded. Once again Thareous threw himself into a mental turmoil. He was fast becoming the warrior everyone sought him to be, but was far from interest on anything threatening him.

******

The next morning the Four Suns hid behind storm clouds. Without their light the world looked light a waxen creation. The skies teemed with teardrops. The clouds mourned for the imminent danger. Thareous awoke, aching and drenched. He sat up and wrapped the deer pelt over himself.

Inching back beneath the branches of a maple, he shivered. All about him elves took in the beauty of the woodland. They seemed to be enjoying the rain.

Aildeimor appeared at his side. "Are you ready?"

"When the rain clears, I will be," Thareous said.

The elf tore the deer pelt away. "You are ready now." Helping Thareous to his feet—sore as he was—he led him away from the leaf-bed. "Fret not over the weather. It shall pass as the forenoon dew."

Thareous remained silent, knowing further argument would rouse another lecture. Elves flew past them, as nimble as a stream passing over rocks. Karthaiz and his archers were back, or at least most of them.

"What happened?" Aildeimor asked, letting Thareous go. Curiosity and concern made him stay.

"Telekinetic hands reached out and snatched us one by one!" an elf snapped.

"I feared we would all be taken," Karthaiz went on. "So we retreated. Ten were caught. Ten have most likely been killed."

"An example of the enemy," Aildeimor said. "We let them pass or fight and die."

"No," Thareous said, "not an example."

All eyes turned to him.

"A warning."

Truth

They started the day by running. "Focus!" Aildeimor shouted. "Do not let your legs do the work. Allow your mind!"

Thareous had to dash around a lake above Leaftorn like an elf. Aildeimor taught him the art of running as his people, never learned by any other human. This human, it seemed, lacked the prerequisite concentration.

"Quicken your pace, Annihilator!" His student's legs did pump faster. Thareous rocketed forward till he was a blur that could hardly be made out. He caught up to Aildeimor. "Keep it up!" The elf delighted at the progress. "Do not stop! Keep going! Good! Now follow me!"

He turned and charged over the water of the lake. Thareous tailed him, shocked at his pristine ability. Fear crossed his eyes; he forced it away. To his relief they came to the other end in a flash.

He expected Aildeimor to stop there. Instead the elf kept pressing on into the forest. They passed through Leaftorn and over the waters of the southern lake. Forest crossed them in a vague impression. Their footfalls made no sound as they ran.

At the upper shores of Kalba Lake, they stopped. A large herd of moose drank a few yards away. Aildeimor beckoned Thareous in the opposite direction. "If they get startled, they will stampede." They settled upon the sandy banks to rest. "Were you ever told how you were born?" The question came from the elf.

Thareous shook his head. "Is it pleasant?"

"Not at all." The elf-archer sighed. "I am going against your father's request of me. Haverin asked me to never tell you. That is all he did: ask. You deserve to know."

"I want to know," the Young Mage said.

"Very well," Aildeimor said. "I shall tell you it from the beginning. Haverin came here when he was twenty-five. We talked and he told me of your birth, saying you are the one. Galthoria came to him in a dream. This is how I know you are the Preordained One. I lied to you. For that I am sorry.

"At any rate the story begins when Haverin is at the age of fourteen. His parents, Frendur and Dareila, were strict Magicians. Your grandfather was the Master Magician of the time. He wished for Haverin to take after him. Each day they set out to train him.

"One day as your father headed to the training fields, a hand snatched and drug him into an alleyway. Five youths and a girl—who treated herself as one of them—stared at him, all armed with crossbows. The leader opened the purpose of his seizure. He said if your father refused, he would die right there. Anazeil Wharansdotter was the target.

"The fairest and most admired lass in Galgon at the time, the ruffians wished to have her court a man. Their leader, Quaron we suspect, would arrange the two to meet. Haverin agreed, fearing what might happen if he did not reach the fields in time. So they let him go.

"In the morning Haverin awoke. Once focusing, he saw Anazeil bound to a pilaster. She was gagged by a rag stuffed into her mouth. He got up and undid the ropes, gazing her down. Blonde hair cascaded to the floor. Sea green eyes reflected his face. After being untied, she removed the rag.

"Haverin's voice calmed and reassured her. He told of why they abducted her. She listened without insecurity. Both had heard of the municipal gang of troublemakers. Anazeil ran into them three times before. She struggled to restrain herself. She wished to thank him somehow. So she leaned forward.

"I give no further details. Only know it was grateful. I shall go to an hour later, when they lay in Haverin's bed. By this time Frendur grew frustrated at his son's lateness and went to investigate. Once he returned home and went into your father's room, he threw himself into a tantrum.

"Anazeil got up to run. Frendur blocked the exit. She had only to give up. Haverin admitted what happened. They set up limitations and conditions between the two. The parents convened and instituted a plan to catch the gang. No one ever found or identified any of them.

"Two years later, as Haverin still saw your mother, she became pregnant. At the age of sixteen she was to bear a child—you. Her parents were confounded, knowing not what to do. They met back with Frendur and Dareila to discuss it with them. They decided to have the two wedded.

"To this day, as you know, they are paired. Haverin is the Master Magician of Galgon. Anazeil is the caretaker of the house. And, Thareous, you are the hope for our endurance in war. Do not forsake us. This story may affect the way you fight. Do not ignore your vocation." Aildeimor fell silent at the last word.

Thareous waged an internal battle with himself. "Woe to the coerced ones! They have fallen into the Pits of Love by means of force. I shall not rest till they are avenged." In the distance tramps of footfalls sounded to their ears. "The enemy already?" Thareous inquired.

"Nay, the women and children heading for Veilzanor," Aildeimor answered. "It is still midmorning. The Dark Legion is not expected until tonight. Therefore we shall train here till midafternoon, then head back to Leaftorn. Let us start with the blade." They got up, clapped swords, and begin to spar.

******

Midafternoon happened in a trice. Aildeimor and Thareous opened their minds to the meaning of haste. They ran faster than the winds ever blew over the vast plains, faster than the comets that flew seldom overhead. When Leaftorn arrived, they stopped. The elf-archer led Thareous to the point where Ianvorr stood. The warriors gathered there also.

"This night war is cast our way," the Ice Dragon said. "The enemy has trespassed into these woods. They hack at trees to open new pathways. This forest is yours; the Dark Legion must be stopped here."

Elves and leviathans whooped their agreement.

"Zakumahk shall be forced to reroute his way back to Valvassa," Ianvorr said. His tone procured confidence. "His forces are to be scattered. His lifeless body will be dashed upon the ground. The Omnipotent Ones are not murderers: we are protectors."

Another cheer would have gone up had Nahilmara not interjected. "What of Quaron? Will he be relocated?"

"It is being done as we speak," Karthaiz said. "Booby traps are being set about the area as well. Even if he calls to his comrades, they are to be ensnared."

"The additional traps are ready?" Ianvorr asked.

"All are set and prepared for usage," the Elf Commander said. "There are pitfalls, crossbows situated in the trees that fire when the enemy trips over a line, and rock-slings fashioned in the latter. We should get the upper advantage."

"If everything is well positioned," Kyjre said.

"Silence, Wyvern!" Ianvorr cried. "Keep the muscles behind your teeth inactive. Your witticisms are disapproved by us. I hope you better think your words. Optimism is a necessary element here, not ill statements."

The Fire Dragon shrunk back.

"Now," Ianvorr said, dignifying some patience, "the time approaches. We are well trained. There is nothing further to bespeak."

"Form the different divisions to their assigned areas," Karthaiz said. "We await the enemy and attack in a pincer motion."

They divided into the groups. Thareous was set in the same unit as Vellar and Aildeimor, led by Ianvorr. Nahilmara managed the troops to the right from the opening of the two lakes and Karthaiz the ones to the left. They all marched out, having plenty of time to set up. It would end if the Legion broke through their lines.

******

Nighttime neared. The skies darkened. Stars shimmered overhead. The moon, pale green and eerie, loomed above like an impending danger. Thin clouds roamed unfathomable firmaments. Heavy treads thundered under the twilight. They tolled as the drums of doom. Their rhythms could be felt under the heels of the anxious companies. No one breathed, should they be shot in the nightshade.

A loud horn cried in the woods. The enemy announced the invasion. Thareous wondered what Zakumahk planned. Something made him gaze upward. A fleeting shadow shot across the inky dome. Wings of an indescribable creature spread out. "They have sent out scouts ahead of them!" he shouted.

His company shifted, awaiting Ianvorr's signal. It came less than a minute later. "Charge! For Keeiirrraaatthhaaaaaaa!" Thareous heaved a suppressed sigh, unsheathed his blade, and ran forward.

The Battle of Leaftorn

The armies collided, swords clashing, wounds opening, and dead or injured falling. Blood splattered to the ground. The elves hacked enemy armor open, exposing the rotted flesh to more wounds. From all sides the sounds of the battle knelled like a death-bell.

Before an antagonist ever reached Thareous, he caught sight of an ominous warrior. He was tall, steady in movement, and armored in black. A saber, made of an ebony alloy, slew any foe in his path. A sable cape swayed to the point of his feet. Atop his head sat a crown forged of the same ebony metal. It stood erect, the top coming up to three long spikes, the middle one longer than the sides.

Whoever this paladin was, Thareous resolved to stay away. But it spotted him and headed his direction. To face him would mean death. So the Young Mage backed away. He knew the warrior was Zakumahk.

Straying northward, Thareous entered the point where the fewest numbers fought. His blade speared the heart of a goblin, which matched the scout he saw earlier. Yataghans flew everywhere, beating even the quickness of the elves. Evasive parries held them at ease. Invisible hands hurled several enemies back. Thareous advanced to where they landed and slew them. Awaiting the next wave, he repeated this tactic numerous times until Zakumahk neared.

Ianvorr flew overhead, seeking him out. Once spotting him, he dove, snatched Thareous, and soared up again. "You must stay away from him. If he ever gets the chance to speak with you, it is all over."

"What do you mean?" Thareous shouted back.

"He will try to inveigle you to his side," Ianvorr said. "You might say you could resist his persuasion. But you have not heard what he has to say."

They watched the roaring tide of battle. Elves and fiends, zarjkakons and leviathans were interlocked in battle. Many ill-lucked bodies fell onto the forest floor. From his perch in Ianvorr's paw, Thareous caught sight of Vellar and Aildeimor surrounded by the enemy.

"We have to help them!" Thareous cried out.

"No, we must get you to away," the Ice Dragon said.

"He is dead in your care, Brother," a sinister voice hissed from behind.

Ianvorr glanced back. Thareous did the same. Zakumahk rode upon a black dragon. "Thareous," Ianvorr said. "We are never past wellbeing. For the Dark King can follow even us in the sky!"

Then, for the first time, Thareous heard Zakumahk's voice. "You shall never pass about victory either. Fall to my allegiance and I shall spare yours and Nahilmara's life. If you refuse, Amarzrell the Shadowhunter, on whom I ride, will blast you from the heavens."

The Ice Dragon attempted many evasive maneuvers. Amarzrell kept tailing him. Among these endeavors Ianvorr pulled up, hoping to plunge back down in a circle and freeze the black dragon from behind. His foe only barreled away and got behind him afterward.

"My patience declines!" Zakumahk shouted. "Land. Order your men back and bow in obeisance before me."

"I would spit in your face," Ianvorr said.

But then Ianvorr did go in for the landing. Before he touched the ground, he turned. Amarzrell let his ebony flames escape. An icy bombardment froze the blazes into a massive blockade. With great fury the black dragon ceased the emission of fire and sent his claws to the ice hunk. It sundered, sending chunks over the emptied battlefield.

"I have failed you, Your Majesty!" Amarzrell cried.

Zakumahk growled and threw himself off his steed. He landed without even having to bend, but tightened the grip on his saber. "Get back to the zarjkakons and keep them from fighting over the corpses. Magic shall succeed where they bested you."

******

Thareous detached from Ianvorr, housing orders to find Aildeimor. Material obstacles lay before him. He ran as an elf. A sea of faces, evil and elvish, swam by. He probed them. None were the elf-archer. As he passed enemies, he stroked out his sword and felled them at the legs. Then he stopped. *Surely he has not fallen!*

An arrow whizzed past his head. A shriek sounded behind him. He turned to spot a dead fury, then spub to where the reed came from and spotted Aildeimor. The elf beckoned for him to follow. Over a field of carnage the two sped past contending waves, razing them with their swords.

Seas of yataghan swung out, but went through them. Blood spurted to the ground. Heads flew in the air. Limbs were abridged. Wounds opened up; bones cracked. Lifeless fiends crumpled over the death-stricken terrain.

"Where are we going?" Thareous asked, decapitating an imp.

"Away from Zakumahk," Aildeimor said, parrying and jabbing the heart of a hobgoblin. "Ianvorr knows not the woods like me. I am your guide. Cover lies a few hills from here."

They continued through the enemy lines until coming to the strongest remnant of defenders. Karthaiz loped to them. An arrow snapped in two extruded from his shoulder. "Fiends pour still from the Fire Realm. We need to regroup and charge at them."

Aildeimor nodded his understanding. "Keep Thareous with you. Zakumahk is seeking him out. I shall implement your orders." With that he ran off.

"Come with me," the Elf Commander said. "Airalus has prepared a shelter where you can wait out the fight."

"I do not want to hide. I do not want to desert everyone here to death," Thareous said. "I am going to stay."

"We have orders from Ianvorr to see you to safety," Karthaiz said. "Please, for your own security, come with me!"

Before Thareous could raise a new objection, an arrow pierced the elf between the eyes. Fiends overran the area. The elves charged, but could not summon their powers in time. They had to retreat. Thareous got slung over the shoulder of a troll. He only watched the Elf Commander be swept away. He did not use his sword to endorse an escape. Almost an entire group was wiped out. The elves would be uprooted and thrown away like weeds. Thareous wept, for Karthaiz's death came by him.

******

That contingent of fiends carried him off to an isolated grove. They bound Thareous's wrists in stringy ropes easy to break. He did not act. He only reflected over his obstinacy. This was, with conviction, to be the end of the protectors of the Nyran Forest. Hope was as dead as deracinated roses.

The fiends stood at attention. The Dark King tramped his way to Thareous. His helmet was removed, tucked at his side. A black, well-kept beard swayed over his breastplate. Dark eyes stared down at the brooder. A scar, twisted like a rope, ran down his left cheek to the bottom of his jaw. "You impose the wrong cause."

Thareous did not reply.

Zakumahk glowered some. "Pathetic. Do they care about you? Did they not refuse anything you wished to do?" He paused and went down to a crouch. "I can save you from this torment. If you help me depose Jaldor, I shall give you Nalla. You may be the prince. She can be your queen."

With that said, the Young Mage looked up into the dictator's eyes. "If you were a good ruler, and King Jaldor a bad one, I would join you."

"He is a rash fool!" Spittle rained from Zakumahk's mouth. Thareous ducked his head to avoid it. "You buttress a king who can tear this nation apart by his *impetuosity*! I am its reviver. This land deserves better. Together we can enforce it."

"Deriving this land by cajoling? Now that is pathetic," Thareous said.

Zakumahk backhanded him, knocking him on his side. "Insolence is repaid by execution. For you I make an exception. Only if you join me."

"Interesting," Thareous said, pulling himself back into a sitting position. "You went from wheedling to forceful."

"That does it!" the Dark King growled. He unsheathed his black-bladed saber; his helmet landed on the ground. "Meet Kielthavra—the Shadowbiter. One more impertinent answer and I shall slice out your tongue. Join me, or so help yourself, this blade will be of your innards."

Right then an elven sword landed in Thareous's lap. He swiped it up in his right hand and jumped back, landing on his feet. At that time Zakumahk struck out. Thareous lifted his hands as if to stop the blade. In actuality it went between his wrists, slicing the ropes.

Terror masked the faces of the fiends as volleys came from unseen archers. Whirlwinds arose in the center of the grove and chased the fleeing demons. Blurs cut them down. Reed arrows whistled to the unarmored areas of their backs. The elves and leviathans struck back for their losses.

Amidst this Thareous and Zakumahk clashed. Though the Young Mage had less experience, the Dark King was livid. Clangs ripped into the air, the metals of their swords vibrating. Each matched in deftness, switching turns to show off their footwork. Thareous waited for Zakumahk to strike each time, the secret of his survival. The Dark King shoved Thareous back and he stumbled over a corpse of a cacodemon. Kielthavra's tip prodded his heart.

"Any last words?" the Dark King asked.

"Aye," the Young Mage said. He smiled. "Do not look up."

A radiance like white-hot fire gleamed on Shadowbiter's blade. "That does not deter me. Clever as though you may be, I am no toy to be played with."

Then a massive shadow of draconic form made Zakumahk's eyes bulge. Not daring to look up, the Dark King knew who was over him. Ivory claws encircled his torso, carrying him heavenward. Kielthavra slid off Thareous's chest. Ianvorr glided up and above the treetops.

Thareous got to his feet, his elven sword in hand. An ogre brought his bludgeon down toward him. A blur passed and a gash appeared in the ogre's stomach. With a pained bawl it freed the club from where it had stuck in the ground. The club flew up and landed on the ogre's back, its own weapon crushing it. The blur came to a halt in front of Thareous.

Aildeimor's sad, vengeful eyes glared at him. "Karthaiz is dead. We now have no Commander."

"I am sorry," Thareous said. "He died because I refused to go with him to the shelter. Had I not argued with him, he would still be fighting alongside us."

"How should I mourn since a friend was killed by a friend's denial?" Aildeimor cried aloud. "I can only forgive him, for this was not intentional. He did it so he could continue in the flow of battle, should death have taken him. May his spirit rejoice for leaving times of hostilities behind."

Though conflict raged still, the two companions bowed and prayed a silent prayer to Galthoria. They asked for Karthaiz's sanction to Kallenalza, for him to never again taste the bitterness of war. When they finished, an assurance mingled in their hearts. They grasped their swords once again and got up. Before and behind them fiends were being overthrown. They ran already to join back in the battle for Leaftorn.

******

Miles away, still within the field of skirmish, Ianvorr glided over the emerald canopies. Zakumahk squirmed in his grasp. "Let me go, you maggot-spawned lizard!"

"If I do, then you will fall to the forest floor," Ianvorr said.

Kielthavra's bite afflicted his paw's tendons. He let Zakumahk go, who hung by the blade still lodged in Ianvorr's flesh.

"Come after me and I shall harm you further," the Dark King said. Then he dislodged his sword and fell into the trees.

******

Thareous and Aildeimor soon met with Vellar. He displayed only a few scratches. The three combatants formed a triangle with their backs together and defended each other from every side. Blades lunged out like a viper's tongue.

A muffled lowing sounded. The fiends stopped fighting and looked back. Their king walked past two mighty oaks, wielding an ox-horn. Elves also halted their swords from striking out. "Come now, my Legion! Our work here is done. The elves and leviathans are dissipated enough. Let us go while Ianvorr deems me dead."

The Dark Legion assembled, coming in endless streams. Before they marched away, Zakumahk turned to Thareous. "Boy, the next time you see your father, give him my regards. It has been too long since I have seen my brother."

He turned, leading on his scourge. Elves desponded when they learned his true purpose—to deplete their numbers. Thareous even more was shocked—Zakumahk was his uncle? *No, he is lying. Father never could be brothers with one so contemptible.* Yet, deep down, deeper than the depths of understanding, he knew it to be true.

******

Ianvorr returned an hour before midnight. "I searched for the remains of Zakumahk, but found nothing. He still lives, I assume."

"He does. He appeared and gathered his fiends, then departed," Aildeimor said. "Thareous knows now Haverin's gravest secret because of it."

The gentle glow of Ianvorr's eyes arrayed Thareous in a light-blue radiance. "This is unfortunate. It is irrevocable, the same. We must rest. In the morn the bodies shall be cremated. Any wounded must report to the healers, who will keep them overnight."

Everyone gathered their belongings and found a pile of leaves for their beds. In the night chill Thareous laid down his bloodstained sword. It felt like bricks had been stacked upon his eyelids. Still, he could not sleep. He could merely wonder what kind of fate might be ordained from this knowledge. Not even the fortunetellers could determine this.

Next Move

Great thunderheads swirled into a single eye. Lightning struck out with thunderous fists and pounded out its fury over the land. A black dragon rode into the eye, bearing a rider donned in heavy ebony armor. Voices arose.

"Great lord of the Way of Magic, long have we awaited your coming!" This voice belonged to Zakumahk.

"My coming is the punition of fools," a darker tone said. "Those who partook in my death are these fools. Those who refute my kingship are these fools. I will not abide by this any longer. Kill them all."

"Lord, I wish to save one soul," Zakumahk said.

"One soul," the other said. "Do you not wish to obey my orders?"

"Just this one from harm," Zakumahk said.

"Thareous Haverinsson is to slay me once I arise! If you fail to slay him, I shall appoint another in your place. Do not object to my command again. End his life and the Resistance will dither."

Then the black dragon Amarzrell and the Dark King Zakumahk were cast from the eye. The thunderheads dissipated, leaving them to wander for their quarry.

******

Thareous sat up, his mind racing from the dark dream. *My uncle is searching for me. He spoke right last night. If I dare tell any of my allies, they will send me back to hiding. I have heard the voice of the one that I am to vanquish too.* From the distance he whiffed the odor of smoke. *The elves must be burning the bodies. May the Fates provide shelter for the defenders of the forest who died last night.*

He got to his feet and let the deer pelt droop off him. Taking up his sword, he noticed the bloodstains still etched over its blade. *This needs washing. There is a lake a league from here. I should be able to get there and return before the others worry.* Sheathing the blade for the moment,

Thareous ran off, scabbard in hand. He stopped at the lake in two minutes. The waters shone, every outline of ripples as definable as a shadow. Its floor could be discerned; even the creatures it covered.

However, as he crouched and slid the blade from its sheath, a glaive stroked the skin of his neck. "Do not bloody the Tears of Eildon," a female voice said.

"I know not what you mean," Thareous said. He swept the glaive from him. Its blade concaved near the hilt and then curved back up to the tip. "The origin of it is unknown by me."

Soft hands caressed up his throat until coming to his chin and lifting it. "It was of yore that Eildon the Intrepid fell in love. The woman whom he admired was smitten to another. Jealousy led him to murdering her love. She became devastated by this and killed herself. At that time Eildon realized what he did and wept until his end."

Thareous was not listening to her. He reflected only on her features. Black curls writhed like snakes in the lakeside breeze. Sapphire eyes, so much unlike Nalla's, mirrored solemnity. A buckskin dress, restrained at her waist, draped near her ankles. Wide straps carried its top to her back.

She drew back her hand, the other fingering her tool. "Annihilator, you are not to be infatuated by me. I am no fairer than the Princess Nalla. I release you from this spell."

"This is no spell, Milady," the Young Mage said. "It is love. I cannot help it if I become drawn to you."

"Love is the reason I am here," the elf said. "I am Lefanarí, the widow of Jalläthre. Because of murder, like that of Eildon, but by witchcraft, I am an exile before my kindred. Of late the Tribunal has been unjust. I wish to overthrow them."

"I am Thareous Haverinsson, the one predestined to stop an evil," he said. "Aildeimor told us your leaders were not the same. We could not question them of their eccentricity since they ran away before the battle. I presume you know of it."

"I do," Lefanarí said. "I have watched you ever since Ianvorr returned. Eftsoons, when you trained with Aildeimor, the last of my kin, I noticed your control over magic. You are the Appointed Archimage indeed."

"I am not ready to face my destiny," Thareous said.

Lefanarí cocked an ear as if to listen. "I must go. Someone nears." She flung herself into a rowan. Aildeimor emerged at the edge of the lake, staring at Thareous in alarm. "Why are you sitting there, your imbrued sword in hand?"

Thareous glanced back at him and arose. He assumed Lefanarí would want him to keep her discreet. "I came to wash it off."

"Use the bark of the trees or the blades of grass," the elf said. "The lakes are sacred. We come only to bathe in them, never shedding the blood of fiends into the water. Follow me. Ianvorr wishes to speak with the entire battalion which fought."

"I will clean it while he talks," Thareous said. He looked away, unsure if he should tell after all.

"What is the matter?" Aildeimor asked.

"Nothing," the Young Mage said, already noting it to be too late. "I—I just wondered which path I took to get here."

"Leaftorn is southwest from here," the elf-archer said. "Tail behind me so I can lead you there." Thareous slid the sword back into its scabbard and ran with the elf.

******

Back at Leaftorn, Thareous got a chance to gather some bark and smoothen away all the gore from his sword. To add the former sheen to the blade, Thareous administered spit and polished it with his sleeve. He was left thirsty, so Aildeimor handed him a water-skin. "This is what elves drink when their tongues dry. It is a mixture of berries and herbs, sure to cure your parchedness for the rest of today. Only take a sip or you cannot get enough of it."

The Young Mage allotted the quantity and handed it back. A grin wormed up his face. "You said I could not get enough if I drank too much?"

"It is overpowering, is it not?" Aildeimor asked. He tucked the water-skin back into small sack fastened to his belt.

"Almost unbearable," Thareous said. He fell back into seriousness. "Where is Ianvorr holding this meeting?"

Aildeimor walked more southwesterly. "Over three more hillocks we should come to the head of the crowd."

Sure enough, hidden by the mass of trees, a multitude greater than that of Galgon stood in the clearing. Ianvorr sat at the side of the Tribunals' abandoned platform. "A lot of them survived," Thareous said.

"Most are from Veilzanor," Aildeimor said. "The women and children are to return when the Nyran Forest is safe."

They trudged more hurriedly until coming into the view of everyone. Ianvorr nodded his head, issuing the meeting to begin. "We assemble this day to discuss if you, the elves and leviathans, should continue in this battle. If so we shall fly to Jurtithan's Temple, the Ice Fortress. Also, a new commander should be chosen."

"I nominate Aildeimor, our greatest archer!" one elf exclaimed. Several more voices, about three-fourths of the elven crowd, roared their agreement. Others were either jealous, ill toward him, or did not know whom to support.

"This will be concluded later in our debate," Ianvorr said. "Right now we must decide if you are to persist in this war or not. Both sides have lost many."

"Our ilk remains with you," Airalus said. "Until maimed or dead, the leviathans will defend Keiratha. But the elves must elect a leader if they are to continue."

"Very well," Ianvorr said. "As the acting Tribunal"—he got on all fours—"I hereby place Aildeimor as the new Elf Commander. Lead well your people."

This time all the elves cheered, arms raised, and faces plastered with smiles. The leviathans bowed. The new Elf Commander held up his hands for silence. "Thank you for your support. We also must respect the one who used to manage this position." The atmosphere became silent. All the elves present knew that Karthaiz was firm yet gentle, relentless in battle yet considerate in peace. Of late he spoke about unseating the Tribunal, for they breached partiality. He never got his wish.

"What of Zakumahk?" Kyjre asked at last. "He went north with the Dark Legion. What do you propose their next course is?"

"Serious at last," Ianvorr muttered. He straightened up, hoping no one heard him. "There are two probable ways: by land or by sea. If they go by land, they will be forced to cross through the Keicor Alps. A significant loss shall result then. If they sail upon the seas, Ielyle's Bergs would be a hindrance."

"Can they not just go over that?" Thareous inquired.

"Nay, the Dark King would want to get there as soon as possible," Nahilmara said. "Though many fiends might freeze, he would rather lose them than time. The ways of the Valvassan Tyrants are macabre."

"Wroth he would be if anything went amiss," Ianvorr said. "This is why it is key we get to the Ice Fortress, to talk to Jurtithan. He must settle if we are to beset the fleet."

"Assuming they do not brave the snowstorms of the Keicors," Vellar said.

"That is not likely—" The Ice Dragon stiffened. His snout lifted and sniffed the air. "Fiends! The Dark Legion returns!"

Blades came up, gleaming in the Four Suns' radiance. The elves handed out bows or arrow-crammed quivers. Aildeimor took command of the elves and two humans. Ianvorr assumed control over the dragons.

"Ready your bows!" Aildeimor ordered. He lifted his skean, waiting to give the signal. Iron-shod treads echoed in the shade of the forest. Shadowy forms darted from tree to tree. The enemy entered from every side. "Pick out your targets and fire!" His blade swung down.

The dragons took to the sky to impede any aerial foes. Zakumahk erupted from the enemy lines and confronted Thareous. His armor was omitted; now he was garbed in black garments. An outstretched hand compressed Thareous's heart. He fell back as oblivion overtook him. Before he lost consciousness, he saw a figure warding off the Dark King ...

******

Stars winked at Thareous when he awoke. He lay near the waters of a lake. A cookfire crackled at his side. Catfish simmered on a grate. At the other end of the flame a being huddled next to it, warming her hands.

"Lefanarí ..." His throat was dry and sore.

She got up and went over to him. "Do not speak, Annihilator. You are very weak. Allow me to clarify why you are here and what happened. The Dark Legion shattered the elves. Their numbers were scattered as well. Fiends wander through this vast forest. Leaftorn is taken. Many captives are held there, plus the other human."

"Vellar!" Thareous croaked.

The elf placed a finger to his lips. "I shall be right back." She took a water-skin from her belt and walked to the lakeside, dipping the skin into the liquid. Then she went back. "Drink this. Though they are the tears of an elf, it is potable." Sliding a hand to the back of his head, Lefanarí helped him sip it down.

"Now," she said when it was gone, "I was spying upon Aildeimor, longing to speak with him. The Legion attacked. I saw Zakumahk running toward you. I followed him, jumping from branch to branch. I intervened ere he could lay his blade to you. He is a durable foe. I soon cast him back into his battalion. Fiends ran to retrieve you. I felled them and spirited you here. Your conditions are ill. On the morrow, if my healing works, we are to see someone I know. He may be able to help us."

The Ancient Archimage

When morning awakened, Thareous did feel better. Lefanarí watched over him the entire night, stating she had no need for sleep. This led him to becoming more drawn to her, for she cared for him. Chunks of a cooked bass were deposited into his hands on a large leaf. "Eat," she said. "We have a lot of fighting to do this day. And do not look upon me like a hungered mutt. Your decision to suit me shall endanger our lives."

"How so?" he asked before popping the first piece between his teeth.

"It is against the Celestial Order, the laws of Kallenalza, for one to love anyone out his own people. Therefore stay with Nalla. Life in Annathias is not worth living."

Thareous backed away from the subject. "Who is this person you deem can help us?" The leaf was halfway full at this time.

"Someone I have known since my banishment," she said. "He is a great studier in the Way of Magic. He is referred to as the Ancient Archimage."

"Can you tell me again why you were banished?" Thareous inquired.

Lefanarí sighed. "I wedded an elf named Jalläthre. Zeildan, an elf who envied our marriage, killed my mate. In retaliation I summoned the Unseen, the spirits of another world, and cursed him to his death. They moved him to a lake where he drowned himself. The Tribunal expelled me from my people for witchcraft."

"They forsook the elves before the Battle of Leaftorn!" Thareous exclaimed. "You can return to them—to Aildeimor!"

"My brother has not seen me in over ten millennia," Lefanarí said. "What would he think of me? Besides, there are law-keepers in the elves. I could be beheaded for returning. I plan on proving my worth by rescuing the captives." She turned away, facing the lake. Thareous set down his breakfast and walked over to her. Once he caught a glimpse of her face, he found her to be smiling.

"Even if things do not work out the way I want them to," she said, "I still have someone who cares for me. Life in Annathias, perhaps, is better than this."

"You cannot mean that," Thareous said.

"I mean what I say," Lefanarí insisted. "You said yesterday you were attracted to me. Please do not take offense by me saying this; you are a considerate young man. I am prone to fall for you beyond any limitations one day. Only time can tell."

"We should be heading for the Ancient Archimage," the Young Mage said. He was eager to regain his control over the topics again.

"Yes," the elf said, lowering her eyes. "It is wrong to speak that way. Forgive me. We do have a duty to fulfill. Let us go."

******

They stopped at a grove hemmed off by black poplars. An eerie aura tugged at Thareous's heart as if he desired to walk into it. He glanced sidelong, noticing Lefanarí acted the same way. Mist rose into the sky like smoke from a burning fire, disappearing above the treetops.

"This is where your friend lives?" Thareous asked.

Lefanarí nodded, shivering somewhat.

"What is the matter?" Thareous asked, drawing nearer.

"I have never felt the allurement this strong before," she said.

"Why does it not affect me so powerfully?"

"You have something else to be allured to."

He looked away. "We are not supposed to yearn for the other."

She clasped his chin and moved it back to her. "It is not how we look at each other, but how we treat each other. For example, if I kissed you, we would both be called to Kallenalza and charged forever to Annathias."

"This is like death, except more pleasureful," Thareous said.

"Precisely," Lefanarí said. She let go his chin and turned to the grove. "Egamihcra Tneicna! Open the way and entrust us passage!"

The poplars in front of them arched over. A small hunchback leaning on a cane shuffled from an opening deeper in the thicket. A crimson tunic fit over his tiny form. A belt of leather bound his waist, the choicest gems set into it. Sandals strapped about his diminutive feet. A single eye stared at them. The other was swollen shut under beige tufts. He raised a hand, waving it at them. "Master expecting you. Follow."

Thareous shot an inquisitive glance at Lefanarí as they started forward.

"Karz," she said. "The Ancient Archimage's servant. He used to be a citizen of Galgon. The others thought him a freak and harassed him. One day he ran away, braved the blizzards of the Keicors, and came here.

The Archimage found him, cold, thin, and near death. He took him in and nourished him back to health."

"Karz is his servant because of this," Thareous said.

"He does wish to repay him for his kindness," Lefanarí said. "Please do not ridicule him. On the outside he is an aberration, but on the inside, a gentleman."

"This was never my fancy," Thareous said.

By this time, after crossing through a pathway with arcades of poplars on either side, they came to the heart of the grove. Saplings divided the inside into rooms. Hints of habitation showed up everywhere. In the anteroom a huge cauldron wafted odorless smoke. Strange enough, nothing filled its belly.

They entered a room with a desk and papers strewn over the grass sward. As if on the brink of discovery, scads of scribbling filled them. An elaborate inkstand held a swan-feather pen, positioned on a shelf above the desk. Thareous tried to read some of the script. It consisted of foreign hooked characters.

Voices sounded from the next section. "Who else is here?" Lefanarí asked the servant.

"Two elf men and one elf lady," Karz said, peering back. "They come seeking you. Master protect you, he does."

"The Tribunal," Thareous said. He glanced at Lefanarí. Her vibrant face turned ashen at the mention of them.

"Karz, where are you?" a stern voice called.

"Master wants us right away," the hunchback said. "Come. Eyes of search probe the emptiness of the room. We not there. Master's patience short."

They walked on without another word. They came to the lounge area. The Tribunal sat abreast on a long couch. A little fountain of an elf firing an arrow stood in the middle of the room. Water spewed from the arrow. Wands hung on the tree-wall by hooks. At the far end a man sat in a buckskin chair, smoking a short-stemmed pipe. His long black hair was braided. A little net of chains dangled off the back of his head, tied by silvern threads. A golden band girded his scarlet robes, gems set into slots, like in Karz's. He kept a gold-hilted sword with a wavy blade on his lap. A glare of somber firmness bedeviled the Tribunal.

"Lefanarí, we have found you as last," Yeilth said. "We come to punish you—this time in the last phase. Relegation was just the first segment of your castigation. You were seen in the treetops above Leaftorn.

Disfellowshipping you was not enough. We have come to the unfortunate decision to execute you."

"Not in this dwelling of mine," the Ancient Archimage said. "Not in these woods of mine—near my grove—either. Iniquitous is your decision. Though it seems harmless, it is unjust. Lefanarí is to stay with me until you all come to your senses. Partiality corrupts all ilks."

"Do not impugn us, wand-wielding worm!" Talleir snapped. "The elves are the unchanging race. Humans fail to their sin. Dwarves and giants war over the mountains. We are fair and wise. Ill affects those fighting Galthoria's dearest beings."

"Ill is the partial, then," the Archimage said. "Give me a sign of your greatness. Can you form the land to your will? Can you bend time, course fate to what you wish it to be? Nay. The Fates have this power. If you cannot do any of this, how can you sway me?"

Darjein got to his feet and unsheathed his sword. "Through force." Something ripped the blade from his hands and lifted him into the air.

"I am the most powerful being here!" The Ancient Archimage stretched out his hand, making Yeilth and Talleir adhere to their seats. "By the will of Galthoria, you shall leave my presence."

Then all three levitated. Talleir reached into a pocket in her garment and pulled out a dagger. She tugged an individual hair from her head and slashed it. Then she replaced the dagger and let the hair dangle away. "Lefanarí, you are hereby cast from the elves! Intrude upon them and you will be killed."

The Ancient Archimage led the Tribunal members to the entrance of the grove. He shut them out forever. Turning to Thareous, Lefanarí put her head on his shoulder, sobbing and shaking. He hugged her for comfort. Karz was silent.

"What has happened?" Thareous queried.

"Exactly what Talleir said," the Archimage said. "She is banned from her people. This hair"—he bent to pick it up—"represents her being cut from them."

"They no longer have charge over the elves," Thareous said. "They are acknowledged as traitors. By Annathias, this universe houses countless sinners! None will ever avert from their wicked ways. They are lost. Is there naught you can do?"

"Not of this," the Archimage said, stroking his beard. "Alas, this universe is lost. Lust for power corrupts the mind. *We* can alter their greed, starting with Zakumahk."

Lefanarí pulled herself away from Thareous, straightening up. "This is why we have come. Leaftorn is overrun by fiends. The Dark King plans on toppling Keiratha."

"We shall leave this instant," her friend said. "Come, Thareous, Son of Haverin. I shall teach you the way of teleportation."

Thareous stared in wonder. "Teleportation? That is only a myth—something from the Legends of Leathí. How can it be real?"

"I have learnt it, so it is real. To warp yourself from one place to another, begin by exposing your mind to the Unseen. They shall open a portal. Just walk in. At the other end you will come to your locality. I am a self-teacher—you are your best teacher."

"Is this not an act of Black Magic?" the Young Mage inquired.

"That depend on purpose," Karz said. "What you do with power, that how you determine category."

"Correct," the Ancient Archimage said. He spread his arms upward to until he looked like a Y. An oval doorway materialized before them. The inside flashed thin lightning in a black oblivion. Outlines of a stairway proceeded into the darkness. "Stay here, Karz. Protect my grove while we are gone."

"Karz will, Master," the hunchback said. "Farewell!"

"I hope we do," the Archimage said and stepped into the portal. Thareous and Lefanarí followed. It swirled and vanished in an explosion of light.

******

It reopened nearly in the heart of Leaftorn. The trio walked out. The Ancient Archimage plied his sword. His allies did as he. The area was infested with shadows. "Fiends," Thareous said. "The Dark Legion surrounds us."

The shadows parted ahead. Zakùmahk strode in front of them. "Thareous, you are unwise to have returned. Three to thousands? By what power do you aim to rout me?"

The Archimage pointed his blade at him. "By the power of Galthoria."

Kielthavra's blade met the Archimage's sword. "You have handed your head to me," the Dark King said. "If it is a fight you seek, it is a fight you shall receive. Prepare to die … all of you."

WIZARDS DUEL

As Thareous and Lefanarí disappeared into the forest, Zakumahk smashed his blade into the Archimage's. Magic played at their fingertips, both emitted small barbs of lightning. It coursed up the swords, but ebbed after linking. The blades circumvented and parried. Sparks fled their wrath. They caught blades, issuing their strength to knock the rival down.

"We fight with steel," the Ancient Archimage said. "Magic proves might. So let us use it."

Zakumahk backed Kielthavra away. "A wizards' duel?" In reply the Archimage cast away his blade. The Dark King sheathed his. "Do you know why they call this Shadowbiter? Because out of the shadows it comes to bite you."

"With my infallible powers I could sense your presence," his crimson-clad foe said. A series of lucent orbs nodded at his sides.

"We shall see how efficient your 'powers' are," Zakumahk said.

They took ten paces back and harnessed to their ensorcelled methods. As honorable duelers they turned and readied themselves. Barriers formed at their bodies. Around them fiends fell to Thareous and Lefanarí. The Young Mage tried to work his way to Zakumahk. Fiends kept blocking his way. Despite the numbers they cleaved through the endless lines. Thareous ideated a spell and engaged it between attacks.

"Begin!" the Dark King roared.

Orbs and beams of pure energy assailed both force fields. Tree branches reached out, stones lifted from the ground. Telepathic wails erupted into their minds. The Ancient Archimage faltered. He found a tree root under Zakumahk and brought it to his use. It coiled about his barrier. The walls pressed in on the Dark King. In panic he invaded the Archimage's mind, endeavoring to take it over. He found a weakness. Fear.

So you live, Prince Deil, Zakumahk said in his enemy's mind.

The Archimage stepped back, alarmed. "Jaldor is ruler, not I."

"He thought Ianvorr killed you." The Dark King commenced his influence. "Join me. We can conquer Keiratha. You may become second-in-command."

"Second-in-command?" The Archimage snorted. "You give me the rule of a beggar. I am to be king and eradicate you from the face of this universe!"

"Not while the Darkest Dictator reigns," Zakumahk said.

"The Darkest Dictator?" Deil inquired. "Impossible. He can never be aroused from his sleep in the grave."

"He can," his cajoler said. "He has suffered in the pits of Annathias. Malluesaer is cruel to him. He wishes to escape. He wishes to make the universe a better place. Help us free him. You shall be rewarded beyond your imagination."

"To revive those already dead?" the prince questioned. "It is occultism. I am not an occultist. Demonry you may control. The power of Galthoria I sport. I shall not fall in league with Malluesaer."

The idealism on Zakumahk's face waned. Darkness enveloped his arm. He released his barrier. Brandishing Kielthavra, he deployed the shade to its blade. As swift as the winds of a typhoon, he released it over the Archimage's force field. Bereft of the ability to see his enemy, Prince Deil probed the terrain for his sword. He discovered it at the feet of an oak. He picked it up with his mind and found the Dark King a step in front of him. Keilthavra was above his head, electricity playing over its blade. His sword blocked the black blade of the Shadowbiter.

Zakumahk succumbed with a curse. Bearing his eyebrows down, he parried a blow from the invisible warrior wielding the weapon. Sweat dampened his brow, capturing the light of the Four Suns. His concentration began to decline. The shadow prison of the Ancient Archimage faded. Sword came into hand once more. Fire leapt to the tip of the blade. As steel clashed, tiny flames flew into air and flickered out.

"Yield!" the Archimage demanded. "Thus far I have beaten you. You are to die." The flats of their blades tagged and the duelers swung away.

"Your tongue is made for lies," Zakumahk said, standing his ground. "If you wish to claim victory, you shall have to kill me first."

Thareous appeared at the Ancient Archimage's side. "Family or not, I will kill you with pleasure. Megalomaniacs die with their greed."

"Where is my Legion?" the Dark King asked.

"Scattered," Thareous said. "Teleported by means of magic. They wander through the Nyran, leaderless."

"No matter," Zakumahk said. "I do not stand alone."

The vibration of a snake's tongue tickled Thareous's ear. He turned to see the serpent head of Quaron dressed under a cowl. Wearing his usual armor and black cloak, he somehow appeared fiercer. "You ssslayed my father. Now I shall ssslay you!"

My uncle has been spreading lies through this snake's head, the Young Mage thought. He brandished his blade just as Quaron brought his down. The wizards' duel ended. They were out for blood.

******

Receiving Thareous's blessing to search for her captive kindred after the Young Mage teleported the fiends away, Lefanarí wandered through a clearing crowning a hill. She looked up. The Four Suns crept closer. Her stomach gnawed her insides. For the last day and a half she went without food. Events kept her more upset of her kindred than eating.

Returning her gaze to the clearing she noticed a foot sticking out of a bush. She parted the limbs with her glaive. Underneath lay a dead elf. She let the branches swing back and bob as if in the wind. Further examination took her to a struggle. She uncovered more corpses. Anger swelled into her eyes. She muttered a name: "Quaron." It was where her people had kept him. The Dark Legion had attacked the sentries and freed him.

I must find the others before they, too, are killed. Unless Zakumahk has some devilry planned for them. Escaping the prison of trees, she strode down the slope to a dingle. The blood of the sentries dried over ling. She glared at it; wrath suffused her gaze.

A growl made Lefanarí turn and almost fall on the ground. A troll stood before her, a taupe giant over eight feet high. It bore a bulbous club with a slim handle in both hands. Over his sinewy chest fell a tangled beard plaited near the base. Arm muscles bulged from the effort of hefting its weapon. It wore only a breechcloth bound by a ceinture. Sallow, glowing orbs acted as its eyes.

When it neared, the elf had some reaction. The cudgel raised behind his head and swung down as she moved. Lefanarí knew she could not floor so fell an enemy with her glaive. She glanced back for a flash, tripping over a root arching from the ground. Turning on her flipside, she backed away, her grasp deprived of her glaive. The troll loomed over her again. Reed arrows sailed into his brow. It roared and shook its head. Eyeing the new enemy, the troll hurled its club. A skean deflected it.

The creature ripped up a birch sapling by its roots. Holding it like a whip, it twirled it in a hand. Two arrows impaled its wrist. The troll bawled and tugged the reeds from it. A snarl emanated as it examined the new arrival.

Lefanarí also looked back to spot her rescuer, Aildeimor. Tears blurred her vision. Noting the danger her brother faced, she whirled over to her knees and took up her glaive. She jammed the blade into the troll's tough hide and removed it. It struck again till the troll spun on her. Aildeimor charged and emulated his sister. Their target lashed his birch-whip at both sides. They evaded it. Desperation augmented inside it.

The two elves whizzed past him, unharmed as the whip melted through them. Their blades wounded the troll further. Its moves weakened. They could hear its breath shallow. Lefanarí anticipated it to collapse. It saw her and pulled back the whip. Aildeimor halted and hurled his skean. It plunged tip-first into the heart. The troll took a step back and fell on its side. The birch-whip loosened in its grasp. Immobile eyelids covered pale eyes.

Reclaiming his hunting knife, the Elf Commander went to clean off the blood in the grass. He took no notice of Lefanarí, leaving her in a shocked state. "Aildeimor," she said.

At length he faced her. "Why did you not let me know you lived? I awaited your contact for ten millennia. Now you return …"

"I had no choice," she said. "I was to stay away or die."

"The Tribunal could not have stopped you," he said. "I would not allow that."

"They would have had you executed!" Lefanarí exclaimed.

"Life is better in Kallenalza than the universe," Aildeimor said. "All are avaricious and self-seeking. Pride has distorted our populace. Men seek pleasure. In the end it will turn to be eternal slavery in Annathias. Very few comprehend this. The elves do for their wisdom."

Lefanarí was disconcerted. "You speak truth. My Brother, there is hope yet. We cannot save the entire universe. We can save a few. We are, after all, immortal."

"Not if we do not find our kindred," Aildeimor said. "This is the time most have fallen. Before we were strong. Even the elves are diverted."

"Have you any army with you?" his sister inquired.

"Only you," he answered. "The ones that remain to us cannot be found."

"We should not allow them further rest," Lefanarí said.

"To free our ilk from death," Aildeimor said. "Or worse."
They clanged blades and were off.

******

Magic ruptured and scorched the area. Several tree roots reached like fingers from the fissured earth. Bodies of fiends littered about them. Thareous and the Ancient Archimage held in with their respective fights. Zakumahk backed away from his crimson-clad foe. "For hours have we fought, only to succeed in wearying ourselves. You cannot keep this up forever," the Dark King said.

Only steps away Quaron and Thareous persisted in their struggle. Spheres shot toward the other. Their swords struck in a tireless cycle.

The Archimage drew tall. "There is no need, Dark King. By the end of this hour, you shall be defeated."

Zakumahk smirked. "How be you so confident? I have proven the better Magician already. You, most of our skirmish, have struggled to evade my attacks."

"And you have no army," Prince Deil said.

The Dark King saw what he meant. Massive shadows passed over them. His beam overturned into fear. Dragons from the Ice Fortress alighted into the Elven Capital.

Leaftorn's Revival

The dragons landed at all sides, hemming in Quaron and Zakumahk. A silver dragon, above two hundred feet tall, towered over them. Eyes of pure light shone like the field of stars at night. He was immeasurable in length. "Where is your power, Zakumahk?" Jurtithan asked. "Where is your might? How do you usurp a land with no army to fit it? Why did you challenge us?"

"Like an autumn leaf you will be detached from the tree," the Dark King said. "For we would be the wind to ravage your society. In the spring, later in time, you would grow back, or regroup. By then I would have a hundredfold of your numbers!"

"Riddles do not answer questions," Jurtithan said in a guttural voice, "the same way questions do not satisfy questions. Fools come to challenge us. Fools die challenging us. Never have we been broken."

"It is not strength that holds an army together," Zakumahk said. "It is numbers. New forces come to the Legion each day. Soon we will not be referred to as the Dark Legion, but the Numberless!"

"Indeed, you shall be the Numberless," Ianvorr said.

"Sssilence!" Quaron hissed. "Thareousss is sssupposed to be the great 'Annihilator,' is he not? Have him challenge me. If I die, you may dispose of our lord. If he diesss, we go free."

"Be you silent, Viper-tongue, ere *I* kill you," Zakumahk said. "Send us back to Valvassa, I plea. I have not committed any wrong."

"You and your fiends slew a battalion's worth of elves and leviathans," Airalus said. "You wish to go free? The path out is death."

"A punishment shall be sought over time," Jurtithan said. "I find it suitable for us to question him, meanwhile."

"We know already who he aspires to awaken," Ianvorr said. "Interrogation is out of the way, Silver One."

"Who is it that he desires to revive?" Thareous pried.

"Your answers will come later, Young Mage," Jurtithan said. "At present we must discuss taking him to the Ice Fortress since my suggestion has been revoked. We can talk to him there."

"If he does not escape," Kyjre said.

"Hold your tongue, Wyvern!" Ianvorr snapped. "Jurtithan, I only tried to point out earlier that we know who his target is. We have only to slay him so we can hinder his invasion further."

"That is superfluous," the Silver One said.

"Stop it. Everyone!" Thareous yelled. "Your debate is prattle. He is my uncle. I should choose his fate. *Objections* are unnecessary."

"Decide then," Jurtithan said.

******

Aildeimor dashed behind an elm, his bow in hand. He peered around the trunk examining the grove beyond for an ambush. Nothing neither came to nor disturbed a probing spell. He beckoned to Lefanarí, who hid behind an oak. They ventured out into the open, always wary and ready. Most of the area had to be skirted as hemlock festered. A red wasp paused in midair to spy the two, then darted away to its nest in a tree somewhere.

Lefanarí put a hand on her brother's tunic and tugged it back. He met her with a tortured and relieved gaze that racked her heart. It faded into a questioning glance before he peeled his eyes away.

"Please, listen," she said. "I am sorry for never showing myself."

"You did what you had to," Aildeimor said. "You did what you thought right. It is because of this your reasons are justifiable. Once again you are correct. Returning would only have killed you. Our kind is the one who stick nearest the laws."

"Thank you, Brother, for those words of comfort," she said. Pulling a hand away from his bow, threw herself at him. She squeezed with the likeness and determination of a boa. Aildeimor tapped her to let go.

A rumbling made them face the left. It came from the other side of a hill, so they hurried up it. At the top the sound proved to be growling. They peeked over a line of bushes to see zarjkakons fighting over a deer. About them were the elves of Leaftorn.

******

"That is preposterous!" a gray dragon snapped.

"You would die!" a leviathan cried.

"It is Thareous's choice," Jurtithan said. "If you wish to duel with your uncle, so be it. Know that demise can seize you in an instant. The Jaws of Death consume all, even the immortal."

"I have fought him before," Thareous said. "I can do it again."

"Beware," Ianvorr said. "Overconfidence can get you killed."

"This is not overconfidence," the Young Mage said. "It is knowing what happens if he escapes. I would blame none of you for that, of course. The accusation is to be heaved over me like a net."

"And should he defeat you?" the Ancient Archimage asked.

"He may leave, unharmed, yet unarmed," Thareous said. "These are my terms, Silver One. You have only to renounce them."

"Do as you will," Jurtithan said.

Aildeimor burst through the circle of dragons. "Silver One." He bowed. "We, my sister and I, have found our people. They are bound by the Chains of Mondoria."

"Those cursed bonds will turn them into witless beasts," the Ancient Archimage said. "We must unchain and then re-chain them to reverse the spell."

"You might need half of your dragons," Aildeimor said. "Zarjkakons are abundant as guards in the thicket where they are being held. Amarzrell is there, as well."

Jeers of displeasure and abhorrence came from the dragons. "That traitor is mine," the gray dragon, Karjan, said. "He shall never again walk this universe when I am through with him."

"Enough," Jurtithan said. "I will take a small force. Meanwhile you should ready your bow. Know there are still fiends wondering the forest. Perhaps they have to be hunted down before the entire wood is razed."

"After the others have been revived," Aildeimor said. "Let us hurry ere the Four Suns rise into the heavens and the moon falls in their place. It shall be the time for Leaftorn's revival."

The Silver One chose his battlers and left. Ianvorr remained as the overseer of Zakumahk's retention. Thareous and the Ancient Archimage wished to also go along. The Ice Dragon denied them. "Zarjkakons are too powerful, even for Magicians. Let the strength of dragons bring them down."

Whatever dragons stayed made a circle. The Dark King and Quaron whispered amongst themselves. Ianvorr heard with his sensitive ears every word. "Thareous, it appears your uncle wonders when you are to duel him."

"Never. Nothing is to happen to him. There is hope for his repentance. He is a worshiper of Malluesaer. He can still find life in Kallenalza just as easy."

"Compassion is what kills one in battle," Zakumahk said. "You can keep your 'Glorifier,' that Galthoria. I am beyond help. Hope for anyone is sucked into the endless oblivion known as sin. Sin is pleasure. And pleasure I love."

"Yesss," Quaron said. "Pleasureful is sssin indeed, though apt to sssend one to infinite pain. The universe burns by thisss pain. Ssstill we can enjoy it for a time."

"You both wish to see the universe burn," Thareous said.

"You do not?" the Dark King asked. "Nephew, you are the one without hope. Face it; the mass of lands are past saving. Why would you strive to save any soul that cannot be saved? What could *save* them?"

"The acknowledgement of their sin," the Young Mage said. "To exchange pleasure for displeasure. The universe may be burning away piece by piece. At least we have our dignity. It tells us of our character."

"Someday sin is to be rescinded," Ianvorr said. "I believe influence can specify change. People are not so blind-sighted as most deem. Some net this incorruptible danger. It can destroy us if not disposed of."

Zakumahk glowered. "Change shall never stimulate anyone! Compelling are your points. Just look about you. Do you both not find it ironic? War is upon Keiratha and Valvassa for the motives of greater power. Who can repeal this?"

"The universe," Ianvorr said, "if everyone is willing to atone."

******

Jurtithan sat behind a group of trees as the invading dragons swarmed the copse. The zarjkakons rose with shock, hissing or roaring. They leapt at the dragons, which had larger numbers and sizes. Tooth and claw met the hides of both sides. Ebony flames contended with the elements of the Omnipotents.

The great leader watched how the fight went in their favor. Then he caught something moving along the skirmish, headed for the nearby trees. Amarzrell attempted to slink by them. It was good that Jurtithan had hung back. Elseways his traitorous brother would have escaped, the others too engrossed by the attack. He got up, deciding to confront the whelp.

"Amarzrell." The black dragon whirled on him. "Why have you done this?"

"Zakumahk overtook my mind," the Shadowhunter said. "When he released me, he gave me two options: serve him or die."

"You chose the obvious," Jurtithan said. He sat up on his forelegs and brought his head down some. "Come and join back with us. I shall ensure your safety. He will not get to you under my protection. What say you?"

"I return to your behest," Amarzrell said, giving a slight nod.

By this time the last zarjkakon fell. The champion dragons greeted their revived brother. Even Karjan, the brusque Dragon of Stone, welcomed him. Meantime Aildeimor and Lefanarí set to freeing Vellar and the elves. Jurtithan smiled at their triumph. In one short week they had overturned the worst invasion in Keiratha's history.

******

Elves and dragons stormed back to Zakumahk's makeshift prison. Vellar rode upon Karjan. All was well, bar Ianvorr's rage below. "Why do you not listen to us? We try to spare you from infernal slavery!"

"What is happening?" Jurtithan asked, landing beside him.

"A discussion of our principles," Zakumahk said. "Your Ice Brother does not agree with me."

"I have not any reason to!" Ianvorr thundered. "Are we to stand by while you speak ill of Galthoria? Nay, we must kill him for ignorance!"

"Ignorance?" the Dark King questioned. "It is ignorance that sent you on that rampage—a decade-long stage of fear and destruction."

"Speak to him that way again and I will butcher you!" Nahilmara yelled.

"Peace, Sister," Jurtithan said. "He does not insult you."

"Your presence insults us," the Sapient Serpent said. "You take the side of the enemy. That is not any excuse for the execrable sin you committed."

At this all of the dragons protested, defending their leader. Ianvorr still argued with Zakumahk. Thareous tried to contemplate why everyone was fought and his uncle so calm. It came to him like a fist to the face.

"Everyone stop!" he boomed. "The Dark King is about to escape!"

Amarzrell lurched forth. Zakumahk and Quaron charged up his outstretched wing. Ianvorr attempted to freeze them. The Shadowhunter's flames overpowered him. He did this to any other endeavoring to stop them. Despite their numbers they could not impede the black dragon.

The Dark King fell into his place between two spinal spikes. He lifted a hand to Thareous. "Farewell! May your last hours be ill!" Then his fingers closed about his palm. He watched his nephew shudder as Amarzrell took off.

Next Thareous clutched his heart and fell backward as if pushed. Zakumahk turned away, a leer plastered to his face. The dragons were too aghast to do a thing. At this time night sidled in, concealing their flight.

Vellar slid off Karjan's back. "Thareous! Something has happened to him."

Jurtithan's head hovered over the body. "The Crafters target the wrong being. He is unconscious. His thoughts are covered by an imperceptible fog. Nothing can rouse him, even if we cannot contact him." His jaws tightened, fitting like two sawblades.

"Wherever his mind wanders, let us pray it is not an ill place," Ianvorr said, rising. "We must leave him here. Whatever evil disturbs him, he must fight it alone."

"If we cannot do a thing, how are to continue?" Vellar queried.

"We shall stay the night here," Jurtithan said. "If Thareous has not awakened, we will have to carry him away."

Lefanarí strode to her friend's feet. "I wonder what he sees …"

Visions of Destruction

Thareous awoke, finding himself outside a cavern. Behind him platforms bobbed in the air with a slight distance in between. A void extended to nothing below them. Two gems wedged to the side of the entry shed yellow light. Curiosity led him into the cave.

Inside snaked a tunnel. Ocean blue gems glowed alongside the walls. Thareous touched one of them. An image of a witch about to be burned flashed into his mind. It was in Nalla's form, except it had albino skin, raven hair, and wore black robes. He did not touch another gem. The tunnel went on until ending in a spiral staircase heading underground where bloodred gems blushed. Thareous noted the stairs to be worn and cracking. He descended, quick yet cautious. Loose chips bounced down the steps.

As he went down, the air chilled. Jade gems replaced the red ones. He saw the staircase's ending and hurried down to it. A fork with three anfractuous tunnels continued to his right, left, and frontage. He took the one ahead. In the dim light of violet gems, Thareous came to a chasm. A rainbow of colors fell past it. *What is this place?* Walking forward, he crossed into the next section.

Here a chamber stood. Walls of clear silver pulsed every few seconds. Thousands of tiny gems glittered at his feet. The center of the room held a stand supporting a diamond-shaped ball. A being, cloaked at the face, gazed up at him.

Why are you in my lair? The cowl fell, showing a girl about his age. Blonde locks spilt over her shoulders. Emerald eyes espied him. *Do not tell me. I have foreseen why.*

Thareous opened his mouth. He could not speak. Words, clear to his ears, echoed in the chamber through his thoughts. *Where am I? Who are you? Why am I here?*

You ask questions I cannot satisfy. Who am I? I go by two callings. One is kept subtle. The other I can tell. I am the Dark Deliverer. I convey many terrible things. What is this place? It is the Cavern of Mystery. Why are you here? That is for you to answer.

I am not sure, Thareous said. *You say you predicted my coming. I wish to know why I was sent here.*

There is one purpose for your being here, the Dark Deliverer said. *An image that I am to show you has been passed into your mind. The one you love, of regal upbringing, is to become a witch. For heresy she is to be burned, or, in another way of speaking, stopped. The images are analogies.*

Thareous walked to the diamond-shaped ball. *What is this?*

A Tanazian crystal. It gives off the images I am to show you. Gaze into the walls of silver to see a remnant of your future, soon to come.

The walls rippled like a sea after the storm. Thareous rode a white unicorn to an unclear destination. He was older. Stubble infested his chin. It altered, showing him beating an older man. Fire, black as the night ere dawn, then ate away that image.

Ianvorr swooped from the clouds, ebony instead of milk-white. His eyes looking wroth, he crooked his jaw and unsheathed his claws. Many depictions whirled by, casting a decade's worth of destruction. In one image he thought to have seen Prince Deil, whom he glimpsed in paintings before. Next he saw Ianvorr thrown to the earth and caged.

Cease the flow, please! Thareous cried.

The images disappeared. *Are you weary of this?* the Dark Deliverer queried. *Of course you are. One your age cannot take such pain. Alas, misery is to follow you for all time. There is one whom can change this course of history.*

Who? the Young Mage asked.

This being's name is to be unsaid. Others do not agree on his past. I can give you one hint: he is my lover. In the room where he sat as king, he was stricken down. He stays in Annathias, where he awaits to be redeemed.

Thareous gazed deep into her unmoving eyes, seeking any hint of who this may be. He received none. *I refuse any help to people I know nothing of. If you tell me aught of why I am here, I will leave.*

Only I can grant you departure, the Dark Deliverer said. She spoke orally: "You cannot continue elsewhere. Go ahead, seek help. You will find none. We are alone."

"I will have to kill you if I cannot leave," Thareous said.

He lifted the crystal from its stand and hurled it into the silver walls. A hole opened where it was spiked. Argent fluids gushed out. The pulsing of the walls slowed, having lost some of its "blood."

"No!" the Dark Deliverer shrieked. She pulled a dagger from her cloak. Thareous's sword met it. "The Cavern of Mystery is to be flooded. If I drown, you are to as well."

Their blades crossed and parried. The contents flowed at their ankles. Tiny, multicolored gems crunched beneath their heels. When the fluid was knee-high, Thareous lifted the Dark Deliverer. He jerked the dagger from her hands and put it to her chin.

He sheathed his blade, looking up at her. "Let me go or die."

She cackled. "Fool. I am mannered as well in the Way of Magic. I was taught by the greatest Magician to ever walk in this universe!" She lowered herself with Thareous struggling to maintain his focus. The poniard zipped back to her hand. "Prepare to die."

She controlled his mind, not his thoughts. An illusion was cast into her mind, making her see him running at her. The spell then pulled back. He knocked her over while she swatted the false image. She still held the dagger.

They both came up for air. Thareous sent out both hands to grab her neck. She lurched forth and seized his face. She forced his lips to hers, not out of lust; just to make him settle. Then she plunged the dagger into his heart and let him go. Crimson strings intermixed with the waters. The Dark Deliverer watched the body float away. Thareous was ridden of. But not to her benefit.

Upon Awakening

Sunlight filtered over Thareous's eyes. He opened them to find the first glimpse of dawn over the forest. He lay upon a bed of leaves, his sword-belt at his side. A damp rag stopped running on his brow. Two cobalt pupils coddled him with concern. "Nalla? How long have you been here?"

"Since late last night," she said, stroking his hair with her free hand. She leaned down and pecked his lips, then pulled away. "They told me what occurred."

"And he must tell us what he saw." Ianvorr lumbered from a grove. "Come with me. The elves are preparing the morning meal. You may recount your tale while you eat."

******

Hundreds of deer were collected, enough for each dragon. For the humans and elves there were leaves full of fresh berries, roasted fishes, and boar meat. As they ate, Thareous related his account. Once he finished, the crowd stared at him.

"You know not whom you have met," Ianvorr said.

"I do not," Thareous said.

"Nor shall you," Jurtithan said. "Galthoria's grace you should not. The Dark Deliverer is the wife of the one we fear Zakumahk aspires to resurrect."

"The Dark Legion heads northward," Ianvorr said. "They are out of our reach. We can still influence an ambush."

"Later," the Silver One said. "For now let us set a time when we leave." He broke no silence until he decided. "We depart at noonday."

"To where do we hie?" Thareous asked.

"The Ice Fortress—for further planning," Nahilmara said.

"Jurtithan," Airalus said, "we are to remain."

"If the Wind Dragons wish to stay and guard the forest, they may," the leader of the Omnipotent Ones said. "We have three hours afore our flight. Brother … this may be the last time we speak. May the Crafters be with you."

"May patience live in every choice you come across," the head leviathan said. "This universe endeavors to sway us. Do not fall for them."

"Your rede will be taken to heart," Ianvorr said for Jurtithan. "Those who are done breakfasting, gather any necessities for the trip."

With that the dragons, having finished the morning repast, turned and ambled into a clearing. The elves scattered throughout Leaftorn. Thareous found himself alone with Nalla and Vellar. "What do you suppose is so terrible about this Dark Deliverer?" He leaned against a holly and rubbed his chin.

"She must be the dowager of a tyrant," Nalla said. "Your uncle means to revive him. How she falls into play, we know not. Her powers are unbeknownst to us."

"I wish the dragons would take the time to elucidate everything," Thareous said. "There have never been so many secrets held against me."

"They have their reasons," Vellar said.

"Their reasons dispirit me," the Young Mage said. "What is my ultimate destiny? How is this to end? *Why me?*"

"Only the Fates can answer that," Nalla said. "We do not know what tomorrow holds in store for us. We cannot even assume the outcome, whether fortune or doom. So what right has you to carp?"

"I know a part of the future," Thareous said. "It opens to you this day. Vellar, I need you to act as a witness. Nalla, I cede you from anything save friendship. We rode and have seen much of the land together. It must end. I am sorry. We could never be."

The princess was in utter shock. A sob broke her inhalation. Tears rolled off her cheeks. Her face flushed—either from grief or anger, neither male could tell. Her fists clenched, her lips contorting into a scowl. Thareous took her cheeks in hand and kissed her for the final time. Their heads swayed until they parted. Nalla softened some, but remained livid. The Young Mage turned away, walking from the holly-infested copse. Vellar could not decide to comfort or avoid her. He delayed, seeing wrath in her eyes.

******

"You have made a most influential enemy," Aildeimor said, after Thareous told him of his decision. "Doubtless she will speak to Jaldor about this." He looked up from a stack of reeds, his skean in one hand and unfinished arrow in the other, and to Thareous. "It has been told to me she is to be returned to Galgon soon."

"Who informed you of this?"

The elf carved off a few more chips from the arrow-tip before going on. "Ianvorr. It appears Jurtithan wishes to negotiate a treaty with King Jaldor. He aims to have him exonerate all charges of assumed treason."

"Treason," Thareous said in wonder.

"High treason," Aildeimor said. "Resulting in the death of you, Vellar, and his eldest daughter. The disbanding of the Omnipotent Ones is also to take place."

"My uncle was right—he is rash."

"He is the King of Keiratha," the Elf Commander said. "He deserves respect. This can sometimes, leastways, influence the hastiest to make better future decisions." He fell silent and chipped at the cusp again.

Thareous also basked in the still until: "What does my prophecy say about my life after the war?"

Aildeimor dropped his skean and reed. "You are to wed an elf beyond all beauty. Men shall envy you, for you won her heart in place of them. Your years will be filled with happiness and great wealth. You will not live in Keiratha. Yelva foresaw millennia, a hundred to be precise, flow by. What fortune you behold can be seen then."

"Do I dare discredit this blessing?" Thareous asked.

"A blessing from Galthoria is not to be discredited," Aildeimor said. "Nor are you to pursue this elf until the appointed time."

"You know who she is," Thareous said.

"Aye. She is my sister," the Elf Commander said, looking away from Thareous to the forest. "Come out now."

The sagging leaves of a weeping willow swayed aside. Lefanarí emerged, a coronet of sapling-branches crowning her curls. A dress fashioned with embroidered gold lacing snaked over her top. Its purple skirt hovered about her legs. Two straps carried over her shoulders, fastened in the back. Her feet unshod, she strode to the observers. Thareous was speechless, yearning to arise and take her. He restrained himself.

She turned upon him, cupped his cheeks in her supple hands, and lifted him to his feet. He did not move. She leaned forward, lips parting in a beckoning gesture. His command fell fast. He was incapable of reaction. Then, to his surprise, she took a tread back. "He is controlled but fails."

"It must do," Aildeimor said.

"This was a test?" Thareous questioned.

"Yes, and you must pledge your abstinence to her," Aildeimor said.

"How?"

Lefanarí took his cheeks again, this time pecking his forehead. "I hereby pull myself away from this human to follow Galthoria the Glorifier." She backed away again.

Thareous realized it to be an illustration and fell onto his knees. "Under the obedience of the Celestial Order, I separate myself from this elf until the appointed time." He bowed low and slid a hand off her right foot as a symbol.

"May the Fates respect this," Aildeimor said, putting the stack of new arrows into his quiver. He took up his bow, shouldered it, and found his skean upon the ground. Sheathing that, he turned to Thareous. "Come with us to gather meat."

"And warmer raiment," Lefanarí said, removing the sapling-circlet.

Thareous glanced up to the Four Suns. They had still an hour to merging. "If it is of no trouble to you."

"It is not," Aildeimor said. "I trust you since you have made a vow. Keep to it." They unlocked their mental capabilities and took off.

******

Meanwhile many leagues to the northeast the Ancient Archimage trampled through gorse-bush. He snagged his robe on an underlying bramble. As nimble as a frolicking deer he charged over tussocks of ling and stones covered with lichen. Birds chirped their anticipation.

A rivulet came underfoot. Its waters trapped stones in the bottom. It was not wide, so he stepped over it and continued up the side of a hill. An orchard where the elves took care of their fruit crowned it. The same stream at the base flowed in a dike near the trees. Blossoming leaves exhibited a cheery atmosphere.

He passed through it and went down the other side. Another, larger hill met him, guarded by two hummocks at either side, acting as shoulders propping up the head. Boulders rested on its incline, in the perfect position for eyes. Tufts of grass sprouted from its head. The boughs of a cedar stretched out to him like probing fingers. He grasped onto one to hoist himself onto the hill. Beyond it lay his grove, his home and haven from the temptations in the universe. Smoke rose like fog over the treetops.

This cannot be. Here he stopped; the smokiness burned his nostrils. Trying to peer to spot his thicket, he succeeded only in making his eyes water. *Karz!* Dashing down this slope, he shoved aside the branches of a sycamore and crashed through the underbrush. More smoke whirled past in incessant streams. All of a sudden he came to a clear spot. The black poplars guarding his home inside were either uprooted or ablaze.

Using telekinesis he choked the flames and drove them down. A host of ashes lay at his feet. They were of trees, not a human. *Where is he?* The Archimage went closer to examine the damage. Scraps of the papers that he used to record his studies on still had fire on them. *My office. This was either done by the Tribunal or Dark Legion. They both shall pay!* More telekinesis poured from his palms as he lifted the smoldering poplars. If Karz was still alive, he would be near death.

Running with the Elves

Aildeimor, Lefanarí, and Thareous stopped under a cottonwood. "This is where the meat is stored," the Elf Commander said. "I shall go up and retrieve it, then toss it down."

Thareous was unsure of how they could store anything, save drying clothes, up there. He caught sight of a house-like structure mingling with the lush limbs. A platform supported it, wide enough that no bear or other animal could climb onto it. A series of knobs protruded from the trunk going up like a ladder. Aildeimor used these to climb onto the base by a trapdoor fastened at the bottom. He disappeared into the treehouse for a second and came out. He had three packages of meat in hand.

Two he cast down to Thareous and Lefanarí. With the last slung over his shoulder, he leapt off the platform, snagged a tree branch, and was weighted to the ground. They went off again.

Back in Leaftorn they came to a gathering. Jurtithan was at the head with Ianvorr and Nahilmara at his sides. Behind them the Tribunal dais was overturned. "As we all grasp, the councilmen are traitors," the Silver One said. "They no longer lead the elves or Wind Dragons. Hence, the leviathans are indeed to stay, to ensure they never return."

"In pain of death this is to be," Airalus said.

"Do not applaud!" Ianvorr said to the crowd before the thought could reach their minds. "It is vital we proceed to the Ice Fortress now, though it is not quite midday."

"Why the abrupt change of plans?" the Stone Dragon Karjan asked.

"For the reason you said last: plans," Nahilmara said.

"We head there for that exact motive anyhow," Kyjre said. "If we need to go there earlier, then I suppose we do."

"We do," Ianvorr growled. He sniffed at the wyvern and shot him a malicious glance. "If everyone shall hold their tongues, we may be on our way."

"Prepare to leave," Jurtithan said. His wings expanded and began to flap. His bulky form rose up, ascending over the treetops. The other dragons followed his lead. The elves, along with Thareous, soon followed on the land below. They passed through grove and clearing. Their legs whirled like grinding wheels. A sense opened in their minds, showing the upcoming obstacles. Also it provided an aerial view from the dragons' sight.

Thareous made mental contact with Ianvorr. *Have we left Nalla and Vellar behind? Are they with us?*

They are atop my back. You could not see them since my wings were up, ready to take to the heavens and return to my long-lost home. Even then I will not be able to enjoy it long. War separates me from this.

Do not let this depress you, Thareous said. *Though you have been away three decades, you still have a very extensive life to live. Dragons are known to live longer than even the elves. Once this is over, you and Nahilmara may settle.*

Perhaps, the Ice Dragon said. *There is a fire in my heart, a yearning for us to settle, as you put it. I await the day when the dragons fly out, declaring the mating of us both. With the voices like strident trumpets this is to be made known to all. Like you I feel the affects of lovesickness.*

Interminable it seems, Thareous said. *Come now. This should not dishearten you. I warrant, as every day passes, there is to be an irrepressible intimacy atwixt you both. Do not let it overtake you at any time.*

Ianvorr's connection waned. A reassurance warmed Thareous's bosom. The dragon would accept the warning and advice. Great was the stamina to bear such obsessions. Greater were the alluring beauties that went with them. Nahilmara and Nalla, or preferably Lefanarí now, were those beauties.

At this time they came to the southwestern mere of the Eildon Lakes and careered over its waters. The crisp air over the lakewater's surface refreshed their lungs. They saw fish swimming away in an aimless flight. The other end neared in a trice. Once there they erupted into a clearing of evergreens, overrun by conies and leverets. Off to the right a clutch of deer perked up their heads and scattered. To the left a flock of bluebirds spotted the speeding blurs and took to the skies.

Lefanarí fell in step with Thareous. "After we reach the Keicor Alps, Aildeimor and I are to meet with you. There is a danger nigh the entrance to Jurtithan's Temple. Nothing lethal, but a precipitous crevasse that plummets hundreds of feet. It is called the Eternal Gorge. More details will be given to you then." She whizzed ahead to Aildeimor's side without a backward glance.

Thareous knew that if they could be together, then they would. It was no matter of being told. Just a confident intuition. Somehow he knew, deep down, she admired him. Someday he would find out how much.

Soon the area became marshy. Alder trees sprouted from the sludgy waters, their roots arching over the surface. Thareous found it more difficult to run in this terrain. Despite his greatest venture to keep going, the fen held him back. So he opened a portal ahead of him and walked in. It exploded into a flash of light.

******

A sound like thunder bellowed outside the Keicors. Great winds swept over the ground, ripping away leaves and branches. The portal reopened and emitted a flash a second time. Thareous walked as it spun shut. While waiting for the elves, Ianvorr contacted him. *Young Mage, what happened? Jurtithan said you skipped miles ahead!*

A bog slowed me down, he said. *I had to teleport to catch up. This was not meant to delay us any.*

No procrastination has evinced, Ianvorr said. The Ice Dragon was silent for a moment. *Prepare: the elves are upon you. Let your sense guide you when you cross into the snowy veil.*

I shall, Thareous said and cut the connection. He turned and began to run. *The elves will keep up.* Before him the snow clouds exhaled snowflakes. With his sense he could make out mountains or mounds of snow in his mind. The terrain was flat yet icy. At that instant the elves surrounded him. Aildeimor had the lead still with Lefanarí at his side. Thareous thought them ghosts in a ghoulish mist: undead and prowling. The intuitive sense deceived his mind.

Lefanarí fell back again. "As I have said before, there is a zigzagging gulf known as the Eternal Gorge ahead someplace. At its bottom end lies the entrance to the Ice Fortress. To reach its underneath, we must go down a sloping ledge along the eastern side."

"This is how we get there?" Thareous inquired.

"It is," Lefanarí said. "We must go singe file. If two go at once, one will fall."

"It is hundreds of feet, as you said before," Thareous said.

"Aye," the elf said, laughing. She flashed him a fond gaze, which he could discern even through the snowfall, and sped away. Above, the wraithlike forms of the dragons alighted from the dense clouds, appearing to come in for a landing.

The Eternal Gorge is nigh, Thareous thought. *The Ice Fortress appears to be underground—possibly right beneath us!*

Anxious to see the sanctuary of the Omnipotent Ones, he quickened his pace. It seemed that by running as an elf, he did not grow tired. Though it required more effort than usual sprinting, he felt the same as when he started. Then coming to his mental eye, a jagged maw yawned before him. The elves checked their paces and glanced over the edge. It had an undetectable base. Aildeimor led them to an inclining path jutting downhill. It was hewn smooth.

One by one, hundreds of elves shuffled down it. The dragons swooped into the prodigious gap and stretched on their hind-paws. Jurtithan descended first to the plane below. The territory was sleety, but at the very least dry and firm. At last the remainders of both groups reached the base. They advanced southward, proceeding in a slow progression. Thareous followed his two elf friends. Off to the side moseyed Ianvorr. Upon his back Nalla glared at her former lover. His gaze shied away.

Precipitous walls overlooked the area. Snowfall did not agitate them, for these cliffs warded away most of the storm. A gloom overshadowed the Keicor Alps. The dimness within the Gorge was much darker than above. If not for the light of the dragons' eyes, it would be impossible to probe the abyss.

"Why do they call it the Eternal Gorge?" Thareous asked Lefanarí.

"Long ago, nigh the derivation of time, an Ice Dragon named Voran lived. He discovered this gap and opened the Ice Fortress. At this time he watched over Ianvorr. Goblins overtook Voran when he was called upon to aid his brethren. Before he died, he said this gulf would never collapse. If it ever did, then the entrance to Jurtithan's Temple would be lost."

"So Voran also gave the Ice Fortress to the Silver One."

"Nay, that was Ianvorr. He is the architect."

Thareous's right eyebrow arched. "Architect?"

"He froze great ice columns to hold up the ceiling of the Fortress," Lefanarí said. "Otherwise, in time, the weight of the snow and rock would have caved in atop us. It would not hold forever." She became silent and looked ahead.

Aildeimor glanced their way. "A promise is something to be kept always. Is it not to be you wish to respect this?"

"I understand that, as her brother, you must protect her," Thareous said. "Can we not have a simple discussion?"

The Elf Commander glowered at him. "In time you shall come to the point where you no longer care for your vow." He walked away from them.

"He fears for our well-being," Lefanarí said. "Against life in Annathias." They strolled into the mouth of a tunnel. Behind them the rest of the concourse followed.

The voice of Jurtithan met them. "Fear not, all who travel with me. Elves who have not been here before, this is the tunnel to the atrium of the Ice Fortress. Just walk forward. No other passageways adjoin this one." On for another little while they went. Thareous was alarmed to see wedged into the walls the same luminous gems from the Cavern of Mystery in his vision. "What are these gems?" he asked Ianvorr.

"They are called lightstones," the Ice Dragon said. "They crystallize within the Ice Fortress and are excavated for the dwarves, who live in a series of burrows. If you ask since they are also in the Cavern of Mystery, know they were stolen. The Dark Deliverer tricked us very craftily."

The procession halted all of a sudden. "Beyond this point lies the bowels of the Ice Fortress," Jurtithan said. "For those who have never seen it, prepare to be amazed."

The Ice Fortress

They emerged into a large room sustained by ten ice pillars, each crossing it lengthwise in pairs. Two thresholds stood across from each other at the long side. A frozen tapestry draped over the wall athwart from the tunnel, bearing a picture in which Jurtithan sat. A plinth was located in the center of the room. The air above it vacuumed a translucent blue light from it. Silver glitters twinkled like stars in that.

"Behold," Ianvorr said, "I give you the Ice Essence. It holds the power of the Ice Dragons intact. If ever it is taken from its perch, we lose our elemental breath. The six clans each have an Essence hidden within their territories. Each is guarded by magic."

As they advanced nearer, Thareous could see undulating traceries on the side of the plinth. He tried to reach out and touch these. His fingertips went numb when they inched forward. He pulled away and rubbed the life back into them.

Lefanarí, at his side still, giggled at him. "Perhaps Ianvorr should have warned you of palpating that. You see, the magic he meant would be the same effect as after you felt ice. Except in this way the outcome is magnified about five times."

"I see," he said, half-smiling at her. Their eyes locked in a tender gaze. His hand reached out for hers. She accepted it. They moved closer in two steps to hide the connection. They forgot morality as they pressed forward with the crowd.

Thareous wanted this. His heart bent toward gaining her. In letting this occur, he broke the heart of another. He cared not. Nalla had been replaced by a more ravishing beauty. Their first real kiss was out of itch as well as farewell. Not a whit of regret probed his soul as he thought of this. It seemed like the magic of the plinth: the idea was numbing, the intent pleasing. He disputed Zakumahk because of his care for others. He knew he was past hope, so he did not delve into false dreams.

He recalled first meeting Lefanarí. Her mellifluous voice drove deep into the sensations of his bosom. He longed to stroke away the tears shed for Jalläthre. He longed for her cascade of curls to fall upon him each time they kissed abed. He longed to forevermore inspect her haughty eyes, her imperious cheeks, her sculpted chin, and her unstinted lips. And she said he should not gaze upon her with lust?

It is not lust, but need, he said. *She means everything to me now. For her I shall fight. Weakness will take me no more. Ianvorr will not be disappointed in me again! It is to be that I meet his expectations.*

By this time they had passed under the threshold to the right. The room tapered into a large corridor. Indigo lightstones lit the passage and cast shadows against the walls. A gloomy atmosphere beset the column. They trudged on like an army of silent specters. Ice crunched beneath their feet, giving a resounding chewing.

Thareous squeezed Lefanarí's hand and was rewarded with a smile. He avoided her eyes and risked a glance at her lips. *Such a marvelous smile! No wonder Aildeimor does not wish me to woo her. He wants her for himself, though he cannot.*

Then an onflow of memories engulfed him.

You follow your own opinions, secular opinions! Vellar's words from many days ago ricocheted off every corner of Thareous's mind, and he became aware of his indulgence. *These do not certify your safety; they increase your deficiency!* Self-reproach set in at the thunderous statements. *Imprudence is an empty path. Where this stops is not a dead end. It is at a hellish life in Annathias. Is this your want?*

He gasped and let Lefanarí's hand go as if holding a snake. She peered at him but looked away once seeing his timidity. He moved away from her against his will. He did not know what did this to him. It was beyond his control.

Not a minute later they turned into an immense room where a colonnade of ice pillars lined down the sides. A single archway served as the entrance. A large icy dais rose over the main floor; a ramp aided the hefty dragons from toppling when boarding it. To the right of the dais, when facing the front, stood an ice-wall map of Keiratha, carved by Ianvorr. This room had plenty of space for everyone.

"What is this place?" Thareous asked Lefanarí.

"The Assembly Hall, I think, where meetings are held. Also, if an Omnipotent becomes insubordinate, a trial takes place here."

Jurtithan mounted the dais, Ianvorr and Nahilmara at either side. He faced the assembly, his head hanging. Then he addressed them. "A plague is upon us for there being such times. Our enemy, the Dark Legion, has headed north. Whether it is so they can turn west and go into the Keicors from there, I know not. It is more likely they advance to the top of the forest, where a fleet would await them.

"If so, they will take the route through Ielyle's Bergs. For over them the course would take too long. So, in no more than a fortnight, if we be fortunate, they are to land. I would like to suggest that the krakens fly to Merlandis and request King Pharsus' aid. Then the Seafolk can wait for the Legion and surcease this raid. Sister Nahilmara, what say you?"

"If the duty falls on me, I must accept it," Nahilmara said. "My Sisters of the Sea shall go as bidden. Though it could mean our lives, we do this for Keiratha."

The Silver One bowed his head. "Since that is out of the way, another thing must be imposed. Should the ambush atop the brine go ill, who else can we turn to? I, for one, propose the giants and the dwarves."

"Call upon the fairies as well!" a wyvern shouted.

"They would not come!" Karjan snapped.

Like gentle trickles of water from a leak, a golden orb formed and hovered over their heads. Then a rapid flash filled the Assembly Hall. A gold-robed being stared at them. Brilliant blue wings of a butterfly suspended him in the air. Hair as yellow as fresh hay streamed over his shoulders. Tiny hands clutched a wand with a crescent-moon top. "I am Osaurius, herald and ambassador of Galthoria the Glorifier."

"Well met," Ianvorr said. "Prithee, why have you come? How happens it that you descend to an immoral world?"

"My purpose is not to dispense judgment," the fairy said. "I was sent to offer you the assistance of my kind. We are ordered to aid you in the war and defend the throne." A grimace screwed his face up at the mention of a cause of death. "Now I must go. Indeed, time there is little of. You should not worry. The Fates are yet to be merciful."

Osaurius whirled away in a dazzling radiance. Jurtithan stood taller, his ligaments written with joy. "Look now on the new dawn! The night has passed and this threat will never reach us. Zakumahk has come to prepare the throne for the Darkest Dictator. It is to prove his ruin!"

Thareous threw up his arms, glowering at the three head dragons. "All right, I have taken enough. Tell me who this Darkest Dictator is. I am to defeat him, so I have a right to know who my enemy is."

"We know, Young Mage," Ianvorr said. "We planned to tell you this day anyhow. All of you." He sat and tucked his forelegs between his hinds. "It is Varkin, the greatest yet gravest Magician ever."

Before Thareous could react to this, a roar of thunder shook the floor. The rays of an opening portal extended to his sight. The crowd shifted as a cry matched the booming. "Make way! Make way for a bearer of the dead!"

Those at the front deemed it was Varkin. The voice disproved their suspicions; the Ancient Archimage stalked toward Jurtithan. He held a large bag in shaking arms, bound by a leathern cord. He bowed to the three on the dais and looked down. "Silver One, I returned to my grove. It was destroyed. With it went years of research, discoveries, and my most beloved friend."

He held out the rucksack. Blood dripped from the bottom and stained the snow. Lefanarí screamed and ran to her friend. "By Annathias! No!" She stopped in front of him and fell on her knees, weeping.

"I am sorry, my dear," the Archimage said, putting a hand on her shoulder. "I could do aught for him this time." He moved the hand to her chin and lifted it up. "I have much power. To bring the dead back is demonry."

"Archimage, may we speak with you … alone?" Ianvorr asked.

"Certainly," he said, looking away from Lefanarí.

"Everyone else leave," Jurtithan said. "The meeting is adjourned." He watched as they filed out. When the last of them exited, Nahilmara flew from the stand and landed near a huge ice door. Putting her head to it, she eased it shut. She trotted back, the others awaiting her.

"We wish to know who you are, Archimage," Ianvorr said once she joined them. "Your hermitage has made us suspicious. What have you been doing in your grove all these years? Preparing a battalion worthy of invasion?"

"I have naught to do with the Dark Legion," the Archimage said. "I shall have something to do with their death." He showed them the sack containing Karz's corpse. "I promise upon this."

"You wish to appear obsequious because of your servant's parting," Nahilmara said. "You swear upon his corpse to fulfill the Legion's destruction. Why? Of what importance is he to you?"

"These questions are mere decoys," the Archimage said. "Later you aim to trap me with my own answers. Why should I betray you? This is my land as well. I wish to defend it. To me he was an innocent. He did not deserve death and does not still. Neither do the other denizens of Keiratha. We must defend them all."

"Why would a hermit care?" Jurtithan queried. "They do not concern themselves with the affairs of others. Why should you, unless you were not always one."

The Ancient Archimage grew stern, somber, silent. "You have forced my hand. I did not wish to tell you, for fear that you might rush to make me king."

The last word silenced the dragons.

"Yes, I am a prince, the last to be beheld. My brother Jaldor knows not of my living. I became more attracted to magic than regime, anyhow. I am Deil, one eager to put this war to an end, to overthrow Valvassa. Even unto death will I go. Should King Jaldor die, I must assume the crown myself. I only seek is peace."

Ianvorr was the first to find words. "Your Majesty, we did not acknowledge this." He went down in a quick bow. "I speak for us when I ask forgiveness from you."

Deil broke into a grin. "Friends, I have no regal influence. How might I punish you? Just know that I am with you … to the very end."

******

Meanwhile, in the corridor outside, Thareous sat between Aildeimor and Vellar. He contained a bowl of venison soup in both hands, which Kyjre had warmed for him. He sipped from it to avoid the glare of Nalla across the way.

"Why do you not go speak with her?" Vellar asked. He had been watching the connections between the broken couple since the beginning. He grasped what might occur if they did not amend things.

"As I said: you have an influential enemy," Aildeimor said. "Leniency is needed."

Thareous downed the last of his soup. "This can wait." He got to his feet, about to leave until he felt a slight tug on his pant leg.

"You face the murderous fiends of the Dark Legion but will not go to her?" Aildeimor asked. "This makes you a coward."

"I can outlast her."

The Elf Commander lowered his brow. "Beware, Annihilator. Though the true danger is upon the sea, she can be more a threat than that. Make the proper amendments now ere it is too late. You would do the same with Lefanarí."

Letting the empty bowl drop at his feet, Thareous turned away. The mention of Aildeimor's sister hardened him. He strode to the princess. Her scowl wavered; chagrin entered her eyes. Whatever dour feelings she harbored before, she gulped down.

Thareous gazed at her like a master would his defiant dog. "Take heed, you are not to expect anything from me I cannot give you. I have a destiny to complete. This is stopping a tyrant from obliterating our land. After that you will be already wed. Albeit, I wish for there to be no ill will, for we cannot be."

The princess's face developed into a reflective moue. "Will you not reconsider this? I mean, how would you have us be, if not together? Lifelong enemies? Distance-keeping friends? Maybe even total strangers?"

"The second is what I would have," Thareous said. "I fear, for the sake of you, that we should not see each other. Jealousy impounds your heart. The jailer is bitterness. You know of my fascination for another. I choose her."

With this he returned to his friends. Nalla's gaze, now morose, held no more spite. Aildeimor patted Thareous on the shoulder. "You did what you had to. Now I must disappoint you. Drop *your* lust, for jealousy is your keeper."

They waited an hour before the great door to the Assembly Hall opened. The dragons ambled out, voicing their opinions of Deil's identity. "Where is the Archimage?" Lefanarí asked. She sat at the other end of the hall.

"Cremating his servant's body," Ianvorr said. "He wishes no one disturb him."

Jurtithan separated from them. "We should ready for bed at this time. It has been a long and fruitful day. We merit it. Good night and pleasant dreams."

Thareous tagged with Ianvorr and Nahilmara. They tailed the Silver One, who led them to a titanic room called the Heart. It was very toasty, the Young Mage noticed, though he could find no source of the warmth. It made him tired and he lay down in an empty area. This was close to an ice column in the center.

A scaly snout nuzzled his forehead. His eyes opened to see Ianvorr over him. "May your dreams be light and unburdened. I will see you in the morning. You have earned well this rest."

"Sleep well," Thareous said, reaching out to pet the Ice Dragon's nose. Cold breath snorted out at him as he probed the outskirts of a nostril. His hand drew away and grinned. "Oops. Sorry."

"All is well," Ianvorr said, chuckling. He shrunk away, back to the side of Nahilmara. Then slumber took Thareous. He beheld visions of great battles beside his milky friend. They ended in victory. As a reward for their courage, the Omnipotent Ones were pardoned. Thareous became King of Keiratha and wedded a shadowy bride.

THE RETURN

Later around midnight while Thareous slept, a finger prodded his shoulder. "Annihilator, awaken!"

He sat up straight. Strands of curls veiled his eyes. "Where are you?"

Lefanarí brushed the hair over her shoulders and onto her back. Her sapphire eyes glimmered in the darkness. "Enough of that. Come with me."

"To where?" Thareous asked, noting the urgency in her voice.

"A room across the hall. I have not the time to explain."

"What—"

A hand clamped over his mouth. "Keep silent and come with me." Dragging him to his feet, she led him over reposing bodies and through a rectangular doorway. The hallway snaked to the right and left. A doorway untouched by light waited for them, straight ahead.

Her hand slid away from Thareous's mouth. "Now if you shall be so lenient to not speak, I can tell you one thing," she said. "My reason for arousing you is to forewarn you of a danger I saw go into there. She might provide us with information of our future."

"She?" Thareous asked.

"You will see," Lefanarí said and strode across the corridor, into the tenebrous room. Thareous paused for a second and followed. Uncertain what lay before him, he just stared at the darkness. Who could possibly give them information regarding their future? Going in was the only way to find out. Against his better judgment, he opted for this.

As soon as he stepped past the entry, something snagged Thareous's arm. He let out a short gasp. Two eyes sparkled in the shadows, though no light penetrated the room. They belonged to Lefanarí. She had her hand on his forearm. The glinting pupils turned away, toward the wall of umbrage.

Thareous could barely make out a figure standing in front of them. It appeared a hood covered "her" head. Though Lefanarí had said the person was female, this could still be Quaron. Who else did he know to wear a cloak?

The being pushed the hood from her face. The outlines of light-shaded hair fell over her shoulders. She turned her head from Lefanarí to Thareous. "So, again we meet, Young Mage. Tell me, have you reviewed what I proffered?" The tone of her voice sounded familiar. "About joining Varkin in his benevolent cause?"

Then Thareous remembered her name. "The Dark Deliverer! You were a dream. How is it you live?"

"Do you not know who I am, fool?" she questioned. "I am Jallaca, dowager of the Darkest Dictator Varkin! The Cavern of Mystery, where I resided all these years, is a pocket dimension. He put me there so that I could live when he returns. That is to be soon, so I promise you."

"Say no more!" Lefanarí yelled at her. "It is not yet time for him to know."

Jallaca reached into his cloak and pulled something out. "I intended not to tell him a thing, elven wench." She brought the item up for them to see. Shadow disallowed them to even make out its form. "I intend for him to find everything himself."

All of a sudden light filled the room. Thareous held up a lilac lightstone, which he had taken from the tunnel leading into the Ice Fortress. He gasped when seeing the object in her hand. A dagger. Then he chuckled. "You hope to fight us with that?"

"There is to be no fight," Jallaca said. She lifted her arm, only to catapult it forth and let the dagger go. It sailed for Thareous and sunk into his left shoulder. He fell to the iced floor, the lightstone slipping from his hands. Spots danced about his eyes. He fought to stay conscious. Thus far he was losing.

"Annihilator!" Lefanarí dropped to her knees at his side. She had her glaive in hand. With it she pried at the dagger's blade, careful not to cut him. He moaned from something sticking out of the weapon. He knew what they were: barbs.

Out of the corner of his eye, Thareous saw a shadow move. Jallaca—headed right for the elf. "Lefanarí, behind you!" His mumbled warning came too late. The former Dark Deliverer had kicked her in the temple. She now lay atop him, her body searing his. The contact made Thareous hold on a moment longer.

Then Lefanarí's form fell off him. He felt hands slide under him and sit him up. Thareous groaned and rolled his head. Jallaca knelt beside him, hefting him off the floor. An opening portal forced him to blink as it spilt light. A second later he was on Jallaca's shoulders, staring at a black ceiling. Again his world skidded toward darkness. This time he accepted it, hoping to never awaken.

******

Ianvorr led Nahilmara from the Heart. Before he was encaged, they would go on walks throughout the Ice Fortress every day. Their conversation circulated about many things: how the kingdom fared, what traits the present monarch had, why people did what they did, and so on. This day he wanted to be special. It could be one of their last together.

Or so Ianvorr thought. His sensitive ears picked up a soft grumble. He turned to a doorway across from the Heart's entry. Lefanarí crawled from the dark room. At once he padded toward her. "What has happened?"

She glanced between him and Nahilmara. "Where is Thareous?"

"Was it he whom harmed you?" the Sapient Serpent asked.

"Nay, it was a being long thought dead," Lefanarí said.

Ianvorr then listened with the utmost intrigue while she recounted the event. When the elf mentioned Jallaca's name, he shook all over. Rage permeated his soul, impelling him to take action.

The Ice Dragon thrashed his jaws together. "By Annathias and all its decadence! Malluesaer be condemned alongside his kingdom! Jurtithan must be informed. The Dark Legion has possession of our only hope."

******

"This is intolerable," Jurtithan said. "He must be found. Our cause would fail otherwise. Getting amends with King Jaldor is most important. Therefore we shall split up. An elf will return to the Nyran forest to notify Airalus of this. We must divide the groups and go to our own habitations."

"The sea is ours," Nahilmara said. "We—the Seafolk and the krakens—shall seek out the Legion's armada and ambush them underwater."

"I will send Ieldru, my fastest companion on foot," Aildeimor said.

"Very good," Jurtithan said. "Now I shall have the wyverns be led by Kyjre, who are to search the Fire Realm. Éilicil and the Ice Dragons will search the Keicor Alps. I myself will lead the remaining dragons to the Brimstore Mountainrange."

"What of me?" Ianvorr asked. "I cannot go with my kindred, so you must have something else in mind."

"I do," the Silver One said. "You shall take the elves and head to Galgon. On your way there try and spot the centaurs. Seek out Uhrar and tell him war is to sweep across his plains." He paused, overlooking the small gathering before him. "Spread out now. Report that we leave. Thareous must be found; tell this to all you meet. The Omnipotent Ones are not to fall on account of ignorance."

Ielyle's Bergs

Zakumahk stood on the foredeck, a hand guiding an iceberg to the side so the ships did not run aground. Behind him the unseaworthy fiends toiled to keep sailing, opening the masts, and pulling up dragnets. A bulky changeling called Izra lashed a whip to the back of any idler.

So we set sail two days ago and stray over the Darrien Ocean, the Dark King thought. *Thareous is aboard my craft. Jallaca rests in my private quarters. We are still days away from Galgon. Thank Malluesaer that Xyllanor led the ships to the northern tip of the Nyran.* He smiled as he shoved another berg aside. *At least Izra could take over till I arrived. Xyllanor was a fool anyhow. Quaron would be more a fool if he learned of his father's true reason of death.*

A commotion erupted behind him. "My Liege, mutiny!"

The grating voice belonged to Izra. Turning, Zakumahk stretched out both hands and lifted the changeling from the insubordinates. Then he claimed the whip and strode down a set of steps. "Sedition is repaid by one hundred lashes per mutineer."

A goblin stepped forth. "Milord, we only rebelled since we are beaten for naught. This buffoon you have as whip-boy extends his strip of leather more than needed. We did not mean mutiny."

"Of course you did not," Zakumahk said. "If you attack one of my 'buffoons,' that still counts as mutiny. Now every one of you line up. Izra, see to it they get their usual punishment and cut their rations in half."

With that he set the changeling to his feet and handed him the whip. He strode to his quarters under the helm-deck. He twisted the doorknob and walked inside. Jallaca sat in his desk chair, looking over his notes. "Those are confidential," he said.

The former Dark Deliverer faced him. "You have interesting plans for the future. Why can they not be shared with me, a lover?"

Taken off guard, the Dark King was rent speechless. He found his voice nonetheless. "We have just met, Milady. I am not your instrument to toy with. Not even by seduction can you sway me. Therefore, if I say it is secret, it is secret."

"You forget who I am," Jallaca said, setting down the paper she read from. She got up and strutted to him. "I am the dowager of Varkin. Throb your tongue at me like a snake and I shall cut it out."

"I lead this fleet!" Zakumahk cried. "I am its captain. Devoid of me the ships would drift over the seas till they came to be rotting wrecks. Do *not* tamper with me."

Jallaca came to stand in front of him. "You are a strong, forceful man." She set a hand to his bosom and began caressing it. The other slid over his shoulder. "Love bereaves the potency of men."

Her torso leaned to his. The Dark King stood there, transfixed by her honeyed tone, despite her last pronunciation. She wove together more flatteries, moving his anger away and introducing lustful sentiments. Admiration mirrored in his eyes. He gaped at her ample lips.

"You are the most estimable man I have ever met," Jallaca said. "Varkin is not worthy to surpass you. Many women may be desirous of us. What should this matter, as long as we are lovers?" Her emerald eyes bore into his, unnerving his gaze and forcing him to look away. "Nay, my love; stare upon my beauty."

A knock on the door sundered the spell. "Leave us!" Zakumahk growled. He glared at the ex-queen of Valvassa. The door slung open anyhow. Izra entered, jerking Thareous behind him. "This scum wishes to speak with you, My Liege."

"Keep him where he stands and get out," the Dark King said. When the changeling left, he pushed Jallaca away from him to place the glare on his nephew. "Who is pathetic now, 'Annihilator'?"

Thareous, bound in chains at his wrists and ankles, merely stared at the older man. His shoulder was wrapped in clean linens.

"I have been patient with you," Zakumahk said in a softer tone. "You denounced the life as a prince that I offered you. Varkin will not spare you. I suspect you heard him command me to kill you in a dream. His tolerance is shorter than mine."

"You care nothing of me," Thareous said.

"Because you are not acquiescent," Jallaca said.

"I shall not be a traitor to my country," Thareous said.

The manacles snapped open and fell to the floor. "Come with us," Zakumahk ordered. "Do not try to escape. The wound is poisoned. This poison can be lethal if set off by magic. You would not go far."

They walked out onto the quarterdeck, but ascended up a flight of stairs to the helm-deck. Thareous watched his feet go ahead of him until he had to stop or stumble over the railing. When he looked up, he gasped. Ahead, an innumerous armada sailed over choppy waves. Dark gray masts flapped in the wind. Icy mists surrounded them, making them appear as ghost ships. Fiends moved over its decks like apparitions.

"Gaze upon them, Thareous," Zakumahk said. "Let your eyes mirror your terror. This ship, *The Firewave*, is the least crammed vessel. In the other one hundred and twenty-nine the fiends overflow their decks like water. Uniting with me would not be double-crossing Keiratha. It would be saving yourself."

"You had best kill me," the Young Mage said. "For if you try to cajole me again, I shall smite you."

"Did I say saving you from death?" the Dark King asked. "Nay! I meant sparing the life of Princess Nalla. Alas, as I said before, the Omnipotent Ones must fall. They endanger my cause."

"You care nothing of them," Thareous said. "There is not a single nefarious rotter who cares for anyone!"

"Again we get philosophical," Zakumahk said. "Avoid this pointless discussion. Join me. I do not desire to kill you. Do not be wroth at me. Let not malice envenom your ill-mannered tongue."

Thareous shook all over. "*Malice*? You call this *malice*? This is not of the sort! You detestable cur! May the rest of your years be wasted away by your stupidity. Condemn your dreams and aspirations! Omit your petty plans!"

Zakumahk backhanded his nephew, knocking him off his feet. "Enough! You are a demented whelp. Stow your tongue, or so let your life be spent."

Thareous got to his feet and chortled. "You have allowed your anger get the best of you. Now I know you have ill plans for me if I accepted. Galthoria protects me from the corruption that Galgon would have housed."

This time the Dark King kicked the Young Mage in the side of the head, rendering him unconscious. "Izra!" The changeling whizzed up the stairs. "Take this churl back to the brig. Once you get there, beat the warden so he might be sure of no escape."

"It shall be done," Izra said, bowing. He straightened, went to Thareous's comatose form, hefted him, and marched away, his whip coiled over his shoulder.

******

Thareous awoke in a cell. Light seeped through some broken boards on the hull of the ship. He peered to his left and there stood a door, providing view into the hallway though a barred porthole. He sat up on a cot. *I must get out of here.*

The tramping of a fiend outside his cell dashed his plans. *There is one way out of here. Nevertheless this hope is far from attainable since I am being guarded. Therefore I can only teleport. But to where?*

Drowsiness overcame him. Hunger gnawed at his stomach. "A place where I can eat and sleep in peace …" He mustered what focus he could. A light opened up before him. He got up, vertigo plaguing him. Onward into an arcing portal he went. Keys jangled into the lock and the door swung wide open. He entered as the jailer, an ogre, lumbered into view. By then it was too late, for the portal flashed its light and vanished.

The Centaurs

Ianvorr cracked his wings and scanned the prairie underneath. Elves zipped over the grasses, which appeared silver from dew. Galgon was five leagues away. Calan Lake sparkled to the west; its waters rippled in a zephyr. The Four Suns descended from the heavens, lighting the grounds below. *Aildeimor, tell the elves to keep going*, Ianvorr ordered. *I must search the area for the centaurs. When you near Galgon, stay a furlong away to not be spotted.*

I shall, the elf-archer said.

The pampas extended farther than Ianvorr's telescopic eyes could make out. Farm houses dotted it. Horses galloped about their wooden corral, frightened by him. Chickens caused a ruckus. Farmers came out of their houses. They froze in their doorways. Ianvorr turned right and headed northwest. *Where are they? They used to keep nigh the lake. Perhaps the farm-folk drove them away. Argh! I have not the time for this. Nalla must be returned as soon as possible.*

A form shifted, drowsing on his back. Vellar held Nalla so she did not topple to the land below, then shifted her so that she lay comfortably between Ianvorr's spinal spikes. Ianvorr frowned. They could not delay much longer. Ianvorr was about to give up until he perceived them. Riding in a ring around a group of obscure horses, centaurs charged ever on. In their hands they bore sharp and twisted weapons. Their leader had unruly black hair that continued down his back like an equine mane. Sunlight glistened on his chestnut horse body, blemished by several lengthy scars.

Ianvorr glided down, so to not land hard or the humans might fall. His paws touched the ground. The leader, Uhrar, and his company halted in front of him. "Is this the ghost of Ianvorr the Powerful I see?"

"It must be, Lord, for we see it as well," another centaur said.

"I am no specter," Ianvorr said. "The Silver One has sent me to relay a message: your plains are in danger. The Dark Legion, under Zakumahk's behest, sails here to invade Keiratha. If it is overtaken, Varkin shall be resurrected."

"This is a lie," Uhrar said. "You have no proof."

"Not with me." Ianvorr said. "I bear only Jurtithan's command."

"Jurtithan would have to come to me himself for me to believe you," Uhrar said. "Move aside now. We go to present these unicorns to the females."

"As an Omnipotent you are to take the call instead of fretting over your desires!" the Ice Dragon exclaimed. "If you wish for your plains to burn away under the Dark Legion's torches, that is not my quandary. You are to be regarded as a renegade. You will want it the other way. It, by then, will be too late."

"I am not to be made a fool in front of my own herd," the centaur leader said. "Of course I have not the worry for embarrassment like you … Rampager. You will never share in any renown, not even as a legend."

"Do you deem I seek fame?" Ianvorr asked. "Nay! I look for the well-being of others. Give up your minor efforts to irk me. I am past irritation for I used it on you."

"Still you persist to persuade me," Uhrar said. "Even a being of your superiority you cannot force us to join. If there is a war at hand, let it come to us. The centaurs are more apt to stop it alone rather than with allies."

"This would be self-murder," Ianvorr said. "Turn away from that inclination. Fighting is the sole way you may live on. What *renown* will *you* gain from folly?"

Uhrar did not answer. Another voice replied in his place. "None!" Vellar shouted, sliding off Ianvorr's back. "Only death will find you. Resign this folly, join back with the Omnipotent Ones, and protect your prairieland."

"You bring a human to our parts?" Uhrar growled.

"Nay, I carry him back to Galgon," Ianvorr said.

"A Galgonian?" the centaur leader cried in disbelief. "They have tried to steal our unicorns. We warred whilst you devastated the land with a black fire. My herd would be tenfold had they not attempted this! The Capital deserves to rot."

"So does your corpse," Vellar said.

"Enough," Ianvorr said. "Uhrar, we ask for your assistance. If you refuse, we shall go to others—the Anathemas."

"The children of Malluesaer?" Uhrar questioned. "Rocs, fauns, griffins … anything but fiends themselves? Accept them and they will strike you down during the war. This in itself is folly."

"Whereunto we have no choice but to trust them," the Ice Dragon said. "Now are you with us or against us?"

"I am loath to relinquish my role in the Omnipotent Ones," the centaur leader said. "Even more so, I am unwilling to fight alongside them. Thus I must be with you."

"This gladdens my heart," Ianvorr said. "Still, we must invite the Anathemas to our side. Do you deplore this?"

"What must be done must be done," Uhrar said, sighing. "Let the Legion come, let them fall. Naught can they do to stop us. Far afield shall their cadavers spread, unable to ever be meted by the yardstick. We will stand over them, united and indivisible."

"May it be so!" Vellar cried, scrabbling back up Ianvorr's back.

"Indeed," the Ice Dragon said. He spread out his wings and looked skyward. Before departing he said, "Listen for the Call. Once it thunders into the sky, we gather at Galgon. The king shall condone your feud then. Farewell!" With that he beat his wings and took to the sky.

******

Nalla awoke then and asked what had happened. Vellar related it in a flash. He was anxious to ask Ianvorr this: "Do you think Uhrar will keep his word?"

"This I know not," Ianvorr said. "He could have said those things just to be rid of us. I saw a light in his eyes—like the burning bodies of the enemy. He is ready for war. I just hope he meant us not."

Far off to the south, Galgon and its splendorous walls dominated the land. Never before had any true enemy set foot into the city. Nor did the king plan for this to transpire. The bulwarks gleamed in the sunlight of the ninth hour after midnight. Ianvorr wondered what would befall them.

HOME

Thareous opened his eyes to a familiar place. He lay upon a pile of straw, stashed at the far end of a room—where he grew up. Here he would run to weep when aggrieved and brood when wishing to be alone. Haverin would come up to comfort him even when he could not be comforted. Once he tried to confess his feelings to Nalla here.

Noise flowed up from downstairs—from the lounge, if he assumed right. It sounded like a heated argument. Picking himself up from the straw pile, he crept over to the flap separating his room from the hall. He pulled it aside and listened.

"My son would never betray Keiratha," he heard Haverin say.

"Whether you like it or not, King Jaldor wants him brought to his court if found," a familiar voice said. The name of that speaker was at the brink of his mind. Try as he might, he could not place it.

"Commander Greilph, I tell you he followed that blue dragon to the white one's court. They forced him to leave with them," the Master Magician said.

So the father of Yal, Blugn, Temnar, and Rhamahl is here, Thareous thought. *He searches for me. If I even approach Father, he is sure to turn me in.*

"This proves nothing!" the commander growled. "He shall be caught in time and executed for treason. You have many powers, but no control over fate."

"Neither have you," Haverin seethed. Thareous heard footsteps, the turning of a handle, and the front door creak open. "If my son is found, I shall report him. As for now, get out of my house."

"This is not over," Greilph said.

Thareous pictured them glaring at one another for a moment until the tramps of the commander left. The door, to his surprise, eased shut. He heard Haverin sigh and steps ascend the staircase leading to the second floor of their compartment. Thareous backed away, the wine-red curtain flapping as though agitated by the wind. The footfalls stopped a moment in the hall. He held his breath and stood unmoving. Then leaning back some, he made a board creak. The treads resumed, heading his way.

The flap jerked out of the way. Haverin stared at his son in doubt as well as anger. "Where have you been?"

"Father, do not be cross at me, for I did what I had to do," Thareous said.

"I am far from that," his father said. "I am relieved to see you hale, but harmed." He pointed at his son's bound shoulder. "Where did you get that?"

Thareous told it best he could. He had difficulty in explaining that a dead queen had reawakened. After he finished, the Master Magican bowed his head. "So the Dark King sails here. The Omnipotent Ones strive to muster their forces ere his advent. You were taken from them."

"You address Zakumahk the wrong way, Father," Thareous said.

Haverin's face became a mask of consternation. "You know of this?"

"He ... told me himself."

Silence parted them until Haverin went over and embraced his son. "I am sorry to never have told you. He is your adopted uncle. My father found him in a gutter when he went to sail away on business. Your grandmother was with him to say farewell, so she took him back to Galgon. He was just a babe at the time."

"Were you not born yet?" Thareous asked.

"Nay, I was not. Five years afterward I was. This gave Zakumahk plenty of time to gather more knowledge than me. In the fields he would watch Frendur train the other Magicians. One day he asked if he could learn—at the age of four or so. My father agreed. They trained the day after."

"Something terrible happened," Thareous said.

"Indeed," Haverin said. "He showed an awful power that day— something that gave away his former lineage ... and cult. Have I ever told you of the Ausrahlian Sect?"

The Young Mage nodded. "I remember a little."

"They are the worshippers of Malluesaer the Malicer. They offer living humans as sacrifices lieu animals. There is not a single misfit amidst them. They kill and eat the flesh of anything dead. They are always encrusted in the blood of their victims. Their streets run with gore of the corpses. The skins of their prey are their coverings."

"What happened in the fields?" Thareous asked.

"A dragon of blackness was made. It flew away, never to be seen again. That is until Ianvorr struck Galgon. I stood in the center of a street playing with other children. Dareila was speaking with the other mothers in the marketplace. Even though I was a child, I never forgot what Ianvorr looked like." Shuddering, the Master Magician turned away from Thareous. "At any rate your uncle ran away less than a week later. He left a note saying he went to find the dragon that he 'created' and to stop it. As it turned out, he became King of Valvassa at a young age. A fiend told a soldier once that they accepted him."

"Why?" Thareous questioned. "Who would be so naive to?"

"Because he bore great power, for Black Magic flowed in his veins. They *feared* him, and so permitted him the black throne." His hands tightened into twin fists.

"Haverin?" a female's voice called. Light paces treaded up the staircase. "Is Commander Greilph here still?"

Before either of them could answer, the flap pulled back. Anazeil stood in the doorway a moment, looking at the stunned expression plastered over his face. She swapped her gaze to Thareous and gasped. "He is being hunted by the soldiers."

"Settle down," Haverin said. "Thareous is our son. We shall hide him here until help arrives."

"Help?" his mother queried.

"The Omnipotent Ones," Haverin said. "He has stayed with them for all of this time, if I gather everything."

"You do," Thareous said. Recounting his tale, he told Anazeil of the Battle of Leaftorn, meeting Lefanarí, traveling to the Ice Fortress, and his seizure. Also he explained that he found out of his birth and Zakumahk's relation to them.

"Almost a week you have been gone," Anazeil said, going to him to caress his cheek. "King Jaldor has been mustering his forces to war with the Omnipotent Ones. He may have to adjoin with them to save the land."

"Mayhap your decision to travel with Ianvorr has saved us," Haverin said. "Now we may warn the king so he might use his army just for that purpose. I have an account to settle with."

"Greilph and his sons must be hurled into the darkness of the dungeon," Thareous said. "Otherwise the citizens of Galgon are to never rest in arrant peace."

The Master Magician struck a palm. "First Division Officer Rhallanas can help! He is second-in-command of the Keirathan Army: third if King Jaldor is put in the list."

"That yellow dog Greilph must be executed, not confined," Anazeil said. "He forces every commoner than him to obey the law. They fear him and therefore cannot inform the king. We should act for freedom."

"Aye." Thareous's eyes flashing like a galvanist's. "No longer should tyranny plague our land. No longer should we be bound by unseen chains and led as a leashed dog through the streets. We are not to be duped. We choose our own ways in life. Let his kind be sent to the deepest, darkest pits of Annathias, forever to toil in fear."

"A fire has been kindled in our hearts," Haverin said. "It burns brighter than the Four Suns at noontide. Alas, that fire wanes when we have the chance to change something. O Fates, why must you allow this? Permit this fire to erupt!"

A still expunged their electrified moment. Nothing was going to occur.

Thareous sighed. "We praise them, we worship them, we obey them. Why do they not listen?" Pain shot through him. Haverin grabbed his underarms and helped him back over to the straw pile.

"You must be healed," he said, lowering him down as Anazeil studied their son. "I sense poison inside you. Magic can nullify it, still."

"How long should it take?" Thareous asked.

"Only a moment," Haverin said, removing the linen covering and peering into the wound. "Teilem, as I feared. Leechcraft is my weak link. I can only heal you by frustrating the poison's flow."

"What makes it so potent?" Anazeil inquired.

"The root of a plant called Taveni. Its leaves can counteract its effects as well as heal any wound. Since we have not this herb, it shall have to have to be done by magic." He let a hand hover over Thareous's shoulder and a white essence wafted toward the wound. He clenched his hand so the deep gash would close off.

Thareous could feel the healing magic enter his bloodstream. He exhaled as a yellow gas flowed from him and steamed in the air. Even the gas was safe to breathe. They relaxed as Haverin focused on healing his son. Next he worked on mending the wound. Pulling the skin together, he remade the atomic constitution. The skin wove to its past stature.

His father moved his hand away. "Lie and rest. The result of healing with magic does leave your body weak. For I have used conjury to swiften you back to full health. This takes great toll upon you since only your body should heal itself."

Anazeil relinquished her edginess. "I shall go and fix him a platter of fruits and cheeses." She thanked her husband with a whisper and departed.

Haverin, too, arose and walked back to the flap. Before he left, Thareous sat up. "Father ... do you regret the way I was birthed?"

The Master Magician gave his son a half-smile. "Not at all. I thank the Fates for delivering me such a son as you. Rest now, for rest is what you necessitate." He pulled away the curtain and disappeared into the hall.

******

Thareous wolfed down his food so he could find sleep fastest. Indeed, he did find sleep. While he dozed, a dream, dark and grave like the one he had in Leaftorn, came to him.

In the shadowy remnants of the dream the Four Quarters of the universe showed. Like looking into the lens of a telescope, the land magnified, but was illustrated from the sky. His view overlooked Galgon. In the east Thareous averted his eyes, thus spotting Ianvorr.

The Ice Dragon's thoughts opened to him. How shall we win without Thareous? His true position is undisclosed to us. Galthoria does not send word. Darkness trails behind the Dark Legion's fleet. There is no escape. Without him we are doomed.

Shadow fell and swallowed him whole. Two crimson eyes opened in the shade enshrouding all the land. A deep, baleful voice echoed over the entire universe. "I see you. You are lost, Little One. Join the Legion to be found again, lest darkness devour you anon. Come to me, coooommmme tooooo mmmmmmmmmeeeeee!"

The eyes closed. Shadow ruled the land as the years swam by. Never again did a

single pupil lay their probing sight upon a thing of beauty.

******

Thareous awoke, his face drenched in sweat. The voice seemed so close, so real. It beckoned to his as someone calling his name. *Was that Varkin? What hope am I if I cannot even resist the darkness? Who can answer my questions?*

I can, a voice, gentle and caring, said to his heart. The Young Mage quailed and blocked his head from all mental contact. Now he knew not whom to trust.

Conciliation

A servant raced down the hall outside Jaldor's Court. Unheeding the guards' shafts, he shoved them aside and rushed in. The King of Keiratha sat amid a conclave with his military advisors. When the servant entered, all attention was divided.

"What is the meaning of this?" Jaldor demanded.

"Your Majesty, live forever," the servant said, offering him genuflection. He arose to fulfill his master's command. "I am Shielden, a menial of Commander Greilph's household. He wishes for me to report something comminatory."

The king extended his scepter as the guards took Shielden in hand. "Let him pass. Danger is upon us. What it is, only he may tell."

"Sire, the White Dragon has returned," the servant said. "In the plains there stand elves. If it is true can run through solid objects, your life is in utter peril."

Jaldor was quick to act. "Return to your master and tell them to hold this dragon off at any cost. Loose as many projectiles as can be spent upon him. If even this does not impede him, the city is to be destroyed."

******

Ianvorr neared the precipitous fortifications of Galgon. Many soldiers stared at him. All of a sudden they reared bows holding reeden arrows over the embrasure. A gruff-looking commander bellowed out the order to fire at will. The first hail was let loose.

"Hold tight!" he yelled back at Vellar and Nalla. Stilling his wings, he swerved left, gliding just over the brink of the eastern walls. Arrows whizzed past him. Some landed in the membrane of his wings. He persisted. A spear hurled past his underneath and lodged into the joint of his shoulder and right foreleg. Wincing, he soared to the left again. *Aildeimor, invade the city. We require a diversion. Draw not your blade; have your kindred deprive the soldiers of their weapons.*

It shall be done, the Elf Commander said. He hailed the elves forth. They charged over the moat encircling the city.

"They decide what fate we have now," Ianvorr said to himself. He continued east, out of bowshot, but kept watch from the distance. In little time he saw the defenders of Galgon screaming atop the ramparts. The archers and pikemen lost their arms to the elves. "So we make it this far to be victorious."

Flapping his wings to gain speed, he circled over the bulwarks. Multitudes of spectators stood frozen in place by the inexorable seizure of fear. His draconic shadow flew past them like the black beast of two score ago. It appeared to return with a wrath. His eyes searched for a place to land. In the entire city he found the Square the suitable spot. Soldiers marched there, armed with ballistic weapons. As they set up to attack, the elves came and disarmed them.

"Where is your commander?" Ianvorr asked.

Seeing that all was lost, the company parted so Greilph could make his way to the front. He stopped a few yards away, unsheathed his sword, and threw it aside. "Go ahead, beast; kill me."

"I have not come to kill," Ianvorr said. The soldiers were unsure. "The king was told war surfaces in Keiratha. He mistook it. We are not the enemy, merely forgotten protectors. I wish to see him—for conciliatory motives."

He lowered his left wing. Nalla and Vellar slid off his back. The soldiers gasped upon seeing them. One broke from the company and ran to Vellar's side, throwing his arms about him.

"Son, you are safe!" Rhallanas cried.

Confusion sprung on Greilph's face. "They were not dead?"

"As you were, Commander," Nalla said. "We chose to come with them—to escape my father's rage." Rhallanas let go his son and peered at her. "The Omnipotent Ones are not traitors. Valvassa sails over the Darrien Ocean ere coming here."

"One is missing," Rhallanas said. "Thareous Haverinsson. Where is he?"

"We know not where he is," Ianvorr said. "We only know he is not with us."

The elves joined them, bearing armloads of weapons. "Where should we put these?" Aildeimor asked. "I feel they will not use them now."

"Set them where you stand," Ianvorr said. "Princess Nalla, will you ensure these men they do not lay a finger upon them? Till all is straightened out?"

"Do as he has said," she ordered. "Should anyone defy my directive, I shall hold *you*, Greilph, responsible."

"Milady, we have already our instructions from the king," he said.

"Alas, this cannot be refuted," Ianvorr said. A smile lit his snout. "Elves, move aside." He breathed over the weapons after they did. "May we now see the king?"

Greilph glared at the iced pile. "No one is to see him unless summoned." He bore his cold gaze upon the elves. "Curse you and your speed! Now the city is to fall."

"Of which you care not," Vellar said. "You always watch for chances of self-gain. The like of you ever is caught. The king will not be befooled by your soldierly appearance, you two-bit knave!"

"We shall see who be the knave," the commander said.

******

"Thareous! Thareous!"

Opening his eyes, Thareous saw Haverin approaching him "The White Dragon is here. With him came elves, Princess Nalla, and a young soldier. I was on my way to the fields. It now seems we will not be practicing today. Come, let us be off to the coliseum."

"I should not go, lest I be executed," Thareous said.

"Nay, not under my influence," his father said. "Do you not wish to regroup with them? This is the quickest road."

"I still have a life here," the Young Mage said.

"What life? The life as a criminal? Under my roof no criminal shall stay. Mayhap the Fates have brought them here for a reason—to prove their innocence."

Thareous lifted himself from the pile of straw, seeing truth in Haverin's words. "One day I must have the mind to outrival your tongue." He glanced back at his makeshift bed. "And get a real place to sleep."

******

Trumpets announced the triumphant return of the city-state's lost princess. Half of Galgon had joined the Royal Family in the stadium for this proclamation. The latter sat in regal chairs upon the emperor's box. On the field below, Ianvorr and the group of elves awaited the upcoming declarations. These would affirm the rescission of former accusations hurled over the Omnipotents. It would also be a public statement to the multitudes. This would hold either side—the kingdom and the protectors—from going against each other.

These wrought from the insistences of Nalla. She had bedeviled her father with the factual happenings until he gave in. Then, when Ianvorr struck, Jaldor decided it best to publish his retraction that day. Or at least certify no ploy on the White Dragon's part. Since he knew none of this truly occurred, he would merely humor them.

Now the king arose to address the assemblage. "Citizens of Galgon! You may rejoice this day, for all evil is beyond us. The Omnipotent Ones—who we feared to be our enemies—have been proven innocent. Like a phoenix they are reborn from the ashes of the past. We live in an age of peace, undisturbed by war or sickness. Thus credit is due to them, our guardians, for ensuring Valvassa has not struck these years."

Behind him he heard Nalla say, "Father, what is it you do?"

Jaldor's voice only rose. "For those in Valvassa are cowards! They know their populace could be razed if they so much as set a toe upon our land. Zakumahk is, after all, a fool." He noticed a doubtful shake of the head from Ianvorr. "So you see, any possibility of an invasion is void. Our eminent protectors have guaranteed this in their absence. Though they claim Valvassa comes already."

"Valvassa does come," Ianvorr said, extracting astonishment from the crowd. "We have fought Zakumahk once, in the Nyran Forest. He escaped to a fleet on the north end of the woods. He sails over the Keicors. It is only a matter of days ere they arrive."

"Oh, so?" the king scoffed. "And why did you allow this?"

"We allowed nothing," Ianvorr said. "This transpired without any of our permit or preference. Only the Crafters could sanction so tragic a thing to betide us. Therefore, should anyone be the blame, they are."

"Who are you to implicate the Fates?" Jaldor questioned. "They have blessed us with no hostility nigh a generation now. I do not doubt that you lie."

"For what reason would we lie?" Ianvorr queried. "There is no reason; we do not lie. The Omnipotent Ones have no aspirations of usurpation. We only remained hidden because we avoided war. Now we are forced to reemerge into the world. Our greatest enemy is on his way with an innumerable army. He wishes to depose you, Fair King. He desires your throne for a nefarious purpose."

"What purpose would that be?" Jaldor asked.

He watched the Ice Dragon's sides bulge from a sigh. "Zakumahk plans to unseat you in order to prepare for the revival of Varkin." Mixed responses flew from the masses, ranging from outrage to disbelief to denial. As if expecting this, Ianvorr spoke louder. "This is truth! I know every one of you is familiar with the Yelva's prophecy. I am fain to announce that our hope exists. He is Thareous, the Son of Haverin."

"There have been many Thareouses in Keiratha," Jaldor said. "They were all frauds. How is this one different?"

Two beings ran out onto the field in response to him. Gasps erupted from most of the throng when they placed the younger person. Jaldor squinted to make out their faces but had to ask Mareinia. "It is the Master Magician Haverin and Thareous," she said. "He abided here all the time!"

The king stiffened his muscles. "Seize them!"

Soldiers descended the many flights of the amphitheater. At the base they dashed onto the field, weapons drawn. Then, upon seeing a monstrous shadow above them, they stopped dead. Ianvorr landed between them and the father and son. He faced Jaldor. "Your Majesty, Thareous is innocent!"

"Innocent of treason, perhaps," the king said. "He is an oathbreaker. He courted my daughter during his time away, so I know."

"Where is your proof?" Ianvorr inquired.

Jaldor ignored his impudence. "Nalla has told me. Not by tongue, but by the way she sulks." He turned to her for a moment, noticed her sadness, and looked back. "Galgon knows of the promise he has made and broken. Ere this time I was lenient. Now I must take action." He motioned for the soldiers to proceed.

Ianvorr resisted their progression, continuing to press the king. "Jaldor, Son of Vellar, you make your gravest mistake. Galthoria shall punish you. Thareous is the Appointed Archimage, the Magician to free us from the bonds of Varkin. If you do not let him be, I believe you are to die in the war."

"Enough of this talk," Jaldor said. Ianvorr's last words shook him but did not break his composed facade. "The battle shall be won without him. The Omnipotent Ones are to fight Zakumahk and overthrow his menacing army. This meet is over."

With that the king smiled, turned, and shifted his crutch to another hand. Much to his bewilderment, a man in crimson robes stood over him. A white beard dangled to his knees. Hoary hair circled around a bald pate and fell past his shoulders. He gripped a wicken-staff with both hands, stormy eyes staring back at Jaldor. Authority emanated from those eyes, instilling fear inside the old ruler. How had nobody seen this interloper?

The man raised his body some and pushed his staff's knotted end into the king's brow. Jaldor heard Ingrezl shriek as he fell. He quivered under the man's unrelenting gaze. A long silence stretched between them. At last the mysterious figure looked up and walked past him. "Order Thareous freed."

Jaldor spun on his stomach and peered over the platform. "Release Haverin and his son! Right away!"

Without questioning, probably fearing for Jaldor's life, the soldiers charged out of the field. The king glanced back at the old man. He found his attacker to be focusing on something below. Following his sight line, Jaldor realized he stared at Thareous. They were studying each other, as if trying to recall where they had met before. No, deeper. As if sharing a secret.

All of a sudden the man spread out his arms and his staff. "Galgonians! I am no usurper. I come from Kallenalza, the City of Glory. My name is unknown to all, even myself. I go by a secondary name. At any rate a fire spreads through Keiratha. Zakumahk has spent the last three decades mustering an army worthy of this invasion. If there is hope, it lies within Thareous. He is the real one, as foresaw by Yelva. Do not deny it."

Then the stranger glanced at Thareous again and turned away on his twisted staff. He stopped only once to regard Jaldor. "Shame upon you, Vellarson. Had you not trained yourself to be reckless, you would have perceived this hope." And he hobbled away, off the platform and down a flight of stairs.

Flustered by the encounter, Jaldor stood with the aid of his crutch and Ingrezl. He lowered his eyes to the field and saw Thareous speaking with Ianvorr. Ire burned Jaldor's insides. How could that boy amount to anything great? He had never shown any special promise of distinction. This mingled with the reason he did not want Nalla around him. He would drive the kingdom to total ruin if ever he took the crown.

******

Noontime was upon them as the crowds emptied the amphitheater. Nalla and Vellar went home with their families. Ianvorr took the elves with him. The elves would find shelter in a tavern. Ianvorr would return to his courtyard. Thareous departed with Haverin, where they walked with the streaming crowds to their home. Along the way the Master Magician noticed his son to be meditating. He did not interrupt whatever thoughts he bore.

Reaching their large abode between two others alike it, they stepped up onto the stair-porch. Haverin opened the door. Into the small vestibule they entered, where the steps leading to the second floor were at their left and the parlor ahead. The Master Magician shut the door, but cocked his head afterward. "There are voices in the kitchen."

His son tamed his abstracted stage for a moment. "One belongs to Mother. The other I recognize." They hurried into the kitchen. Anazeil chopped onions and talked at the counter. A cookpot hung over a crackling fire, water boiling inside. In the corner where the table was stationed sat the old man from the amphitheater platform. He stared at Thareous as he had done from the platform. Deaf to Anazeil's chatter he arose, taking his staff in hand. A long white beard cascaded to his knees. Now that he was close, Thareous could see his crown was bald, his gray eyes more calculating. They mirrored wisdom, perception, the probing of the Young Mage's longings.

Haverin went over to his wife and gestured her to silence. They glanced back at their guest, noting the eye contact he made with their son. It was a sort of understanding, as if supplying Thareous with unfathomable knowledge. The elder got up, circling their son like a pride of lions to wildebeests.

"Well met, Thareous Haverinsson, the Annihilator so named by the elves, the Appointed Archimage so called by the ancestors. Do not fear me, for I fear also you, Young Mage so entitled by Ianvorr the Powerful. You outrank me as an archimage."

"Who are you?" Thareous inquired.

"My name is unknown to all, even to Galthoria and me, as I stated when facing King Jaldor," the man said. "I mentioned a byname though. It was stolen by a deceiver, an alleged friend. I am the Nameless Magician of Kallenalza—the Ancient Archimage."

Endowments

"You are a Demigod?" Haverin asked, taken aback.

"A denizen of the Highest House, I am," the true Ancient Archimage said. "The one whom deceives the Omnipotents as the Archimage calls himself Deil—but that Deil is only an illusion. He is a puppet to the puppeteer: Zakumahk, Son of Karz."

Thareous could only blink. "Hold … Prince Deil?" he queried. "Karz? The hunchback who abided with the deceiver? He appeared to be only a young man!"

"All Ausrahlians appear young, for it is of their powers that they do this," the Archimage said. "As for the real Prince Deil, he is truly dead. He tried to interfere with Ianvorr's rampage once and died during doing so. He abides in Kallenalza, in peace."

Thareous shook his head, feeling the weight of this newfound insight.

"There is a traitor amid the Omnipotent Ones? They know naught of it?" Haverin inquired. "This is very hard to perceive. But how did Zakumahk find out of your peculiar attire to make the deception so believable? Have you shown yourself before him?"

"Nay, a fiend of Annathias arose from his grave up to Valvassa with a tapestry," the Archimage said. "The tapestry bore my likeness upon it, which the Dark King has recreated into an illusion. He sought the most unsuspected name for his false Archimage and came upon Deil. Therefore he forged one to mislead anyone he met and is undoubted thus far."

"Jurtithan must be warned," Thareous said, taking a step back.

"In due time," the Archimage said, raising a slow hand to check the movement of Thareous. "As of now I bear gifts for you."

Going back to the table, he reached down next to the chair where he had sat and hefted a rucksack. Parting the mouth, he stuck his hand inside and pulled out a sheathed sword wrought of gold. The pommel was pointed, the guard horned, and the hilt segmented. Thareous took it and unsheathed it. It had a long blade, the edges sharp as a new-honed dagger. It seemed to give off light, though it might have been a reflection. Where it met the guard, the blade curved inward. It continued on up, thinning until reaching the top.

"Theldaneru, the Lightkeeper," the Ancient Archimage said. "Forged by the elves for their warrior Artheil. It was passed unto the Demigods at his downfall. Now I give it to you, Young Mage."

Next he pulled out a shield of silver. It had a painted golden eagle head on its face. On the other side two silver straps dangled, awaiting an arm to be slid into it. At the fringe it split into two divided slots. The Archimage strapped it onto his arm and swung it. Spikes jumped out of the rim and began to gyrate.

"Kielkanur, the Thornwhirl," he said, shutting it off. "This used to be Artheil's buckler, also sent to us via his grave. Inside is a series of gears. When powered by magic electricity, barbs come from the side and revolve around the circumference of the shield. It is able to hack armor or cleave a sword in two."

Taking out the last item, the Archimage gave Thareous a shining silver and bright green corselet. He unbuckled Kielkanur and set it on the table. "This is armor from the scales of Asbestos, the only dragon to resist fire. Alas, he was cut down in the air and drowned in the sea."

"This is all you have to give me?" Thareous asked. "Not that I do not cherish such gifts. I have been well supplied. Have you nothing else?"

Drawing aside part of his cloak, the Archimage clasped a radiant gem and slid it out. "Will this lightstone not satisfy you? I found it in the room where you encountered Jallaca and fell to her dagger. I now return it to you. Use it well and wisely."

Taking them in hand, Thareous and his parents marveled at the gifts given. He unloosed his belt and slid out his former sword, replacing it with the shining scabbard bearing Theldaneru. His shirt he removed and donned the Asbestos armor underneath it. After reclaiming his shirt, he slid Kielkanur over his shoulder.

"Thank you, Nameless One," Thareous said. "These endowments shall I treasure till my dying day. Galthoria has done me good, despite my apostasy."

"Call me Ancient," the Archimage said. Then his head dropped. "O alas, alas to these next tidings I convey! The Glorifier is to be replaced in five years. It is nigh the end of his kingship, for the Fates will appoint a new ruler."

"Why must this be?" Haverin questioned.

"Because, the Celestial Order demands so," Ancient said. "At the end of every one hundred millennium, no matter how just the ruler, he shall be replaced. May it be evermore ere his deposition."

******

After lunch they talked for another hour of remnants of Keiratha's past. Thareous paid his main attention to Theldaneru. *Lightkeeper. Why would they call it this? Kielthavra, the Shadowbiter—my uncle's saber—bears a sable blade. But this* ... Pulling the golden sword from its scabbard, he surveyed its conspicuous craftsmanship. *Aildeimor would be astonished to see Artheïl's former blade. I will show it to him if possible.*

"That sword is of more power than can ever be conceived by you," Ancient said, dividing him from his thoughts. "Long have the elves sought it out in Artheïl's grave. As I said, it was taken up to the Demigods. Do not fret. As long as you wield its power, through wisdom and caution they shall not look for it."

"Why?" Thareous inquired.

"Because they know you may be trusted not to besmear its blade with innocent blood. Artheïl endorsed it to murder hopeless lechers, such as prostitutes, adulterers, and homosexuals."

******

Why must we waste out lives in lechery? Thareous asked himself, going out to the streets. *Of course, who am I to judge, for I have also felt its effects? Lefanari has enraptured me with her beauty. She has feelings for me, just as I have feelings for her. How came she to love me? I am of no great position or fame, other than prophecy.* Turning in with the crowd's main flow, he walked down the streets. *I must find her and ask her why.*

A half mile walk took him to the Jolly Dragon, the closest tavern to his house. He made slow progress because of the crowds. As soon as its wooden sign came to view, dangling from a thin bar mounted on the stonewall, he cut to the sidewalk. He opened the door, a small bell ringing in his ear. Fixtures second-rate to the Royal Quarters furnished the lobby. Straight ahead was the desk where the customers signed in. Noise flowed from the room to the left, a boisterous bar. To his right a stairway curved up to the next floor.

Elves are here! Thareous thought as he glanced at the names above his on the sign-in sheet. *One is Lefanari. Let me see ... room three-two-*

two. Turning to the right, he walked up the stairs, where it climbed to the second story. He rounded the next corner to a well-distanced corridor and came to the next stairway. A small family descended by him, so he let them pass first.

Reaching the third level, he peered to and fro for the private chamber. He soon spotted the room numbers. Recalling what occurred the last time he entered a strange door, he unsheathed Theldaneru. Then he put a hand on the knob and threw it open. Countless eyes stared at him. His face contorting into embarrassment, he sheathed the sword and explained his intrusion. Aildeimor silenced him afterward. "That man who attacked the king earlier ... we saw him enter your house. Later you and Haverin came. Has he harmed anyone?"

"Not a soul," Thareous said. "He is quite the opposite of a persecutor. He struck the king since the man spoke as a fool. As for us, he came there to clarify his identity to me." He told them of this also.

"The Nameless Magician of Kallenalza," Aildeimor said. "The one that used to befriend Lefanarí"—he glanced at her—"is an illusion." His pointed ears seemed to perk up. "Quick—get in! You look suspicious as you are."

Thareous disappeared inside. The door closed but not by him. Three candles stood atop a small table positioned in the center of the table and scattered shadows. Footsteps padded past the door. Tension let go its straining grip.

"Why do you hide so?" Thareous asked, adopting leeriness.

"The king may be looking for us," Lefanarí said, getting up. She walked to his side. "He could deem this other Ancient Archimage to be an insubordinate. We must remain hidden."

"I wished to speak with you alone," Thareous whispered in her ear.

Aildeimor said: "That would be too risky. Soldiers patrol the streets night and day, through ache or lethargy, or the mischances of the weather. Do not state I have heard elseways, for I know what you said."

"This question I cannot ask amid the company of you," Thareous said. "If the king sends soldiers, I shall fend them off while she runs away."

"From what I recall, the last time you went with her, she was attacked," the Elf Commander said. "Ergo, the answer remains still no. Your coming has endangered us. You should leave."

Tightening his hands into a fist, the Young Mage turned on his heels, opened the door, slammed it, and walked away. *I will not know how Lefanarí came to admire me till my dying day! The only approach to this is persuading Jaldor to not be angry with them. What wrong have they done to him, after all?*

Closing the door to his home, he climbed the stairs to the hallway outside his bedchamber. He pulled aside the drape revealing there to be no intruders and went in. Pictures of famed battles of yore lined the foursquare room.

Removing his sword-belt, he stuffed the black and silver scabbard onto his dresser to the right of the entry. He slid Kielkanur off his shoulder, slanting it against the wall. Grasping the handle of a drawer, he pulled it open. Inside he found a dark leathern shirt and a dark brown pair of leggings. *Tonight I convince him.*

Secrets Unveiled

The afternoon lapsed as if in an instant. Nightshade reached out and embraced the land. Sable clouds obstructed the pale green light of the waxing moon. The last flashes of day upon the horizon melted away. Thareous donned the clothing and went to his window. Unhooking the fastener from a loop, he opened it. He put a foot onto the sill and leapt out. An iron trellis working halfway out of the neighbor's house acted as his fall-breaker. *I have not done this in years.*

Scaling off the trellis, he looked down and saw a garden beneath him. *Dame Marja is still growing things.* He pushed off the latticework and landed feet first into the alley separating their houses. Turning to the vacant streets, he dashed that way, stopping before going onto them, and peered out. No one came from either route.

He continued on down a northern boulevard, always on the lookout. He had Lightkeeper at his side, which would defend him from most weapons. Thornwhirl had to be omitted; its clanking would draw attention. At the end of the avenue he paused for a few breaths. Gazing up at the parapets, he noted the number of guards. He remembered there not to be so many. In his mind he counted Aildeimor's fears as true.

Eager to be on his way again, he took a detour east, where the street split between a bathhouse. Two more avenues circled the building's corner. He chose the one heading straight, going into the neighborhood of the rabbles. Higher royal servants such as eunuchs and cupbearers lived here. The buildings arose, tall and proud, yet hailed a gloomy air. An upstairs fire in the hearth lighted one window. Smoke wafted from a smokestack. The others that he could see just gawked at him.

Peeling his eyes away from the edifices, he went on. His ears ever vigilant, he kept a mental watch for the iron-shod treads of the gold-clad soldiers. Often he peered behind him, should he be followed. Soon that district fell abaft to him. A greensward stretched out at his feet, divided by the cobbled street. He trod down that street, certain that no danger would come his way. A plot of assorted nocturnal flowers bent at his side. Beyond that stood more structures.

From here I go to the left into the Square and begin heading north again. From there comes Bakers Street and beyond that the Royal Quarters. King Jaldor's bedchamber is at the eastern wing. At its base is the Royal Garden. There I can climb a tree to his window and sneak in. He began to run again. The ways he reminisced flashed by just as they had in the memories. His life would be endangered this night as he ventured to face the king.

******

The high walls leading to the Garden towered over Thareous. Soldiers often patrolled this area, keeping watch for possible regicides. He wished only to find something out. His own actions could expose the Omnipotent Ones' trust. He had to do this; he felt the Fates were leading him to it. No niche in the wall could serve as a handhold. He had examined it before the patrol returned. At this he groaned, for any damage to it they repaired. So he evaded the guard and sought out another way in.

Sidling along the high barrier, Thareous kept surveying the top. As he wandered on, he noticed it to get lower in steps. Bar-fencing followed over it also, ending in something like a spearhead. This defense discouraged intruders. He pressed on until coming to a lane between two buildings. A large wall barricaded the far end. Within it he spotted two crates stacked on top of the other. *Those will come to be helpful.* An idea sparked in his head. *Everyone makes a mistake. In my case this will aid me considerably. It must do.*

He lifted them with his mind. They rose and floated toward the outer wall. After a long moment he lowered the crates and got onto the first. Careful to not tip over the next, he put his left foot onto that one and lifted his body to the bar-fencing. Over the wall he saw many beds of flowers, just like in the greensward. It consisted mainly of a myriad of trees and even a hedge maze.

He swung one leg over the fencing, avoiding the ends of its pinnacles. Doing the same with the other, he vaulted over the wall. At the other side he landed. For a moment he put his hands on his knees. *There should be a tree where I can get up into his window, if I remember.* Looking about near the towering barrier of the palace, he searched every window in sight. He spotted the one where the royal couple slept. The limbs of an elm stretched out to it.

That tree's boughs slanted groundward also. So he braved the hedge-maze till finding the elm. Leaping to the closest branch, he began to scale it, unheeding of the growing altitude. His eyes lay on to the open window. Already he could hear the steady breathing of the regal couple. He could have spoken with them through the casement. He took another limb overhead in hand and pulled himself onto it. He sat on it, staring at the sashed window, it being open all the way. The cool evening air seeped in to moderate the heat of a bedside fire.

His first foot pushed against the branch. It shuddered, being sturdy enough to hold him. While holding onto branches above him, he shuffled across. The wall neared as each foot was placed ahead. Soon his life was to be tried. Would Jaldor listen or would he be executed for intrusion? He did not have the time to worry about this. Since he was there, he would not resign his duty like a turncoat. A step away from the casement, he paused and leapt. He caught hold of the rocky sill and hauled himself inside. It had been done. He could not turn back.

In the bed Jaldor stirred. Light appeared on Thareous's palm. It glistened like the morning. This deceived the minds of the two rulers, asleep side by side. They both arose to a supposed new day. Thareous clenched his hand and all went dark again.

"What is this?" the king asked.

"I know not," Ingrezl said. "Though I apperceive the Four Suns have yet to come down to us."

The rasping of a sword unsheathing reached their ears. A blade slashed the tiebacks. Teal drapes fell over the open window. They peered that way and caught sight of the black-clad Thareous. He sheathed Theldaneru. "Fear me not. I have come to ask something of you, King Jaldor, O Ruler of Keiratha."

"Thareous Haverinsson!" Jaldor exclaimed. "How dare you enter my chambers in the middle of the night, unbidden, unsought!"

"It is still a young night, Your Majesty," Thareous said.

"I care not of the hour," the king said. He drew aside the covers, clothed in nightwear, and turned over onto his feet. At the nightstand he grabbed a poniard. "Fool! You come in peace. I do not welcome you."

"Husband, stop this madness!" Ingrezl called. "Earlier when you spoke to the people, you welcomed them. Many of them are former prisoners from the Revolt ten years ago. Thareous has done to us no harm. If you love me, he will not be touched."

At this Jaldor stopped and glowered at her. Then he dropped the dagger. "Because of him my entire family has now turned against me.

I shall not lose their love. Nor will I become a murderous tyrant." He withdrew from Thareous. Once again the old king looked as a wizened man, devoid of strength. "I have failed Keiratha. I am rash. Forgive my hastiness, Thareous. I am the fool. May I soon be carried atop the bier to my grave."

"Speak not of this," Thareous said. "I have come only to receive an answer, not have you discuss your personal flaws."

"Tell us," Ingrezl said, sliding her feet to the floor.

"I wish to know if you, Jaldor Vellarsson, deem the elves as traitors," Thareous said, growing serious. "They know naught of my coming. I am here to my own resolve. I must know if it is safe for them to wander the streets."

"This downsizes me," Jaldor said. "They are welcome here as long as I am king. As for your resolve, it is folly. You knew you would not be able to escape. Guards are on their way here right now. You have lost."

"You feigned sincerity," Thareous said. "You have deceived me. I am to be arrested." He paused, keeping his hands from Theldaneru. "I do not resist."

"Let him be!" Ingrezl pled. "You dive back into your madness."

"Silence, trot," the king said. "You do not rule Keiratha. The ward outside will be back with more soldiers. While you are here, I keep you where you stand."

"What of the Omnipotent Ones?" Thareous asked. "They still fight for this country, to defend it from danger. Will you accuse them as well?"

"Thareous, you misinterpret my principle," the old man said. "I hold you against your promise. The Omnipotent Ones restored their trust to me. They would have my crown if I turned that fraternity back to false incriminations. Ergo, I attribute you for courting my daughter."

The door flew open. Soldiers entered, swords drawn. They ran over to Thareous, unbuckling his sword-belt and depriving him of Theldaneru. His hands were forced behind his back and into shackles.

"Farewell, Thareous Haverinsson," Jaldor said. "In the morn I shall see you. We will talk then ... just us two."

"Get this stray dog out of here!" Greilph barked. He turned to the king as they led away Thareous. "Your Majesty, we keep watch on the elves. Not a one has left the room. Should we further our observations?"

"Until morning," Jaldor said. "They will hear of Thareous's arrest then. There is sure to be a protest."

"Unfortunately so, Sire," Greilph said. "If I may now, Your Highness. The life of a soldier has only a few days of rest."

"Be on your way home," the King of Keiratha said. Before Greilph could leave his chambers, he said, "Commander ..." The highest-ranking officer glanced back. "Keep up the good work. Keiratha needs men like you."

Beaming at his commendation, he nodded and egressed the bedchamber.

******

Thareous barreled over as the guard heaved him into his cell. The door slammed shut. Moans of the ailing or calls of others wishing to get out interspersed. Snoring fell and rose from the jailer's room at the left end of the anteroom.

Growling, Thareous stood and examined his cell. Underfoot, the reek of sewage rising from between the stones beset his nostrils. A lump lay upon the only cot. A barred window at the other end provided him the view of the darkened street. To the left a lit wax candle stood atop a nightstand, emitting little light.

Home has never sounded so good. He went to the center of the room to lie down and sleep the night away. He knew could not escape by teleporting through a portal, as he had done from Zakumahk's fleet. For then suspicion might be cast back over the Omnipotent Ones.

Disagreements

"He did what?" Zakumahk roared, upending his desk. Papers scattered everywhere like a flock of frightened birds. A large chunk from the back left corner flew off. The morning after Thareous's escape, he had just heard the news.

The jailer stood like a hill over his master. "He has gone, Milord."

"So will follow you and your failures," Zakumahk said. Unsheathing Kielthavra, he hurled it at the ogre. It wedged itself in his heart before he could lift a protective arm. "There is no room in the Legion for failures."

Jallaca, who watched from the side, looked at the corpse. "Disappointing. I brought him here for aught."

"That is what your life will come to if you do not shut up, tit," the Dark King said. "We are becoming underhanded. Malluesaer has sent us dabblers. I cannot conquer a nation like this. Should we retreat?"

The former Dark Deliverer half-smiled. "Never. That would make us appear as pusillanimous puppies. By our numbers shall we subjugate Keiratha. The Dark Legion sail not through these dangersome waters for naught."

"Of course," Zakumahk said. "The fallow soils in Valvassa need time to heal. We are doing Malluesaer a favor. His fiends require a place where they can remain and rest so they may keep up their might."

"I am not here to provide the Malicer's fiends a refuge," Jallaca said. "Varkin was promised to be resurrected—to rule Keiratha."

"You will not address the Lord of Death so!" Zakumahk snapped. "Your dead creep has lost all his power. This I know. Malluesaer himself has told me in a dream. Give up your foolish ambitions. Varkin will never slink over a living land again."

Jallaca pulled a poniard from her vest. She wore now clothes fit for the sea, provided by Zakumahk. In no mood to beguile him, she poised her weapon. "You stand there, the tip of your blade in an oaf."

"This may be so," the Dark King said. "I have still the Dark Arts within me. What has you, save a scrap of whetted iron?"

An urge to complete her smile prodded up her lips. "I have the Black Magics of Varkin. He tutored me in his ways. Yield, ere you be afflicted by pain."

"My will is bent not upon pain, so pain cannot beleaguer me," Zakumahk said. "What else have you? You convey a poor choice of magic. If aught is with you, back away before I am forced to harm you."

Jallaca's eyes hailed vacillation. A mandatory fear drove her to this. *Zakumahk!* Two florescent spheres of a phosphorous hue came over her prone palms. She hurled them at him.

Before the Dark King could react, they made contact in front of him and exploded. Flames exploded above the oaken floorboards, and Zakumahk fell.

Jallaca stormed outside. "Attention, every fiend! Your captain set the body of the ineffectual jailer afire for failing him. Before he mustered a spark, the ogre struck him."

"Is he whole?" Izra shouted from the foredeck.

"Aye, just unconscious and burned," she said. "Lo, his chambers are ablaze! He must be rescued!"

"Abandon ship!" the Changeling Commander enjoined.

Goblins and vampires flew off, seeking anything they could use to hold water in. Izra transubstantiated into a wave and washed over the decks. As if with invisible eyes he directed his entire mass to flow toward the rising flames. Jallaca charged to the floor over Zakumahk's quarters, where other fiends gathered. The torrent carried many fiends into the sea. Those still aboard tossed out lines to the survivors within reach.

Inside the chambers Izra battled to fend away the claws of the inferno. He fought them back, waiting for the chance to rescue the captain, until scattering them. He reformed, hefted Zakumahk, and ran out, kicking open the door. Oxygen burst in, rekindling the fires. Jallaca dashed down the stairs to the quarterdeck after him. As fiends slashed the ropes to the lifeboats, she shoved Izra aside when he tried to set Zakumahk inside. "This one is taken." A dagger impaled Izra's arm.

The Changeling Commander cried out and fell back. The dagger did not go with him, so Jallaca cut the lines holding her yawl. It fell to the waters below. She took the oars in hand after setting aside her weapon. Smoke shrouded *The Firewave*. She still saw the flickering fires on deck, fiercer now. It busied the fiends, disallowing them a chance of escape. Some fell prey to its flaming hands.

In her little boat Jallaca watched with delight as the fruits of her plan flourished. A few fiends extracted from the main group. What did this matter as long as they could not report to the others? *Let it be that I might accomplish my task in peace.*

Abaft to the yawl came a hulking ship, *The Courser,* to her rescue. A line thudded at her feet. She snatched it ere it slid away. Being hauled in by a gnarly-bearded troll, she swung onto the foredeck. Its captain, a lich, welcomed her.

"Yer 'ighness!" he called, though she was near. "W'at 'appened? We saw t'e s'ip

go up intuh flames. W'ere is t'e captain?"

"Still aboard," Jallaca said. "Below deck the cook set himself on fire. In desperation he ran around, seeking something to put out the flame. It caught to other things. Above the kitchen lay Zakumahk's quarters. I was in there at the time. The fire spread through the boards and his desk gave way. I ran outside to warn the others. Izra, the righter of wrongs on *The Firewave*, asked me what happed. I told him and he became water, for he is a changeling, and flowed inside. Meanwhile the crew prepared a yawl for me and I got aboard. They lowered me onto the water and I drifted here."

After sensing the silence to be a pause, the captain of *The Courser* swore. "Is t'at all? W'at became of the Dark King?"

Jallaca lowered her head. Her voice depicted sorrow. "I fear the worst for him. *The Firewave* may now be a blazing jetsam. We still need a leader."

"I nominate Jallaca, Dowager of Varkin, the new warlady!" the lich claimed. "It s'all be so to our graves!" Roars of consensus followed.

She held up her hands for silence. "Please, hold your tongues. As the new leader I want to make a few things clear. To begin, there is going to be a change in plans. We will not vanquish Keiratha first, but free Varkin. Hence, we are to sail to the Brimstores and march to the Gates of Time. You know what we must do from there."

THE DOWNFALL

Anew day dawned over Keiratha. Somewhere in the city a cock let out its hoarse crow. Hectic crowds filled the streets. Dawn-to-dark sentinels relieved their nocturnal brothers. The officials of the king came to his courts, having been summoned.

"I have convened you all to inform you that Thareous Haverinsson snuck into my bedchamber last night," Jaldor said. "He did not try to harm me, but instead to speak on behalf of his elven allies. He is now being held under my order for defiling the oath he took a month ago. You were sent word of it in your own fiefs."

"My Lord, should we not prepare for war?" asked Jarsh, the baron of Ceilvre.

"It would be wise," Hemner said, his highest vizier.

"I am the king," Jaldor said. "This we will speak of first, over breakfast." He clapped his hands and servants rushed in with platters of various cheeses, a roaster, and mead. Cupbearers brought the drinking-horns or goblets for those who preferred them, filling them to their brims. To his servants the king said, "You are all dismissed."

Lord Aüshamer watched them leave and double-entry doors be closed. He focused then on Jaldor. "Your Majesty, I deem Commander Greilph would rather discuss tactics. You must agree to them, after all."

"This he knows!" Greilph growled at him. "Our king is not a dotard. You are a crass imbecile to speak to him this way. Never again try to arouse animosity amongst us. Though you may be of a higher rank, I have still the right to verbalize my thoughts."

"Thanks to you, Commander," Jaldor said. "Once more I laud you. Never before in all the lines of leaders in the Keirathan Army has there been one like you. Upright, just, meek … Why cannot even the peers under my behest be as you?"

The noblemen looked at each other, noting that they had been set up. At last stood up Barakuim, duke over the city Yarer and a bulky, broad-shouldered man. "King of Keiratha, we heed your words and accept them to our hearts. Continue."

The king shoved a gobbet of ham into his mouth. They waited for him to stop eating and leered in disgust. Further glances asked the subtle questions: *Is he ill? Do we support a sick king, a demented dotard?*

At length Jaldor spoke: "Fellow noblemen, though you are disagreeable, I remain firm in my actions. Thareous must be punished for reneging his promise."

They ate and listened as he retold his plans. At times Greilph shot them malicious looks, a triumphant luster in his eyes. He had his own plans—which the noblemen later discussed to be to undermine one of them by the king's favor. He could take that person's place and ravage his appointed town.

"So," Jaldor concluded, "all shall be well once we eliminate these trivialities and win another war! We will send Valvassa back into the shadows." Clapping with affected conviction, the peers exchanged uneasy looks. They could not waste the debate with objections on the king's behavior. His poise would get himself killed.

******

Thareous awoke by a red beam of sunlight shining in his eyes. Then a massive form blocked his view. "Well, look what the dogs cast in here last night. You know, friend, I have not had a single cellmate for two years. The only lug in this compost I can talk to is that jailer."

"I sympathize for you," Thareous said.

"What did they get you for?" the bulky man asked. He wore no shirt, had no hair on his pate, flashed gray eyes like a hawk, and sported a gut that stuck out like the foot of a boot.

"Naught which concerns you," Thareous said. He got up and walked to the cell door. "Has the warden not fed us breakfast yet?" This he asked aloud, to remind the jailer of the morning meal. Footsteps answered in from the anteroom. There appeared to be more than one, almost ten to twenty men. One tapped the ground with a stick. *It is not the Royal Kitchen Staff.*

As he gazed out the barred window inset within the oaken door, a sword blade pointed at him. "Breakfast is going to be a little late, pig," the jailer said. The keys slammed into the lock and the door swung open.

Before an escape could enter either of the prisoners' minds, soldiers flocked the cell. Outside Jaldor watched as they bound Thareous and the other man in chains. "Take this cur to a different cell," he ordered Rhallanas. The First Division Officer led the bulky man away. Most of the soldiers went to guard him. The king put his attention back on Thareous. "So you did not attempt an escape. I have underestimated you."

"I would not escape unless my allies protected me," he said.

Greilph laughed. "You would not escape anyhow, not with this efficient security."

"Yes, you would not," the King of Keiratha said. "If you did, certain precautions would be taken."

Jaldor snapped his fingers. Sounds of a struggle took place. More soldiers jerked a hooded being inside the cell. The victim sounded female, from her muffled murmurings. Thareous did not recognize the voice since she surely was gagged—he knew her still.

"Remove the covering," Jaldor commanded.

Thareous's heart sank when the hood lifted. It was indeed Lefanarí. "How did you know?"

"Nalla told us you parted with her," Greilph said. "She suspected that you might be in love with an elven maiden. So we went to the Jolly Dragon and snatched the most beautiful one there. The leader, her brother I presume, did not even try to stop us. We bound and gagged her and then brought her here."

Thareous stared at Lefanarí for a long time. His gaze darkened when he eyed the king. "What is it you want from me?"

Jaldor began to pace the cell. "A very interesting question. Since I am king, I could order anything from you. I am a fair man. All I want is your life."

Lefanarí spat the rag out. "You cannot do that! He is the one appointed to slay Varkin once resurrected! Spare him; take me in his place."

At this Thareous's breath eased out with her name. "Lefanarí ..."

The king smiled. "You are wise ... Lefanarí. I am as well-versed in the Celestial Order as you. It states if a king kills or has killed an innocent elf, he is to be sentenced to the Pits of Doom."

"What will we do, Lord?" Greilph asked. "If we kill the whelp, the Omnipotent Ones will rebel. If this war is indeed true, we shall not have any stronger allies. The Keirathan Army cannot win alone."

"Indeed you cannot," a voice said from the cell doorway. "For by the will of Galthoria, they would have the Capital Galgon torn down, brick by brick."

All eyes turned that way, discerning an old man in crimson garments leaning on a wicken-staff. Jaldor familiarized the distorted head. "You!

You fiend, you devil! How dare you speak of Galthoria and strike a king at the same rate."

"Be silent, Jaldor Vellarsson," the Ancient Archimage said. "In the war you are to die. Malluesaer has misled your mind in the last four decades of your rule. The Chief Entity is incensed with you. Where you go, he has yet to decide."

"Who are you?" Jaldor demanded.

"I am the Nameless Magician of Kallenalza, the punisher of the violators of the Celestial Order. Thareous is the Appointed Archimage, the slayer of the Darkest Dictator Varkin. Free him or so be dead *now*."

Jaldor gave the order to unchain Thareous and in addition Lefanarí. He turned to the Archimage and quailed. "You are mightier than me, so I could impart. Can we not settle in peace?"

"We can," Ancient said. "Only for what time you have left. You are old and pliable, Son of Vellar. The one who has used you to find his gain is with us. Now should come his downfall."

"Now shall come it," Jaldor said. "Tell me his name. I will see he is executed."

"The Commander of the Keirathan Army, Greilph," Ancient said. "Do you still wish to see the blade hew off his head?"

Gasping, the king spun the commander's way. "So! After these years of service you have *manipulated* me. *Deceived* me. *Used* me. Greilph, you are to stay in this cell, replacing Thareous till tomorrow. I relieve you of your post."

Shadow passed over the commander's eyes and he unsheathed his sword. "I go not until vengeance is taken!"

Glaring Ancient's way, he charged. The Archimage clasped his staff in both hands and slammed its butt unto the cobbled floor. A green, ghostly arm stretched from the knotted tip and seized the heart of Greilph. His face blanched, his grew skin cold, and his eyes no longer moved. The body dropped to the floor, the sword clattering near it. The spectral arm receded back into the staff. "So passes another knave. Who is next in line to be the commander?"

"Rhallanas, the First Division Officer," Jaldor said. "He leads the garrison atop the northern battlements. There are Four Divisions, if you understand, so we number them by how it moved in a circle clockwise. Because of his experience and dedicated service, I appoint him the new commander."

The Archimage's eyes closed for a moment and reopened. "He heard your words as I. He comes. Once he gets here, dub him with the sword. Give it to him, as is custom."

Rhallanas appeared at the cell door. His eyes fixed on Greilph's body. "What happened here?"

Ancient's hands tightened. "He attempted to kill a Demigod. I stopped him."

"Who are you?" the First Division Officer asked.

He told him and reiterated also the occurrence. Then Jaldor claimed Greilph's sword. "Rhallanas, come forth."

Rhallanas obeyed, as if they had disclosed some long-kept secret. When he stopped, the king tapped his shoulder with the flat of the blade. "Bow to me. By the power submitted to me, I dub thee commanding officer over all soldiers. Arise."

The new commander remained upon his knee. "Sire, I am blessed by this! Lo, there is a new dawn over us! A danger has passed, ended like the outcome of death. No more fear shall overshadow us, for our renown is to be reinstated."

"Indeed this is true," Ancient said. "There is still danger nigh, one that is greater than any single heel's deeds. The liable downfall of Keiratha is upon us."

Answers

The mixed company came out of the dungeon. Jaldor departed with the soldiers. Ancient led Lefanarí and Thareous back to their habitations. The Young Mage held back most of the way. With her being so close, he could not find words. In minutes they intermixed with the cramped crowds. Theldaneru had been returned to Thareous's side. He looked forward to asking Lefanarí how she came to like him.

Moving with the crowd's rate, they made slow progress. The Archimage made sure Lefanarí stayed by his side.

He knows what question I desire to ask her, Thareous mused. *Why would he not want me to? Why is he so guarded?*

The answer came without a responder. *The more time you are with her, the more you will be incapable to resist her.*

So he stayed back. How could he approach her with this mindset?

Soon the Jolly Dragon came into view, with its wooden sign presenting a childish dragon beaming over a mug of overflowing beer it held. Here Lefanarí would depart. Like a silent observer Thareous lingered.

The Ancient Archimage turned to him. "Will you not say a few words of farewell before returning to your house? You know the way." Without another word he disappeared back into the crowds.

A sense of unease appeared in Thareous's heart. They were alone. This he wanted. He had waited for this. He scanned the facade of a cobbler's shop to avoid any amoral emanations. The moment brought hesitancy and shyness to him. A hand, set on his cheek, turned his face her way. An angelic smile toppled his guard. Into those round sapphires he peered, wishing to go closer.

Lefanarí withdrew her hand, diverging his attention. "Yesterday you told me you had to speak with me. We were interrupted. I can talk now. There is no doubt we are being watched, for the elves' room is just above us. All the same, go ahead."

Thareous sighed and looked away once more. "We have known each other for a week now. Upon seeing you, I came to love you. I cannot help but wonder … if you feel the same about me. If so, then how is it this way?"

"Of course I love you," Lefanarí said. "I even respect, regard, and revere you. If you talk about another way, I must say no. For I follow Galthoria. He would not have me pursue my wants. I pray you can understand this."

"You looked at me with affection!" Thareous shouted, gathering attention. "As we went to the Ice Fortress, you smiled at me. When Aildeimor said we should stay to our oaths, you tried to avert the conversation elsewhere."

"I care for you," she said, putting a hand on his shoulder. "A lot. If ever it came to a time where a sword was upon you, I would get between it. The concern you seek is unlawful. I am sorry. I must remain whole to my oath. I hope you would join me, despite this news. It would heal my heart to a great extent."

"My prophecy!" Thareous exclaimed, neglecting her words. "It says we are to wed. Countless will become jealous of us. We can start our relationship at any time. How sounds this to you?"

"Heeded you not a word I said?" Lefanarí whispered. "Well, hearken it this time, for I shall not repeat it. My allegiance lies with Galthoria, not Self. Since the death of Jalläthre I have found none who surpass him. You do come close. By the pity nestling in my heart, I wish you would think else."

"I come close," the Young Mage said. "This you have said not a moment ago. Can I not be more than a friend? If I kept my feelings in check, could I not fraternize with you? I love you. I do not wish to lose you."

"We can be friends, and no more," the elf said. She sighed and took his hands. "It is not my volition that it is this way. The Fates have mandated us to abide by their laws. I see no other path for us to tread. For if we step off the trail, we are apt to wander far from it. In accordance I cannot go to you since you would mislead me."

This statement brought anger to Thareous's face. "How dare you portray me so! I do not plan on guiding you to death. Far from that! Instead I now wish to institute an understanding betwixt us. I crave only your friendship and trust—as it has been voiced. Even more so I request you not seek another mate."

"It is obvious Galthoria lives in you not," Lefanarí muttered. "He does not allow us breath so we suspend it when kissing. Lust is wrong. That blade you bear has killed those who sought lust. It is not the Glorifier's wish. We are so fallible when it comes to sin. He uses pleasure to test our devotion to him." Her hands clutched his tighter, sending a chill flitting through him. "Let me lead you to him."

At these words Thareous scowled and unlaced his fingers from hers. "I will never bear that yoke again. My life was tragic ere I let him go. Then I met Nalla. The days have been easier because I charge my own actions."

For the first time ever he saw hatred enter Lefanarí's eyes. Her beauteous pupils were shattered by it. "May you think better of your future. In time you shall see the truth in my words. Then, and only then, will I consider courting you."

She whirled from him and sprinted into the Jolly Dragon. The dragon's smile on the sign seemed to mock Thareous. Bitterness jabbed his heart and hardened toward Galthoria. A series of imprecations disparaged his worth. Malevolent evocations quelled Thareous's hopes as the waves pushing a ship to jutting rocks. He felt alone, even betrayed by himself. No reassurance from his inner being could stopper his maelstrom of thoughts.

On the way home he reflected the conversation. It seemed to him more like a debate. How could Lefanarí be so rapt in an entity who allowed suffering to his people? He did not understand. It frustrated him. He had to clear his head. He pined that Ianvorr could not have been there as a witness. The Ice Dragon would have offered him gentle advice. Although it might not go his way, their amity would have them be forbearing.

The door to his abode was open when he walked in. As usual the small vestibule held no one. So he strode into the parlor. Not a soul occupied this room, either. *Where could they be?* Voices arose from the kitchen. He entered there and began to ask what they conferred over. Once he saw they had company, his tongue halted.

"Thareous Haverinsson," Commander Rhallanas said, coming over to shake his hand. "At last we are at a place where we can talk amongst friends. Vellar has told me much about your discovering the dragon could speak."

Thareous withdrew his hand after a terse shake. "Ianvorr—the White Dragon—decided it best to disclose to me his ability."

"We have other business," Vellar said from his seat in a kitchen chair. "The four sons of Greilph are to be jailed this day. The king ordered their arrest after hearing their reprehensible deeds. It is time we take them down. They alone can ravage Keiratha from within."

Deliverance

Rhallanas set the original plans of the late commander's house atop the table in an abandoned edifice. A group of armed soldiers stood around him, scrutinizing it. "Men, we are assigned to apprehend the sons of Greilph. These designs designate the area surrounding his domicile and its inside. Do you have any questions or comments so far?"

Thareous raised a hand. "Aye, it appears that an alleyway disconnects any contact with other locales. For that reason there could be a side door there. We can post an archer on the roof across from it."

"That is a good suggestion," Rhallanas said. "I agree to this. The best bowmen are saved for the garrisons, should the enemy donate us a surprise attack. They do not involve themselves in petty assignments."

"Then allow me to appoint an elf," Thareous said.

All of the company watched the commander for any sign of refusal. He showed only a dim approval. "Very well, we shall ask of him of this favor. If you wonder of our reserve, know we have contested over who is the better warrior for generations. Anyhow, let us finish our briefing."

They drew the posts and dispensed everyone into groups. They marched off to fulfill their duty. Thareous went to accomplish a harder task.

******

"Over my dead body," Aildeimor said. "Not after what they have done to Lefanarí. Our rivalry with them has become more virulent since the last generation. They wish to make us appear as fools, especially that decadent rotter Greilph!"

"Who is now dead," Thareous said. "A wiser, more considerate fellow has taken his place. He does not cow anyone, not even for pleasure."

"His name is?" the elf-archer asked.

"Rhallanas, the Father of Vellar," Thareous said. "Having you be placed atop a roof is a grand idea. Those scamps are homosexuals, molesters, and even murderers. They deserve to be imprisoned."

"Do not be critical because they know not better," Aildeimor said. "These scamps, as you call them, are wrongheaded. They do not identify the truth of Galthoria's mercy to all who are fain to follow him. Malluesaer has them in his claws."

"What do you mean?" Thareous snapped. "They have harmed people, even going so far as intimidating Nalla to deliver a message to her father. This was to drop laws so they could have 'fun.' They are malicious. The malicious merit death."

"Fret not: that is where they go after being caught," Aildeimor said. "Execution. The lords in their tower-rooms stuffing their faces till they could burst. Their heads drown in their vanity. They are the true enemy. They sit back while others suffer. Keiratha is dying."

"You speak truth," Thareous said. "We can help nurture it by ridding of its problems, such as hooliganism. So are you still with us, even in this?"

Aildeimor stared at him for a long time, unsure of what decision to make. His friend was right. Ruffianism tore down Keiratha's columns. Such was the gnawing pretentiousness of the noblemen. They took their positions, their power too heavily. Rogues running amok in the streets threatened the lives of innocents. "I shall do it."

******

"Yal, when do we get to go upturn another covered shop?" Blugn complained.

"Or start a fight in the Jolly Dragon?" Rhamahl went on.

"Or throw rocks through an old dame's window?" Temnar ended.

"Will you three shut your orifices?" Yal retorted. "I am not interested in your yearnings. Something is afoot outside. Even though *I* wish to ravish another wench, we cannot." He peered out a window, his voice toned to a whisper.

"What is it?" Rhamahl asked.

"Soldiers," the eldest brother said and closed the shutters. "They are isolating this area. It will either be us or another creep nearby. At any rate we must get some weapons. Blugn, fetch them. Temnar, watch the door. If anyone knocks, then answer it, *casually*. Respond to any questions or conversation. Let us go!"

******

Outside Rhallanas checked his men's positions and walked to the door. Knocking, he saw a grille inset in the oaken door slid open. An eye peeped out. "Off-officer Rhallanas, wh-what are you … do-doing here?" Temnar stuttered.

"We are here to find an escaped prisoner by the name of Thareous," the commander said. "Your father was injured when he went to interrogate him. Do you mind if we scour your home?"

"Well, um, do you not require a search warrant?" Temnar queried.

Rhallanas reached into a wallet tied to his belt and pulled out a folded piece of paper. He grinned. "Signed by the king himself and sealed by his signet ring." Handing Temnar, the third oldest, the warrant, he waited until he had read it twice over.

"It is real enough," Temnar said and swung the grille open some more. "Come in.

I shall explain your entry to my oldest brother." He paused. "Oh, is Father okay?"

"Just a little roughed up, but whole," Rhallanas said. "If you do not mind, we have business to undertake." Waving a hand, he summoned a band of soldiers who forced the door open. They found entry and caught Temnar off guard. Inside they overturned furniture, pulled up rugs, and broke doors off their hinges. The other three brothers ran down a curving stairway.

"What is this?" Yal demanded.

When Rhallanas saw them armed, he ordered his men to draw their swords. "You and your brothers are under arrest for murder, homosexuality, molestation, vandalism, and stealing from the bazaar. The consequences shall be your lives, for you have taken those of others."

"Wait until Father hears about this!" Blugn exclaimed. "He has the influence to bring anyone down."

"Not anymore."

"What does that suppose to mean?" Rhamahl questioned.

"It means he died for trying to slaughter an innocent," the commander said. "Give yourselves up or it shall be done by force."

"The side door!" Yal cried. "We will escape through there!"

The brothers flew down the stairs, exiting the parlor via a door to the left of its last step. The soldiers seized Temnar, for he still stood near them. Chains snapped at his wrists. Rhallanas stopped his men before they could follow. "Nay! Let Aildeimor finish them off from there. He will not shoot to kill, but impede them. Bring Temnar to the main company."

******

Meanwhile the other three brothers threw a door leading to the alley open. Yal ran out first. As soon as he lay foot outside, an arrow perforated his ankle. "Annathias!" He limped back inside. "They have bowmen outside. Get this damn shaft out of my foot! Whoever that yellow dog is out there will pay."

Blugn and Rhamahl helped him onto his seat. They tried to pull the arrow from his ankle. Their brother moaned so much they could not stand it. "If Mum were still around, she would know what to do," Rhamahl said.

"Shut up and pull, idiot," Yal said. "We have to escape."

"Your injury complicates that," Blugn said.

"I said *pull*!" the eldest repeated and heaved his good foot into his brother's jaw.

Then soldiers armed with crossbows and falchions charged into the dining area. "Halt!" Captain Ahlk commanded. "If you resist, you will be shot. Drop your weapons."

Yal made a growling sound like a demented man. "I shall not be taken down! Not now, not ever!"

Despite his ankle he arose, brandishing a dudgeon and bill. He charged at the soldiers. As he neared, they parted. A golden blade came out to meet him. It parried a blow from the small dagger. A fist of Thareous's landed across his left eye. The lead scamp collapsed in a heap. His subjugator focused upon the others. "Do you two wish to challenge me as well?"

They shook their heads and threw their weapons down.

"On your knees!" Ahlk barked. "Put your hands behind your head!"

At last they cuffed the sons of Greilph and led them away. The Captain of the Guard and Thareous shook hands when exchanging a few words. That company left as Rhallanas entered the room. "You did that well, from what I heard."

"It was mainly the collaboration of everyone," Thareous said. "I, for one, admire that idea you came up with about me escaping and hiding away."

"A reason was needed," the commander said. He put a hand to the pommel of his sword. "This appeared to be the most credible one."

"It was ingenious," Thareous said, shaking his hand as well. He went to seek Aildeimor. His elf friend stood outdoors, seeming a recluse. He went to his side.

"That is that," the Elf Commander said, noting his friend's presence. He gazed into Thareous's eyes. "I must say I did not enjoy it."

"For what reason?" the Young Mage asked.

"I fired an arrow that impaled the ankle of an endeavoring escapee," he said. "I do not enjoy fighting. I do not enjoy war. Always we fight, never seeking peace, a break from hostility. All folk are akin in one way: they seek power."

"Are we to endorse another philosophical altercation?" Thareous asked.

"Not by my tongue," Aildeimor said and walked away.

Thareous followed like a spaniel. "Why are you so cross?"

Aildeimor did not slow his pace. "Because my sister told me what you said. An unsaved warrior cannot live without Galthoria." He halted and faced his shadow. "Malluesaer can take you in any instant. Devoid of the hand of life, you would join his forces. Beside Varkin, your greatest foe, you would fight us."

"Life is much easier without Galthoria," Thareous said.

"I shall not press you to repent," Aildeimor said. "That is your decision. I do urge you to reconsider it. People think they can rule their own lives. In truth they find misery. You right now, for example, feel deceived and lost. I should know this feeling, for it was once a part of me."

"You too have denounced Galthoria?" Thareous shook his head at the thought. "This is unlike you."

"As it is to any who misread their friends," the Elf Commander said. "Yes, I had an empty soul at one time. I had also the same concept as you. I later found it to be a derivation of the Malicer. Thus I keep my thoughts pure and my life of good morals."

The Young Mage sighed and tailed him back to the Jolly Dragon. They stopped and spoke a bit more before Aildeimor went up to his room. Prior to his departure Aildeimor once more spurred Thareous to cogitate on penance. This heartened Thareous at first but then, after the elf left, befuddled him. *How does one return to a style he had long renounced?*

Back in the confines of his room, he sat to ponder. Something eroded his resentment and made him weigh on the chance of return. It had been a possibility, he said to himself, but no more. Of course the arguments of his elven friends stimulated him. He wondered if the Glorifier would even accept him.

Off Again

For the rest of that day Thareous stayed in his room. He looked over the tableaus of battles of yore. Great kings in their chariots or on chargers extended their swords toward the enemy. Castles under siege, cracked with sections aflame. In one a prince-knight rescued a fair maiden from the sword of her despotic captor. In the last a white dragon alighted from the heavens to a flowery meadow. Probably in the Nyran Forest.

How can I be like them? Their blood was blue. One under the nobles cannot be famous. I care not for glory and veneration. I fight for a peaceful nation. Always we fight, never seeking peace, a break from hostility, so Aildeimor said.

The flap pulled open. Anazeil walked in with a tray of food. She went to the far end and placed it on a nightstand. Then she pecked Thareous's cheek and ruffled his hair. Her playfulness subsided when she noticed his lack of response. "What is the matter, dear? You look despaired."

He took her hand and enfolded it. "Mother, how does one accept destiny? I mean … what can he do once he sees what is happening? Say it is unpleasant—he has no remedy—no solution. How would he continue?"

"I would need more details to answer," Anazeil said.

"Very well. I am, of course, having trouble bearing my kismet. There are distractions that pull me from it. These are certain doubts and worries, even love. I told you of an elf, Lefanarí by name. She has eyes like a moonlit pool fed by a glistening waterfall. Her guise is pensive and heartsore, bequeathing to her the air of a weeping willow. And her hair—it matches the boughs of the same."

"You cannot consort with one outside your race," his mother said. She sat beside him, seeing this would take much explaining. "Artheïl had men and women bed with him. Henceforth, he could discern the licentious from the righteous. Galthoria grieved at his salacity and had the Fates form the law."

"This Artheïl did to all lechers?" Thareous asked.

"It is so. Furthermore, once he found them guilty, he killed them in their sleep. The elves did nothing to stop him. They deemed he did right, as did he. In truth he would lead many to think unconditional immorality pure. Nonetheless he vanished one day and no one saw him since."

Thareous bit his lower lip. "He must have been sent to Annathias when the edict was distributed. He must have not been informed. Only days after his disappearance, a voice announced that statute from the heavens. Thus Artheil was taken since he heard not of it."

"This is the most probable course," Anazeil said, then stood. "Eat now, and rest. You must keep up your strength for the departure." At his confusion she added, "The Omnipotents cannot stay here. You have likely foreseen this. They must disperse so they can watch for the Legion."

Her son nodded. She left. He grabbed the tray and positioned it on his lap to where it would not fall. He took a cheese square and munched on it. While doing this, he ruminated everything over the last two days. Everyone he loved seemed to be turning on him. They pressurized him to return to Galthoria. How could he? Only one friend had not done so. If he agreed with the others, Thareous would repent.

After finishing the meal, he lay down. With a sigh he contacted Ianvorr, who he found to be in his court. He recounted the previous events and discussions. He said he needed counsel from someone he could trust. Then he disclosed his regression of faith and pleaded for no reproof.

The Ice Dragon just chuckled. *Young Mage, I would never have it this way. Indeed, I would prompt you to review your feelings. If they say you should recover your fallen belief, then hearken them. The best thing you could do is be patient. You will sense Galthoria probing your heart when you feel you should discard Self. Tell me what you undergo now.*

My bosom seems to be made of air, Thareous said. *I have experienced this before. I got it after a heavy burden was lifted from me. I could breathe easier, discern the life in the air. It is restrained, as if the burden has been picked up but not disposed.*

You have still a choice, Ianvorr said. *Great or grave things are to come from it. It is that you must relinquish sin. Yes, temptation will haunt you after this. You have just not to listen. Light you will be after this. Your treads are to possess an airy strut. The world shall seem as you would have it. Yet there is one thing.*

Thareous's brow furrowed. *What would that be?*

Sin is to always thrive till the end of ages. It is up to you to repel the evil forces that invite you back to depravity. Of course, you shall be given a conscience to perceive these ills. Use it well and wisely so you do not degenerate. In any event, now that you see what you are up against, you must decide where you will go.

A moment passed as Ianvorr scanned his friend's mind. He found it to be blocked and him unresponsive. *Thareous? Be you there still?*

I am, and ready to rejoin him. Though I know not what to say.

Elation fell into the Ice Dragon's heart. *Repeat what I say.* "Galthoria, I am sorry for regressing from you. My life has been challenged by wrongdoing. I have failed you. Please accept me again, for I regret my faults. Let not the lures of the world bother me. I wish to serve you now, Self no longer. May the Fates heed you."

Thareous exhaled to test Ianvorr's theory. Indeed, he did seem to have a new thrill in life. It could best be described as freedom. He felt like a convict pardoned for capital offenses. His heart beat with invigorating drumbeats. Bliss spread over his face, manifesting in a beaming smile.

Ianvorr, the burden is gone! he cried.

I told you it would be. Now there is something you must do. Aildeimor and Lefanarí require apologies. When it is done, get to bed. For the shadows lengthen afield; darkness descends. In the morn I am to take you away—to Draer-Vollith. There the giants dwell. Jurtithan is with them at the moment and needs proof you live.

I will do as you instruct, Thareous said. The euphoria waned some, but soon got replaced in stimulating waves. He bid Ianvorr good night and let the connection melt away. He felt aversion to this new quest. At least he would see Lefanarí again. *No! I am not supposed to think like that anymore. Galthoria directs me now, and I choose his way.*

He got up, shouldering Kielkanur and sheathing Theldaneru. He sighed and went out of his room, then plodded down the stairs. In the small vestibule he stopped and looked at his feet. Should he go through with this?

He decided it best. The longer he delayed his trust from his elf friends, the longer he could not be with them. Something told him their time was diminishing, thus precious. He could not establish it on the bedrock of reasoning. So he thought it a pettiness and went on his way. It persisted to nag him without concession.

At the Jolly Dragon he halted once more, this time uttering a brief prayer. He felt like he could do anything and continued to the third floor. He walked down the corridor till coming to room three-two-two. With a shaky fist he tapped the door and stepped back. It opened to reveal Aildeimor.

The two stared until the elf nodded a greeting. He seemed not to be as cold as he had been. "Well, this surprises me. I did not think you would be coming anytime soon. Just the same, why are you here?"

"Lefanarí must be here ere I can answer that," Thareous said.

Aildeimor disappeared back inside the room. Murmurs flowed from under the closed door, sharp and direct. A moment later it opened again, this time both elven siblings coming out. Lefanarí looked intolerant. "Speak your piece so I can leave."

Thareous leaned back at her deportment. He was glad to have settled into his previous face before showing himself again. "I am not here to argue with either of you, but rather apologize. I have not been fair with you, Lefanarí. My own intentions and sentiments got in my way. For that I am penitent and cry your pardon."

Then he faced Aildeimor. "To you I admit I have not been right with your sister. I sought to misuse her. She resisted me. I know am failing in keeping my side of the vow. Please accept my justification. It is meant to maintain our friendship. May no more struggles come atween us."

The Elf Commander peered sidelong at his sister. They had noticed the same thing. He smiled and put both hands on Thareous's shoulders. "Brother, something has died within you. Something malefic, we have marked. Could it be Self?"

"It is," he said, also raising his cheeks. "I have a new master now. He guides me over treacherous waters, where I will not crash nor go astray. He shall never abandon me as I have him. By him I swear to uphold his precepts and not impose them to others."

"Thareous, this is wonderful!" Lefanarí took his chin and the back of his head in hand. She pushed her lips at his jaw-hinge and pulled away to see him blushing. She and Aildeimor laughed. His face reddened all the more.

"Leave your mirth," Thareous said. "You have still to forgive me."

"Of course we forgive you," Aildeimor said, lifting a fresh smile. "So let us dwell on that no longer. We do bid you to leave. The elves still do not trust the king. This could attract attention. Fare thee well."

"Have a pleasant sleep, Thareous," Lefanarí said. She pulled him close, her chin perched on his left shoulder. "I am very proud of you. It seemed the impossible would never come true. You have proven me wrong."

"Good night," he returned. It was all he could say.

Back at his house he dined with his parents and Ancient. He recalled each incident up from his release to the apology. They rejoiced upon him mentioning his contrition. After the light celebration Thareous went up to his room and removed his weapons. Then he lay on his straw mattress and fell into a fitful sleep.

******

A shaft of light penetrated through Thareous's dreams. He opened his eyes, blinking. The Four Suns just fell into their places. It was about the seventh hour of that day. He remembered what Ianvorr asked of him and gathered his belongings. Once done he went downstairs to eat breakfast. Little conversation passed in the kitchen. More adieus came than talk. None of which were from Ancient.

"I shall see you anon," he had said, "so here there is no parting."

At last he found his congé and joined the morning crowds. They carried him to the street he needed to go and he exited there. He headed down a southern avenue with fewer pedestrians until coming on the portcullis. His made perfect timing, for it was raised and an oaken drawbridge lowered. At the end of it Ianvorr waited for him.

Thareous dashed to him and embraced his pearly friend by the neck. "Thank you so much. I am indebted to you. Trust my word: if ever I find a way to repay you, I shall."

"You owe me nothing," the Ice Dragon said. "Galthoria placed me here to help people find him. That is what I do. As to your gratitude, you are welcome. It was my pleasure." He straightened his neck and stood up. "Come now. We must be on our way."

Soon they were off, Thareous astride his back. Ianvorr wound toward the west, following the circuitous Diran River. In a half-hour the serrated environment known as the Brimstores rose in their wake. The mountains suckled at the watercourse, the supply never running low. Thareous watched as Galgon dissipated in the distance.

"What of the elves?" Thareous asked. "Are they to leave Galgon?"

"Jurtithan has said they must stay in the city. This way, if any of the towns are under attack, they could go to their aid. You must not worry about them—particularly Lefanarí. For where we soar to, you have something to fear. The giants hate mankind more than they do the dwarves. By my claws and teeth you shall be protected."

COUNCIL OF THE SEAFOLK

Nahilmara dove beneath the silvern surface of the Darrien Ocean. *At last back to my habitat. Not that seeing Ianvorr again was not worth it. He has come to be more arrogant than the last time we spoke. Is this his way of covering up his pain?* Splashes broke away her thoughts. "Follow me! Victory is at our doorstep, if we summoned it loud enough. This shall end the war ere it ever begins."

They swam down deeper and chanced upon the seabed. Colorful reefs spread out to every side. Clefts led down to the deepest depths. Not even a Water Dragon could endure there. Schools of fish overran the area, outnumbering Nahilmara and her like. Light bent into a translucent web as the waters above rippled.

Following the seafloor more closely, the krakens westered, spying familiar landmarks. Rows of stalagmites and stalactites circled outside a cave: Jaws of the Shark. Gas-filled bubbles rolled to the surface in the Air Fields. The Seafolk came to relax themselves here. A long-feared shortcut to Merlandis, the Trench, loomed ahead. A fabled beast lived in a cave at the other end. The krakens had passed through it many times before. So they feared it not.

Between the walls Nahilmara led her kind. Ridges, broken or sea-worn, spread out from the sides. Murk lurked here, making them appear as the ghosts of those devoured by the beast. Sharp jags lay at its base. "Swim faster!" Their dim shapes sped through the eeriness of underwater haze. It twisted and interwove like octopus limbs. No light fell here—only deep shadow.

The other end was about one hundred feet away. The cliffs narrowed, so they had to group into a line and go out single file. Nahilmara ordered a younger kraken by the name of Gaal to oversee that each them did this. They saw no "monster." A huge rocky acclivity arose before them. Crags jutted from it. Fissures housed many animals.

At a peak a bluish light reflected off it. The krakens paddled stronger, anxious to see the missed sight. For decades not one of their eyes had lain on it. They made it to the top and their eyes widened to the glory. A bubble of a lost magic spread out thousands of fathoms across the ocean floor. It kept away saltwater and defended the dwellers from predators of the sea. Housing a civilization, it shimmered in the faint light. Merlandis sat before the krakens.

Donning cloaks of joy the Water Dragons surged forth as they came upon the lost splendor of the sea. Wards in the city, wrought of the rock of the seabed, went to inform their return to the officials. A huge archway held up by the encasing bubble opened up. When the krakens entered the city, the water drained into outlet ducts.

Nahilmara entered first, her wings outspread as if going to embrace one long-unseen. The officials of Merlandis came to see them. There were King Pharsus and Queen Éiden of the Merfolk; Lord Gŭruden and Lady Änsha of the nixes and nixies; and the Duchesses Merkeil and Laindel, the Nereid Sisters. Amphitrites loomed outside since their enormity disadvantaged them in the city.

"Hail, sky-dwellers!" Pharsus exclaimed. He and his wife swam in a canal. "What news from above?"

"There is a danger moving over your waters, Great King," Nahilmara said. "We must destroy it ere it reaches land. First let us converse." She noted the collective crowd. "In private, if it can be managed."

******

The Rulers of the Seafolk met in their great chamber. Six thrones sat below a monolith, each pair on a lower step of a three layered platforms. This way no ruler forgot his or her place of power. Four windows—one pair to the right and the other to the left—provided partial view outside.

King Pharsus swam up to his throne via one of the canals lining the floor, then took his scepter—a golden three-pronged trident. "You may speak, Sapient Serpent."

"Zakumahk plans on attacking Keiratha so he might resurrect Varkin."

"That fool would pollute the seas!" Lord Gŭruden cried. "If Keiratha falls, so will the rest of the universe. It is by that land all is held in order."

"The Fates' first creation, devastated by Black Magic," Laindel said. "Your Kingship, our food supplies would be terminated. Action must be taken."

"So it shall be," the King of the Seafolk said. "Let there be resistance so that destruction may not find us. Zakumahk's fleet will not make it to shore."

"Idle chatter leads us nowhere," Queen Éiden said. Her hair billowed long and red with tinges of orange and yellow. A top nit of kelp wove around her bosom, skintight at the waist. For emphasis, her fish tail splashed the water that rose in the canal, platform after platform.

"Wisest and Fairest of the Seafolk, you are accurate about this," Merkeil said. "We believe our Sister Nahilmara. She has never feigned danger before. Let it now be we do not mistrust her."

"We go astray!" Änsha said. She glowed blue, with lucent fins falling from her arms and ankles. Also her hair, of the like, did not disperse into individual strands. "Yes, we know she is trusted always. It is not the time to laud her, in respect."

"I came only to seek your assistance, not an argument," Nahilmara said. "Since I have your pledge of aid, I shall leave so we might be ready."

She was about to turn, but the voice of Pharsus stopped her. "We still require a location, argument or no."

Her fortitude left her when she glanced at him. "As soon as you are in armor, come to the point a fourth away from the Brimstore Mountainrange. There you will find an armada sailing the cold waters of Ielyle's Bergs. In a day, ere comes the fleet, we must meet. They shall pass above us. We will have only to attack it."

The King of the Seafolk summoned the Royal Charter and his commander, both mermen. He told them the spot Nahilmara gave and said to ready the troops. They bowed and went to complete his orders. Then he called on a Recorder and had him put down the date of war. Doing this provided the future lines a way to learn the importance of protecting their people. He engraved it on a slate and returned to the archives.

"We have our place and preparations," Éiden said. "Sapient Serpent, you are clear to leave. We shall arrive a day ahead of you, at most. If this fleet is where you said it would be, all is well."

"The meeting is adjourned," Pharsus said, sliding back into the canal. Wading his way down each platform, the King of the Seafolk swam out of the chamber through an opening in the far wall. His wife followed. Nahilmara departed with the other nobles and returned to her sisters.

"Well?" Gaal asked when she came back. "What had them to say?"

"The Seafolk are with us," Nahilmara said. "We must go await the Dark Legion. So I suggest we search the waters for food and then be on our way." The krakens spread out their wings almost in turn and flew over the architecture. They glided from the archway to the sea till the last had gone under. In the distance they saw a school of flyingfish. The hunt was on!

Rebellion

Jallaca set her tricorn on the desk to her new living quarters. She sat down in the desk chair. "At last things point my way." Leaning back, she put her feet up and rested her head on the top of the chair. "No more trouble is to ensue. Any dilemmas in the plan are dead. The fiends have chosen me."

You are mistaken, Dowager of Varkin, a voice said in her mind.

She fumbled to sit upright. *Who are you?*

I am the Ancient Archimage, wrought by the Dark King's mind. You deem to have killed him. He is not dead. Once he finds you, you shall be.

What is it he wants with me?

Your life, for attempting to take his.

Ha! You are only an illusion, purported Archimage, for the Dark King created you. You are him! Zakumahk ... how fares you and your crew?

Far better than yours, the Dark King said. *Look out your door. See what Malluesaer beholds. He controls fate, doom, your death. So will its advent dawn soon. Go on! Do not sit and gape like the fool you are.*

Arising, she went to the door and opened it ajar. A hand snatched its side and heaved it open. It seized Jallaca's throat. She came to face Quaron for the first time. "Foolish. You left the Dark King upon that hulk to die. As a result, you have arrogated the right to captain upon yoursssself." The grasp of his gauntleted hand tightened, though allowed her to breathe still. "How sssad that a wench like yourself mussst die. Your lips are ssso close to mine. Just a kisss of departure before you die?"

She glared into his snakish eyes. "You mean a kiss before *you* die?"

"I can sssnap your neck in two with a single sssqueeze," he said. "There shall be death aplenty in the war. Ssso I will let you go. The lich-captain is pulling assside *The Firewave.*"

"Release me or I shall plug this dagger into your gullet," she said.

Quaron chuckled. "Pretensssessss are not to save you. Our Lord Zakumahk comes to avenge your deceit."

"At least *I* am no buffoon," Jallaca said and swept her dagger cross his cheek. The tip grazed it. The shock made him let go. She shoved him aside and scurried out on to the quarterdeck.

The fiends split between the task to make Zakumahk warchief or keep Jallaca where she stood. Upon seeing this, the rebel group broke away from their antagonists and chased her. The lich-captain wielded a cutlass longer than himself. Swiping it, he knocked the dagger from Jallaca.

"Yer 'ighness, we 'ave made a c'ange in plans," he said. "Instead we feel yuh s'ould be t'e one tuh go tuh t'e grave." He threw the cutlass forth.

She skipped to the side, grabbed his arm, and wrenched it off. The captain of *The Courser* lost his weapon also. "Fool. I do not fall to the swoops of an incompetent corpse." She jerked the cutlass from the hand still on the arm and cut through his spine.

"Turn this ship away from *The Firewave*!" she cried. A vampire flew up and took the tiller. "Get archers and spike the crew with your arrows!" Fiends ran to challenge them once the order was passed about. Jallaca tailed them, slashing their backs, surpassing most of them. *The Firewave* pulled closer, less than three yards away. Fiends dipped arrowheads in tar, lit them with fire, and discharged them at it. A rising swell doused the little fires left on the hull.

Shafts shot from that ship, striking enemy and allied fiends. A man clad in black armor stood at the foredeck, a saber darker than ebony hanging at his side. His pinnacled helmet masked his face. *The Firewave* pulled next to the ship's side. Boards were positioned on the railings. Fiends filed across. Izra ran on to the quarterdeck of *The Courser*, maiming the enemy until they moved. The devilkin fought each other till a voice stopped them.

"That is right, my children," Zakumahk said. "War is a pointless thing. The Omnipotent Ones do not grasp this. They seek to stop us. We can do this through some sort of agreement, other than death. Those who serve me, bow before me so that we might end the lives of the procrastinators." All but three fiends and Jallaca paid him obeisance. "So you are the cretins amongst us. Why do you resist peace?"

"Tyrants do not bring peace!" one of the rebels, a hobgoblin, cried.

"This is sad," Zakumahk said, face torn with pity under the helm. He extended a gauntleted hand and squeezed it shut. The hob's heart stopped. It fell to the deck. "Let this be an example to the traitors. Why do you disregard me?"

Jallaca threw down the cutlass. "Why do you not just dispatch us? What stays your hand? You know we will not rejoin you. Be done with us!"

"Dowager of Varkin, I was just getting to," Zakumahk said. Kielthavra slid from its scabbard. The fiends parted, allowing entry to the scattered traitors. "I am not to be trifled with. Nor are any of you to toy with my power any longer." He felled the second rebel, an imp. "Winds of change flow through the very sails that carry us to victory. These sails are not to be torn, not by blade nor shaft. We ride onto peace, ever intent upon a better universe."

He approached the third fiend, a jinn, and slayed it. "A fire spreads over Keiratha. The Center of the Universe is burning. It holds everything in place. Should it fall out of order, the rest of the universe would go with it. We are here to douse the flame."

Then he reached Jallaca. Here he sheathed Kielthavra. "Death should not touch you. I come to change the ways of the universe. Why be you against me?"

"Because Varkin is change," the Dark Deliverer said.

"Alas, you must be gone." The Dark King clamped a gauntlet over her mouth and darkness she became. The shadow floated up into the heavens, vanishing in the noonday azure. "Back to the Cavern of Mystery you return for all eternity."

Attack upon the Sea

Waves rolled away from the icy shores of the Keicor Alps. Icebergs bobbled up and down as the roller barreled beneath it. Ripples moved about as an upsurge pulled from the shore. Sunlight shone through the silvery clear waters. Nahilmara lay under the concealment of a reef. *The Dark Legion is to approach soon. The Seafolk have still a far distance to travel. How are we to win without them?*

Her thoughts turned then to Ianvorr. *Bless him, Galthoria. He comforted me on the night he went away to hunt. Then came Jurtithan to my nest, eyes fixed upon me. How dare he!* She struggled to dam back tears. Sorrow overwhelmed her and immobilized her concentration. She lowered her hardened gaze with a sob. A fire seemed to flicker in her cerulean eyes. Her wings drooped, tightening and shaking from the effort.

"Sister Nahilmara," a voice said behind her. She glanced back, turning away the disconsolation. Gaal floated in the water. "They are here."

******

The prow of *The Courser* dipped in the water. A robust wind pulled at the sails, reeling them closer to warmer waters. Fields of floating ice spread out farther than any eye could conceive. Light spilt over it like radiance through glass. Zakumahk slept on a bunk in his office. His armor lay at its side, omitted until the time of war. His breathing was silent and steady. He had his eyes shut, yet his mind expanded to the world.

A noise under the hull made him open his eyes. He sat up, looked at the tip of the bed where Kielthavra leaned, and reached out to take it. *Whatever danger lurks in the sea, let it be finished. The Dark Legion is not to be scattered.*

******

"We attack now," Nahilmara said. The krakens surged surface-ward, their wings unfolding. They crashed out of the choppy waters and took flight into the skies. They split up, gliding toward individual ships. Arrows loosed from the bowstrings and gaffs from arbalests. The battle had begun.

Nahilmara swooped down to *The Courser* with Gaal at her side. Their group divided to either side of the ship, intent on ravaging them. Fiends appeared at the portholes to fire shafts. They waylaid ten unsuspecting krakens. A tip struck Nahilmara as she dove to eradicate the archers. Many fell in a single swipe. The decks, though, never seemed to be rid of them.

Saber-shaped teeth opened to the enemy. Then water streamed out onto fiends. The torrent poured overboard; with it many foes. The krakens attacked with greater ease, for they had shattered the defense. With its empty floors *The Courser* looked like a ghost ship. Now a door on its deck swung open. Zakumahk walked out.

Eyes wroth to the center of the pupils, he glared at the destruction around him. Fiends that evaded the flood gathered at his side. Izra, who was amongst them, morphed into a gruesome zarjkakon. Wings encased in tiny spines, he took off after the krakens. Fire bolted out of his maw, overtaking a Water Dragon. It shrieked and fell into the sea.

"On which ship is Amarzrell kept?" Zakumahk asked a goblin.

"Upon *The Outrunner*," it said. "Being one of the last ships, he shall be in the skies afore those harpies overwhelm him."

An abrupt screech diverted Zakumahk's attention back to the battle above. Izra's form dropped onto the deck with a crash. His eyes turned to the Dark King. "They are too strong. Can you not see this is hopeless?"

Zakumahk's admiration toward him declined. Kielthavra met the Changeling Commander's heart. He shut his eyes. "Keep up the attack!" He turned away and watched the onslaught. His dark gaze averted from one kraken to the next until falling upon Nahilmara. "At last the leader." Pulling Kielthavra from Izra's heart, he smirked.

Black fire scrambled up the saber's blade. "Breathe the burning flesh of the Kelp-guzzlers, my fiends. Taste their smoldering meats." The fire blazed into an insatiable inferno. It formed in the head of a dragon. "Feed, my beast. Devour the bones of my enemies. Crush the marrow that molds them. Fire has no coequals. Water is your enemy. *Feed*!" The dragon head only smothered and became smoke.

Fire is not with you, though you may be an archmagus, a voice said. *Let it be known to all after you: my element is not to be used for injurious purposes. It was issued to help warm the skin. Black Magic it is not associated with. Begone!*

Zakumahk slammed Kielthavra on the deck boards. "Annathias! Does anything work?" Thrusting his sword into its unbelted scabbard, he charged up the stairs to the helm-deck. Taking the tiller in hand, he swerved *The Courser* landward. *If we cannot take them upon the sea, we must do so ashore.*

******

Nahilmara gasped when she noticed the fleet's change of course. *No! Zakumahk has outwitted us. Where are the Seafolk? It nears the time that they should appear, lest all be lost. What hope have we then?*

"Everyone dive! She swooped down, going again to ravage *The Courser*. Bolts of

lightning went to greet her. She looked down to spot the one responsible. *Quaron.* She spiraled about the next shaft. It shifted course, striking her this time. It numbed her blood and seemed she had felt death ten times over. After what felt an eternity the unspeakable agony receded. Her wings could no longer hold her up. She fell to the sea. The supportive paws of Gaal took hold of her.

She waged a war between herself in which consciousness and unconsciousness fought. In the end darkness overtook her.

A short time later her eyes reopened. Gaal peered over her. They sat upon an iceberg. "The Dark Legion still war with us, but flee toward shore. We are not sure if we should continue or let them go. The shores are ice. Many fiends are wounded. What say you?"

"Finish as many of them as we can—even to the death," Nahilmara said. "Come now; we are still needed. Weakness cannot hold me back."

"B-but—" Gaal stuttered.

"I said come!" the Sapient Serpent cried. "Death we should not fear. All that we can fear is Zakumahk making it to shore. Let us ensure this fear is not carried out. Let us ensure his death." The two krakens spread out their wings and launched off.

******

The armada was about two leagues away. At the rate of a dragon's flight it took very little time. The tattered masts swayed like torn flags in a battle over land. Fiends readied their bows and discharged more arrows at them. "Now comes the time we must fight," Nahilmara said. She let out a roar and advanced.

Shafts flew to meet them. They went over or under the volley. As they neared the first ship, indigo energy from underwater sundered its hull. Something like the tentacles of an octopus wrapped about it and pulled it under. The heads of horses arose from beneath the waves. Dolphin tails slapped the water, connected to the equine body in the middle. Hippocamps, the steeds used to pull the chariots of the Seafolk!

A vehicle made of the bottom jaw of a giant clam emerged. Pharsus and Éiden, her fiery hair waving like a comet's tail, sat on a carven bench. The King of the Seafolk held a pair of reins in one hand and his trident in the other. Smoke whirled into a cyclone. Its power had been triggered. Behind their chariot the merfolk, Nereids, nixes and nixies, and sirens leapt from the sea. Amphitrites ascended to the skies. Many trinkets from the ocean encircled their arms by laces of kelp. Seaweed also composed their attire. They wore unfathomable skirts at their legs.

The king and queen each flicked a hand and a great wave amassed at their sides. These grew to be the size of tsunamis, anxious to charge like a bull. They willed the waters to flow forth. As it neared the first ship, a barrier enclosed the fleet, even under the hull. Zakumahk's ship neared the icy shores as the others docked. Krakens swarmed overhead. The Seafolk surrounded the impenetrable bubble.

Nahilmara dove into the sea, surfaced, and paddled to Pharsus. "My king, it appears you have arrived late. The fault is not yours. Much preparation had to be done. For you the battle was short. By it could have come death."

"Death to me is of aught concern," Pharsus said. "If Éiden and I died, our daughter, Thierueal, would take my place. Woe to those who have departed!"

"May they find rest in Kallenalza and be favored by Galthoria evermore," Éiden said. "By his grace shall they never chance upon hostility again."

"Thank you for your blessing, Fairest of the Seafolk," Nahilmara said. "More of us have fallen than those of our enemies. Since they have made it to land, there is no hope of assault. Hence, the battles are done. Next comes the war."

"Spend your last days with us—in Merlandis," Pharsus said. "There is to be a time of requiem for the deceased. They led lives of compassion and care. This they deserve."

"Your offer must be surpassed, I fear," the Sapient Serpent said. "With respect I must return to the Omnipotent Ones. There I will report what has crossed us. Also I search for a human."

"A human?" the king asked. "There is no human in our waters, save those who dive for pearls. Yes, I know they make a living from it. They steal from the ocean. Vast as it may be, it has still a limited supplies."

Nahilmara sighed. "He might be with the Dark King. At any rate I must go. It has been a pleasure to see you again. I must gather the krakens and aid the land-dwellers. Fare all well!"

With that she took to the skies, her sisters mustering. She turned southwest—toward the Brimstore Mountainrange. She would have to report their failure to Jurtithan, and Ianvorr. Her heart sank, for she deemed Thareous still with the Legion.

DRAER-VOLLITH

Thareous captured his first glimpse of Draer-Vollith, the giant's stronghold. Many spires pointed heavenward. Tied to the tips, pennants—of great hawks swooping down—flapped in the wind. Arcing bay windows, tainted by colors of purple, red, and blue, stretched open to admit sunlight.

Draer-Vollith was carven from the mountainside. Though it bore the shape of a castle, with many tiers jutting out as ledges, it appeared as the mountain. Crenels, tall enough to hide a giant save its head, curved over the three tiers like claws. Sculpted to look like an eagle head, the peak watched the two near.

Ianvorr landed in a glen near an edge dropping off to a shallow river. Scree lay at the feet of the mountains surrounding them. Thareous swung himself off Ianvorr and walked to the edge. He peered at the other end. "How do we cross?"

The Ice Dragon led him down a ways. They came to a causeway hidden by a protrusion near a mountain's base. It sloped to the other end, wide and sturdy enough for a giant to walk across. They traversed it, looking down to spot the snaking streamlet below. Jags awaited them if they fell. At the other end lay another glen. Two mountains arose at either side, blocking off any incursion that might transpire. At the other end of the vale Draer-Vollith transcended them. There the giants could hurl boulders at their enemies or meet them. This made the defense almost impregnable.

"What now?" Thareous asked once he made it halfway. "Do I continue—going ever nearer death?" He remembered what Ianvorr told him and feared it.

"Under the order of Jurtithan you shall not be harmed," the Ice Dragon said. "Fear is unprovoked, Young Mage. Let it not taunt you."

The pair continued down the open area. Thareous looked up to the tiers, expecting to see espying eyes. There was nothing. His gaze wondered back to the entranceway of Draer-Vollith. An octastyle portico stood about fifty feet from the ground.

"How is Jurtithan able to fit into that?" Thareous queried.

"There is a side entrance at the eastern wing," Ianvorr said. "It consists of a slab that can be pushed out or pulled back in. It fits into place, so it looks like ordinary rock. A sizeable corridor leads to the vestibule, wide enough for the Silver One."

"That is very ingenious," Thareous said.

"The giants tend to be, though they look as mindless brutes," Ianvorr said. They stopped outside the portico. The Ice Dragon faced him. "Be strong, Thareous. I am here beside you. I know what makes you wish to fly. You must enter, so Jurtithan will know you are whole."

With that he turned and headed down the archway. Thareous looked at the ground a moment, acknowledging his words. *Fear must not obstruct my continuance. I have made it this far. I will go the rest of the way.*

Pulling the silver straps of Thornwhirl up his shoulder, he took his first step into the portal. Convening more daring, he brought up another foot and tramped it down. His feet resembled blocks of stone: they refused to move. He forced them on. Whether harm or worse awaited him, he would face it.

The end came to him in a trice. Voices, indefinite to him, arose, loud and bellowing. They came from an enormous atrium. In he walked to see giant men bordering the height of fifty feet. Jurtithan towered over them, his spinal spikes grazing the ceiling. Marble pilasters held the maximum up near the walls. Bars of red, blue, and purple light lanced from the bay windows. Two corridors branched out past the western and eastern sections.

Between the pilasters stood sculptures of giants, about their stature. They had war-armor on, a chiseled coat of mail dropping over their torsos. In each of their hands they bore halberds and pavises with the swooping hawk emblem. At their sides a sword and a dagger sheathed through the belts. They wore capes, an eagle brooch holding them in place. A helm covered their heads, visors lifted, showing eyes. Their jackboots pointed at the toe. A few had leather jerkins covering their chests and hauberk underneath. Feathers extended into the air from their heaumes.

Thareous marveled at these carvings, his apprehension waning. That is until he was nudged from behind. He turned to find Ianvorr standing at the edge of the entryway. Then he walked to Jurtithan's side. A supposition erected in Thareous, telling him he had to follow. Reluctance knocked that pole over.

"Come, Thareous," the Silver One said. "I wish to speak with you."

The giants stared at him as he stalked their direction. They bore no hatred or acrimony in their eyes, only an inscrutable bearing. As he neared, they backed away, as if in fear and reverence. Perking his head up, he looked deeper into their eyes, trapping flashes of terror.

"You see, they venerate you. You are of greater power," Jurtithan said. "King Harvok of the giants welcomes you as his guest. As does Chieftain Orkon of the dwarves, Lord Hadres of the fauns, and Commander Aralles of the rocs. We gather now to discuss future affiliations."

Harvok, the giant in front of the group, bowed. "Well met. I have waited for your arrival for days, once the Powerful One reported you were found. Bless me, for I have at last laid eyes upon our rescuer!"

"Arise," Thareous said. "I am no idol for you to entertain. You and your kind worship the ones called 'rocs.' Why?"

"They symbolize our redemption from Varkin," Harvok said. He gesticulated to the effigies. "We are a proud folk. All the same, we are inferior when it comes to supplies. You see our clothes? They are patched together with deerskins. Each pelt of our kills goes to the needle and thread. Until our garbs are done, we wear aught but skin."

"Size has its advantages and disadvantages," Thareous said. "At least you do not waste anything." He paused. "Where are the rest of my hosts?"

"In the assembly hall," Jurtithan said. "They would prefer to tarry there than welcome you. They wish to discourse things over by themselves, it seems."

"They have waited long enough," Harvok said. "Let us moot new strategies."

The giants turned and routed them down the western hall. Hanging above the guides' heads, braziers threw off a constant light. Jurtithan had enough room to squeeze through, crawling on his belly. The braziers scraped his spinal spikes, issuing sparks. This hindered the procession several times. At the other end of the long passageway, they emerged into a parlor. Furniture filled most of the room. Tapestries draped over the walls. A large bust of a giant at the far end of the parlor frowned.

"Who is that?" Thareous whispered to Ianvorr.

"Arahmur, Harvok's father," he said. "There shall be also a figurine of him one day, when he, too, comes to pass."

"Harvok is the second king of the giants?" Thareous asked.

"In this land, he is," the Ice Dragon said. "Because of their sizes they have longer durations. King Arahmur was killed by a rebel giant, though he was fair and impartial. That giant lusted for power. He only received execution."

Thareous's curiosity desiccated at the mention of this. The company reached and went under a threshold sustained by rocky beams. They entered ahead of Jurtithan, waiting for him to again squeeze through. The chamber spread out wider than the vestibule. Rows of stone benches lined its side. Hawks near the size of the giants perched atop them. Dwarves and fauns sat underneath them. A host of giants and giantesses dominated the room. Dragons stood near a podium.

As Harvok passed, the assembly moved aside so that they might go by. All eyes appeared to be facing Thareous more than the Giant King. The Young Mage walked by, oblivious to their gazes. They ascended to the top of the podium. Two pillars held up the ceiling next to the stairs leading up to it. Jurtithan had to stay off since he filled desired room. Galthoria increased him in size after he had killed Varkin.

"Omnipotents alike"—Harvok raised his arms for emphasis—"we gather a new company. More groups have joined us though we used to be enemies. Will the leaders of these clans please come forth and state your reasons?"

Hadres and Aralles approached the stand, stopping at its base where they found room. "Despite our differences, I shall not see this nation torn apart by invaders," the Faun Lord said. "Too long has Valvassa threatened to overturn Keiratha. It is time we rise to send them all back into the Pits of Despair."

The Roc Commander bobbed his beak. "My kind has seen what tyranny can do. Halleír, our late commander, my deceased father, died since we rebelled. We tired of fascism. I have decided to reinstate our renown by joining you and fighting for a cause."

A gruff voice drained away the stimulation. "What of the griffins?" Orkon, the Dwarf Chieftain, treaded toward the steps leading up the stand. He, being short and thickset, ranged to the height of Thareous's knees.

"We are out of contact with them," Jurtithan said. "If the Griffin Master knew of our plight, he would send help. He is more sagacious than any of us."

"If so he would have already dispatched them," Orkon said. He turned to the observers. "What say you? Aye, I conceive they reside under that extinct volcano, Malmeir. Should they not come as well?"

"If they come, they require time," Harvok said. "Let us not fret over this. Galthoria is on our side."

"Is he?" Orkon wondered aloud. "For I have seen we fail to keep Valvassa at ease. May he not be angered by these words. I only make a point."

Thareous leapt off the platform, landing on the highest step of the stairs. "You have no faith in him!" He jumped to the next. "What has tainted your mind? I am here, though I am not of his likeness." After this he leapt to the third and final step. "If it is proof you want of hope, then I am it, allegedly."

"Allegedly indeed!" the dwarf cried. "You are of brave ambitions, lad. You are no more than a young adult. It could take years to vanquish the Dark Legion."

Without warning, wind swirled with a dazzling light. An archway opened up before them. An old man stepped from it, grasping a twisted staff for balance. "It shall take years since you have not faith." He looked at them all. "None of you do."

"Wh-who are you?" Harvok asked in consternation.

"I am a light in the darkness—the voice crying aloud past deafness. I am the mouthpiece of Galthoria the Glorifier. I speak against all sins, all folly. Even more so I speak against those who have forsaken faith, given up hope. Because of it the universe burns. Have any of you a care even?"

Thareous answered first. "I do! I am with you."

The Ancient Archimage looked about him. "Any others?"

Jurtithan and Ianvorr came out with it next.

"How about you?" Ancient continued, pointing at Harvok.

The Giant King hung his head. "I am both ashamed and embarrassed to not have spoken sooner. Whatever lies ahead, whether pain or death, you have my collaboration."

Everyone but Orkon followed. He looked like he would faint on the spot. Instead he cast himself down upon the tessellated floor and wept. "Galthoria help me! I have disowned you through lack of faith!"

The Archimage walked over to him and knelt at his side. Setting a wrinkled hand on Orkon's shoulder, he lifted the dwarf up. Kindness showed in his eyes; forgiveness reflected in his gaze. "Truly your heart rues. Deplore no more. Galthoria has heard your pleas and pardoned you. Arise and live in peace."

The Chieftain got to his feet, wiping away the tears. No one laughed at or mocked him. Ancient arose also and led him down the aisle to his kind. At his side he would stand until the meeting adjourned.

Harvok found it hard to form words. He let Ianvorr take the pulpit. "Let this be an example to you: have faith in whatever plights you. I know what I speak, for when I was still encaged, I lacked the belief that I would ever get out. Here I am. I shall never doubt Galthoria's glory ever again. He prefers the same from us."

He turned away and took back his place with the giants. Thareous inspected the crowd's faces. They portrayed a solemn recognition. Orkon's wanting confidence had supplied them with a new outlook. At length Jurtithan spoke up. "Through this remorse comes pain. It is good pain. None of us should judge or deride one another. If we do, we may remind ourselves with this experience. We have admitted to not bearing faith. Now we have it to be sure.

"I rebuke none of you by saying these words. I only set forth an acknowledgment—one that has yet to be grasped by the universe. Will the bards or songsters spread this episode through their works? Not likely. We can pass this down as an example to our offspring, though, and them to theirs."

HARVOK'S COURT

After the meeting Thareous decided to walk through Draer-Vollith. He went into a passageway supported by arches. Large doorways led into an assortment of differing rooms. Busts of giant-warriors from long ago lined across from another down the hall. Thareous reached a threshold where two sculpted wings smiled at him over it. An extensive drape swept the floor. Harvok's voice came from inside, along with a female's. He walked to the curtain and shoved its hem aside. He wished to speak with the Giant King.

"… and this human shall free us!" Harvok bellowed. A tree was in his hand. Seated, he spoke while whittling it into a war-club. "He will drive the groups to the lowlands so we might have supplies aplenty."

A beautiful giantess lifted Harvok to his feet and kissed him. The circlet atop her head fell over her brow. She pulled away and adjusted it. "True are your words, Husband! From then on are we to live in utter peace."

"King Harvok!" Thareous shouted. "You aspire to use me for personal gain. I am the Appointed Archimage, not one to be befooled by the likes of you."

"Eirmrasha, leave us," Harvok said. The Giantess Queen sauntered into an adjoining room separated by a stone door and closed that. "What is it you want? I would even give up my crown to you, would it fit."

"I come here not to partake in your merriment," Thareous said. "I fight for a greater cause—to defend those who are helpless. If Varkin were to overthrow Keiratha, would you fondle with victory so? I should hope not. In the same manner should you capitulate joy."

"Joy is our symbol of hope," the Giant King said. "If we jettisoned it, what would strengthen us? We cannot fear you as a deity, so you cannot be our strength. How appeals you to this?"

"It is like the refuse that we cast out unto the streets," Thareous said. "I refrain from your worship and manipulation. Mayhap I should choose to abandon you."

"You shall be renowned as a dastard, then," Harvok said.

Thareous shook in his anger. "*A dastard*? Why do you hide behind these walls? What have you to fear? You are aught save a brood of recluses! What right has you to call me such an untrue thing?"

"Accept my apology pardon for naming you so." Harvok paused. "Shall my indiscretion disconcert any troth atween us? Are you to begrudge me? Have you such abhorrence toward me that this is what you chase?"

"What must be done must be done," Thareous said. He looked about the court, noting the decors. The throne room had massive furniture like in the parlor: a couch and chair at one end and a settee at the other. Shades closed in front of bay windows, leaving six braziers about the chamber to light it.

"I have no alternative save to heed your words," the Giant King said. "Thus we will remain here forever to combat the dwarves. This you have heard, so I grasp. Can you not discern we tire of war?"

"I discern naught concerns you. Therefore you I shall leave you to your conceit."

Thareous turned on his heel and tromped to the flap. Coming upon it, he brandished Theldaneru and cut an opening for himself. Then he hurried out to a light-blue radiance. Icy mists chilled the marrow of his bones. "Why are you wroth?" Ianvorr said.

He explained, sheathing Lightkeeper.

"I see where you evoke indignation," the Ice Dragon said. "Come, let us walk while we discuss this. Unless you are loath in doing, we may tarry here."

"Let us be off," Thareous said. They started down the hall.

"Now," Ianvorr said, "the giants wish to use you to gain their own ambitions. Your duty is to not be treated so and you hence threatened to run off. Alas, we require your assistance. I shall put in a word to Jurtithan."

"I thank you for suggesting it, but I need advice," Thareous said.

Ianvorr looked down upon him. "Of what kind?"

"How I can inspire others to alter their viewpoints—their self-seeking habits. I have observed sin from the distance. Most of all, lust in many forms. I was afraid to speak up in a remonstrating voice. I feared them calling me judgmental."

"The answer to this is simple," Ianvorr said. "Tell them you wish to be as a leader to them. For leaders create change and influence others to create change. Only through keenness can you entice this."

"Bless you, Powerful One!" Thareous exclaimed. "Your philosophies are brilliant. I have yet to accomplish change. How might this be brought about?"

"By commitment—by will," Ianvorr said. "Few have found this answer. I am one of them. Of course I do not swank about this. There are more principal things in life, such as work and raising a family."

To these words Thareous sighed. "I have one more thing to ask of you. Though it is against Galthoria, I lack counsel. Lefanarí dwells in my thoughts daily and is always in my dreams at night. I wish to know how it is possible to surrender an elf. Despite my apology, I feel she is pressing my heart."

"You ask something great," Ianvorr said. "I should say revealing your feelings for her should help. So tell me what you think of her."

"I see her as one seeking a mate. For she lost her former to a jealous admirer. In retaliation she murdered him. Thus I wish to comfort her with compassion and pity. At the same time, I do love her. Before you saved me, I felt like she was a need. It is *she* who needs someone that will look after and protect her from harm."

The Ice Dragon inclined his head. "Because I also admire one of my kind, I can relate. Even I cannot give you a satisfiable answer. Still, you must tell me more. Disclose to me what you would do for her. How would you treat her—support her?"

Thareous watched his feet go ahead of him. "If ever she is ill, I would be at her side, whether war tore at us or not. If ever she is stricken down in battle, I would leap atop her to take the killing blow. For my care for her outstrips that even to Nalla. I am, after all, unfit to be King of Keiratha."

"With this I can offer you some insight," the Ice Dragon said. "Lefanarí is the one you are ordained to wed. You must resist her for now. She can only lead you down a path of misery and agony. She knows you should not consort. Hence, petition Galthoria for self-denial and caution. There will come a time when your actions are unknown."

"Yes," Thareous said. "Each time I see her, I become more attached to her."

"In that case," Ianvorr said, "you should relinquish her."

******

He had seen the protruding tiers, for Ianvorr had flown him up many stairs. He found that giants crouched behind the claw-like crenels. Embrasures also opened up, admitting view over the glen below. The parapet curved back into the outcrop on both sides. At the other end, another tier wound about, forming a complete circle.

Once the two finished sightseeing, the groups settled for lunch. The banquet hall looked like an expanded version of Galgon's. The benches and stone tables were fit for the giant-folk. The smaller kinds gathered at their feet. They used flat rocks for dishes. King Harvok and Queen Eirmrasha sat on thrones with wings carved at the sides. Because of this they had to sit far apart. This was the closest they usually could get, it seemed.

They ate smoked deer meat, apple slices from an orchard close by, and hunks of cheeses. A fire roared in an immense hearth. Cool mountain air vented into a skylight above. Everyone swapped songs, cheery or cold like an elegy, and riddles.

A tower guard rushed in. "King Harvok, the krakens are here."

At this Ianvorr arose and charged past the guard. Thareous went to Jurtithan's side. "Have you called the searching dragons back yet?"

Jurtithan's gaze flashed with astonishment. "Galthoria's grace, this I have forgotten of! They look for you still. Kyjre and Éilicil are in their own lands. Airalus hunts for you in the Nyran Forest, where he remains to guard till the war."

"Have you spoken with Ancient?" Thareous asked.

Jurtithan glanced at the aged man in red robes sitting by Orkon.

"Aye," Thareous said. "He is the real one."

The Silver One arose to his full height, his spinal spikes pricking the ceiling. Chips rolled off his back. "What of the other Ancient Archimage we have already dealt with? They wear the same attire."

"He is a puppet, an illusionary spy for Zakumahk," Thareous said. "He thrives in the Ice Fortress—the very place the Omnipotent Ones are stationed."

At this time the krakens entered the room. Ianvorr was in deep discussion with Nahilmara. She reached Jurtithan, but peered at Thareous. "You are a wonder, Young Mage. Not even Zakumahk can hold you back."

"Speaking of which," Jurtithan said, "what have you to report?"

She held her gaze on Thareous as she spoke. "The Dark Legion has regrouped with more fiends. There must be a hundredfold more than before. We sunk a score of their ships, whereas they demolished a fourth of my sisters. In the end, as the Seafolk arrived, they reached land—the coast of the Keicor Alps."

The Silver One growled. "The time for war draws nearer. We should not tarry here much longer. There are others to assemble."

"The Seafolk has done as they were required," Ianvorr said. "They can no longer aid us. We shall look to the griffins and the centaurs for further succor. I have invited the latter to fight. Their oaths could be forgotten."

"They are complacent since they have not anyone to war with, save the humans," Jurtithan said. He glanced between Harvok and Orkon and continued in a drawl. "I say unto you now both of them have battled ere your birth."

Thareous gazed at each of them before replying. "This explicates why they welcomed me so. Something that I have already deprecated." He felt a presence and looked around, catching the stare of Ancient. It seemed to say, *Do not judge*. He whipped his eyes away. Selfish anger swelled. He burst it.

The dragons talked among themselves, too engaged to notice. "I must call Brother Kyjre and Éilicil," Jurtithan said. "The Ice Dragons shall return to us here while Kyjre goes to the griffins' den." With that he went out of the banquet hall.

"I must greet my host and inquire where we are to bed for the night," Nahilmara said to Ianvorr. "Shall you accompany me?"

"Aye, but Thareous may come also," the Ice Dragon said. His lightsome eyes darted to his human friend. "What say you, Appointed Archimage?"

"I deem to tarry where I stand," he said. "I have another affair of which I must attend to. I shall meet up with you later."

"So be it," Nahilmara said.

As soon as the dragons departed, a wizened hand pressed down on Thareous's shoulder. Turning, Thareous spotted the Ancient Archimage. "You are easier to read than a scroll," Ancient said.

"Anyplace save here," Thareous said.

"Nay. We shall speak here. One must deign himself to truncate his pride."

"Then"—Thareous spread out his arms—"let us speak here."

"In the eyes of others you are to demean yourself. You do not fear slander or gossip behind your back. How came this to be?"

Thareous smiled. "I wish to be as a leader unto others. My pretension is to lead them to change—to stand up if a busybody gets in their way—to follow their own dreams. In this way that is wrong. Therefore I do not judge the giants, but count them as ignoramuses. Can you read my look only?"

"Not alone," said Ancient, "I can also read your heart—by the way you speak your words. They are not ill-enunciated. They tell me all you wish to do. I suppose this feeling spawned when you witnessed the callousness outside Galgon."

"This is so," Thareous said. "I note the helpless more oft and wish to help them. Once I aided the capture of Greilph's sons, I swore to myself

I would do this. Since I am an important figure, then people should hear me."

"With a voice as powerful as yours, they shall indeed," Ancient said. "My friend, if you are satisfied to the gullet, let us leave."

"To where?"

"Elsewhere. The merger of these voices gives me a headache."

Thareous gathered his things and followed the older Magician out of the dining hall. They came to a prodigious corridor. To their left a large boulder held an ironbound door of oak against the wall. Giant suits of steel lined up past each arc, ten yards apart. They stood there as watchmen. Thareous conjectured they might bear an actual wearer. Some had lengthy swords that they held at the pommel and stuck into pedestals, which they stood atop.

After a while they detoured through a passage that had doors leading to bedchambers at either side. Torches were placed in their sconces by each threshold. They passed through, hearing a snore. At the end they found themselves in a large library. Racks fashioned from the walls contained stacks of scrolls. Rows of bookcases, paved in the floor, lined in twos. Multiple desks pushed against the wall held clean parchments and giant inkstands. All this amazed Thareous.

A shadow fell over him. He whipped around on his heel, facing back to the hall that he entered. Ancient joined him in the movement, clenching both hands on the twisting shaft of his wicken-staff.

"It is incredible, is it not?" Harvok asked. He gazed at Thareous, holding up the war-club he had carved earlier. "I wonder if you meant what you said about abandoning us. You cannot intend upon it. For the sake of Keiratha, you cannot!" He snarled and a hand swooped after him.

"Run, Thareous!" Ancient cried. He conjured red orbs and launched them at the Giant King. This gave Thareous a chance to flee. He took off between two bookcases. Before he could find a place to hide, the voice of Harvok followed him. "Go as you may, Son of Haverin. This is my palace. I control everything here!"

MADNESS

Ianvorr's head jerked as bellows ricocheted off the walls in a corridor. Nahilmara was with him. They stood near the stables, their resting place for the night. He turned to her. He had heard because of his sensitive ears. "Something is wrong. I must go."

Her head perked up. "Only the reverberations of our converse meet me. To where do you deem to go?"

"Wherever they take me," he said. "Hearken: though you hear not what I do, let me remind you that I have the lion's share of the curse. Ergo, you sense nil, for your malediction is less grave than that of me." He put his snout to hers, withdrew, and followed the echoes.

******

Harvok shoved the books in the lowest row of the nearest shelf with his club, for it had no back. He assumed Thareous hid there since the door at the other end was closed and had no cracks. As he drew back the knotted club, a telekinetic lasso wrapped about its head. He looked back and caught Ancient pulling it. A lucent arm extended out of Ancient's staff and held his club in place. Harvok strained his muscles to tug it over his head. It budged not even an inch.

"Curse you, Ancient Archimage!" he bellowed. "Curse your Unknown Arts! I do this for the good of my people. You get in my way." He pivoted, facing the old man, and brought the club a foot away from him.

Seeing the Giant King intended to kill him, Ancient let the arm go and erected a barrier. "Get past this. None bar the zarjkakon Eiljr have broken through a mystical force-field. Mayhap you can best her."

Harvok glared at him. "Fool. I am not to be duped. Omit your manipulation."

Still he kicked the barrier once with his jackboots. A minute fracture was induced, then mended. Harvok turned away, beginning to search for Thareous in the piles of books. Ancient glanced up and nodded to Thareous, who lay atop the nearest bookcase. As he heard a string of curses, Ancient looked back upon Harvok. The Giant King rambled through the shelves again, three down from where his quarry rested.

Ancient let up the barrier and walked toward Thareous. "King of the Giants, give up your search. The Young Mage fled long ago while you and I fought. Cease this ere Galthoria decides to remove his hand of life from you."

His foe glowered. "I shall not until that churl is found. I am to keep him here till he swears unto me that he shall not abandon us. Here I have all behests. Including over Jurtithan himself!"

As Harvok said this, a blur lunged at him from the other row of bookshelves. They toppled over, landing in a pile of books, Harvok first, and they both emitted gasps. Icy breath descended upon the area before the Giant King could behold his attacker. "Powerful One! I wronged you not."

Ianvorr snorted in his face, bathing him in icy haze. He whirled his head to where the war-club lay in Harvok's hand and secreted a stream of pure ice. "Do not plague me with paltry statements, mutineer."

"It is not like that!" the Giant King cried. "I—"

"Save it for Jurtithan," Ianvorr said. He sensed a being above him. "You may come from your place of hiding, Young Mage. All is safe."

A small head poked out from the topmost shelf. Ianvorr spread out a membranous wing. Thareous dove to it. He experienced a brief moment of rushing wind and a soft landing. The wing curved till its tip made contact with the stone floor. He slid down it. As he did, a gauntlet snatched him up and squeezed him. Ianvorr had not considered Giant King's other hand. The same, Harvok had not considered him as a threat. Ianvorr drew out his neck, opened his maw, and plunged down, chomping the giant's arm.

Bellowing, Harvok let go of Thareous, who fell on the floor in an insensible heap. Harvok's other arm tightened as he broke the ice from his gauntlet. Wielding the war-club, he bashed his aggressor upon the head three times before he let go. The open air stung Harvok's wound. Warm blood flowed down his arm and into his gauntlet. He glanced at Thareous. *No,* the giant thought. *Ianvorr is more dangerous.* He averted his gaze back to the Ice Dragon to find he had recovered. A clobber to the dragon's side made his back curve into a bow-shape.

Harvok slid his legs to his side, levered them to his gut, and shoved into Ianvorr's hinds. In retaliation the Ice Dragon exuded a stream of ice into his face. This kept the Giant King down for the time he needed. Picking up Thareous, Ianvorr turned to Ancient and laid him down. "Heal him and leave. If you come to one of my brothers, tell them of my plight with your mind. The giants could come to aid Harvok."

No sooner had he finished saying this did a sound like shattering glass echo into faraway rooms. From the empty shelves they saw Harvok sit up and wipe away crusts of ice from his face. "Hurry," Ianvorr said. He spun to the Giant King once more. His foe did not seem coordinated at the least.

"Ianvorr, be you still here?" Harvok asked in a steady voice.

He did not reply till Ancient was away. "I am."

"You have bettered me, do you hear?" The Giant King felt the shelves and lifted himself by them. "Ice has cut my eyes. I cannot see. I am *blind*. So I need you to lead me as a dog to my throne room."

The Ice Dragon studied him. Harvok's eyes moved about as if seeking something, though his head never turned. He blinked seldom. As he took a step, he was mindful of where he placed his feet, afraid that he might step into a hole. He began to utilize his war-club as a guide-stick. "Where stands you? Be you still here, Powerful One?"

"I am here, Harvok Arahmursson."

Another cautious step and Harvok's club swayed to and fro. It swung to the right, always clipping the side of the bookshelf. Harvok strode forth again, his expression wooden. "Lead me to you by your voice. I must return to my throne, for I am to end my kingship." He discontinued his pace. "Speak, Ianvorr!"

The last phrase concluded his suspicion. "You feign your sightlessness. You wished to deceive so that when you neared, you might land the final blow."

"Nay, I do not," the Giant King said. "Help me; I beseech you. I am blind! I can no longer walk the land and note its beauty. Permit my son, Diermahk, to take my place in this battle. I cannot continue."

His pleas ripped Ianvorr's heart asunder. Pity hardened in his spirit. He forgot all caution. "Put down your club and I will guide you."

"I need it," Harvok said. "I know not the way to my court from here, in this state. From there I can wander with the aid of my attendants."

Ianvorr hesitated as Harvok lifted his foot again, placing it two yards ahead of him. "If this is a skullduggery, I shall ensure your blindness. I am loath to aid you in this way. You have attempted to steal away a friend of mine. I will help since you are in this titular condition. May you think better of treachery."

He ambled to Harvok, his body sideways to him as if a man were to mount atop a horse. He felt an imbrued gauntlet grasp a neck spike and started walking. Then he saw the shadow of a knobbed stump be lifted up, betrayed by the light of sconced candles. Pain jolted his back and unconsciousness took Ianvorr …

******

Ancient leaned over Thareous's form. "Young Mage, come back! All is well. Awaken!"

Thareous clenched his eyelids for a moment, lifting them. "Whe-where am I?"

"Among friends," another voice assured him. He faced the place where it came from and his vision made out the outline of Nahilmara. "Ancient has told us what occurred. Jurtithan is on his way to face Harvok, should he be alive still."

Sitting up, Thareous turned over and pushed himself to his feet. "I will go as well. I tire of that manic rambler. Have either of you any objections?"

Nahilmara shook her head. Ancient took up his staff and rose to his full height. "No objections, only advice. Do not get overconfident, unless you wish to be captured."

Thareous nodded. "I heed you." At that he ran through the wall as an elf.

******

Jurtithan stooped over Ianvorr's broken body. The light of the candles caught in the sheen of his scales, manifesting him an argent ghost. He lifted his snout, inhaling in faint whiffs of Harvok's trail. A time passed before he procured the scent. With his nose he followed to the oaken door guarded by two dugouts holding scrolls. He butted it twice to smash it open, then wound his head and neck in. Only these would fit.

Here the scent was strongest. Inside, the room was dark, unlit by any means of light save the rays that lanced over him. His white eyes served also for means of light and searched the room. A desk at the far wall had a stack of papers on it. An inkwell keeping the feather of a roc also stood there. Besides this it looked empty.

Then two hands seized his horns. With untold strength Harvok wrenched his neck to the side. This took a great deal of willpower out of

Jurtithan. In addition to twisting his neck, Harvok tugged it. In several places Jurtithan felt the tendons of his neck strain. The nerves in him screamed. Soon the screaming found its way to his voice. He bellowed so long and loud that the ceiling trembled, threatening to collapse upon them. He burned for the throe to cease.

A second later his head went dead. Harvok let it go and wept. "Why must I do this? Why can they not just believe me?" A sob choked off further words. He went to the side and took up his war-club.

"Harvok! When shall your destruction cease?" Thareous stood on Jurtithan's body, which he then slid from.

The giant's eyes narrowed. "Thareous. You are the reason for my insanity. *You* are the reason I defend myself as well as my people. Prepare to die."

"You prepare."

Harvok threw back his head and relished a moment of laughter. "A human would be so bold as to say this to a giant? One that is friendless? Your temerity amuses me!"

Thareous smiled. He had an ally, one as powerful as his will could make. *Magic.*

THE GRIFFIN MASTER

Kyjre stood at the opening of a cavern at Malmeir's base. *By Annathias, I have never met a griffin in my life. I do not know what their temperaments are like. I am not even sure if they like intruders.* He lumbered in, his ligaments masked in hesitance. Already he missed the heat outside, the deep rincons in the land known as the Fire Realm. It was a barren wasteland, devoid of plantlife or underprivileged beasts.

The wyverns, the Fire Dragons, lived in dug-out rocky knolls. Their chief village, Zahkrahm, lay at the foot of Malmeir, which had not erupted in several millennia. Over holes filled with lava, they would roast their catch, fiends who strayed from Valvassa. As for Kirtchaz and Mallaem, they had fewer residents. They found caves to live in. Wyverns at Kirtchaz ate fish that swam too close to the polluted shores. They beset fiends sailing from or into to Iszalli and ate their corpses. They could only survive this way.

The most miserable had to be Mallaem. The Three Elders of that group appointed the strongest and bravest from there and sent them to hunt for stray fiends. Some simply escaped to Zahkrahm. Females kept most of them there.

Kyjre pondered over these things as he delved into the griffins' den. His thoughts turned back to Jurtithan's mental conversation with him. *At least Thareous was found. Though we have not spoken, I revere him for his bravery.* He reminisced about the Silver One detailing him on Thareous's adventures. The one in which the lad spirited himself away from the Legion fascinated him most.

By now he crossed out of the longish tunnel. A colonnade of cave formations lined the sides of the chamber he entered. Between each partition a griffin sat, but did not disturb him. With his ebony eyes he kept watch upon them until coming to a threshold. A causeway stretched past this. It tapered as it continued to the other end in a slight camber. The ceiling curved into a dome. The bottom bore stalagmites. The protrusion upon which Kyjre stood was almost too small for him.

I remember this used to be our base of operations. Brother Ianvorr convinced the Silver One to relocate and moved to the Ice Fortress. I do not care. I prefer this place to be occupied by one race.

Spreading out his wings, he took to the airl, the narrow bridge too slim for him to walk across. He expected his flight to be thwarted by magical means. Nothing out of the ordinary transpired. He made it to the other side in utmost safety and ease.

Ingressing under a curvature, he came to a lake of bubbling lava. The shore split off in both ends, leading to three passageways. Two twisted pillars of rock held up the cupola. Kyjre selected the right-hand way. At the other end he could not choose which doorway to take. He had to find the Griffin Master, one who taught those who visited him to live in perspicacity. His indecision left him immobile. For all he knew, one of the ways could lead him through endless tunnels.

Then he spotted a griffin running to meet him. "Welcome, Braveheart. I am Purnus, sent by the Master to escort you to him."

"He has my blessings," Kyjre said. "This is one intricate place, if you do not mind my saying. Come, let us not linger because of my prattle."

Purnus nodded his understanding. "This way."

They went to the passage across from the one Kyjre had come. Amber lightstones set into little braziers stuck in the continuous walls and lit them. Stones crunched under their feet. They came to the other end. They entered the largest chamber thus far, with no entryway save that one. An accumulation of gems like no other mounded to the ceiling. In it aggregated diamonds, gold ingots, silver, jades, emeralds, and golden staffs with magical zircons for the head.

The claw of greed gripped Kyjre's heart. Being a beast that hoarded treasures to entice mates, he bounded toward the trove. "This is incredible!" Then his eyes widened. He moved away.

"Go ahead," Purnus said, "take some. I shall tell none."

"Nay," he said, "This is a test. If I took a gemstone, I would not be able to do what I came for." As these words ended, a golden flash, like the sunlight of dawn, imbued the room. Kyjre's eyes filled with awe that disabled his tongue.

A griffin twice the size of Jurtithan stood before him. The riches had vanished. By him the test was created, for he was the test. Everything they garnered went into his body, fused into this essence. Two feathers serving as eyebrows slanted down, their tips drooping. This gave him the semblance of having ageless wisdom. With great eagle wings ringed in the rays of golden light, the Griffin Master flew into the air, touched down, and sat. "Ye hast past the test, Kyjre Braveheart. Ye came here quicker than a fire could burn a leaf. This I know. How doth ye plead?"

"Through a voice of importunacy," Kyjre said. "The Omnipotent Ones cry for your aid, O Wise One."

"Forgiveth me for not addressing myself eft," the Griffin Master said. "I am Lánoch. Ye, Kyjre Braveheart, hath passed rock and fire to see me. Erewhile ye came, I sent Purnus to retrieve ye. Thine mission is done. Albeit, I hath yet to answereth ye."

"Time is short, Master," Kyjre said. "Zakumahk has landed—"

"Beeth patient," Lánoch said. "I must pondereth this decision. Thou shouldst not hasten me. All thilk, I shalt not hasten ye, whilst the Dark King nighs Galgon. Time is short indeed. Permit me to reflect mine great thoughts." He closed his eyelids, hiding the golden orbs inside. Not a minute later he opened them. "Valvassa lieth nigh here. Its numbers hast trekketh over the Fire Realm. We hast let them passeth. Vengeance wilt be taken."

Kyjre's eyes widened to a tenfold. "You mean?"

Lánoch let out a trill crow. "Time is short indeed. I pondereth my thoughts in a brief spell. Ye hast not passeth this test. Ye hast passeth the ultimate one. Hence, let the others knoweth that in spite of our differences, we shalt defend Keiratha."

The wyvern beamed. "May all things that are old come to pass."

Lánoch bowed his head. "This is ever-true. Byeth the end of this century, this millennium, in five years, Galthoria shalt be replaced. I shalt be replaced. Every being that important shalt be replaced."

"Master Lánoch, these tidings I have heard before from my kin," Kyjre said. "I yearn for advice. Tell me, what is the secret to gaining wisdom?"

"Many hast asketh me this question," the Griffin Master said. "Ye are the one hundredth. Whilst they longeth for the answer, I concludeth one thing: what wilt ye doeth with such insight? I asketh thee this question."

"I perceive where you go," the wyvern said. "The universe asks for it. It is a sacred gift. They use it for their own gain. The meaning behind it is very subtle. I shall use it to help people."

Lánoch drew his breath in and out with a sigh. "So it beeth. Prepareth thyself, for these art strong words. The answer to attaining wisdom is to useth knowledge well. Wisdom is how ye decideth to run thine life. Live it well. Bear in mind you art optimistic. Do not let that downsizeth ye."

Kyjre congeed as Lánoch dematerialized into light and reformed into the mounds of riches. He turned away so to not revel in his avarice. He busied himself by ruminating his last words. *Brother Ianvorr thinks me to be a fawn since I admire him. My admiration should not get between us. I must speak with him.*

Purnus escorted him back to the entrance where they said their farewells. Kyjre unfurled his wings and took to the sky. *One mission is complete. Another, more personal one awaits. I shall not let this keep living as a voracious blaze within.*

Battling the Storms

A shiver ran down Zakumahk's spine as he drew his cape about him. Wind and cold beat at his helmet, trying to best him. Nothing could, as hardened as he was. They traveled over the shores between the sea and the Keicor Alps. The last fiend reached their abandoned fleet, still in sight. It felt like an eternity passed with each step. The storm kept from him the sibilant utterances of Quaron.

Zakumahk peered out the eyeholes of his ventail. To the left the Keicor Alps arose, heaps of snow twisting about to the top. The summits appeared as spearheads, their glacious slopes smooth and precipitous. Thick clouds bandaged the peaks. At the right a boundless ocean raged, tamed only by the Fates. Icebergs floated into each other. Glaciers broke off into the brine. Ice-isles, less frequent, ported near the shores. An icy route curved on the outside of the mountains. A biting mist clung to the ground. Heaps of snow piled at either side.

Despite the onerations visiting the fiends, they were silent. If the Dark King caught their petulance, there would be a massacre. He cared not how many he slew as long as they did not complain. He just wanted a crew that revered him.

At times I got rid of more than five hundred. Not even that flagged additional fiends to cease their kvetching. He kicked sleet off his jackboot. *There is one that will not carp.* He caressed the hilt of Kielthavra. *You have remained with me since my coronation.* Not daring to release its blade for fear rime might freeze inside the scabbard, he drew his hand away. He reached a finger to the brooch pinned to his cape.

"Massster!" a voice cried. "The cold chills our bonesss. Let us ressst."

He swung on his heel and struck the snake-head. The hood fell. Quaron's human face hit the snow. "Fool! No one is to eat or break. If they do, they get left behind."

Quaron trembled as he gazed into the Dark King's eyes. In his human voice he said, "Yes, Sire. This is understood. Earlier I did not consider it. You reminded me."

"Of course I did." Zakumahk seized his cloak and jerked him up. "Do not speak to me again so long as we are here, whoreson." He dropped him, dusted off his hands as if he touched filth, and walked on.

Quaron got to his feet and swung the cowl back on to his head. "Thisss is not over." The fiends had to remain behind him since he was second-in-command. He wished it different.

******

The environs darkened as if the sky above drowned in deep umbrage. The air chilled to an arctic windstorm. In the dead of twilight they began to spawn snowflakes. Fiends fell, defeated by the cold. Their comrades left them to freeze. Even they respected the dead. Zakumahk rode Amarzrell. The black dragon's wings erected to deflect the chill. He ordered his lackeys to quicken their paces. His steed's rate exceeded theirs.

Black smog pervaded the area as Amarzrell strove to keep his body temperature. Without any unease he denoted the wintriness. "My scales protect me from many things, Lord. Not this."

Zakumahk lowered his eyes to the back of his steed. "Hurry then, you slowcoach. I do not tolerate crosspatches." He spurred his side.

Amarzrell grunted and did as instructed. The crests over his eyes dropped.

Through a dingle between two snowy mounds, they wound. A snow-hare bounded from a small aperture under one of the piles. The Shadowhunter yearned to chase after it. Another kick to the side made him abstain. Hunger persisted in his stomach. Then he felt water at his paws. A half-frozen puddle quaked like a diminutive ocean, carrying with it vessels of ice. The Dark Legion stopped as he did. Those in front prodded his tail with their weapons.

He lifted his head, trumpeting a roar. He charged forth, the ice forsaken. He flew. Ahead the clouds dissipated. He broke free from the mists, leaving it to curl as a column of smoke. Beyond him loomed iceless mountains. Zakumahk beamed as he familiarized what had taken place. "Yes!" Lurching Kielthavra from its sheath, he held it skyward. The twilight donated on its blade an inky hue. The Four Suns vanished into the heavens. The Legion emerged from the Keicors.

"Now for blood," Zakumahk said, lowering Shadowbiter. "Now for revival. Now for the coronation of Varkin, our beloved king!"

The Black Night

In a flash Thareous pulled Theldaneru from its black and silver casing. Glyphs from the Dragon Script rose off the scabbard's side. They stood for Protection—protection for his golden sword. It was indestructible to his knowledge.

Harvok answered with an overhead swing of his oaken club. It smashed in front of Thareous. The Young Mage got an idea. He leapt onto the bludgeon and jabbed Theldaneru's tip into its head. The giant lifted it, starting to shake it.

Thareous summoned fire. It ran down the gold blade and onto the club-head. The Giant King shifted his weapon toward his lips and blew. The inferno spread, staying sustained by mystical means. A swift motion with the club-hand made Thareous flip into his own fire. His shirt fell prey to the flame. It burned away, but not anyplace underneath. Instead a bright corselet of green and silver glistened. The armor of Asbestos, the only dragon to resist fire, protected him.

In his surprise he let go of Theldaneru and slid off the club. He dropped ten feet, landing on his upper back. Growling, he rolled over and sprang to his feet. Being shorn of his sword angered him. To his relief Kielkanur broke the worst of the fall.

Harvok threw away his cudgel. It was too charred, still conveying raging fires. It broke into large burnt chunks, issuing a spray of sparks. Theldaneru wedged into the remains, the in-curved blade showing. His enemy stood between Thareous and his blade. He lifted a hand, motioning at his foe. "Come, if you have any courage. I deem you to be a poltroon when you are bereft of your weapons—a bravado-invoked braggart." Kielkanur the Thornwhirl slid into place as he spoke.

"Do not affront me!" Harvok thundered. From underneath the folds of his patch-threaded cloak, he produced a kris. "I am not without a tool for defense."

In one stride he leaned over and swung the dagger at Thareous. It clipped off Kielkanur's surface. *Next time, I shall be ready*, Thareous thought. While Harvok righted himself, he buckled the silvern straps, inducing in them magic. Spikes shot out and whirled like a tornado.

The kris swooped again. Thareous answered with a swing of Thornwhirl. A flash of light dazzled them as both weapons met. Asbestos' armor glowed, dazing Thareous and Harvok. When it dispersed, they heard a clang upon the stone floor. They had to both blink to regain their sight. After recovering, they peered to the ground. Half of the kris's blade lay at their feet. Harvok held the remains of the dagger up to his eyes. "This cannot be!" His glare averted to Thareous. "You are a nuisance."

"At least I am not an irrational tyrant," he said.

Rasping his voice, Harvok jabbed the kris downward. Thareous had just enough time to block it. It came down again, this time faster. Kielkanur set up again. The next time he was not so fortunate. Harvok landed a fist against the buckler.

Thareous flipped over his head and came to rest on his back. The breath rushed from him. The shadows about him deepened as the Giant King loomed over him. "Why do you fight? Why do you resist?"

"I believe in a better universe," Thareous said.

"It is hopeless," Harvok said. "Every class Galthoria watches over drown in their sins! Can you not accept that, accept defeat?"

"Let me ask you: why do you fight?"

The Giant King lowered the half-kris. "You have forced me to. I do this to protect my people. Your words could undermine my authority. They would aspire to depose me. They need my leadership. You stand between us."

"Think of them as the universe. Feel no ill will to me," the human said, levering himself up. "Is it worth fighting amongst the Omnipotent Ones?" He indicated toward Jurtithan. "Look at what you have done. Is this to be your life?"

Harvok's grip on the hilt tightened. "Curse you, Haverinsson! I said I do this for my people. Yes, we shall be extracted from the Omnipotent Ones. Yes, your death might cause another war. At least I might uphold my dignity."

Thareous could not believe his ears "This is your reason for aspiring to kill me? To keep some pride, some respect from your subjects? Your character rots like a corpse."

"Again you insult me!" Harvok cried. His face twisted in enmity. "Let it be the last time. I impeded our fight so that I might convince you to see things my way. You withstand me still." The kris overturned in his hand, the half-blade facing Thareous. "It is the time for you to die, Forsaker."

Without a sound but a stifled breath, Harvok jammed the weapon downward. Thareous rolled to the side and assumed a standing stature. He faced his enemy. While they spoke, he had healed his hurts with magic.

Fighting with a shield, he found out, could only get him killed. He unstrapped Kielkanur from his arm and cast it aside. "I need not any weapons to conquer you. Fight me as you will."

Harvok stretched out a foot in order to crush him. Again Thareous circumvented his endeavors to slay him by summoning a barrier to ensure his protection. It moved as him. He decided to let it go. A new plan formed in his mind. He set the magic to work.

Conjuring up a dozen other facsimiles of himself, they stood abreast in a line. They took off, running as elves. Harvok gawked at this peculiar sight. No one had ever stopped an elf while he or she ran. *Because they did not know how.*

Lifting a jackboot, Harvok sent it crashing down. The room shook and the ceiling gave in. Shafts of twilight cut away the darkness. The dimness showed the illusions for what they were. Thareous lost his footing from the tremor and fell. He whirled onto his back and spotted Harvok over him. The giant raised his kris to throw it. The illusions Thareous took back into his mind. He gazed into the giant's eyes, finding his will to be exposed.

Thareous shut his eyes and an awareness of his surroundings showed him a dimmed depiction of the room. He saw Harvok, his breathing coming in drawn-out gulps. With this intuition he searched for entry to his mind. Soon he found it. Drilling an opening into the giant's thoughts, he found hesitations, the pangs of regret forming. He found in his memories the picture of a young giant. His son Diermahk. Harvok feared what would become of his only child because of his actions. Despite the findings Thareous began to bend Harvok's will to submission.

Sensing something in his mind, the Giant King prepared to hurl his weapon. It was too late. His self-choice abandoned him, betraying him to the mind of his enemy. He felt as a void. He stood there, staring into oblivion. "What is your first command?"

"Drop your dagger," Thareous said. He watched as the giant did. "Turn and take three strides to the right." Here Jurtithan's comatose body rested. "Step over the Silver One, duck your head, and walk into the library."

Thareous retrieved Thelaneru then followed as he continued to give orders. He paused to probe Jurtithan's neck and set the muscles to their initial arrangements. He turned his attention to Harvok.

"Walk across the room until you come to Ianvorr. Stop to wait for me." He heard mumbling, that of a soul trying to break free of its prison of stupor. Harvok proceeded without dithering. Upon reaching Ianvorr, Thareous searched his body for injury. He found three fractures in the head and his spine to be broken. These he healed also. When he finished, the Ice Dragon trembled and his eyes open.

"Young Mage. I sensed your presence. Thank you for healing me. It was unnecessary. Time would have done the same."

"You would not have been revived for the war," Thareous said. "Come, I must see to it that this traitor is punished rightfully and justly."

"The giants' edicts state if their king goes mad, he should be banished," Ianvorr said. "Lead him to his people. They shall judge him."

"What of Jurtithan?"

"He is here?"

"Past the bookcases, unconscious."

Ianvorr paused. "I will see to him. Go … do as you must." He got to his feet, trembling, and went to check on the leader of the Omnipotent Ones.

Thareous led Harvok out of the library, down the hallway leading to some giants' chambers, and into the main corridor. Using memories of his former trip, he followed it back to the parlor. Giants sat in here discussing what they did. They stopped after seeing their leader and his blank posture. Then their gazes fell upon Thareous.

"I can explain," he said.

Punishment

Harvok stood to the side, his wrists bound in large irons, his head bowed. His people stared at him in disbelief, in disgust that he had shamed them. Eirmrasha wept. Diermahk comforted her. Few dwarves and fauns abided with the predominating giants.

Jurtithan and Ianvorr stood on the podium next to the traitorous king. Thareous, Ancient, and Nahilmara were between them. They assembled in the throne room, also the lawcourt to offenses, great or small. Harvok usually served here as judge and prosecutor. Jurtithan assumed the duty in his place.

"For the first time," Jurtithan said at length, "one of your kings has rebelled against us. He is the second to rule the giant-folk. It still counts to me as more than one, I say. If Arahmur lived this day"—he glanced at Harvok—"he would be mortified. I deem him to still be amid us all. I deem the entire giant race to be him. Harvok's outcome is up to you—giants and giantesses alike. Undifferentiating my power, his life is in your hands. You should listen to the accounts given, first."

He bade Ianvorr to begin his narrative. The Ice Dragon related his arrival, the struggle between them, Harvok's ploy of blindness, and the club being sent to his back. Ancient relayed his side of the story. Then Thareous informed them of his hiding, his unconsciousness, and the fight.

Nahilmara spoke next. "I was in the stables, where the pet dragons of the giants used to abide—when we used to be their mounts as we flew into battle. It is close to the library. The Ancient Archimage charged toward me and told me what was taking place. Thareous hovered in at his side. Jurtithan, leading a pack of dragons, heard the account. In a great hurry he flew out of the room. Before leaving, he told us to remain." Despite her acrimony for him she told the episode. "I followed Ancient to a giant stall where he laid Thareous. He knelt to his knees, put his staff at his side, commencing to awaken him. In due course his eyes opened." She recounted the ensuing conversation to end the accounts.

"You have heard their sides of the story," Jurtithan said. "Harvok, you must now convince your own kind you do not deserve punishment."

Raising his head, he gazed at everyone before starting. "Brethren, I did what I did for I believed it to be required. This speech I do not speak to persuade any of you of my innocence. I wish to inform you of my reasoning for attacking our most respected guest. My guilt overburdens me. Earlier, ere the midday repast, Thareous came into my court, unbidden. He began to reprimand our kind for adulating him as a deity. In our discourse he warned me he might abandon us if we did not eschew from such worship.

"I swore this could not befall us. After the meal I followed him and Ancient into the library." He told them of the exchange, going into Ianvorr's advent and the argument. He reiterated their fight, now from his point of view. He told also of his trick. "Once I saw Ianvorr fall to the floor, I realized my actions and was afraid. I had seen the Archimage flee down the hall, conveying Thareous with his staff. I knew the Powerful One would impede me again. So I did the one thing I could: hide.

"Showing my face to Jurtithan could endanger me. I thought, *What if they already informed him when we met?* I recalled the door beyond the bookcases. I ran to it, hoping none would follow. As I reached the door, I heard echoes from the hall. In haste I turned the knob, stepped in, and closed it. I sidled to the corner and lifted my weapon. I heard Jurtithan's voice. I cognized his body could not fit through the entry. Thus I set aside my club and awaited his ingression.

"Not long after this the oaken door fell to pieces. The Silver One slid his head in, the light of his eyes silvering the room. A few rays from the candles in the library assisted him. Before he could turn my way, I jumped in front of him. I snatched his horns since they are about my height. He tightened his neck muscles. I began to wrest his head to and fro, jerking all the while. At length his stamina seemed to give way. He collapsed. Soon a shadow blocked off the light that fell over him."

After this he related the last conflict. Then he fell silent, again looking over the assemblage. "To my choice I wish to receive Thareous's leniency ere I am tied to your verdict. I could not continue without it."

Thareous nodded his affirmation. "Your attempt upon my life is forgiven. Were the decision mine, you would go free. Since it is not, I fear the worst."

The Giant King lowered his head; bobbled in grief.

Jurtithan thumped his tail on the podium for attention. "You heard the accounts and beheld forbearance. You must now settle on a judgment.

Whatever this choice, the accused must accept. If it is not to his favor and he rebels, he will be treated to death."

With these words said, the giants left the throne room to debate. After the last of them had passed under the threshold, Ancient gripped his staff in both hands. "I have something tragic to report."

Everyone present looked at him. His eyes closed. He reopened them and explained he was enclosing sound from leaving the room. "There are many eavesdroppers amid that crowd. Giants tend to be prying." Despite the slighted glare of Harvok, he went on. "In any event I am troubled to inform you the Dark Legion has emerged from the storm."

Ianvorr was thunderstruck. "We must move quicker than ever. The Dark Legion are to arrive at Galgon in half a week maximum. Tomorrow morn we should set out and return to the Ice Fortress before flying to the Capital."

As soon as he said this, the door swung open. The giants filed in. Eirmrasha and Diermahk worked their way to the front. The Giant Queen knew what had to betide her.

"Jurtithan, Highest Dragon of them all," Diermahk said, spreading out his arms and bowing. His vociferous and eloquent tone extended through the room. "We have reached our verdict through majority of vote and hence decided my father's wyrd."

He fell silent, it being Eirmrasha's turn to speak. "I am not pleased to utter these words upon my husband. Since his actions led him nigh to madness, we agreed on one thing." She lowered her gaze. "Banishment."

Harvok's eyes widened at this. Jurtithan cut off any protestations. "If banishment has been decided, banishment shall be to him. Harvok Arahmursson, through the laws erected by your father, you are ousted from the giants as well as the Omnipotent Ones. Surrender your crown."

Full of rage at his race's betrayal, he lifted the crown and flung it at his son's feet. "May it be a curse to you!" He stormed off the stand, shoving giants out of his way as he fled the room.

"The law is not yet fulfilled," Jurtithan said, reclaiming their awareness. He focused upon Eirmrasha. "Your Queenship, Arahmur's decrees state if a Giant King is ejected from his kind, you must resign. You may become a commoner, wed a commoner, and have commoner children. Your son must choose a queen for himself."

Eirmrasha's eyes filled with tears until they could contain no more. They spilt into runnels and branched off into deltas. Then they ran off her jawbone and splashed into pools at her feet. Those behind her patted her on the back, trying to allay her grief.

Diermahk tensed as he lifted her tiara. "I present this to Kuarla my lady friend since childhood." He watched a giantess make her way to the front. She had a buxom frame, braided blonde hair and jade-green eyes. A long dress made of deerskins flowed to her ankles over unshod feet. She bowed as he set the tiara on her head.

"I give you King Diermahk the Regal," Jurtithan said, "and Queen Kuarla the Beautiful. A coronation must be set for another time. The darkness outside deepens. The stars glow brighter. We must rest. It has been a long day. The meeting is adjourned."

******

Outside the precipitous walls of Draer-Vollith, Harvok stumbled over the scree-laden glen. He wept, his thoughts a turbulent storm. Anger seethed in him as he pressed on toward the causeway. He paused at its nearest end and turned back to his former home. "Demons! *Traitorous bastards*! I will not be *forsaken*! I will not be *abandoned*!"

The heads of the tower guards appeared at the merlons. Harvok scooped up a boulder and catapulted it at them. It caught one of the guards on his nose. Blood spraying into the air. They disappeared behind the crenellation. "I shall return! I *shall* return!"

THE FLIGHT

The next morning the dragons, two humans, and rocs prepared to leave. Diermahk met them in the atrium, Kuarla beside him. Orkon and Hadres stood at their feet, a war-hammer tucked in the dwarf's belt and twin daggers in the faun's.

"Farewell, Silver One," Diermahk said. "Farewell, Powerful One."

"Farewell," the two dragons said.

To Kuarla, Ianvorr said, "May your days be lived through abstinence and your womb never fail to give life. Your beauty and charm exceeds the bindings of restraint, so beware. Others shall seek you. You must avoid them."

Orkon grunted, his thick-accented voice echoing through the chamber. "No offense, Milady. The dwarven women surpass your beauty, even. To the eyes of a dwarf anyhow." He fingered his hammer's head, hoping to not have affronted his hostess.

She looked down at him and blinked. "Oh, what are they like?"

He pointed at his beard and stomach. "All the qualities the dwarves seek." Everyone save his kind chuckled.

Jurtithan cleared his throat. Their ears turned to him. "Now we depart. This is not to be the last time we see each other. War still awaits us."

"So to war, so to death," Aralles said. He cocked his head, peered at his feet, and picked at a beetle crawling over a talon. He straightened back up. "This will be us if we do not act."

"All in good time," Hadres said. "For now I would advise you get moving. I surmise the Dark Legion will try to dominate some villages."

Jurtithan stiffened. "There are six towns from the top of the Brimstores to Galgon. They lie open to attack. Aralles this mission might not please you. I need you—"

"Speak not another word," the Roc Commander said. He turned to his kind. "Let us fly as the wind."

They took off, flapping their wings until they were over Jurtithan. They sped under the arched entryway, out the portico, and into the sky.

The Silver One ordered his followers to wait for him outside. He exited through the side outlet. Ianvorr led the others down the longish archway, having bade the giants, fauns, and dwarves a last farewell. Thareous rode atop his back, clutching a blade-like spike.

Seeing past the covered portico, past the veils of translucent light, they emerged into the glen. Thareous spotted deep footprints extending from Ianvorr's paw to the causeway about a mile away. "Harvok?"

The Ice Dragon grunted and went forward.

******

By noon the dragons stopped at Calan Lake for a drink. Krakens dove and caught fish for those who were hungry. Thareous studied Ianvorr lapping at the waters, his tongue curling to sustain his load. When the Ice Dragon finished, Thareous bent down and cupped the water in his hands. A cold thrill ran through him. It cured him of the heat of the flight and even freshened in his mouth. Two more scoops sated him.

The rest lasted for a half-hour before they left again. Thareous smiled at the transparent lake till Ianvorr became airborne. It was not resplendent as the Eidon Lakes. It did come close. Rising sediment tainted the waters. They still held a sparkling grandeur. This somehow reminded him of Lefanarí.

Her eyes. They gleam, as two sapphires lit by the stars. She cannot be topped by any barmaid or bawd! She is the one for me. A picture of her entered his mind. He clamped his eyes shut and held the image. Her expression depicted sadness, longing, hurt, and lovelornness. He yearned to comfort her, to elate her with his presence.

"She must not be a part of you, Young Mage," Ianvorr said. His head tilted toward him. "You should think otherways. Consoling her would only reconstruct past dejections. She would remember Jalläthre and have to face reality."

"This I know," Thareous said. "I am sorry. I should reflect more on Galthoria."

"He has forgiven you, as will I always," Ianvorr said. "For now let her go. There are times when we must sacrifice our most beloved things. From this good results. In times of rebellion we are blinded by our wants and strike out at everyone."

"Until they are met," Thareous said.

"Alas, it is this way," Ianvorr said. "The universe is racked by desire. It is a place no worse than Annathias, in some countries. Kingdoms are roiled by the hatred in their hearts and launch vendettas. Keiratha is neighbors with such a kingdom. Zakumahk aims to pull down the pillars supporting us because he hates this land."

"Why is that?" Thareous asked. "What have we done to him?"

Ianvorr let out his lung-choking haze. "The Omnipotents did nothing. The Regime forced him from this country. They discovered him to be associating with the Malicer. He used me as the first stage of his retribution. This invasion is his second. This is why it is crucial we stop him."

"Retribution," Thareous said, furrowing his brow. "To think my adopted uncle would do it for that reason. He is insane. How does he plan to overthrow us? As far as I could tell, he has not that power. The Magicians could rout him with ease."

"Do not be so confident," the Ice Dragon said. "He has the Darkest Dictator on his side. With that much sorcery they could have us. I do not say there is no hope. It is just that presumptuousness undermines our focus in war."

His rider frowned and lowered his head. "Is there no escape from this? It is not I am disinclined to fight. Why must this take place? Why can there not be peace?"

"If we stood down, Keiratha would be soon as Valvassa," Ianvorr said. "Thus we should remain firm. The hardest thing in battle is the killing. At least to the caring and the humane. I must tell you to be strong. Have Lightkeeper in hand at every moment of the war. It is a mighty tool, if kept clean of innocent blood."

After this neither found any words. Thareous pushed Lefanarí from his mind and hugged the spinal spike in front of him. His eyes scanned the countryside. Seas of bluestem and sage extended to the azures or mountain-borders. Farmhouses miles from the nearest villages stood alone and unguarded. Few of them had neighbors. Soon a town surrounded by a tall palisade came below them. Rundown shanties stood within the walls.

"Kazsham," Ianvorr said. "This is the poorest habitation in Keiratha. The penury of its tenants is due to Greilph's attempts to take it over. He used King Jaldor's name to arrogate the authority of the village to himself. Our old ruler knows aught of this. The people were overtaxed. So they live like dogs fighting over scraps."

"This is a sad place," Thareous said. He watched the palisade for a bit before spotting movement near the tips of the stakes. *Something is not right.* He shut his eyes and found men with bows to be nocking arrows on the strings. "There is an attack!"

"Be at ease, Young Mage," Ianvorr said. "I have sensed it and contacted Jurtithan. He wants us to scatter as the shafts pass us. Earl Harleman, the official of Kazsham, must not have heard of our pardon."

Jurtithan flew over the settlement first. As soon as Ianvorr passed it, the archers discharged their shafts at them. At the Silver One's roar, the dragons rolled to the side. They circumvented the village and met back at the other side. Women and children rushed into their hovels, shrieking and bawling. The men at the ramparts hurried to restring their bows.

"Keep going!" Jurtithan shouted. Straight ahead the Keicor Alps sat beneath their perpetual storms. The dragons now pressed in as close as they could get to avoid another barrage. None came. Nahilmara said they had few arrows and would save it for the second assault, if it came.

Soon, after the dragons toppled their anticipation, they pierced the veil of snow. Jurtithan turned to avoid a sudden icebound mountain and set his course straight. He perceived familiar landmarks. Their route headed toward the Eternal Gorge. Winds howled in Thareous's ears like a hundred packs of wolves. Despite this he could make out the groans of Ianvorr and Nahilmara.

"We will get there before dusk," Thareous said. "That is not an hour off. Have strength! Let not your curse worry you; it shall not kill you." He awaited a complaint. Instead he heard the moaning die away. He thanked Galthoria for no incommodiousness.

As Jurtithan had said, they reached the Eternal Gorge before the Four Suns rose back into the heavens. They swooped into the zigzagging orifice and alighted at the bottom. The Silver One faced them. "I hear something echoing throughout the Ice Fortress. It is the voice of the false Archimage—this much I can tell. I advise you to be ready. We could be attacked by our own guardians."

REDEMPTION

"Let there be freedom! Let there be deliverance! We, my gathered ones, have been accused for deeds we did not commit. High treason! My brother, the king of this majestic land, is rash. He is a senile clown under a crown he is not worthy of. I, Deil, the rightful owner of the throne, wish to restore peace to Keiratha. By taking his place, I can do what he will not. Lead an army into war!"

A united roar brought a smile to the illusive prince's face. He saw his plan being fulfilled before his eyes. *Mayhap my objective shall be victorious after all. With the leaders away, I can lead these pawns against Galgon. Then their defenses can be weakened and the royal seat made ready!*

At length he raised his arms, silencing the band of dragons. "I would not be so quick to celebrate. There is still an obstacle: your fraternity. They shall not inspirit you to be done with the ennobled bungler. Now is the time to make a choice. Will you help institute a better future or watch the kingdom crumble? If we can get them to see our purpose, we can unify and defend the Capital.

"I fear we must fight to the last man if they resist. This is for the good of our country. We could be its final hope. Henceforward, if we are to turn away Valvassa yet, we must remove all resistance. Be willing and unopposed to this. By *your* claws this can be settled. End this threat ere it ends you. As one this can be accomplished. Omnipotents alike, help me uphold peace. What say you?"

A kraken stepped forward. "I speak for everyone when I say we want change."

Deil beamed. "It will be given to you."

They turned to leave the Assembly Hall, where they met. As they neared the threshold, a silver dragon blocked their way. Jurtithan eyed them one at a time until his gaze came to the prince. "What conspired you, Zakumahk? Where were you to take them? To Galgon? To frame us once again?"

"I know not what you mean," the false Archimage said. He saw a figure slide down the Silver One's side. He wore red and had hair white with age. He leaned on a knotty staff. Lines formed at his face. They formed a scowl, not elderliness. "Wh-who is this impostor?"

"Impostor?" Ancient spat. "I am not of that sort. It is you who are the fraud. May it be heard to you, Dark King, that your dissimulation shall be disclosed. These innocent creatures will not fall prey to the palms of a needless battle. As to me you may know I am the Nameless Magician of Kallenalza."

For a moment Deil's teeth clamped together. They opened to a loud fit of merriment. He threw back his head and let out long cackles. Ancient extended his staff toward him. Deil began to choke. The illusion faded but soon regained its tenor. "That being is not real," the false prince said. "He is a spurious concoction of children's tales."

"Speak not of a Demigod that way!" Ancient cried. His voice rang with such authority that Deil breathed in, almost choking again. "For too long you have denied Galthoria. Fool I label you and mean it full well. You have failed. You will face the Omnipotent Ones and not deceive them."

"Shall you not fulfill your duty?" Deil screamed at the seditious group. "They are here to impede us!" Upon seeing their lack of response, he growled and turned away. "*Asses*! I will succeed yet. Your precious land is to come under the banner of Varkin. He is to be your king!"

"Waste your breath no more, Uncle," Thareous said, entering atop Ianvorr's back. "You have still a chance to return to Valvassa. Go back to your ships and sail to your kingdom. Forget this aimless duty. It will mean only your death."

"Silence, you whelp," the prince sputtered. "You have not control over time nor fate. You have no power of death, that you may choose who remains or departs. To the same way, you are to not force me out."

By these words Thareous was saddened. "If only you could see the truth. If only you could discern the mercy shown to you. I force you to do aught. I know I have power over no such thing. Galthoria does, and him alone. He speaks on our behalf that we might be in favor of the Fates. We are bless—"

"Oh, shut up!" Zakumahk's illusion disdained him with a glare. "Keep your blessings, for they are malisons. It is visible you have regained your faith. Religion is an aimless duty. There should be simply one master— Malluesaer. He gives us what we crave and need. How can you serve a god who takes from his subjects?"

"Galthoria is no god!" Ianvorr thundered. "He does not seek attention like your heathen entity. He adores us as a father does his sons. He hates his enemies and loves his friends like any being. He bears no grudges. He merely waits for his children to gather back under his roof. There we are met with many embraces and talk."

"Save your sermon for the dogs!" Deil stormed. "It promises an afterlife of misery and monotony. Our cupidities are more important."

"This Malluesaer causes you to think," Ancient said. "In Annathias you are to labor night and day whilst you rue over your decision. Self is your worst foe. For from him you encounter your destroyer. Sin is an immense vacuum that can never be satiate. It sucks at your blood like a leech you cannot be rid of."

"Futile are your attempts to convince me," the false Archimage said. "Your pity and mercy are ill-spent. You have squandered time with feckless persuasions. Failure you have met since this scheme is a mere ruse. At this moment Nalla prepares to dine with a soldier from Ceilvre. Their meal is about to be delayed."

"What are you going to do to her?" Thareous demanded.

"So the youngling still has feelings for her. Well then, perhaps you shall not mind going to rescue her. She is about to become my tool. I knew you would thwart this invasion. I comprehended it because Malluesaer told me this crimson fool entered the Bottomlands. My felicitations, Ancient Archimage. You, a Demigod, have fallen under my expectations. Farewell now, dupes! Our meeting is not far off."

The illusion laughed as it whirled into a cyclone. Wind pulled at the tiny grains of snow or loose ice on the floor. They whizzed toward it and shot out of the top. Soon the air chilled like the blizzards outside. Then the twister thinned and flashed in a pervasive crimson light. The bystanders blinked to recover their sight.

Thareous scrambled back onto Ianvorr and spurred his side. "We have to get to Galgon. We must save Nalla ere she is taken."

"It is too late," the Ice Dragon said. "Any hope of intervening is disobliged by the distance. We would only get to the entrance before—"

"Something must be done!" his rider exclaimed. He turned to Ancient, who glowered. "What about you? Can you say the same? Is it hopeless? How would teleportation appeal? Could it be quick enough?"

"The spell has already been cast, Young Mage," he said. "Since we do not know where Zakumahk is camped, we could not follow her. Therefore I should say it is hopeless. I do not disregard your haste."

"I have broken up with her," Thareous said. "She is no more than a friend."

"I meant it not this way," Ancient said. "The word I should have applied is care, not haste. Indeed, you have dropped her. For your heart yields to another. Lefanarí, the Daughter of Yelva." He took full notice of the human's shock. "That is right, she is the descendant of the one who prophesied you. As is Aildeimor."

"Wh-who is their father?" Thareous quizzed.

"Artheil," Ancient said, glancing up. "He tested Yelva to see if she was lustful. As it became, they fell in love and had two children. He continued his killings, alas."

Jurtithan lowered his head. "It is so. We contain other problems now. I see it fit we rest for the night and then leave in the morn." He paused to scrape the floor with his claws. "We head for the Capital."

******

Zakumahk watched his fiends set up their encampment as the pink sunlight turned gray. In his hand he held a large rounded diamond. It glinted from the collecting stars above. He held a Tanazian crystal—the same magic trinket Jallaca used to spawn her images. He would use it for a darker purpose. He enclosed a barrier about it, extracting its underlying power to his mind. *Master?* Zakumahk inquired within his thoughts. *Are you there?*

I am. What is it now?

I report my mission was a success. Your plan has ravaged their hopes. The throne is to be yours ere the week is done. That is about two days from now ... if you cannot tell it from there. But that is not the matter! I can tell you Keiratha is ours!

Very good. I applaud you for your victory, Varkin said, voice dripping with sarcasm. *You fool! The Center of the Universe is not taken! So do not rejoice, and stay to the plan. Your duty is far from done.*

Fear not, My Lord, Zakumahk said. *We shall triumph. Malluesaer has blessed me with a worthy force. The princess's abduction will cause Thareous to come at me. I can then dispose of him as you ordered and affect the Omnipotents' certainty.*

He is not to pursue her. We have aimed at the wrong target. That elven wench is the one we should have gone for. Do not abort the spell. With Nalla in our ranks we can use her as a bargaining power with the king. He shall decree no attacks be sent so long as she is unspoiled. Make sure that is so.

With that the connection petered out. The Dark King sat on a pile of stones made to be a throne. He started to watch the fiends at work again and fingered his beard. *Nalla, you are the key to my conquest. At last I can prove my worth to Varkin. He can help me take my revenge. At dawn we march and overthrow the villages. Then we can use the townsfolk as captives as well. Jaldor will pay for what he did to my father!*

CHOICES

The face in the cheval glass winced as a brush tugged Nalla's hair. She fidgeted in her seat. A swarthy hand restrained her. Mulsa, the queen's old chambermaid, fought the entanglements in the gilded strands. The princess laid her hands on the lap of a cerulean gown. Bands of silver fastened around her underarms and under her bosom. She had to display her form to the soldier this way.

A complaint eluded her patient side as Mulsa pulled out a hair. The mulatta apologized more than sought. Nalla just stared in the mirror, studying the designs of her dress. Milk-white traceries ran about the top of it to the waist. There a belt-like trimming rounded to her back and rose into a tree. Embroidery of tulips adorned her skirt. Silver glitters coated maroon slippers.

"Milady, you look stunning in the absolutest," Mulsa said. She set the hairbrush on the dresser holding the mirror and analyzed her further. "That young man from Ceilvre is sure to admire you. Oh, what a blissful day it is!"

The princess frowned at her beauty. "Why would father want me to meet him? I do not plan to wed anyone. This is a waste of time. I am not going through with it."

"You have to," Mulsa said. "The king would have it no other way."

Nalla's frown deepened into a grimace. Rebellion sat on the pupils within her indigo irises. "My introduction to this man shall spawn a courting period. I would soon become troth-plighted to him. Then what? Marriage! The end of feminine freedom. Men make us think we are in love. They treat us like riffraff afterward."

"Your Ladyship, they—"

"They what?" Nalla seethed. "I will tell you. They deceive, use, beguile, tempt, tantalize, and ensnare us. We are their garden. We can be planted in any spot they choose. Once our roots are embedded, our hopes erected, they desert us to the weeds. Our water is stolen, the life sucked out from us, and we wither."

"All men are not bad," the chambermaid said. "Some care for their gardens."

"That is what I thought once," Nalla said, her scowl loosening. "The boy I loved forsook me. He chose an elf—a wench he could not consort—over me. So my affections toward his kind have soured. No man will claim me again."

"You should go now, Milady," Mulsa said, looking out a bay window. Pink rays seeped through clear violet drapes. She could tell the sky darkened. "The king shall be expecting you. May you depart with my blessing."

"Blessing," the princess said. "There is no blessing in what comes next. There is no profit in wedlock. Only *misery!*" She dug her hands in her face and sobbed. "Thareous, why did you force me into this corner? Why could we have not wedded? Why must we be separated by our ranks?"

It took Mulsa ten minutes to settle her down. By the time her tears ceased, a reddish gray tint pervaded the room. Her beautician handed her a handkerchief, which she wiped her face with. Then she got up, lifted her skirt, and went out the door. In the hall her cheeks flushed with indisposition. She fought with herself to return to her bedchamber or go on. She knew she had no choice.

So she ran down the passage to a spiral staircase. At the bottom she found another corridor where she took a left. After a while she came to the banquet hall and went inside. She wove about the tables until reaching an entrance at the far end. For one last time she entered a hallway, this one being the most decorated. Here she turned right and continued to the throne room. The two guards lowered themselves as she slipped by.

Inside, Nalla plodded toward her father, his back turned to her. He revolved his top half, coming to face her. He gripped his cane more firmly than usual. "Daughter, you have decided to show. I am pleased that it is at this time. We are behind schedule."

Gazing past him, she saw a mahogany ladened with a melange of foods. Servants milled about it, bringing in several flasks of wine. Two chairs were positioned at the head and foot of the long ovoid table. She glowered at them, knowing what it meant. Then she saw the menials pour zin into two chalices and shook. "Where is he?"

Jaldor smiled and put a hand on her cheek. He turned it to the right, toward his throne. A man sat in it, the royal scepter in hand and crown on his head. A monarchical purple tunic garbed him, laced at the top to fit his frame. He was able-bodied and broad-shouldered, but not hefty. A wine-red cape cushioned his back against the rise of the throne. He stared at her in awe. He soon became timid and dropped his examination.

In a rage she jerked her head from the king and glared at him. "Father, what is this? Why is he in the royal seat?"

"Because my term is to be over soon," Jaldor said. "Someone told to me three days ago I would die in the last battle. Therefore I am in need of a replacement. I give my rule to him, for he used great military strategy to protect Ceilvre from the Defenders. A leader such as him could do what I have failed to."

The man got up and walked to them. He reached for Nalla's hands, deeming it to be fine with her. She kept them at her side. So there he put his also and gazed at her. It chilled her bones and summoned impassivity.

"I am Kathar Lielesson by name," he said. "By the series of invasions of that rebellious mob, I see the country's safety first and foremost."

"That is not all you want to see," she said.

"Nalla, be a lady!" Jaldor ordered. "You shall treat him as you did Thareous Haverinsson. If you do not, your mother's crown is placed on Mareinia. Is that understood?"

"Completely, Father," Nalla said, hanging her head. She would have proclaimed she did not want to be queen had he not mentioned Thareous. Her heart tore in two as she pined it could not be her way. Once again she cursed him for giving her up.

"Please, Your Majesty," Kathar said. "It is not my intent for there to be strife. She does not have to wed me. We can control the people apart. Not that I am going against your will, I should hope. Somehow … I prefer it that way."

"Your words are reasonable," the king said. "That is another basis I want you in my place. She needs someone who can tame her. I lack in these resources. You, on the other hand, attain the authority necessary. Now I must leave you alone. The night is young. The war is close. May your discussions be merry!"

He hobbled out of the room with his servants behind him. Kathar took the chair nearest them and offered it to her. Nalla went to the other end and sat. She took her plate, piled it high with greasy chicken, and jammed the first leg into her mouth. Though against her nature she wished to do anything to disgust this gallant. Juices poured down her chin and trickled onto her plate.

Much to her surprise Kathar did the same, even if he seemed hesitant. Every action mirrored hers in a parody of punctiliousness. She clenched her teeth and breathed out. Her eyes bore him down so that he stopped and dropped the chicken. It clattered on the side of his plate, the thick end leaning on the tabletop. "I-I am sorry. I have not the manners to grace the meal as you," he said.

In his state of insistence Nalla beheld what she could not through insensitivity. She trembled as he looked at her with slate eyes. A brazier above them illuminated his dark hair. It went below his cheeks in spruce sideburns. Still continuing, it stopped and split about his lips. He kept mustache and beard well-trimmed also. She then gazed at his brow, which furrowed in concern.

"Milady?" Kathar asked.

She closed her eyes and shook her head. "All is well. You are pardoned."

"I worry now of else," he said. "You appear ill. Should I cancel the dinner? I could arrange it for another time and—"

"N-no," Nalla said. "I rather we complete this tonight." She took a napkin and pretended to wipe her face. She covered it to conceal the redness. *Thareous, you have been bested at last! Now my heart is mended and my hopes replenished. You may love who you will. I have found a gentleman who cares about me.*

They ate for a few minutes without words before sitting back. Nalla lowered her chin to where her neck ached. She closed her eyes, recalling the reverie she savored. She longed to be among it again—and if so, for it to never decrease. Then footsteps approached. Opening her eyes back up, she saw Kathar standing over her. A frisson raised goosebumps. She did not erect her wards as amid most men.

"I must go," he said. "The morrow brings with it many preparations. I do hope to see you again." He smiled, forcing her cheeks to elevate as well. "This time, I mean not for your body."

Nalla dropped her gaze and sighed. "I ... I too would like to meet again."

The king-to-be took her hand. "There is no other way I would have it." For a moment he stared at her slender fingers and back at her. He leaned over, never having done this before, it appeared.

Get on with it! she thought.

Then she felt something tugging in her stomach. She fell from her seat with a cry. Rolling on the flagstones, her arms and legs flailed. Darkness overwhelmed her gaze so that she saw no more.

Only Kathar's voice penetrated the void. "Your Highness! Galthoria's grace! Guards, get in here! Guards!"

She could not discern the outer world. Nalla saw her being for what it was. In one dark section an entity of beauty stared back; in the other a shadow, an unloved thing. She shrieked as she saw the second move toward her. She flung her arms in front of her. Against all hope she burned to repel this aberration. It would not be so. As she took a peek from between her arms, she spotted a monster that snatched her in its jaws.

Inside Nalla sensed her body changing. A charge of electricity lunged through her. A numbness overtook her—a numbness she wanted to go away. She felt like a creature frozen in ice. She could not move. Whatever deviltry controlled her also imprisoned her. She caught sight of the end result to her transformation in her mind. And she wished she had never disdained her beauty.

Without warning the darkness receded. Or at least total darkness. Now she lay under the pall of nighttime. Whitened skin looked irregular against her cerulean dress. Inky strands of hair fell over her shoulders. She picked it up and wailed. A hand placed on her shoulder made her stop. She looked up.

"Fear not, my princess," Zakumahk said. "All you have to do is help us win this war and I shall change you back."

THE LAST DAY

Dawn the next day, Jurtithan led the dragons from the Ice Fortress. They took to the skies and flew into the blizzards. The snowfall kept tugging them back, for they flew against it. Ianvorr's body shielded Thareous. Frigid drafts still floated at him. He pulled about him a flannel coat provided by Orkon. He laced a hood, almost too tight for his head, at the neck.

A few hours elapsed before they erupted from the clouds. Daylight glared off the snow-clouds and refracted on the dragons' scales. The prairieland appeared as a wavy sea of green. In the distance Galgon was but a speck, Thareous noticed. It would be awhile ere they got there.

He breathed deep the cool and unpolluted air, enjoying the freedom. The clouds held a flamy tinge as they ambled across the sky. The fringes of the horizon appeared to be streaked with fire and purple. A flock of sparrows chirped in the distance, giving warning of the dragons. They set course for the Capital and did not wander.

Ianvorr gazed forward and perceived a long line strung from Galgon. "Silver One, there is a strange activity near the city. I cannot make it out. You are the one with the stronger eyes. Perhaps you can tell."

"I have seen it too," Jurtithan said. "It is aught to fear. They are the Galgonians, not a procession of fiends. This is the exodus emptying Galgon and making for Albra. The Royal Family, save Jaldor, is probably with them."

"What about Nalla?" Thareous inquired.

"You know the answer to that," Ianvorr said. "She has been taken, without a doubt. As soon as we touch down, the king will have us look for her."

"And will you?"

"Of course not. We would not choose one life over Keiratha."

******

211

Jaldor seethed at these very words when they finally came before him. "I have ordered you to go! How is it you repeal the command of a ruler? I brought your order back from the depths. This is how you repay me? Risk my daughter's life in the hands of that *maniac*? Why do you allow this, unless you are all traitors?"

"We are not," Jurtithan said.

"Then go and retrieve her," the old man said.

"King Jaldor, with respect, you think not of your country," Nahilmara said. "This is a choice that you must examine. What might happen if we did go? Zakumahk would have an ambush waiting for us. He would use magic to disperse our forces. His fiends would finish us off while we fled. We would be weakened. I have seen their numbers and can tell you we are too even."

"There is always a chink in armor," the king said. "Therefore, Jurtithan, I shall see to it you leave at once or I will disaffiliate with you."

"That would be even greater folly," Ianvorr said. "Should you do this we would turn to the Dark Legion and depose you. Then we could see a new government is set—one that does not involve a lifelong ruler."

"You are a part of the Defenders, then!" Jaldor exclaimed.

"Nay, we work against them, best we can," Jurtithan said. "They are but a trifle to what is coming. The Dark King brings demonic enforcers that will burn villages and oppress your people. We need your collaboration to pinion this. Keiratha used to be a land of strong-minded men. They have lost the sense of duty that used to drive them. They have lost their faith in Galthoria, as have you."

At this the king began to wheeze and convulse. "Galthoria … my master! I have neglected you for many years! I have cursed your servant who foretold of my death. My heart is weary of sin. Dotage has brought my mind to forget you, thus becoming rash. Oh, Friend, I am ready to come to you. Still, I must petition you keep Nalla safe." He closed his eyes and bobbed his head in grief. "Away from me, now. All of you! I give my daughter's life in the hands of the Glorifier. Malluesaer has bonded me to old age for too long. No more!"

They had met outside the entrance to the city. As Jaldor rode across it on his dappled roan, the drawbridge raised and the portcullis lowered. The Silver One sat on the ground and respired a windstorm. "What is done is done. A dotard has been made well by the mere mention of the Chief Entity."

Thareous picked at grass for a while. The others spoke in secret. He had been listening to the conversation with the king in interest. None of it had to do with Nalla. He decided long ago she was not for him. He did wonder what would occur if they did go. Then the others dispersed and he went up to Jurtithan. "What are now we to do?"

"Prepare for the war," the Silver One said. "The elves are scrapping wood from a lumber depot since the city is empty. We are to build three fraises in front of the city. This is where the Legion should attack from. Aildeimor will be behind it with the best bowmen. The centaurs shall defend both sides. The Magicians, along with you, are to be at the back. This way you can protect the drawbridge."

The elves came with the timber a short time later. They took out daggers and began to whittle away at the ends. Shavings soon littered the ground. They made perfect stakes. Their tips looked like sharpened pencils. Next they distributed rope and cross-tied the posts. They selected a large tract ahead of the northern side of Galgon for planting them there. Soon they completed the fraises.

Everyone broke for lunch. The female elves had found ingredients within the city and set up soup stations outside. The males brought large slabs of salted meat out from several shops in the marketplace for the dragons. Lines proceeded from about five miles from the moat. They filled bowls of the vegetable stew and passed out to those preceding.

After Thareous got his bowl, he skirted about those already seated. His eyes scanned the crowds for Lefanarí. He saw Vellar heading his way, so he stopped. "Hullo! I have not seen you since I was here last."

"And you have not seen Nalla since your disappearance," the flaxen-haired soldier said. "I suppose you were with the Omnipotent leaders when they spoke with the king. The enemy took her."

"I have heard," Thareous said. He put up a ward to hold off any eavesdroppers.

"It may interest you to know she met the king's surrogate," Vellar said. "When the war is over, they are to be wed, doubtless. If she lives to see that day, she might remember you. Then she would ask the crown-king to arrest you. Under what charges I would not know. You could be a fugitive."

"Why are you telling me this?" Thareous queried.

"Warning, more likely," Vellar said. "I am warning you of what could happen. It would be best if you went into hiding for a spell."

Without another word Thareous set down his soup and straightened. He looked straight into his friend's eyes. Truth seemed to emanate from them like the day he first met him. Any master illusionist could capture that. So he rolled up his sleeve below Vellar's eyeline and hooked him under the jaw. The soldier lost his bowl as he fell. "What was that for?"

"I had to be sure you were you," Thareous said.

"To the expense of my lunch," Vellar said.

Bending over, Thareous picked up his soup. He handed it to the flaxen-haired soldier, who rubbed his jaw. "Have mine. I am not hungry." After Vellar accepted it, he turned and treaded off. A little ways off he found Aildeimor and Lefanarí amongst the elves. They chattered and laughed so much he could not catch their conversation. For a moment he stood there. Then he joined the group.

"Annihilator!" the Elf Commander cried. "Sit with us, will you not?" He patted a patch of grass between him and his sister. "Tell us what occurred in Draer-Vollith." The sapphire gaze of Lefanarí inspired the request.

Thareous recounted every detail since his arrival to the departure. He even threw in the incident at the Ice Fortress and how they learned of Nalla's abduction. This he said with lower spirits. Once again, he did not love her. His concern for his new pick outdistanced any visitations of the past.

"You have been through much," Aildeimor said. "Alas, that the giant-clan should be shamed so. They are apt to fail in renown one day."

"Indeed they did," Thareous said, "with their idolatry."

"This was not their fault," Lefanarí said. "It is not our place to judge them. They believed what they did because Harvok convinced them into it. He misled them by his creeds. It is no wonder they have declined in their preeminence. Their kind should be pitied, not maligned. Their pride should not have sentenced Harvok to ostracism."

"It cannot be undone," Aildeimor said. "Though we can pity them at present. In any event let us speak of merrier things. This course could darken our mood." He faced Thareous. "How is your heart? Has Galthoria counted you immune to temptation?"

The human glanced at Lefanarí. His blood warmed. "I feel still the affliction of my past. It is alluring. My faith is thus far insurmountable. I cannot believe how free I seem. How could I have foregone this for so long? The dolor in me makes me fancy a lamentation. There is aught to lament over. Something holds it back."

"That is the Glorifier's hand," an elf said. "He is at work in your heart. You can sense his presence if you close your eyes and focus. He is all around us. In the forest the trees can be felt breathing. This is his gift of life."

"Yes," the voice of Ianvorr said, who came up to the group. "All you have said is true. My friends, Galthoria has directed this discourse so it did not go ill." His eyes shut into slits. "Not to disparage this, there is a message I must herald. Aildeimor, you are needed to trump the Call. Now our forces must gather."

The Elf Commander nodded and reached for his hunting-horn. He stood and put it to his lips. Then he inhaled and blew into the mouth of it. A euphonious note rose, resonating in the distance. Another followed, this time louder and more melic. One last melody sounded, continuing on in the same pitch for many seconds.

Distant reverberations trembled the ground in the west. Giants, dwarves, and fauns marched from the mountains. To the east the outlying snow-clouds of the Keicors parted. Leviathans, wyverns, griffins, and more elves flew between them. From the north came the rocs and centaurs. They made haste as if being chased. Black lines arched in the sky and fell within their numbers.

"Galthoria's grace!" Lefanarí cried. "The Dark Legion is overrunning them."

"Should we prepare to attack?" Thareous questioned.

At that moment Jurtithan charged up to them. "Hold your ground! We shall not act without knowing they mean to beset us. This may be a time of parley. Although the rocs and centaurs fly from them, the Legion could just be protecting themselves."

"Zakumahk is not that merciful," Ianvorr said

"I must agree with you," the Silver One said. "Once everyone gets here, they shall assume their positions. It appears the war may start early. Slight is the chance the enemy could spare us." He moaned and watched the bolters.

Aralles came into view after a few tense seconds. Dark shafts whizzed past or struck his thick feathers. He appeared to be gasping for breath. He still moved with exigent yet dilatory beats. As he neared, he swooped and landed, devoid of any grace. "The villages Liekle and Famor have been taken. The Legion was too many."

Uhrar stopped next to him and bent over, hands on his forelegs. His face reddened from exertion and his bare body drowned in sweat. When he regained his composure, he straightened up and clenched a sword in his hand. "Those black-hearted demons will not pester us any longer since we are here." He clomped his front right hoof for emphasis. "By my blade not a single devilling shall live!"

More rocs and centaurs poured in as he said this. The horse-men huddled together, being vigilant of the crowds. They turned northward to spot the torn gonfalons waving like sable shadows. At the brink of the land they saw the Dark Legion stop. Some fiends strung their bows, roaring and screeching at them.

"Aildeimor," Jurtithan said, "inform the king of our plight."

"It shall be done," the Elf Commander said, then ran off toward Galgon.

Thareous watched in utter shock. He peered at Ianvorr. "Do you think Zakumahk will attack us tonight? Or could it be he has to make preparations that should take till morning to set?" His heart went out to this hope.

"I do not know, forsooth," the Ice Dragon said. "All that can be discerned is the last battle is about to commence. We decide by how we fight for Keiratha's fate. If we fail, the Center of the Universe dies. Thus every country and continent is to crumble."

By now the other classes began to arrive, save those of the mountains. By foot they were much slower than those on wings. Kyjre landed with the wyverns. He went to locate Ianvorr. He searched every wall of the Capital until he spotted him. Thareous conversed with Ianvorr, but spotted Kyjre and excused himself.

Ianvorr, confused by Thareous's departure, looked around. Then when his eyes fell on the wyvern, they hardened. He sniffed; icy haze covered his vision.

Kyjre did not give up. *To be wise is to use knowledge well. I have been wise, but in a different sense. I used my "wisdom" to irritate others. This ceases now.* He proceeded through the stinging cloud and stared at the astounded Ice Dragon. "Brother Ianvorr, I would like to speak with you."

"Speak as you may," he said. "Just be rid of your impertinence. It insults your kind and shames their pride. In this way you are a shame to them."

"I come not to fight," Kyjre said, "but to explain. That is, why I am always so uppity. Or this is how you view it, at least. I hide behind a mask of jollity and endorse waggeries when I can. I mean no harm by this. Though it appears I am boasting, in truth, I veil my pain. This pain is the anguish of war. I cannot abide the bloodshed. I pray you can understand this. None of this is for annoyance or abhorrence."

Inclining his head, Ianvorr watched the Fire Dragon like a master to his dog. He considered the words and saw their sagacity. Somehow his soul warmed and melted away the coldness of his heart. The contrition on Kyjre's ligaments told him the apology was candid. "I believe you, Braveheart. For you have cut into the very roots of the problem and removed them. Ice and blaze are not meant to mingle, I suppose."

"They are this day," the wyvern said. "The day ere our probable end."

Catching his insinuation, Ianvorr raised his snout heavenward. A beam of ice shot from his maw and scattered into snowflakes. Kyjre emitted a mushroom of flame that overcame the mist. Steam hissed upon contact. A warm cloud descended upon them. Thus they mitigated past belligerence.

******

For the rest of the day Thareous mixed with Aildeimor and Lefanarí. They talked seldom, focusing on the remote camp of the Dark Legion. As evening neared, they lit tiny campfires. In case the Dark King decided to attack that night, they erected ground torches near the fraise. Jurtithan decided a watch cycle should be set up. It consisted of dragons and elves.

Everyone out of the vigil went to bed early. Thareous slept at the feet of his elven friends. His eyelids became heavy and his stomach felt sick. He dreaded the morning—also he dreaded the night. Of late his dreams had grown to be disturbing. He fell asleep in little time.

He found himself in a world of darkness. Then two slanted eyes of a scarlet radiance opened before him. A voice rumbled like the thunder of the heavens. It said that he was "the Summoner," manager of a realm called the Yolmakz. He told Thareous the Fates had become cruel. He had a plan to dethrone them. Another voice roared down, ordering the Summoner to be gone. And the eyes closed …

Silence followed. Before long, Thareous felt the ground below break apart. He fell into deep shadow. Eons of his life seemed to pass. It all ended in an instant. He blinked and saw he had been transferred to a new place. He had no recollection of undergoing a landing.

Light, streaming ribbons of light, distracted him from this. They were red, blue, white, green, brown, and gray. He noticed that the room held these colors in different sections. The wall reached up toward a tunnel of blackness. Where I fell through, *he guessed. Next he observed the bases. Curved dividers separated the areas. Between them six orbs bearing the hues of the streamers hovered.*

In a golden flash six dragons replaced the spheres, bowing in turn after a red one. They arose, formality and regard in their movements. The scarlet beast spoke. "I am Malmeir, the Dragon of Fire. The place that you stand is the Chamber of the Elements. Ere you are debriefed of your summons, permit me to present my colleagues."

There was Nueasa the Dragon of Water; Kazion the Dragon of Ice; Denorias the Dragon of Air; Vlaedren the Dragon of Stone; and Zolten the

Dragon of Storms. Each was made of the element that they were labeled after but in, of course, a draconic body.

"Now," Malmeir said, "for your being here. Ahtariek, the Dragon of Time, is missing. He was last seen by us on Mondoria, Island of the Cyclopes. We cannot go there. Those one-eyed brutes build weapons that absorb our essences. Therefore you are required to find and rescue him. Once he is in your possession, we shall call you back here. Know that we could ask this of no one else. Only you can be trusted."

"What do you mean?" Thareous queried. "Why could you not send another? I do not even know who you are. What if you are a creation of Varkin's?"

"We do not blame you for being cautious," Nueasa said. "By saying just you could be trusted, we meant only you are able. You see, before Galthoria's withdrawal, Ahtariek could die. Should this happen, time will surcease."

"Someone could assume his entity," Kazion said, blunt.

Denorias sighed and rolled his eyes. "In any event Varkin must not do this. Time is able to be sustained in here. Elsewhere left, it could discontinue. It depends on you."

"I might not survive this war," Thareous said. "I might not be the one. How is it you can tell? For the last time who are you?"

"We are Six Bearers of the Elements," Malmeir said. "Galthoria has told us you are the Appointed Archimage. You are the one to slay Varkin. You shall live past this trial. For he loves you and has forgiven you of your bygone misdeeds ..."

******

Something nuzzled Thareous's side. He opened his eyes to see Ianvorr standing over him. The sky was as black as ink; the rays of the Four Suns peeked past it. "Young Mage, the Dark Legion is on the move. No one reported a thing in the night. Come full daylight, we are to behold what we could not."

Thareous sat up and strapped on his belt. "Where is Zakumahk?"

"He has been spotted in front of the vanguard," Ianvorr said. "He holds a white banner. Jurtithan has gone to meet him. This may be a ruse. He could be killed. Peace must be held for as long as it will."

"You mean a parley?" Thareous asked.

"Aye," the Ice Dragon whispered. "You must join the Magicians now. Hasten!"

The Silver One flew down and landed between them. "Thareous, your uncle wishes to speak with you. He is being held in my mind right now. I shall repeat what he says." He closed his eyes and contacted Zakumahk …

"'Nephew, this day every drop of blood will be put on your conscience. Whether you live or not, your life shall not last long. I keep no resistance. I will take no chance of Varkin falling. He has been restrained from his return to kingship too long. So know that once I topple this kingdom, all of you are to be executed. Then I shall set out and resurrect the Darkest Dictator, who is to not let Keiratha decay'."

A silence followed as Jurtithan dropped his head. "This is his plan, then. To use our land as a second chance. The past cannot be reversed. Valvassa is right next door, a reminder of his failure. In a tide of flashbacks Varkin might ravage Keiratha!"

Then the worst happened. A fanfare of cacophony announced the advance of the enemy. The three of them whirled their gazes northward. The Dark Legion marched toward Galgon. Zakumahk strode in front, the white banner in hand. Now it was ablaze—an emblem that comity turned to ash. Thareous hurried to his place beside his father and glanced out at the decisive skirmish.

THE BATTLE FOR GALGON

From his position amid the Magicians, Thareous saw the centaurs stand their ground. Fiends reached them and hacked at the front line. Most of the horse-men deflected their blows. The elves fired arrows into the oncoming waves. Their enemies responded with their black shafts. Some fiends tried to open the fraise. They got tangled in the pickets or jabbed by their tips.

As for the dragons and rocs, they held an empyreal assault. They fought zarjkakons and Amarzrell. Sometimes they dove to wipe out fiends. Their elements contested against the enemy flyers' flames. Most of the time they used the claws to finish them off. Then they would carry them over their forces and let them go.

Holding his sword to the ground, Haverin glowered. "This is the first onset I have been in. Already it looks unpromising. Do not worry, my son. I shall survive, by the Glorifier's hand. He watches over us."

Thareous scanned the battle before answering. A division of goblins skirted about the defenders and headed toward the city. "I do not doubt Galthoria would keep you alive, Father. Still, I would suggest we leave our eyes on our nemeses. If you look to the right, you will see my mean."

The Master Magician's brow tightened as he peered that way. He brought his sword up and slew it at the goblins. "To the east! The enemy is trying to slink by! Prepare, men. This is where our training falls into play. Onward!"

All of the Magicians charged that way except for Thareous. Over his observation he had seen Quaron amid the elves. Though he opposed vengeance, he wished to fulfill his oath to repay the treacherous guard for his parents' coerced intercourse. He pursued him. Aildeimor joined in the chase. They hacked at fiends along the way till they overtook him.

Seeing them coming, Quaron snatched an elf by the neck and held him in front of him. "Get away if you value thisss blighter's life!" His grip tightening, the elf reddened. He clawed at the gauntlet and gasped for air.

Aildeimor sheathed his skean and took up his bow. He jerked an arrow from its quiver and fit it on the string. Then he aimed it at the snake face. "Let him go."

Quaron put his blade onto his victim's chin. "Indeed, I shall, with his head ssseparated from his shoulders." To prove his point, he pulled the cutting edge in more, bringing blood to the cold steel. A simper spread over his longish face. "You will not even hear him ssscream."

"Try it not, Commander!" the captive cried. "I am content to go. Just finish him!"

Seeing Aildeimor intended to, Thareous snatched his bow and pulled it back. "We need all the hands we can get. This would not do." Seeing his elven friend's indecision, he went on. "Call in for backup. Every man's life is valuable."

At that moment fiends surrounded Quaron. He had heard their conversation. Thareous found that to be plausible. Their foe was cunning and acute. This bordered problematic since they knew not how to counter his wit. Thareous resolved to protect this soul. To the astonishment of everyone watching, he leapt forth.

Theldaneru beheaded a lich. Then Thareous's blade parried a succubus's whinyard and swung it about, then jabbed. A troll clobbered the ground in front of Thareous. He activated Keilkanur and sawed the brute in half. Now those protecting Quaron began to attack Thareous altogether. Albeit, they could not match the buckler's gurging spikes. It hewed their weapons and mutilated their bodies.

Not believing his eyes, Quaron throttled his sword. He removed it from his hostage's neck and eased in front of him. He still clung to the elf. Thareous strode up to him, knowing the captive could be used as a shield. They each waited for the other to make the first move. They perceived their rival's actions could be expected from then on.

At length Thareous angled Thornwhirl and poised it. Then he inched in while Quaron studied his footwork. Quaron's right foot shifted fornent his left and he circled about Thareous. A stop marked that Quaron was about to make his move. His sword was set so that if struck, it would go into the elf.

Thareous hit the blade's side and made Theldaneru slide down to the guard. Spikes jumped from Kielkanur's sides and veered at Quaron. His foe ducked and stepped back. With his sword immobilized by Lightkeeper, he could not ward off the spikes. He would wait and give his pawn to Thornwhirl.

Thareous deactivated his buckler and positioned it at his side. He pushed his golden sword into Quaron's steel. The crossguards snagged. Thareous flicked his wrist and sent his enemy's weapon flying. Then he lunged at Quaron and jammed the side of Theldaneru's pommel at his head. They both fell over. The elf escaped and ran off. A company of his people hemmed him in.

In the interim Thareous and Quaron struck with elbows and fists. The Young Mage overpowered him. He whirled over on the quisling, his knees pinning down his chest, and put Lightkeeper to his chin. They stopped the struggle for a moment to catch their breaths. All the while the victor glared at his prey.

"So here you are, in my grasp," Thareous said. "An inch more and I will cut your jugular. You know why I am this way. You are the reason. I understand you had friends. Where are they?" The tip of Theldaneru grazed his skin.

Quaron threw back his head and cackled. His hood fell to reveal a smirking human face. Tufts of disheveled brown strands fell back over his sconce. He had the complexion of a linen sheet. "We are even now. Family honor besmeared is akin to death. My father has been redeemed, rest his soul ..."

"I did not kill him," Thareous said. "Zakumahk lied to you. He is using you to kill me for something I did not. That matters no more. You are to join him in Annathias. I find no pleasure in this. I must kill you all the same, to uphold my parents' reputation."

"That is what you think," Quaron said. His simper deepened at Thareous's puzzlement. Turning both palms toward him, a net of lightning formed and wrapped about him. He flew back several feet, bellowing as it vibrated inside him. The traitor bound to his feet and set the cowl back on his head. He found his sword near the corpse of a faun and sheathed it. Then he ran into the multitudes, not to be seen for some time.

Thareous growled as he got up and scanned both armies. A goblin jumped at him and opened its mouth, showing webs of saliva and yellowed teeth. He deflected its scimitar and cut off its left shoulder. Aildeimor joined him again and paralyzed a changeling in the knee. He slashed its ghastly face out of his sight afterward.

They delved into the ranks of fiends and Omnipotents. Amid the fray an ogre forced his aggressors back with a massive mace. Thareous went at the ogre as Aildeimor peppered it with arrows. When the ogre noticed them, it lifted the thorny club and sent it toward the Young Mage. Thareous sidestepped in time and grabbed one of the spikes, vaulting on the shaft. Thinking him to be crushed, the ogre hefted it over his shoulder.

Here Thareous jumped on the ogre's head and jabbed Theldaneru into it. Roaring, the hairy brute tried to grab him with its free hand. The gold blade sank deeper, to the brain. This time the mace whirled in the air, about to be aimed at Thareous. He jerked his sword out at the last second. The ogre smashed his head with his own weapon.

Thareous landed on his back. He knew he would be attacked and slain if he lay there, so he got up quick. For a moment he stopped and panted, looking north. Then his breath caught short. In the distance he could make out erected structures moving their way. The light of the Four Suns did not help any. His eyelids closed and next parted to slits. He gasped and pried his eyes open after he saw it.

"Siege-towers!" he cried to everyone. "Siege-towers are on their way here!" His mind buzzed as he dashed from the assault. *There must be a way to warn Jurtithan. Likely he is too busy fighting to have noticed those. Zakumahk is sly to use this against us.* Dread infringed upon his heart. He felt defeated. The Legion would take the city.

Coming upon a circle defended by elves, he sat and shut his eyes again. *Ianvorr?* He waited a while before the Ice Dragon responded to him. *Mark, you must find Jurtithan and tell him siege-towers move in from the north. The Dark King has ployed us. I would not be surprised if this is not the main invasion.*

I, too, have wondered this, Ianvorr said. *He has brought ordnances. That is, catapults, bombards, and the like. To any speed, I will contact the Silver One. Mayhap Diermahk can pull back some of his men. This must stop ere it begins.*

All right, Thareous said, relief smothering his words. The din of war—the clang of swords and the crunch of bone and flesh—resounded like trumpets. Everything blurred by in a tumult of bellows and death. It saddened him there had to be so much bloodshed. *What would you have me do now?*

Fight to the death, Ianvorr said. Another pause stretched out the time before his next response came. *It is all we can do. If the Legion breaches the city, you should go to the king. For his protection. Now I must depart. Thank you much for the information.*

The connection slid out of Thareous's mind. He sighed and got to his feet. "Go to the king. I suppose I am the only one who could guard him. Then again he may already be dead. This could be a trap. That voice could have been a replica of Zakumahk."

He felt it not to be, with conviction. *Fight to the death. It is all we can do.* Those words Ianvorr would use for bolstering. He dropped his wariness and stood up. His weapons still in hand, he charged back into the battle.

For hours nothing out of the blue occurred. Thareous kept an eye on the siege-towers while he fought. Other than that this was a bland engagement. He had presumed it to be worse. He only had to focus on his enemies' moves and expect any artifices. Also, he minded his milieu, making sure no foes double-teamed him.

The day swam on. Midday came and went like a memory. Neither side seemed to be winning. It was a consistent struggle to disclose the underdog. The entire time both sides pushed toward or away from Galgon. Thus far the Dark Legion they kept within a mile near the fraise. Only a few fiends had bled through the main mass. The fauns and dwarves between stopped them.

And then it happened.

The squeaking of heavy oaken wheels made everyone stop and stare. A melange of military weapons was carted behind the Legion. Ogres and trolls pulled them, with a zarjkakon at the catapult. A large wooden tube raised on four wheels and bound by iron was the most to be seen. Wains full of boulders or metal balls stopped by these things and the catapult. The siege-towers pushed on.

Diermahk and two dozen other giants went to counter them. Zarjkakons abandoned their fight with the dragons and flew at them. The ogres and trolls dropped the ropes they used to tug the armaments and unloaded everything. Kyjre led the wyverns to incinerate the armaments. The attack kept on after flying fiends opposed them.

Thareous had just separated the spine of a cacodemon when he noticed this. He turned his full attention to it and growled. He slammed a lich's cutlass away and beveled its torso. Then he gasped as he saw who stood behind the fallen lich.

"Well, you have managed to make it this far," Zakumahk said. He wore his pinnacled helm. The faceplate was raised. A sneer plastered his jaw. Shadows covered the top half of his face. "I figured you would have expired long ago. Alas, since my fiends could not accomplish this, I must."

Kielthavra whirled at him. Thornwhirl knocked it to the side. It recuperated in a trice. Zakumahk chortled as he twirled the saber in his hand and thrust out. Thareous parried, the tip of it an inch from his throat. He repeated the move. The buckler got between it this time. A feint deceived Theldaneru. The Dark King kicked his nephew in the chest. He tumbled over onto his stomach.

Before he could recover, a boot pushed Kielkanur down past Thareous's control. A tingling numbness lingered in his arm. He groaned and tried to turn over. Zakumahk kicked his side. "I offered you a chance!" He leaned over and jerked Thareous to his feet. "More than once. You were forewarned about what would happen if you refused. Now you must die. This time I project no mercy."

Hurling Thareous away, Zakumahk lowered his helm's ventail. His nephew landed with a clunk and rasped in pain. Three strides and Zakumahk stood at his side, Kielthavra turned down at him. "It has been pleasure fighting you. Even more so, it is a pleasure killing you. Farewell, boy." The saber jabbed into his back. It did not go through. He tried it again. Now he stopped. Looking at his target, he saw no barrier. "What is this?"

Thareous rolled over and glared at him. Though he wore no outer armor and wielded no magic, he contrived to stay alive. A smirk came over his face once he locked his legs about his uncle's. Then he rolled over and tripped him. While he fell, he pulled his legs in and got to his feet. He pointed Theldaneru at the man's chest.

"Go ahead," the Dark King said. "Slay me. You have bested me, after all. You merit it. For that I owe you my congratulations. Of course, doing so would inflict upon you the label *Murderer*. Surely this is not your want."

"My want?" Thareous said. "*My* want? This has aught to do with me. It is what I had to do the first time I was able. Since the chance is on me at last, why should I dither?" He slid the blade down the chest plate and to the helmet. With it he opened the visor to see if the face inside held any remorse. It did not.

"You do not have to," Zakumahk said. "You are to make that choice. You have the power to decide the fate of Keiratha. Do it. I care not. After this life I go to a place where there is no resistance. That, to me, is utopia."

"Do not listen to him!" Lefanarí ran up to his side. "Finish him right now. He is instilling vacillation within you. He is the only reason the fiends fight. They are mindless and imprudent." She graced him with a glance of her sapphire eyes. "Telling you what he desires is telling you not to give it to him."

For a few seconds Thareous considered both of their words. His elven friend made the most sense. His uncle had aroused his passion for following Self. *Indeed, getting what you craved is desire.* Since he repented, did this mean he could not have his will? Would it be against Galthoria to kill him—to enforce justice?

Yes, was his decision. *It would be. That is why I must let him live. Another shall one day topple him. By then it might be too late for Keiratha. I have my principles to stay with.* Therefore he pulled Lightkeeper away and sheathed it.

Lefanarí hung her head and shook it.

The Dark King beamed but did not get up. "Thank you, Nephew. Now I know you would have done the same had I confronted you myself. Your naivety has prided me with a longer life. I guess you cannot discern every illusion, like you did Deil." Then, in an eye-sparkling madness, the form thawed away into the ground like water.

"What was this about?" Thareous demanded.

"It was a test," Lefanarí said. "As he said, he now knows you would not kill him. He has duped you. Be more vigilant. This goes to us both." She sighed and rushed back into the fray.

A great vibration came from Galgon. Thareous peered that way and saw a cloud of powder scaling to the heavens. *What could have done that?* Then something from the sky demanded his attention. A boulder being flung from the catapult. His heart sank. The Dark Legion would either claim the Capital or destroy it.

Amidst the ballistic weapons, both armies still strove to keep the other side from advancing. No fiend attempted to break for their destination anymore. They appeared to be holding the Omnipotents back. If a wall collapsed, the Legion might make a dash for the inside. The bombardment of the rocks did not help anything. It instead served to help the enemy. More of Zakumahk's cunning.

I have to rejoin my group. They are sure to be wondering where I am. If any of them are alive. He turned back to the fight and saw Orkon leveling a regiment with his war-hammer. Then they surrounded him.

Thareous rushed to assist him. He could see the fiends falling to the Dwarf Chieftain. Blades flew everywhere within the circle as the war-hammer warded them off. Lightkeeper came to his aid, slashing the spines of a jinn and vampire. It turned two yataghans and ruptured the dwarf's enclosure. He pulled Orkon out with his shield-arm and received mumbled demurrals.

Ignoring them, he backed away and checked more weapons. Then he threw the Chieftain over his shoulders and bolted off. Magical obstructions arose to stymie any pursuers. Once he was a safe distance away, he set down the disgruntled dwarf. "A ruler should not be endangered. He has to stay alive so his people remain strong."

Orkon's brow pinched but nodded. "Thanks be to you. Perhaps I do owe you my life. I mean not to venerate you as the giants."

"You owe me nothing," Thareous said. "It is my duty to protect innocent lives." He licked his lips. "It has also been made clear to me I should uphold Galthoria. This is why I cannot seek worship. This is why I defied them."

"I say you did the right thing, lad," Orkon said. He stuck the haft of his hammer into the ground and leaned on it. The clamor of ringing metal and agonized cries brought him back to reality. "Come! We have still the land to conserve." He upturned his weapon and charged off.

The siege-towers still rolled forward again, unimpeded. They crushed any being that did not move away. At the fraise ogres swept away the cross-tied stakes with clubs. A rondure of fiends guarded each structure. Zarjkakons carried brigades toward Galgon's battlements. More projectiles rained past them, the bulk landing in the city. One boulder hit the drawbridge, sundering it to splinters.

Ianvorr plunged from the sky and dropped beside Thareous. "Get on my back at once. Zakumahk rides Amarzrell. There is no chance of us tailing them." While he spoke, the Young Mage obeyed him. Then Ianvorr bent his legs and launched off.

As they ascended, his rider clutched a spinal spike. Black shafts sped after them. Thareous knocked them back with telekinesis. An iron ball just missed Ianvorr's head and caromed off a wall instead. The Ice Dragon swerved to the side ere a boulder could weigh down his left wing. By now they reached the inwards of Galgon.

Ianvorr stopped beating his wings and perched on a rooftop. He squatted so his rider could slide off his side. Afterward he straightened up and regarded the human. "Find the king. With Zakumahk in the city, Jaldor is in danger. We shall thwart the Dark King best we can, though make no promises."

"Where should he be?" Thareous asked.

"In his throne room," Ianvorr said. The shattering of glass and upending of shops below told them fiends were everywhere. "Go now. We have not much time. Keiratha is hinged on the hope that we should not fail. May Galthoria watch over you."

"May he bless us with victory," Thareous said. He left and let the Ice Dragon soar away. He sighed and took out Theldaneru, which he had sheathed during the ride. His eyes scanned its lengthy blade as he ran to a trapdoor. Power seemed to emanate from his blade, although he could not tell how. Something great resided within it.

A Light Reawakened

On the streets Thareous sprinted past the fiends. He smote one whenever he could, but stuck to his task even more. Any pursuers he once again impeded by the barriers of magic. If any got by them, he finished them off with orbs. Only a werewolf overtook him, which he dispatched with a blast of fire to the face.

A company of elves found their way to him and ceased any more chases. Lefanarí ran from them to meet him. "Thareous, I bear dreadful news! The Tribunal has been spotted in the Legion's ranks. They are traitors after all."

This made him stop dead in his tracks. "I am sorry to hear this. I have been called to protect King Jaldor. I cannot stay to fight them."

"That is not why I came," she said. "They are after you—to stop you from your objective. Zakumahk rides Amarzrell to the Royal Quarters. We cannot hamper our old leaders. Nothing can—save your death."

Thareous bowed his head. "Let them come. I shall confront and try to outlast them. As for now, I must be off. Should they appear, I will stick to my word." He peered into Lefanarí's sapphire eyes, as if for the last time. "Farewell now, my friend. Death may find us. We are then to meet in Kallenalza."

With that he broke away and headed for the palace. Along the way he vanished through walls for shortcuts. Inside, he saw fiends ransacking and plundering what they could. An inclination to stop them made his hands shake. His orders already given, he had to fulfill them. So he continued on, however reluctant.

Galgonian soldiers pitted themselves against the enemy. Most fell or retreated. Thareous veered off course when he could to help them. He cursed his duty, Jaldor being one of the last men he ever wanted to see. These defenders risked their necks for an impractical cause. None of it should ever have transpired. The past was the past. Nothing could be changed.

The city, the place where I grew up, is falling to ruin. I am not able to shield it from further damage. Ianvorr ... H-he does not understand! None of them do. Even if they have lived longer than me, they still do not. This is my home. I have every right to fight for its endurance. They ... argh ... they do not understand.

Still, he proceeded down lanes and avenues. All overran with fiends and Omnipotents. All warred and strove for room. Theldaneru lashed out as Thareous passed a column of ouphs. Each time one demon fell, another replaced it. He was exasperated and weary. Being midafternoon, the day was hot and cloudless. The air did not improve his mood. He wished it would end then and there.

A few minutes later he came to the palace gates. The centaurs guaranteed no fight took place here. He breathed for a spell, hunkering over on his knees. He knew he did not have long and therefore erected his back. After taking one last gulp, he went inside the palace gates.

As soon as he did, someone tackled him from behind. He heard a blade being unsheathed and whirled onto his back. The blade struck his shield as he secured it for the blow. Then he moved it an inch away to see Yeilth, eyes lit with fire. The elf's jaw slanted in a sneer. Slate eyes hardened into the color's namesake.

Thareous noticed two more shadows fall over him. He bent his head back to spot Talleir and Darjein. They pointed their claymores at him. Thareous rolled past them before they could stab down. Getting to his feet, he watched the trio slive up to him. Then they all struck out.

Kielkanur blocked two blades and Lightkeeper tagged Darjein's. They swung away and then somersaulted at him. The action caught him off guard. He jumped back and parried. The Tribunal arose and circled him now. Thareous let his weapons go comatose. Yeilth moved in, dealing lightning blows. Theldaneru kept up the pace. Their duel ended when the elf feinted. Thareous anticipated it and lopped off his head.

As the body dropped, Talleir and Darjein growled and advanced. Thareous had to fight them from side to side. The female tribune took on his shield as the male engaged his golden sword. Their target ducked and their claymores met. While this happed, Thareous had enough time to take one of them down. Theldaneru chose Darjein, slinging his right calf off first and then tearing Keilkanur across his chest.

Before he could strike Talleir, she jumped back and dropped her weapon. It clanged at her feet. "I surrender. You have proven a mightier foe and killed my captors. My brother wanted power and contacted Zakumahk.

Darjein, his best mate, joined him. I did not want this fate. They coerced me to fall in league with the Dark King."

"You mean your own brother would kill you?" Thareous asked. He almost believed her, until he remembered what she did to Lefanarí in the false Archimage's grove. He decided it to be farcical, but would still listen.

"In a sense, yes," Talleir said. "He would kill my pride and honor by having an elf defile me. To this day I have been pure under the gaze of Galthoria. Still ..." She strode forward, eyes staring him down. "I mean to repay you." Another long step brought her to him. "Somehow, and somehow sweet, I do."

An edge of caution poked Thareous's stomach. His leeriness fell, for her tone played his soul like a harp. He let her separate his arms from forming a protection. Her hands slid to the back of his neck, sending a thrill through him. She inched toward his lips. He shut his eyes, hoping to enjoy the moment.

The presence of Lefanarí seemed to be about him. This was why he gave into her intentions. Why he felt so vulnerable—so sentient. While he waited for the kiss, he held her image in his mind. A fall of argent hair ran down a soft face. Her lips, full as rose petals, accentuated under her blue-gray eyes. Her eyebrows arched in a proud manner, like that of a feline.

Just then he sensed a new presence. This one *did* feel like Lefanarí. In surprise his eyes snapped open in time to see her pull Talleir's chin. Wariness returned and he threw the female tribune away. As his elven friend held her back, he swung Theldaneru at her neck. The front half below Lefanarí's fingers sliced open.

Thareous glared at his blade as the body fell between its companions. "No. This is not my resolve. This is not my volition. Lightkeeper, indeed!"

"It is not your fault," Lefanarí said. "That sword is meant to kill fornicators. She tempted you. Every elven weapon has its own personality, it seems. Those have to be discovered in time. We have no control over what that may be. Besides, Talleir would have died anyways, whether by you or another."

"I would have been sent to Annathias," Thareous said.

"You are wrong," she said. "Galthoria would remind you of that at the last second. He is loving and merciful. He prepares us for a new life once we repent. This is when we must take control, though he still assists us." She smiled but soon frowned. "Let us go, now. We have delayed long enough."

They turned and ran toward the palace. Thareous was glad Lefanarí would be going with him, however sudden. She might prove helpful, resourceful as she was. He added no more to the list, or so he hoped. In truth he exulted at this. Whatever time he had left, he wished to spend with her.

✶✶✶✶✶✶

In the hallways of the Royal Quarters, they stopped. Jaldor's throne room sat a few turns from there. They sensed something to be amiss, that they were not alone. They noted every shadow. None looked human. Then a radiant flash dazed them. They raised their weapons. It withdrew a second later. Lowering their instruments, they saw Osaurius in front of about a dozen other fairies.

"Why are you here?" he asked.

"King Jaldor is in danger," Thareous said. "Zakumahk has made it into the city, if you have not seen it. He heads here, although already he might be here. Ianvorr sent me to protect our ruler. Tell me, have you seen any signs of a breach?"

"Nary save you," the Head Fairy said. He turned to his kind. "Let them pass. I feel they speak the truth. They are not illusions." Without warning they became a golden translucent matter and whirled away.

"I do not like it," Lefanarí said. "The Dark King should be here right now. He would have arrived ahead of us. He must be here, just hiding. In the Bottomlands the fairies are not omnipresent. They would not know where every being is."

"Jaldor could be dead right now," Thareous said. "That is, if you go that way. Come on. We are not done yet."

They stalked to the throne room and twisted the knob. The door opened ajar. Thareous inched it the rest of the way. Then they peeked in. An arrow zipped right by Lefanarí's bangs. The Young Mage squeezed past her and upheld Kielkanur. Another shaft made a bowstring sing. It rebounded off the buckler's golden eagle emblem.

At this Thareous ran forth and lashed out at the figure on the throne. Theldaneru severed his tool of defense, a crossbow. A growl of rage sounded familiar to him, not at all like Zakumahk's cadence. He lowered his shield and respired.

"Son of Haverin, why are you here?" Jaldor demanded. "Is it you who are to kill me? Have you been in league with that currish uncle of yours all the time?" He beamed when noticing Thareous's shock. "Rumors do not hide from the king well. A Magician heard once that Zakumahk is a relative. I did my own investigation after he told me. Your grandfather was a good man. He should have known whom he raised."

"Your Majesty, I petition you to not mention that," Lefanarí said. She entered and demeaned herself with a curtsy. She saw Jaldor's astonishment when rising as he identified her. "It is not what you think. We are here to protect you from the man you fear. The enemy is outside the palace. Thus far we have managed to hold them back."

"For how much longer?" the king questioned. Then he dropped his head and put it in his hands. "Oh, what does it matter? I am to die anyhow. I shall have to answer to the Glorifier for my witlessness. Drat this dotage!"

Thareous and Lefanarí did not mind his monologue. They watched the entrance, the floor ahead of that for a shadow. Nothing came. Nothing happened. They stood there for a half-hour, answering Jaldor's inquiries and remarks. He seemed a man with no more friends. He used to be a revered monarch of a great land. Now he appeared as a city of ruins, abandoned and forgotten.

Then, after a while, he fell asleep. His soft snores echoed through the chamber, while the cries of battle roared outside. Thareous told Lefanarí to try and get some rest as well. She refused. They would fight together, she reasoned. They could take the breaks they needed after the war.

The shadows in the room began to lengthen. Dim light entered from the doorway. It bore a pinkish hue, proclaiming that dusk neared. The umbra made uneasiness flood through their limbs, causing them to quiver. Beyond the affray they could not hear a single resonance of a footstep. Hence, they could not be sure about any ambush.

As if by an order, they sat down. A few moments later they lay on their backs and closed their eyes. Conjured awareness made it so they could detect any arrivals. Dreams followed, some depicting what might occur in the morning or what happened right then. In one they thought Jaldor had stopped snoring.

Suddenly they felt someone shaking them awake. Jaldor leaned over them. He could not speak, for he had no mouth. They could see a smile formed over his cheeks. He pointed at his throne and bobbled as if laughing. Then he began to fade. A black-gowned being replaced him.

"Nalla?" Thareous asked in a gasp.

Upon hearing this, Lefanarí rolled onto her feet. She unsheathed her glaive and pointed it at the woman. "Get away from her. The princess is not herself. Someone has made her into this."

Thareous studied her and choked on his breath. She wore a sable dress bound by a milk-white sash. Midnight hair undulated at her back, braided strands and curly tufts giving her a wild aspect. Her eyes were now a dead periwinkle. Albino skin made her as pallid as ashes. The being as a whole roused a horrid memory—the image that he saw in the Cavern of Mystery.

"What has Zakumahk done to you?" he asked.

"She cannot understand you, Nephew," a voice said from the throne. The Dark King arose, his armor omitted. Now he was garbed in an ebony tunic laced at the top. A pair of trews went into ornate jackboots. Most surprising was the item on his head: the crown of Keiratha. "She is only able to translate my voice."

"Where is King Jaldor?" Thareous demanded.

"Ah, you must mean the late King Jaldor," Zakumahk said. He lowered his head and put a hand to his heart in scornful respect. "Well, he hangs from a balcony above the skirmish. Is this not right, my dear?" His index finger tickled Nalla's chin. She shook all over, appearing to giggle. "Yes, you have been very helpful to me."

He turned away then, his hand lying on Kielthavra's pommel. "The two of you should not hold me in utter contempt. I, after all, have won. My minions have only to drive your friends back. As for yourselves, I let you live to hear me gloat. None of the corpses outside would heed me, anyhow."

"The Omnipotent Ones are not to fail," Lefanarí said. "They will never back down till you are conquered. That is to be very soon."

"I would not be so sure," Zakumahk said. "Seeing you do not know the second step of my plan disparages your word. At this moment my fiends exit the city. The Omnipotents deem they are retreating. Nalla is going to make a sacrifice for the good of her country. Magic barriers hold the spell within Galgon."

"What spell?" Thareous asked. "How are you to use her?"

The Dark King simpered. "You shall see. It is about to rise." He lifted a hand. Nalla levitated off the floor. Then his palm went flat and she scudded for the door. Lefanarí hurdled after her. She leapt at the princess, grabbed her, and weighed her down.

Meanwhile Thareous engaged his uncle with ferocious swipes. Their blades skidded off each other and issued sparks like a display of fireworks. Kielkanur averted most of the Dark King's blows. One time as the Young

Mage almost blocked another, Zakumahk kicked his shield. He fell back and skated over the flagstones.

Then, before the lapse of the next second could come, time stopped. Across the universe every being froze as if in ice. A voice cried out to them. Everyone heard it, even the deaf. *I am Ahtariek ... the Dragon ... of Time. I am dying. And if I meet ... my demise ... then life ... will cease. Hasten to find me ... ere it ... is too late.*

The next second followed at that time. Zakumahk sprung atop Thareous. His black saber pressed against his neck, but not enough to draw blood. "I wish to keep you alive to see my conquest. Come with me to the veranda. Your elven friend is failing to hold Nalla back. You cannot stop me and her."

"Maybe," Thareous said, tipping his head to the side. "The way I see it, if I kill you, then the spell will regress." A sallow orb constituted at his side. It zipped into the Dark King's head and paralyzed him. His prey threw him on the floor and got to his feet. By this time he repelled the effect and also stood.

A golden glow filled the throne room. Thareous held up Lightkeeper to see it shining as a mere mirroring sunlight. Then the glimmer flared like a miniature sun, emitting revolving beams. Nalla shrieked while the iridescence ate at her skin. Lefanarí and Zakumahk covered their eyes with their arms.

The radiance developed into a round explosion, extending toward anything it could devour. Galgon was overcast by it. It drew toward the retreating fiends. Without warning it erupted to unknown lands. Now it pervaded the utter universe. The seas illuminated by it, mirroring it to the heavens. To those above, the light reflecting off the waters' surface dazzled them.

Then it retroceded into the contour of Theldaneru. Thareous stared at the sword, his hand wobbling. *This is why you are called Lightkeeper. To force away shadow and depredation. To retain what is good. Or at least what is left of goodness.* His thoughts ended when he heard whimpering. He saw Zakumahk cringing in a corner.

"No, my lord, I have not failed you. Spare me what my enemies will not. Let me run and gather a new army. Yes, that is what I shall do! This time, with the Omnipotent Ones weak—" He jerked his head to the side as though slapped and cried out. "My lord! Exonerate me! *Please!*"

A few feet away Kielthavra raised as if picked up by a hand. Thareous sensed a powerful presence in the room. He trembled after he thought he caught sight of a see-through man. The black saber teetered while floating toward his uncle. A barrier surrounded the shrinking Dark King. Kielthavra, Zakumahk's own sword, tore into the barrier as though it was cloth. Then the black blade raised back and lashed out. A final bawl from Zakumahk pestered the silence before his head split open.

"Get Nalla out of here!" Thareous yelled to Lefanarí. Not looking to see if she complied, he faced the unmanned blade. "Come at me, Varkin! I fear you not. Do you heed? You wish me dead? Ensure it yourself."

The dark saber waved at him.

"Young Mage, do not encourage him," the Ancient Archimage said. He appeared at Thareous's side, his wicken-staff in his right hand and a wavy sword in the other. "Get you gone, Darkest Dictator. You have failed. Your days of devastation shall not be known to us again. Away with you!"

Cackles resonated around the throne room. Kielthavra jabbed into the flagstones. Shady wings enveloped it. Black cracks opened into a web where it pushed deeper within the floor. It sank until the pommel disappeared, then regained normalcy.

A few minutes elapsed with no talking. Thareous and Ancient awaited something to happen. It never came to that. Indeed, the war had culminated. For as they teleported outside, they saw no more fiends. The Omnipotent Ones lost more than half their numbers. Those still alive met out of the city. Lefanarí whispered to a tearful Nalla, so they were unharmed.

Jurtithan turned to his compatriots after seeing the carnage. "There is aught we can do to reverse this. You must understand: everyone volunteered to give their lives in order for peace. It ends here. We have triumphed over the enemy. Despite our losses a corruptive threat has been annulled. Rejoice for this reason! Galthoria has given us a time to rebuild our friendship with the kingdom. Let us spend it well."

"There is another thing we must rebuild," Vellar said. He pivoted on his heel. A great structure of marred walls entered his sight. In some places wide openings grinned back like a gap between teeth. The battlements of Galgon crumbled, threatening to collapse. "This habitation has protected us from many battles. It deserves to be saved."

"All in time," the Ancient Archimage said. "As for now, I must say it, in fact, is not over. Before regrouping, Thareous and I encountered an apparition of Varkin. He slayed Zakumahk himself. That tells me this blasted war was a challenge. A test of your strength and durability. We shall have to confront him another day."

"Although you speak truth, we must not delay reconstruction," Ianvorr said. "The Royal Family must be notified of their bereavement." He glanced upon Nalla. "Do not weep, Little One. Now is not the time. There will be a day where you may spill out all your tears. Your father lived his life out as he should. Let him rest in peace."

Her teeth clenched and cheeks rose to a scowl. "I killed him!"

"No, you did not," Ianvorr said. "Zakumahk did, using you. Still, you did not. You must not blame yourself. I have been in your same position." His snout entertained a smile. "I had three decades in a cage to think it over. You have not the same. Discontinue your tears now. They will never overturn what you did."

To gather attention away from her, Jurtithan said, "Find rest now. On the morrow we shall amass the dead and cremate them. Meanwhile the architects will repair Galgon for the Royal Family's arrival." He ambled off with Ianvorr behind him.

The rest of them dispersed about the city. Again the elves cooked soup and doled it out for the warriors. Thareous got served as one of the first and went to find Aildeimor and Lefanarí. He located them at the eastern end of the fraise. A few feet from them he spotted Nalla sitting by herself. Deciding it best, he went to her instead and sat down. When she dared look at him, he said, "Tell me how you feel."

Epilogue

The Aftermath

In two days they restored Keiratha's capital. The giants, being master architects, had fixed the fortifications. On the inside, elves readied supplies while fauns searched for scraps. The Magicians re-erected walls to all the buildings. Dwarves renovated the houses after doing their best to repair the furnishings. The fliers took the bodies—Omnipotents and fiends alike—and set them alight. The dead could have overflowed Galgon.

Once the Galgonians returned half a week later, most of the groups went to their environments. Dragons and elves constituted most of the remainders. The queen bade them to stay for the coronation ceremony. Their leaders agreed and said they would camp outside. Then they told to her the news. She erected a fortnight of fasting and mourning. Following that were the king's cremation and next the anticipated event.

Volunteers adorned the amphitheater with white lining and archways leading up to a latticed camber. Calla-lilies wove throughout the trellis at the feet of a stairway going to a platform. Here Kathar's future retinue and the Royal Family stood. An old, kind justice named Parthas stood nearest the steps. Galgonians sat in the bleachers above.

Then a tucket sounded from the trumpeteers' box. Commander Rhallanas led a cavalcade down the wide walkway appareled in a red rug. They pranced up to the lattice-work, turned their horses inward, and pointed their swords to the sky. A lane went between them to admit the subsequent arrivals.

Next Kathar stepped from the archway at the tip of the walkway. He was arrayed in a white silken tunic trimmed with gold and velvet slacks. Two servants followed behind him, carrying the rings and crowns on carmine pillows. Thick gilded threads lined their sides and ended in one corner a plaited strand. They stopped beside Parthas.

Murmurs filled the air as their queen-to-be stepped forth. A figure veiled in white strode into sight. Golden hair glinted from the sunlight under an opalescent mantle. A flower girl dashed ahead of her, tossing Tudor petals above her. Behind her, twelve serving girls, six on each end, lifted the train. Unshod feet peeped out from the hem of her pearly skirt.

The walk to the platform seemed an eternity for her. She was exhilarated on the inside. On the outside she was reluctant. And it could have showed, even through that veil somehow had she not hung her head. The soldiers attending the cavalcade examined her; whether for protection or admiration she could not tell. She did not stop them. She would not have anything spoil her wedding day. Not even her late father.

Gulping, she let the flower girl move to the side of the stairs so she could ascend. The serving girls, meanwhile, went up after her and stood in a space kept for them, still holding the train. Kathar hoped to spot the indigo eyes within the veil that enslaved him when first he saw them. Nalla kept them lowered, denying him that privilege.

Parthas extended his hands to the heavens. "Friends, we gather here under the gaze of Galthoria to join this couple in wedlock. Kathar, Son of Liele, and Nalla, Daughter of Ingrezl, he is your witness as well as this fine audience. They may hold you accountable if your vows are misused. May it be it should never come to this."

The judge put a hand on each of their shoulders. "Besides a nuptial gathering"—he brought them closer—"they shall unite to form a new age of leadership. Kathar is to be made King of Keiratha, and Nalla his queen. Until the end of their days they will do what is best for you and their kingdom." He let them go and stepped back.

"Now," he went on, "the matrimony commences. I ask you, Kathar, Son of Liele, do you take this girl to be your lawfully wedded wife? In strife and concord, in illness and health, in misfortune and fortune, till death parts you?"

"I do," he said with a nod.

"Nalla, Daughter of Ingrezl," Parthas said, facing her, "do you take this man to be your lawfully wedded husband? In strife and concord, in illness and health, in misfortune and fortune, till death parts you?"

For a moment her voice became choked. She could not find the right words to say. What was it Kathar used to affirm his avowal? Then Jaldor's face intruded her mind. She shut it out, but knew what to voice. "As my father's last wish of me … I do."

Parthas pivoted on one foot and took the rings. "What do these symbolize in marriage?" They did not know. "The unification and inseparation of each spouse. These bind them stronger than any adhesive and keep them to their vows." He handed the halos of gold to them and they slipped them on.

Nalla's was sculpted into the form of a dandelion. An emerald perched in the top of it. Four fingers held it in place at each corner. Kathar's was flat at the rounded crest and had a star imprinted in it. This, he realized, was his signet-ring used to press down the hot wax on scroll or envelope lips.

The justice's eyes widened, his cheeks lifted under the influence of a smile. "By the power invested in me through Keiratha and Galthoria the Glorifier, I pronounce you man and wife. You may kiss."

Kathar pulled back the veil and touched for the first time his love's face. A fire ran through his palm. It did not burn. It comforted him, a reassurance that this was actual. As the indigo eyes fixed on his sleet ones, he knew it was. Then he leaned over and put his lips to hers. He groped at her face like a potter to the clay. Though he could craft her into anything he wanted, he would remain chaste. So he let her go a second later.

When he did, the justice separated them so he could set the king's crown upon Kathar's head. Jagged rows of teeth rounded the entire head. Inset in it were twelve various gems, surrounding the band. A large ceris quartz in the shape of an oval had been put in the front.

Next Nalla's crown was set on her head. It curved in undulating lines at the sides. Two leaves pushed together on either side. At the back the lines twisted like a rope or lock of hair. The front had a heraldic shield. It signified she would do anything to uphold her country. It had, unlike Ingrezl's, silver on the edges but gold in the rear and face.

"Keiratha!" Parthas cried. "Allow me to present King Kathar and Queen Nalla, your new rulers!" He shook his hands to keep the viewers quiet. "Before we depart, let me go over the king's promises as your leader. He has pledged in the courts of his forefathers to reduce crime. In doing this, new means of punishment are being ideated. This is not to intimidate anyone—instead secure the realm's safety.

"In addition, the Omnipotent Ones are to never be falsely accused again. There may be an audience with His Majesty if Jurtithan agrees. The Keirathan Army cannot engage them without cause also. This does not grant them full impunity. Should an Omnipotent rebel, whatever the means, he shall be dealt with by the Silver One. This is to ensure no usurpery or civil war ever bechances us."

******

Later that day Thareous plodded through the corridors of the Royal Quarters. Yesterday he had requested Lefanarí meet him in the Garden. She said she would think about it. They would be free to tread there since they were Omnipotents. The Keirathan Army considered them higher than any of their officers, after all.

This walk gave him a lot to think about. His future, his decision, his recognition of the only enemy survivor from the war. Quaron was still a fugitive at large. Somewhere in the kingdom he had undisclosed friends. People loyal, or stupid, enough to help him. What made him so dangerous? He could revive Varkin.

The others might not let Thareous go. They would deem him out for blood—for vengeance. He would have to go to the one being he felt he could trust. Not for help. For a herald. He would use her to deliver his intentions to … someone. He had not yet elected in his mind the person who would fight for him.

What would become of him then? Would he be hunted? Would he become as Quaron? He hoped not. Otherwise his purpose might be endangered—and by his friends. He would only do this until he found the fugitive and brought him to justice. Then … His plans did not reach that far. He did not even know if he would succeed.

At last he reached the Royal Garden through a tall threshold. Under a cedar tree, sitting on a bench, was Lefanarí. She heard him coming and looked up, smiling. "Well, now he arrives. Do you know how long I have been waiting?"

He shook his head. "Not unless you tell me."

Her smile broadened. "Not long. I just got here."

"That does not spoil a thing," Thareous said. He sat next to her but kept himself a few inches apart. "I am glad you came. I mean … I am surprised you trusted I will not do anything beyond me."

She put a hand on her lips and giggled. "Annihilator, that should be the least of your troubles. Of course I trust you. We are friends—that is what we do." Shaking her head, she omitted her mirth. "Anyhow, what is it you want of me?"

Seeing her seriousness obliged him to turn away. He stared into a hedge of rose bushes, scanning the next leaf and petal in sight. "I need you to tell Ianvorr I am leaving. Not forever, mind you, but for a time. I hope you understand this."

"I cannot understand what you will not tell," Lefanarí said. "What are you going to do? More importantly, where are you going?"

"Wherever Quaron is," Thareous muttered, facing her again. He required eye contact to adduce his aim. "Wherever the Omnipotent Ones are not. There are some who would try to impede me. This is why I need you—as a friend I can trust—to give them this news. Will you do that?"

Lefanarí took one of his hands and squeezed it. "As a friend you trust, I accept this. I understand you do not mean retribution. *That* is beyond you, saving it could overtake you. This is your option—no one should make it up for you. Go now. Do as you must. You have my best wishes. May Galthoria be with you."

Thinking of no better way to thank her, no words to express his gratitude, he pecked her cheek. Then he embraced her close to him, got up, and ran away. His feelings for her mounted higher than ever. Whatever betided them, he prayed their next meeting would not be far off. The Royal Garden wall passed him as he went through it. Soon he would be out in the open with no supplies save his sword, shield, and wit.

Afterword

Dear Reader,

I open this letter with a woeful heart and weary soul. My life has been tested and decimated because it was tested. Self—our greatest bane—has caused much of my grief. It is the remorse, the knowing, the reminder of what I allowed and supported. It is the most monstrous beast, more feral than a zarjkakon and more grotesque than a goblin. Ianvorr encouraged me to write this whilst we head for Draer-Vollith. I pray you read it with care and note its message. Much can be learned by observing the errancies of your peers.

Deem not that I judge you or your colleagues. Instead I aim to help and direct all who peruse this to morality. Too many of us get our feet caught up as we stumble toward sin. Do not make the mistake I did—following Self and trailing after my every fancy. Autonomy—self-government—this is called. It is when we train our eyes only to ourselves and lose trust in others.

Besides this, we grow incisive and derogatory, dissecting the good from guiltless people. Our words cut deep into the heart like swords. Soon everyone we called friend shuns us, for we are as fiends: vile and malicious. We come to be estranged, alienated from those we love most. Everything we knew once is blinded by our will.

Now you have to decide between Self—Malluesaer—or Galthoria. Life is about making choices. Not only that, but keeping to the expectations of others. By saying this, I mean we should not go amiss through our desires. See what your peers note and aim to pry from you—so long as it is not detrimental. Let your options in life be founded on what you were taught. Never let anyone down, lest they are to begrudge you. The selection to harm people is quicker sent upon you than a blade thrust.

May Light Be Your Path,
Thareous, the Son of Haverin